# HILLARY

## © Thomas Moore

## ALPHAR PUBLISHING

### www.alpharpublish.com

**alphar**

# HILLARY
## ALPHAR PUBLISHING
### Manhattan, NY, Burbank, CA
www.alpharpublish.com

Copyright ©Thomas Moore, 2009

LIBRARY OF CONGRESS
CATALOGING IN PUBLICATION DATA
Moore, Thomas
HILLARY
1 Title
ISBN 0-9786024-04
ISBN 978-0-9786024-06 (at 13 digits)

Published May, 2009 by ALPHAR.
ISBN # 9780978602406

# ACKNOWLEDGEMENTS:

Thank you to my Village of support: especially Steven, Katie, Gabrielle, Michelle, Linzi, Andrew, Rikki, Kathleen Spivack, Anthony Chaytor, Natalie Black, Anna Palliser, Paul Chapman and Tony Lee. Thank you to my mentors, especially Ray Martell, Pat Evans, and the California Writers Club, Diane Brown, Paul Chapman, Robert Free, and members of the Back Beach Writers Club, Murray, Phil, Neil, Jonathan, Max and the Dialogue Club, and to Michael King.

I wish to acknowledge contributions to this text by modern fiction authors, such as: Kathleen Spivack, Philip Roth, Toni Morrison, Michael Riddell, Ben Olson, Phillip Temple, Brian Caldwell, Chuck Polahniuk, Drew Stepek, Nick Hornby, Chris Else, Owen Marshall, Marise Oliveira, Robert Byrne, Peter Hoeg, Hillary Smith, Elizabeth Moon, Nick Cave, Curtis Sittenfeld, Janna Levin, Pankaj Kurulkar, Ezeibieli Kingsley Chidi and Anne Desclos.

I gratefully acknowledge contributions to this text from journalists such as: Mark Magnier, Steve Geissinger, Chuck Plunkett, Anne Hulls, <u>Dana Priest</u>, <u>Gene Weingarten</u>, <u>Thomas Curwen</u>, <u>Steven Pearlstein</u>, <u>Ann Hornaday</u>, Rupert Murdoch, Carl Bernstein, Edward Klein, Gail Sheehy, Brian Williams, Seth Borenstein, Eric Zorn, Joel Stein, Seth Borenstein, Bill Morris, Jim Lehrer, Jim Hightower, Frank Rich and Maureen Dowd of *The New York Times*, Bob Woodward of *The Washington Post*, Seymour Hersh of *The New Yorker*, Michael Isikoff, Jonathan Alter, and Evan Thomas of *Newsweek*, Matt Cooper of Time, David Corn of *The Nation*, Richard Serrano and Ronald Brownstein of the *Los Angeles Times*, Brian Ross of *ABC News*, Chris Mathews, Greg Brouwer of *LA Weekly News*, James Walcott, Joe Scarbotough, Michael Savage, Sidney Blumenthal, Michael Moore, Brent Scowcroft, Al Gore, the following *Newsweek* staff: Richard Wolffe, Mark Hosenball, Holly Bailey, Debra Rosenberg, Jonathan Darman in Washington, Arian Campo-Flores, Catharine Skipp and Carmen Gentile in Florida and Lee Hudson Teslik in New York, Newt Gingrich, Hillary Clinton, and Barack Obama.

I also wish to acknowledge contributions from valued Internet bloggers and columnists, such as Ken Sanes, Transparency, Metro Boston, Ann Althouse, Jonah Goldberg, Katherine vanWormer, Tim Grieve, Jacob Weisberg, Daily Kos, endhumantrafficking.org and The Blotter.

Editing by Anna Palliser and Natalie Black.
Cover design and art by Mathew Tribuhovic of Third Eye.
Photography of Author by Max Lowrey.

## FAIR USE NOTICE

## DISCLAIMER

All characters and events in this work - even those perceived to be based on real persons and events - are in support of a fictional creation. Information on the historical behavior of the iconic characters such as Hillary Rodham Clinton, Carmella Meeks, Barack Obama, Tony Chaytor, and Newt Gingrinch is mostly derived from biographies, (such as *Living History* by Hillary Clinton, *Hillary's Choice* by Gail Sheehy,) media articles, and personal communications. The decision to rely on this material was made because it appears that the published versus real characters of Hillary, Carmella, Newt, Tony Chaytor may correlate with a particular discontinuity between the real personalities of our leaders versus the behaviors and virtual images imposed by the spin doctors. The use of established biographical and media material, juxtaposed with behaviors of literary heroes, creates a massaged reality that competes with the heroic images of literary fiction and the fantasies of imposters. Biographical material written about our characters provides a reference point from which imposters and journalists both enact the scurrilous deviations espoused by spin-doctors. *The truth* sought in this book is relative to the PR image used to represent our leaders and their critical events. The reliance upon previously published material herein regarding the characters and events acknowledges the contributions to this book by fiction authors versus PR media.

# INTRODUCTION:

Hillary Clinton is challenged by the ridicule of her enemies, and by the political success of her rival, Barack Obama. At issue is the lack of integrity in our nuclear program, tall building construction, pharmaceutical industry, information about global warming, and the moral fabric of the national character. These failings evolved from the repetitive behavior of a group of powerful Bosses who invariably got so enthused about their latest boyish program to make their America more powerful, that they lost their moral compass. There is an emotional explosion... Amidst the enthusiasm for pleasure and power, our moral fabric is abandoned. *Hillary* uses the tool of biography; woven with fiction, to extrapolate history in order to discover a new level of reality, beyond the virtual world of the puppet surrogate Simtwo who fronts for Hillary during her successful 2012 election campaign.

Although this novel is structured within a matrix of humor, readers will discover a darker message underlying the hilarity, leading to a more tragic interpretation of the thwarted Hillary character. Even in her heroism, Hillary does not dare to triumph entirely, perhaps confused by too many layers of secrets: "She wants to declassify national security secrets. I want you to produce a *Hillary* script that will destroy her credibility. Democracy is too fragile a flower to risk in the hands of a woman, especially a woman who is a bitch."

There is a disparity of integrity between the professionally spun images of political leaders versus the literary record of endearing public characters such as Carl Meeks, his granddaughter and philosophical prostitute Carmella Meeks, the Gypsy engineer and journalist Tony Chaytor, and the seductive sleaze of Newt Gingrinch.

Just as the *Newton show* offers a grand metaphor for contemporary American culture, *Hillary* addresses the plastic images created for our politicians by media giants such as Newton PR. The message is that we are immersed in a media landscape of lifelike fantasies of our political candidates... and our values, that serves the interests of those powerful people running the PR firms.

Hillary is blocked by a malevolent simulator, by a high-tech manipulator, who is intent upon keeping Hillary inside a plastic bubble—but there are new opportunities for actualizing thwarted ambitions.

Anthony Chaytor, President, Alphar Publishing.

## PART I: HILLARY CLINTON

### CHAPTER 1: February, 2013

SILENCE, always silence! If they aren't going to talk why should I listen? I am silently observed and evaluated each day while presiding from my white room. My psychiatrist, Dr. Elizabeth Moon, is probably no more certain of what the news media said about Hillary Clinton, leading up to the election, than I am. But I saw the results on TV:

*Ladies and gentlemen, the next President of the United Sates of America is… Hillary Rodham Clinton."*

Those words *were* said—I heard them through the SILENCE… yet it is so improbable. The early months of 2012 leading up to the election were discouragingly hot; getting to sleep was impossible. But Barack Obama never called… not once! Fortunately, I continued to endure—until the messages of rejection were as undeniable as in 2008. It was hopeless. However, with a stroke of genius, my friend Tony Chaytor enrolled me as a *write-in* candidate for the election-- just prior to the deadline of August 1. However, Doctor Moon says that my election victory is just another Walter Mitty dream!

Whatever they say, they now have to deal with the fact that I *am* President of the United States of America. It wasn't an easy journey: I prayed with unrealistic hope for enough election ballots to be cast in my favor. As the early results from the Midwest came in, I began to dream of a miracle. Then, two hours later, I waited eagerly for more results. The State of California was yet to be finalized, but it was almost certain that I had won… won the hearts and minds of the people of America.

Dr. Moon, crisp and professional, raises an eyebrow and shakes her head not quite imperceptibly. Delusional people do not understand these signals; the book says. I have read the book and so know what it is that I supposedly do not understand. What I haven't figured out is the range of things *they* don't understand-- the people who wear the white coats. But I do know *some* of what Dr. Moon doesn't know; she doesn't know that I have healed: Every time she asks what my job is, and I say I am doing public service--she asks if I know what *public* means. She definitely thinks I am a lunatic, and even calls me Ms. Mitty. What a terrible name.

But I, Hillary Rodham Clinton, to the disbelief of this moonbeam psychiatrist, have overcome the odds and become President, by a minor landslide, propelled by a minimalist election campaign lead by Tony Chaytor.

Tony telephoned. "What if everything is an illusion and nothing exists?"

"In that case, Tony, we definitely overpaid the company that is planning my Inauguration Ball."

My path to Inauguration had been threatened by a breakdown. But Tony publicized that I was on an extended meditative retreat in New Zealand, *eighty days of solitude before my Presidency of Service, before my healing ministry*. The graduation ceremony for my internment program in Dr. Moon's retreat center was finally over, and the old clock had been chiming the midday hour. I had an appointment in central Dunedin with Tony—He and Carmella were only over from DC for three days, to pick me up. But I'd depleted the rationed supply of gasoline for my borrowed car, so I needed to call the bus company--to find the location of the nearest bus stop. I was in a panic! I had to search the study for the skinny phone book… there it was pinned to the notice board.

It was five blocks to the bus stop! The rain had finally stopped; stopped making that irritating noise on the iron roof. Holy Hell! Tony and Carmella were expecting me for a New Year's Eve party. Now! I grabbed the cut flowers from Dr. Moon's desk vase and a bottle of wine from the pantry. Damn the oil crisis. I was stuck with relying on those fruity electric buses?

New Year's Eve was that day of the year when even an average garage band could command triple-pay for playing at any old dive. Tony has therefore been confronted with a new vision of he and I on stage, rescuing a godless and polluted America--so the opportunity for a triple-pay-gig was too much for Bill and Tony to resist. They were going to put on a show to remember.

I snuck my way to the bus terminus… I was wearing the janitor's ten-gallon hat -- with my collar turned up to avoid recognition. Down Brian Street, along Caldwell Avenue. The terminal was vacant! I had thirty minutes to fill in before the bus arrived. I stepped off the curb into a puddle. The nasty December storm seemed to bring the entire country down. I purchased a Snickers bar from the vending machine. Wap! What a fright. Carmella was in disguise wearing an Arabian robe, jeans, and sandals. She had just poked my chest:

"Hullo President Hillary. I've been stalking you."

The Asian boy accompanying her was wearing a dark suit and a white shirt and shuffled beside this Arab-looking chick that was Carmella. The boy introduced himself as Xiu Zhou. I easily recognized her as Tony's wife, despite her outrageous costume. She must have been on drugs, but I shook her hand in order to keep my distance— Carmella had recently misbehaved, again, and should have been at home in a recovery program. A cold wind blew the fur back from the eyes of a dog watching us from an alleyway across the street. We were the only people at the bus terminus by the ocean now.

"Good to see you two. Thanks for coming." I said.

"This could be your last chance Madam President," Carmella said. " May I offer you this opportunity to repent?" She held a religious tract a few inches from my nose.

"I'm already saved thank you." I pushed the flyer away. I didn't like getting heavy, but they were obnoxiously high.

"You must be waiting for the central Dunedin bus to take you to Bill and Tony?" Xiu

Zhou asked.

"None of your business."

"Come on Sweetheart, I can tell by the shameful look on your face that you don't even know what salvation is. I'll ride with you and explain," Carmella said.

"Go back to your husband," I snapped. Geez!

"Come on, lady! Do a prayer and get rid of that guilt and shame that is rotting your soul."

"I have nothing to be guilty about so behave yourselves."

"I am a good girl now, Hillary--Xiu is gay, a priest. We know about your war plans for China. Get down on your knees now or Allah will strike you down," Carmella said.

"This could be your last day on the planet Madam President. May I offer you this opportunity to repent?" Xiu Zhou asked.

Carmella again held the religious tract up to my face. She was grinning.

"I'm already saved thank you... by Dr. Moon." I pushed the flyer away.

"We know about you Moonies." Xiu Zhou said. "Bill has to play his saxophone tonight, so I came here especially for you, to be Bill's surrogate while he is at rehearsal."

"How kind. Bill can be such a boy, so it should be easy for you to play his part."

Xiu Zhou forced a tract into my hand. "Could be a recipe for a New World Order!"

I screwed the tract up and threw it at Xiu Zhou.

"Come on, Hillary! Change your life. Support the Progressive Youth Movement."

I remained silent and motionless, refusing to look at anything but the puddle of water covering the hard gray pavement where the bus would arrive.

"Damn girl," Carmella yelled, as she hopped off the curb and began moon walking back and forth in front of me. "This could be your Holy Grail, the chance to break free from your Bosses, your peace, love, and understanding of the Lord."

Xiu extended his arm in front of him, allowing another golden flyer to float up and down in the cold air. "This could be your release from the White House spin doctors and puppet masters. Just reach out and take it. If it turns out to be crap, so what! It's not costing you a single, shiny shitty cent."

Carmella halted her dance and jumped back onto the curb, sliding her lips next to my ear and whispered. "*It's so fuh-fuh-fuh-fucking free. Learn about the real Christianity.*"

I spun to face her so quickly that I bumped her.

"Look, I don't want the thing, all right? I don't want it! Did you hear me that time?"

Carmella stared blankly at me. She was the same height as me, but looked much younger than her thirty-five years because of her child-like complexion.

The bus pulled up to the curb and I jerked my torso away from Carmella and stepped toward it. My legs toppled in the sudden motion and my feet slipped off the curb. As I fell, I tossed my bag with the flowers and the bottle of wine, in a misguided attempt to save them. My naked, unguarded face slapped down onto the pavement.

"Jesus freaking nut cases," I mumbled as the giggling Carmella stepped over my body. She deposited her banana peel in the recycling bin.

Avoiding the stare of the bus driver I retrieved my bag, left the broken bottle on the curb, climbed onto the bus, and sat down. Carmella and Xiu Zhou stomped aboard and sat either side of me. The bus pulled out of the terminus and silently steered away from the ocean toward central Dunedin.

9

"Are you happy now Hillary?" Carmella interrupted my thoughts.

"I am healed from my little breakdown... Of course. I am a happy servant of the people."

"And I am born again Hillary, and therefore surely free of my addictions. Here's our stop. The party is being held around the corner, at the Alphar Ranch. But first, the costume store... to get you a funky outfit in which Bill will not recognize you. Your big hat's good." Carmella tripped as she stepped down from the bus.

...What a New Year that was. And here I am, five weeks later, back in the U.S. and re-established in another humble white room, virtually straight-jacketed, alone. Tony Chaytor cannot visit outside allotted hours--but he calls me every morning. When the phone finally rings I am afraid, of course, but I pick up the receiver because I am not so terrified of discovery at this particular time:

"How are you Darling?" Tony uses the word *darling* too often.

"I'm OK. What will become of you now, Tony?"

"I told Carmella I won't be filing for divorce," Tony says. "...But why did I dream about her this morning?"

"Because you love her." That woman is definitely Tony's true love. I put them back together in 2001. But now I wonder if I should have?

"In my dream Carmella visited my room--then excused herself to go to the bathroom. I waited and waited. Suddenly I awoke... and called you," Tony said.

"I'm glad that you called."

"We both have had a lot of bad luck," he says.

"Yes. Both of us."

"But fortunately, Carmella is seeing a darling counselor."

"Good. Come over at three. We'll have a meeting like back in the good old days."

I nominate the conference room located down by the lobby as the ideal venue for us to meet... I call that room the *Café Alphar* for sentimental reasons.

Tony mutters, as if to himself, "OK Darling."

Before my election campaigns, Tony and I met regularly at the original Café Alphar, back in 1996, a few years after he broke up with Carmella for those five strange years. We have all changed so much, so profoundly... the events of the previous eighteen years have left deep marks on our lives. Back then Carmella was a naive young girl trying to make sense of a world in which her daddy, the one person who was meant to make her feel protected.... had repeatedly abused her. We were all there at the Café, except for Carmella, investigating a spate of building failures. At the original Café Alphar—at the Café that became popular during the Second World War with the intellectuals, code breakers and spies. Should we all try to make amends? Shit! Forget about it all that for the moment. Try and get some sanity and then go back. We have all worked hard to remember as close to nothing as possible about our failures. But the brain can be devious...

## CHAPTER 2: HILLARY CLINTON, Café Alphar, 1996

The Café Alphar is old, but it has safe parking, and security guards. Slowly the engineers accumulate tonight. Assembled, they are called 'The Circle' around DC, and even by a few as far away as San Francisco and Los Angeles. At the center of The Circle is a circle: a round marble tabletop. Tony Chaytor selected the Cafe Alphar precisely because of that table. Tony and the other engineers throw their ideas into the mix with those of us lawyers—and we rebound from the journalistic hysteria that followed our nation's 1993 bombing by terrorists of the World Trade Center... and the 1995 bombing of the Alfred P. Murrah Federal Building in Oklahoma City. We all look at the photographs of the bombed section of the World Trade Center parking garage below WTC-7... and then the views from above. The engineers are focused on discerning rationale amidst the disordered column offsets.

They gather here every week to distil their ideas--to distinguish science from hysteria. At stake is reality, and surely one of Tony's precious principles. We lawyers have lost a tolerance for embroidered attitudes. We all want to separate out the truth. The engineers sense, I imagine, a judgement of the entire engineering profession behind Tony's exposure of the structural defects revealed during the recent building failures.

I stand here, looking three hundred and sixty degrees around the table. Some of these people shine brighter than others: The engineer Leslie Robertson is here, and Professor Janna Levin... she is the scribe for the group. Tony's father, William L. Chaytor, is here to form the hub of the Circle. William wears an eye-patch as a consequence of the invasion of an eye infection. He sucks on his mints while Leslie Robertson drinks lethal doses of caffeine and settles himself with a brush of his lapels. The participation of the others present is less imperative... apart from Tony. They are The Circle that can be approximated by a handful of discrete points--and the others do not count.

Outside, a cold wind burns the blurred faces of evening pedestrians. Professional women pin their scarves to their faces with gloved hands. Inside, a grand mirror traps an image of them in a circular chunk of animated glass. On a plain wooden chair in a corner near the wall, almost camouflaged beside the green of a vinyl booth, sits Tony Chaytor. He is an erect man of twenty-eight, his sharpest edges hidden beneath the soft pulp of youth. He informs the Circle that the unexpected and serious damage to tall-buildings that occurred during the moderate 1994 Los Angeles earthquake was caused by the use of a particular but universally adopted Lincoln weld metal to connect beams and columns during construction—and that this scandal has been hushed up.

Although we all now live under the shadowy threat of his new discovery, Tony's name is hardly known. He is merely a signature on a PhD thesis and a few top-secret reports. Here he sits, ready to alter the view of reality that his colleagues have previously formulated around this white table. Tony joined the Circle tonight to tell the members that they were wrong, and that the Government had also lied about Port

Chicago, Pearl Harbor, the Oklahoma City and the World Trade Center bombings. They had lied most recently about the safety of high-rise steel buildings… and he has just proved it.

Tony is introspective, alone even in a crowd, sitting in his corner. He appears reticent yet likable. The attention with which his moussed hair has been casually spiked, hints at his strongest interest next to engineering… women. His carousing efforts often come to fruition, only adding to his mystery for the few engineers close to him. His profile on the local Internet dating site would shock them: *'I search for the woman who is complete within herself, and yet adaptable to living with a creative man who has seen the world and is keen to practice the sauces and spices. I prefer slim, beautiful, intelligent, creative-- a woman who knows who she is and what she wants… someone who knows both great tragedy and awesome joy… A woman who welcomes abundance and carries success well. I am keen to meet a woman who has discovered what is and isn't worth fighting for in this life.'*

While Tony has been known to show off a girlfriend or two, he keeps his real love a secret: His bruised apple, his sweet Carmella Meeks--because he has lost her to misfortune. Tony's face is sweet--hidden as it is behind borrowed thick-rimmed glasses. The round black frames with a thick nosepiece have the effect of accentuating his eyes or replacing them with bright orbs--a physical manifestation of great vision. They suggest, for anyone looking in, that all emphasis should be placed there on those blue orbs, or rather, on the vast intellectual world that lies just beyond the focus of their magnifying lenses.

All twelve engineers that have circled on this crucial Tuesday evening, believe in their very hearts that the structural engineering profession is divinely appointed, like the founding fathers: *Building failures are invariably the result of malpractice by the contractor, and only occasionally does a careless engineer function as an accomplice.* Tony Chaytor cuts through this night to shatter their prejudice--until all that is left of their preconceptions are damning pieces of debris, that when reassembled on the circular tabletop, erect a powerful monument to the fallibility of the engineering profession. Tony has proven that some truths live outside of petty rationale and that we cannot get salvation, or even redemption, by engineering tall buildings. We lawyers are quick to claim that we knew all along that some truths are beyond narrow-minded engineers, pollsters, and campaign managers.

Tony Chaytor never did believe that the truth around the epidemic of building failures would elude us--although he knew the structural engineering profession would mostly deny it. Tony has proven that integrity has chosen to abandon our nation--less discretely as each scandal becomes uncovered… He hasn't invented a myth to conform to his prejudice of the world--at least not when it comes to engineering. He discovered his theory regarding the fragility of our tall-building stock as surely as if it was a splinter embedded in his finger. Look for it and you'll find it where he said it was, just off center from where you're staring. There are faint stars in the night sky that you can see even now, but only if you look back in time—and to the side of where they shine now…

## PART II: TONY CHAYTOR:

## CHAPTER 3: February 2001

I am glad to exit the staleness of the taxi. Outside it is humid and the heat is discouraging, even in February. I squint against the glitter of mangled steel. The EQE building is located out in the country, next to the Fort Pierce Naval Station where Carmella's father is based. There are armed guards. I can look at but must not touch the twisted beam and column steel, the sheared bolts, or the curious weld metal. Two other forensic investigation companies, in addition to Lilly-Thomas, have supposedly been assigned to investigate the building collapse. One is a local company from Miami, and the other is also from Washington DC--but they haven't been here.

The EQE building is owned by a PR firm and is rumored to have been the site of a massive Republican media campaign, a campaign for George Bush's blockbuster election. This doesn't feel like a forensic investigation site; it's like a Reality TV show because a zany film crew is here. But why has there been zero news coverage? Why such personal questions? Why don't they wait for me to finish my sentences?

"One young woman died when this high rise EQE building collapsed--a homeless prostitute named Marise," says the front man wearing a false moustache. "Died on Valentines day, 2001. Dr. Tony Chaytor of the Lilly-Thomas Company is investigating."

The front man rushes on, piling question upon question. I have been hired to determine the cause of the building collapse. It just happens to be near the hometown of my missing girlfriend, Carmella Meeks—I am still visited by wafts of memories.

Even after the body of Marise is loaded into a vehicle from the Coroner's Office, the armed Naval guards remain to patrol the devastated site of twisted metal and concrete rubble, bringing their weapons to shoulder at any sudden movement. My job is to ferret out what caused the collapse: A fire has detonated a gas explosion in the basement. It is probable that the person living in the basement of the building started the fire. I am told that the fillings in Marise's teeth melted due to the intensity of the heat. Poor girl. But neither that fire nor the gas explosion, simultaneously or in isolation, could create enough energy to collapse a properly designed steel building.

My girlfriend Carmella used to be called Marise... But her mom told me in a letter that she changed her name to Carmella a few years ago, after the big fuss with her dad. I hate fuss. It is possible that a terrorist detonated an explosion adjacent to ground floor columns, like at the concrete framed Alfred P. Murrah Federal Building in Oklahoma City. But that could only have caused this type of *total* collapse of the EQE building, if it had been professionally rigged with a TNT-type explosive. Such a planned detonation would have to take out all the critical columns simultaneously-- and would have caused more horizontal dispersion of the debris. Alternatively, the building could have been rigged with a cutter-incendiary such as thermite, which would have resulted in a free-fall collapse. I wonder if the EQE building collapse was a set-up, planned by the powers that be as a trial balloon. I telephone my friend at Testing Engineers and request that his Company take samples of both the beam and column steel.

My lunch of a mango and three Twinkies is not satisfying. I read the *Washington Post* while the crew slink around, filming the testing guys in white coats while they remove samples from the site.

My friend telephones back the yield test results, which confirm that the building collapsed because it was almost certainly flawed. Firstly because, ironically, the beam steel in the girders was thirty percent stronger than the engineers had designed for. Then, when the building was severely stressed, the fuses failed to activate in the beams. Instead, undesirable yielding occurred in the columns. Secondly, because the welds were faulty, the use of the Lincoln self shielded E70T-4 welding system had compromised safety.

The following day the front man has more questions. I answer reluctantly: "Yes. A fire has engulfed much of the building, but heat could only have caused the collapse if the fire had incendiary help from thermite explosive."

"And what does the CIA think about that theory Dr. Chaytor?" he asks.

I am not that well connected wit the CIA. "My client wants to sue the Taiwanese steel supplier. But the Attorney General has ruled that the supplier behaved legally: The specifications require that the beam steel be 36K psi… But the specifications failed to indicate any *upper* bound so there was no illegality in supplying stronger beams."

"But surely the contractor took a cheap bid?" the front man asks.

"No court will blame a construction company for taking the lowest guaranteed bid for steel supply," I say.

"So, what's the big deal that's keeping us here all week?" the man asks.

"Unfortunately, the the same Lincoln weld rods and the same over strength foreign beam steel have been used for most of the high rise buildings constructed in the US for the last three decades."

"Where was the cost saving for the supplier?" he asks.

"They delivered *all* the steel to the US at the higher 50K psi strength, both columns and beams, presumably to simplify production."

"So?"

"So? What do you mean, *so?*"

"What's the damage to our industry?" he asks.

"Massive repairs will be required, involving the strengthening every beam-column joint in most of the high-rise buildings in the nation. The repairs required in the earthquake zones of the nation will cost mega-trillions of dollars. The consequence of this scandal is that America will certainly suffer many deaths following a large earthquake--or when a category five hurricane hits a dense urban location. Such events are predicted statistically to occur in ten or more American cities prior to the completion of the lengthy repair operations. The Government cannot allow the inconvenient disruption due to demolition of *all* such buildings."

"Can I quote you on that?" asks the front man.

"I'll deny it." Geez. This could get the family business in big trouble. Dad has always insisted that Lilly-Thomas keep a low profile. I brush the concrete dust and insulation fluff from my jacket. "You know that the Government is adverse to the risk of scandal." I walk out into the sun after my first day on site.

My yellow cab drives me to the nearby town to visit the parents of Carmella Meeks. I'm hoping that time has healed some of their dislike of me. I wrote two letters to Carmella's parents in 1995, but nothing further until last Christmas. Captain Meeks' reply in 1995 blamed me for his daughter's disappearance. The next reply was from her mom, in 1996, and was more encouraging: "She's written to her sister, and has changed her name from Marise to Carmella--trying to make a new life for herself." Last month Captain Meeks wrote an unexpected letter saying that Carmella seemed to have disappeared again—there has been no contact, and no reply from her last known address. Apparently her dad wants my help, but is too proud to ask directly.

My cab pulls up at the front gate of Carmella's family home. It is waist high and made of wrought iron with a wooden address plate, *1 Meeks Rd,* and has no fence either side of the gate, like at my mom and dad's home back in New Zealand. The gate still swings beautifully on its hinges. A concrete pathway leads through it, marking the distance to the house. The house is empty. The only thing moving is the aluminum coffee pot, simmering gently on the stove. It smells slightly bitter and burnt and the entire house is filled with the smell. Carmella's father, Carl-Junior, walks into the house a few minutes later.

"Thanks for coming. Carmella's still missing... and my wife died of a heart attack."

"I'm sorry... When did Mrs. Meeks die?"

He's going to dump on me. I hate that. Probably got no friends. And poor Carmella. She'd be better off if it was C-J that had died. The still simmering coffee pot sings the bitterness of his pain. He leans on the kitchen bench, his gray-black face distorted.

"I don't want to talk about it. Just help me find Carmella?"

"That's why I'm here. To find her."

We sit on the black leather sofa in the familiar living room with the TV mounted high on the wall. A beam of evening light shines through the hole in the awning. Dust floats in the air and cobwebs cling to the dirty windows.

Carl-Junior has his own Command now, a miniature submarine. Captain Meeks specializes in underwater explosives, but he has been seconded to work next week on demolishing several high-rise buildings in Manhattan with thermite. It cuts through steel columns like a hot knife through butter, resulting in a more controlled demolition.

"I don't believe she's gone too far. All she knows are the Fort Pierce and Vero Beach areas. But Hillary Clinton has called for her twice," Captain Meeks says.

"Why would Hillary Clinton possibly be calling for Carmella?"

"They became pen pals after Mrs. Clinton tried to organize a Presidential Pardon Ceremony for Grandpa Carl--regarding the Port Chicago affair."

"How do you know it was the real Hillary Clinton?"

"She said she was, on the phone."

"Your family never met her?"

"No."

Carl-Junior drives a new Buick. He sits erect in his Navy uniform, chewing gum. "Is thermite as good as they say?" The coolness of the leather seat is soothing. "They tell me it burns only briefly, but at more than 2500 degrees."

"My crew gets the thermite charges for a whole building installed in a day… but it takes a week to wire the fuses," he says.

"I haven't heard about that on TV… must be how the EQE building came down."

"I don't want to talk about that. Top secret. Let's focus on finding my daughter."

He turns his radio on to shut me up. "Shall we start in Vero Beach? Show me the places she knows," I suggest. He nods, indicating he heard me above the radio music.

This bastard raped Carmella, but I gotta ride with him cause he may have information, and I have got to find her this time. We search up the Streets then down the Avenues and venture into neighborhoods where we have to drive down dirt tracks and ford deep puddles amidst blizzards of insects. We check out Bars that are so dark that we have to order a drink to give our eyes time to acclimatize.

When Carmella got pregnant, I was so ready for diapers, feeding bottles, and all the crap. I remember a time just before my sister died, almost ten years ago, when she insisted that I give her twin babies their feeding bottles. They must have been about nine months old and my sister had just finished breastfeeding. My mother Rita would have breastfed me at that age but it wasn't fashionable back then. I was raised on dairy formula, which is what my sister's twins were drinking that time I fed them. It was almost bedtime. Even though it was I who was feeding them rather than their mom, they'd nestled into me, each head perched in the crook of an arm. I still recall the weight of their heads against me. The funny thing was, all the time that the twins were feeding; they never once took their eyes off me. They just stared at me with an expression of complete trust. A small thing like the milky smell of a burp can melt your heart if you are open to it.

That is why I watch the *Newton Show* --because the show has a similar effect to a glass of warm milk before bedtime--relaxing and cozy. I particulaily like the *Hillary Clinton Special* on Tuesday evenings. She is the only Democrat on the show, unless you count that celebrity decorator Martha Stewart. Hillary is clever like Martha… but not just about house decorating, colors for fabrics and party cookies. However, the host, Newt Gingrinch, is abrasive and annoys me.

Captain C-J Meeks and I search from his Buick, stop after insect-ridden stop… knocking on blistered boarding house doors, showing Carmella's photo in coffee shops and corner stores. The photo shows her green eyes and sculptured lips.

…Reluctantly, I have to give up the search. Her father gives me the photograph, saying he has another. Marise is an uncommon name, but the prostitute who died in the basement of the EQE building rubble was not Carmella according to the Coroner. But how could he know that for sure?

The evening flight home to DC from Fort Pierce is delayed. It is hot at the airport, with smells of chili and rotting fruit, the screeching and shrieking of the parrots is as blaring as their plumage is glaring. The trees beyond the wire perimeter-fence are so dense that in the early evening I can't distinguish one from another. When the sun goes down it is silent, apart from the humming of the emergency generator. I had worked long hours on that crazy building site, accompanied by a stoned film crew and security guards, and because of the humidity I had to do my laundry every evening. There were just not enough free hours available to search in a planned way for Carmella.

Tonight the airport terminal is almost empty apart from several slow moving Staff. The PA makes an announcement: "There is a delay for all flights because a truck has knocked out an electric substation nearby." Traveling by plane magnifies my sense of the loss of Carmella. I think of leaving the airport, then glance at the businessman sleeping in a chair at the red table, motionless, his head thrown back. Anyone could cut his throat and he wouldn't be any the wiser. Funny eh? You could die just like that, without having a clue that it is about to happen. Like my sister... She was dead by the time I found her. The fence posts had come off the back of the truck and lay scattered around. At the bottom of the slope the truck was resting innocently on all four wheels, like a cattle beast grazing in a paddock. You wouldn't have known just by looking from the road that tragedy had occurred. You wouldn't have guessed that my sister had just been killed.

I flew out in pain from this same airport after Carmella and I were split-up, almost a decade ago. I stayed over in Florida for several months longer than I had planned. Carmella was pregnant, so I forfeited my air ticket home to be with her. I never made love to Carmella without using a condom. But one night the condom broke and she got pregnant. Then the fuss really began with her father.

I stayed on until the end hoping that we could work it out. But I was just a boy, and none of us could handle the pressure. Her father was violent and abusive, and I wouldn't have visited him today if I wasn't so desperate to find the love of my life. I was with Carmella right up until she was forced to abort our baby by her father--I asked Carmella to marry me that evening. But we didn't get time to make plans... I was evicted the following morning.

I am in no hurry to leave Fort Pierce now. To travel you have to have a home to leave, and a home to come back to. My house in DC is tired. I take one more look at the barman watching TV and at the sleeping businessman. I don't want company tonight. I stand stiffly and stroll outside of the terminal to the parking lot, which is deserted. I sit on a bench in the garden adjacent to the cracked stucco wall at the side of the airport. The quiet continues until a small plane comes in, squeals, and taxis to a hanger. Then the screeching and shrieking of parrots takes over. The forest's tangled mess sucks the echoes into creepers growing up branches, lianas hanging, and the white and yellow orchids that are latched into crannies in the tree trunks.

Carmella and I had planned to call our baby Marise from the beginning—after her mom. I never drink more than one glass of wine with dinner now, not since that awful binge the day we broke up. But I might have done so tonight if the empty bar had appeared more inviting—a drink to distract from the hopeless searching... and the guilt.

The electrical blackout is over the entire region served by the Vero Beach substation. The airport has only minimal lighting, powered by the humming generators. It is dim and humid. I stroll around the airport lounge yet again, to relieve my numb butt, waiting for dawn and a miraculous sighting of Carmella.

Sometime around 5am I go outdoors. A surreal landscape of misty, tropical Florida forest drips beyond the narrow airfield after a gush of rain. I search the perimeter. There I see an image of my Carmella in a white silk nightgown, walking on a lonely road flanked with gnarled trees and withered mangroves. Distant crows caw. A breeze ruffles her transparent nightgown. A peal of thunder echoes as flashes of lightning illuminate the road. The vision of Carmella seems to fuse with reality. Carmella cups her mouth with a palm. Our naked child, Marise, crawls toward her, crying. Carmella stifles a scream, hugs herself and shivers. Her eyes dart left and right. A distant parrot curses. She bites her lower lip and walks on. Marise's haunting shrieks grow louder. Carmella fidgets with her nightgown, panics, and runs away into the darkness of the steaming forest. The dream was so real--like watching a reality TV show. Now I know that Carmella is still alive. If she were dead she would have spoken to me from out there.

I am cold, so return to the terminal lounge. I lean against the wall and drift into a moment of sleep. When I come around the businessman has gone. I'm almost alone, except the barman is watching TV, and a couple is chatting in the lounge--they must have come in at dusk on that small plane. A wallet has been left beside a newspaper. It feels like expensive leather. According to the driver license the owner is a male with gray hair, wide jaw; and puffy face. There are also several credit cards and an ID card. The wallet belongs to Newt Gingrinch from Newton PR. I like that *Newton Show*--but Newt himself is not my cup of tea.

I call the mobile phone number on the ID card and get a bleary greeting, then, "Thank you. You've saved me a lot of trouble. Perhaps I can help you. No one is flying out of there. Where you headed?"

"Home to DC."

Newt talks about the collapse of the EQE building: "It couldn't possibly be terrorism, like the World Trade Center or Oklahoma City, could it?"

"More like the 1994 LA earthquake damage. It's got to be flawed welding metal, and the over-strength beam steel. Could be the fire triggered the vulnerability, along with an explosion. Or it may have been a thermite detonation. More tests are being done."

Newt is no longer a high Government official. He became king of the Congress as Speaker of the House in 1995, and was the leader of the first Republican majority of both houses of Congress. Newt represented the angry white male striking back. His message was delivered in a voice with the swagger of a movie star, pitched to the terror of the times. Newt perfected the politics of personal destruction, as he attacked President Clinton regarding his sexual morality… despite his own carnal affairs. The more outrageous his rhetoric became, the more attention he got from the media; a media regime purchased and aggregated by moguls--almost entirely Republican.

*We are engaged in reshaping a whole nation through the news media*, Newt Gingrinch boasted to the *Washington Post*.

Like Bill Clinton, Newt Gingrinch was abandoned by his real father, an alcoholic, and from the age of three, was raised by a harsh stepfather who invaded

18

his household and took possession of his mother.

Newt bragged that all future Presidential Candidates would have to adjust to a world in which his Congress was *relatively more important than the White House*. Newt, the new Speaker, encouraged speculation that he himself might be available as a Presidential Candidate. Then Newt was caught with his hand in the cookie jar; cheating with election funds and diverting public monies to his own personal promotional programs. Newt is no longer in the Congress. He retired in 1999. But he still has major back-stage influence.

"What about Al Queda, Oklahoma City, and the 1993 Trade Center bombing?" Newt asks. "A remote controlled missile?"

I don't need to know… whatever Al Queda might be. Newt fires questions at me, similar to those that the film crew has been asking, as if he and they are in collusion and pushing me. I tell Newt that it is important for me to avoid reaching any conclusion until all the data is in--*to be objective*. It is difficult because the film crew, and now Newt, only demand the answers they want to hear. Then Newt asks me to explain *objective* over and over. "Is it the opposite of delusion… or illusion?"

The EQE building belongs to Newton PR. (I had presumed it belonged to the CIA or the FBI.) So why does my client care to the stage of being a nuisance? The Fort Pierce Naval Base leased the building from Newt PR to use as a research center. Strangely, the entire building had been vacant prior to the collapse. I suspect there is a devious cover-up underway: the similarity between the EQE collapse and the Murrah Building in Oklahoma City in 1995 is eerie: they both collapsed instantaneously, as if detonated by massive explosives--a much larger explosive force than was reportedly available in terrorist Timothy McVeigh's truck, or in the basement gas supply for the EQE building. I have had some of the molten metal debris from EQE tested for thermite because of the high temperatures involved and the nature of the residue.

"I'm going to DC," says Newt. "All flights have been cancelled out of Fort Pierce, could be hours before electricity is restored. I've chartered a plane, leaving from a private strip ten miles away. Want a ride?"

…I want to get out of this airport and get home, hire a private detective; and plan another search for Carmella, but I am suspicious of Newt. I'm suspicious that the EQE building collapse was rigged to test how a representative of the engineering profession would react if a building came down. Imagine if it had collapsed in a populated metropolis like New York? "No thank you Newt. I'll leave your wallet at the bar."

# CHAPTER 4: TONY CHAYTOR, April 2001

Carmella and I can talk for hours now in the summer twilight, on the patio, in the spa, or lying in bed. Carmella arrived at my door last month, unannounced, wearing only a red summer dress with small white flowers, in the cold of March. The kid was beside her. It has taken a few weeks to get accustomed to calling her Carmella rather than Marise. After all these years of searching and praying and heartache, I am finally living with Carmella now--and the kid. Marise has started school here and her education needs to be planned. Marise looks more like her mom than her father; and is small for her age.

Carmella and I don't debate about current stuff like global warming, the stalled economy, our new President, George W. Bush, or peak oil. We want our own space to build something special. Whether Carmella is talking or listening, her eyes are attentive and steady, her head still. She talks confidently, "We could buy our own mansion soon. Just like the mansion that Hillary Clinton lives in on the *Newton Show*."

I shall persist with my parenting goals despite Marise's initial rejection of me. I buy my child gifts, play board games; and take her on trips to the laundromat. She is slow at board games though and has been understandably cautious with me. The thing is; I don't want to be tight and busy like my father, now that I am responsible for a child. I want to be the kind of dad who has real adventures with my daughter, like Hillary does with her daughter. Hillary and Carmella are becoming good friends, (Hillary insisted upon meeting her right away and has taken a keen interest) taking Marise to the gym and the shops... just small trips—within bounds--just clean energetic fun close to home. There's a widespread notion that children are open. The truth about their inner selves is ripped from many children by frustrated adults struggling with inadequacies. It doesn't just seep out of them. That is all wrong. No one is more covert than a child. No one has greater cause to be that way. It's a response to a world that's always using a can opener on children to see what they have inside.

When Carmella falls asleep with her arm around me, I smell the natural scent of her body, subtle, difficult to recreate the next day, but still easy to recall. The impact of her scent lingers permanently in my memory like a Crossroads dream. It is a scent that smells as God might smell... a little stronger than spring water, almost as strong as vanilla.

Carmella and I wake and drink papaya juice in the dawning summer heat. I stare at the ceiling, watching the wobble of the rotating ceiling fan, and the patterns of water stains on the white wallpaper.

My home for the last five years, and now Carmella and Marise's home for the last months, is outside DC, near where three states converge. Carmella and I shop in Virginia, and work and educate Marise in Maryland and Pennsylvania, respectively--Carmella works at the Annapolis submarine base. She might still be unemployed if Hillary hadn't helped: Carmella can get claustrophobic in confining environments such as in a submarine or in a tight embrace, so she needed some conditioning therapy. I wish I could help Carmella but she keeps secrets from me. I used to be entirely open--until that day I got evicted by her dad. Regrets have haunted me from that day, awaking in Carmella's parent's living room in Florida, too exhausted to think. She was eighteen and pregnant, and I had almost finished my Ph. D. Her Grandpapa Carl was sick in the basement with radiation poisoning from an explosion at a naval base in California they said. Poor Carl. I must have been sick too. I could hear children babbling.

I go back to that memory often; There was light from a dim blue bulb. A ceiling fan creaked and fluttered the curtains as it whirled overhead. Carmella looked peaceful as she slept. The window blew open. Carmella stirred, shivered, grabbed a pillow and hugged it just as an eerie cry of a baby cawed in the distance. Carmella started panting in the middle of a nightmare. A gust of wind tossed the curtains up and about. A bank of cloud scurried across the sky before the flickering moon's light suddenly shone through the window. Carmella awoke.

"Where are we?" Carmella pleaded… "Tony?"

"In your parents' home, Carmella."

She sat up and looked around. We were on the foldout sofa. A large TV hung high on the wall and her brother Freddie and her sister Donna sat in the black vinyl chairs disarrayed around the lounge. Freddie turned the volume up on the TV.

Footsteps trudged down the staircase, getting louder. Mrs. Meeks entered and glanced toward us. She was dressed in a fuchsia nightgown, but wore boots. She clomped to the kitchen. Captain Meeks marched in, his Navy officer's uniform bright. "Darling, is breakfast ready?" he asked.

"Sorry Captain. Soon."

The phone rang. Carmella bit her lower lip. "Don't answer it Mama. I'm not going to any abortion clinic with Buck, no matter what Dad says," Carmella said.

"But…"

"What about Tony's feelings? You talk as if he isn't . . ."

"Men get over things," Mama said.

"But what about me? When will I get over it?" The phone stopped ringing.

"You will. Buck'll take good care of you. But I wish he wouldn't call so early."

"It's Tony that I love Mama. Please, I'm destined to be with Tony!"

Captain Meeks raised his head from a magazine. "Tony is racist. Besides, Buck is Catholic like us. Do you want to be a burden on the family?"

"This is ridiculous. Tony's listening… and Buck is the racist one. I want Tony."

"I think my sis' is right." Freddie said from the doorway.

Mrs. Meeks gave Freddie a warning look.

"Let's give her a chance," Freddie said. "It's time for her to follow her heart."

"Listen to the boy. What do you know about racism and marriage?"

"Enough of this negative talk or I'll cut my stay short," Freddie said.

"More talk like that and it may be better that you travel sooner." Mrs. Meeks absorbed Freddie's glare and continued, "Sweetheart, with time you'll understand."

Carmella covered her face with her palms and sobbed, "It's only been two months. There's still seven months to go. When will I understand Mama?"

"Someday you will. And no seven months! You'll have an abortion this month."

"No, Mama," Freddie said. "This is Carmella's life. She's an adult now for…"

"Keep quiet, Freddie!" Captain Meeks interrupted.

Freddie jumped. "It's a real life Mama. Don't you get it?" He slammed out the door.

"With time you'll get over it Marise." Captain Meeks paced the parlor, scratching his head. "No child! Have an abortion and I'll take care of you."

Captain Meeks looked out the window and then turned sharply on me, "Leave my house... We have an abortion to arrange--thanks to your irresponsibility."

Carmella stared into space, her eyes watering. Her mother, now sitting close to Carmella on the other side of the sofa, threw an arm over Carmella's shoulder and petted her.

"What do you *want?*" I asked. There must have been something more, something better I could have said.

"Father is out of control. You'd better leave."

I quietly shut the door, and listened outside through the open window. My head was throbbing from being treated like I barely existed, just an inconvenience to Captain Meeks' plans--whatever they were.

Carmella was still sobbing--I should have gone back inside. I was a coward.

"C'mon Marise. Buck's an architect," Mrs. Meeks said. "Registered with the State of Florida. Better than a gypsy student like Tony Chaytor. Brighten up. Come on! Smile for your mama. Smile for me."

There was a long silence then. I could have gone back and taken Carmella with me; but instead I walked to the local bar, ordered a beer, took one taste, and spat it out. My anger needed a more bitter expression. So I caught a taxi to the airport... my first taste of that morbid departure lounge at Vero Beach. I learned of a flight due to leave for Washington DC. Contrary to common knowledge it is possible to hitch a ride on a plane: I volunteered to help the crew to repair the plane, and then asked for a ride. That is the way of my life. I never turn down an opportunity for a free ride on a plane or a ship. My father hates me hitching rides, but my mother understands because she is a Gypsy. My dad mostly wants to be recognized as the best in his fields of engineering and ranching: to be famous in New Zealand is insufficient--he wants to be the best in the entire world.

Dad's character drove him to leave Mom for a short period when I was six. Deep within every great love grows a small hatred toward the beloved; she holds the only key to his happiness. Dad left in a state of pent-up rage. Catastrophes such as rage, hurricanes, and earthquakes occur at regular intervals--but what *determines* the frequency? Only the longing to return home surpassed Dad's rage. He was tied to Mom with a fan belt that was invisible to the rest of us. Dad can remember every golf stroke in every tournament he has played. But he regularly confuses Mom's name. It's symptomatic of the narcissistic person: his surrounding world becomes nameless.

I hitched a ride to a bar in the downtown district of DC to reflect on my critical day back in Fort Pierce. Loud people filled the bar, dancing so hard as to vibrate the floor. People shouted to be heard. A few stood close, talking directly into their neighbor's ears. I was there for an hour before I edged across the dance floor and slithered through the crowd near the door. I hauled myself up the stairs.

Silence pushed at me as I staggered through an open doorway and forced my rubbery legs to a vacant table. I sat. My head span slowly. The vibration from the music below my feet finally stopped. I drained my beer, wiped my lips, and sat there, vacant.

A waitress approached me along the polished floor. "Another bottle," I requested. "Will *Near Beer* do?"

...She shook me awake and handed me a chilled bottle. The room was almost empty. A Christian song was singing from the jukebox. The waitress sat down at the table across the aisle. A pretty lady was also observing me as I quaffed the contents of my new bottle. The lady smiled uneasily as she stood, pushed her book aside, and started toward me.

"Hello, my name is Hillary." She leaned over me, "Since you've been staring at me, I thought I may as well introduce myself... I'm *Hillary*," she emphasized. "What's your name?"

I lifted my bottle with intoxicated difficulty and took another mouthful.

Hillary sat at my table. "I've been watching you since you staggered in. A novice drinker. Do you want to kill yourself?"

"I'd be better off dead."

"I didn't hear that. What'd you say?"

I swallowed and tried to untangle my tongue, "My name's Tony."

"Yes. Tony Chaytor," she said.

"Lady . . ." I ogled her while trying to take my eyes off her white tits. She stood so I couldn't look down her blouse. I turned to stand. "Leave me alone." I staggered, spilled my beer, and then kicked the table sideways.

Hillary reached to steady me. "Then who will take care of you Kiwi? Pity?"

"Pity ain't never taken care of no one. So fuck off."

Hillary moved close to ensure that I heard her next words. "Please don't kill yourself. This isn't a bar. This is the drop in center at Downtown Methodist Church."

"How'd you know my name?" I was suddenly sober.

"Many guys come in after taking the wrong turn, with problems similar to yours. We never laugh after they tell their story. What's your story?"

"I'm Tony. Tony Chaytor." I stood again in an attempt to leave, but fell back heavily into my chair.

"Isn't your father's name William? Dr. William L. Chaytor?"

"How'd you know? Oh my God! ...You must be Hillary Clinton." I sat and placed my arms on the table; then buried my face in them, ignoring the spilled beer that was soaking the sleeves of my shirt.

"That man's in heaven but I'm here. I think it's me you need right now. Let's go." Hillary helped me up.


We stopped for Chinese food on the way to the sofa in my father's office at Lilly-Thomas. Hillary knew the way because she has worked on projects with my dad. I didn't puke that night.


Hillary met me the next day--with a ticket back to my University, to attend my final thesis examination--courtesy of my father's account.

## PART III

## CHAPTER 5: Morning of September 11, 2001

Tony Chaytor is not supposed to *discuss* the project to measure long-term effects of radiation in the vicinity of Port Chicago, California. ... the Port Chicago testing was set in motion by Bill Clinton when he was President... and Dubya might have cancelled the project if he were that type of detailed administrator. But Dubya doesn't have a clue with regard to the ongoing data gathering that has already concluded that people living within a twenty-mile radius of Port Chicago have the highest cancer rates in the US.

According to Grandpa Carl Meeks, Port Chicago was a spiteful place to work back in 1944: The air at the loading dock spat static and the bombs that Grandpa Carl Meeks was loading that dry evening were so alive they were slapping him. Alerted by the stones jumping off the roadway, and by the dogs howling through the electric air, Carl ran from the dock ten minutes before the detonation. Carl Meeks was only twenty that night he ran his fastest mile. The explosion that followed was the world's first nuclear detonation. It happened in California, on July 17, 1944.

Hillary Clinton telephoned the Meeks' family after the interview aired in 1995. Carmella was the only one who would take her call that day. Hillary acknowledged the Government racism that lead to the Port Chicago mutiny. Hillary's husband, President Bill Clinton, subsequently apologized for the injustice that the Meeks' family and the other black sailors suffered after Port Chicago, but that long-overdue 1999 apology wasn't enough to compensate for the debilitating shame that the US government had previously smeared upon the Meeks' family.

Munitions Loading Units were all black in 1944. That was because of the Navy's segregation policy: The bunkrooms of warships were reserved for white sailors. Black sailors were mostly assigned to shore units and only performed menial duties. Few duties were considered more menial... or more dangerous, than munitions loading.

The off-duty black sailors who survived the Port Chicago explosion have been forced to endure the denials and the further spite of the Navy. Even today, more than fifty years later, Grandpa Carl Meeks is still suspended between the meanness of the living and the haunting of the dead.

Garndpa Carl's only child, Carl-Junior, was born in Fort Pierce, Florida a year before the detonation. Grandpa Carl moved back to Fort Pierce after he was released from the Navy. He kept the dirty secrets of the war to himself--until the day that the interview aired on the *Newton* Show. The interviewer asked Grandpa Carl, "If you don't like America why don't you leave? Go and live in Puerto Rico with your wife's family?"

"What'd be the point?" Carl said. "Not a house in the world... Democrat or Republican, ain't packed to the rafters with some Colored person's grief."

"It was the Democrats in charge of Port Chicago and Pearl Harbor. Blame the Democrats, rather than *all* of America," the interviewer said.

Grandpa Carl's wife died shortly before that *Newton Show* interview. The interview was aired only once on the network media. Carl concluded that the network rejection was because he had exaggerated his claim that the children of the Port Chicago survivors *all* suffered congenital deformities as a result of the nuclear radiation—and unfortunately the interviewer concluded the show with a put-down of Carl's concerns:
"The *Congressional Record* states that a child of the black munitions loaders, who suffered congenital deformities, suffered them as a result of wartime *stress.*"
Grandpa Carl was still suffering from a continuing Governmental denial of a nuclear detonation!

Grandpa Carl Meeks now lives furtively, thirty miles hinterland from Washington DC, where the winters are rough. The breakfast show on TV provides him some relief, but counting on that duplicity for life's principal amusement is discouraging. Carl doesn't regret leaving the old haunts down in the oppressive heat of Florida. He hid there with Carmella until his granddaughter finally moved. Carmella will marry her teenage sweetheart, Tony Chaytor, soon.
Grandpa Carl doesn't walk the mile across the invisible railway track to Carmella and Tony's house. Instead Carl forces himself to stay at home—voluntarily, staying at home helps Carmella not to worry that he might say the wrong thing about Eleanor's abortion, in Tony's presence. Last week Carl comforted himself by getting satellite TV hooked up – "*So's I can eyeball BBC News, and African and Arab TV. See something mo' real than that white bread American TV.*" When Tony visits him, Carl turns the volume up on his new TV so as to avoid Tony hearing any slip of his tongue about Carmella's prostitution... or her secret plan to hijack a submarine... the plan that Carl isn't suppose to know about.
Carl dresses early today because it is Tuesday. His granddaughter always visits him on Tuesdays, and today arrives shortly after 9am, just in time to see the terrorist plane explode horrifically into the 110-storey WTC-1, twin tower number one of the World Trade Center.
Carl sees the other Trade Center Tower, WTC-2, get hit by another plane half-an-hour later—and collapse before the first tower. Carl continues to stare at the TV coverage for a further two hours. Then he turns to Carmella as she is cleaning his lounge windows: "The United States has brought on them Al Qaeda's attacks because of its own terrorism. Them white breads bombed Hiroshima, they bombed Nagasaki, and them nuked far more than those three thousand got killed in New York. They supported white bread terrorism against Palestinians and black South Africans, and now they got the blues cause that stuff them white breads gone done overseas is now come back to their own front yard. Those white bread American chickens, them chickens o' justice, them comin' home girl, comin' home to roost."

"You're a tad too hard on the Government Grandpa. Nobody deserves to die like that. Nobody! Black or white. Nobody... It's time for your meds Grandpa."

## CHAPTER 6: Evening of September 11, 2001

Grandpa Carl Meeks hurries back to his TV after a quick pee. It is 4.57 pm on Tuesday, September 11, 2001, almost time for the five o'clock news. The British channel, BBC World, interrupts their broadcast. "Listen to this Grandpa," Carmella yells.

The anchor appears on the TV screen:

"We'll leave it there for a moment. We've got some news coming in… The Salomon Brothers' Building (WTC-7) in New York, right in the heart of Manhattan, has also collapsed. This fits in with a warning from the British Foreign Office a couple of hours ago to British Citizens that there is a strong risk of further atrocities in New York and it seems as if there is now another terrorist attack with the Salomon Brothers' Building collapsing. We've got no word yet on casualties. One assumes that the building would have been virtually deserted…"

5:00 pm: The anchor states:

"The 47-story Salomon Brothers' WTC-7, situated just a few hundred meters from where the WTC-2 tower stood—only hours ago, has also collapsed."

5:07 pm: The anchor states:

"Now more on the latest building collapse in New York... you may have heard a few moments ago we were talking about the Salomon Brothers' Building WTC-7 collapsing and indeed it has, and apparently it is only a few hundred meters away from where the pair of 110-storey World Trade Center Towers collapsed. It appears that rather than another terrorist attack, the WTC-7 building had perhaps been weakened by falling debris from adjacent buildings during this morning's attacks. We'll cross now to find out more from our correspondent Jane Standley in New York. Jane. What more can you tell us about the Salomon Brothers' Building and its collapse?"

5:08 pm: The screen is filled by BBC correspondent Jane Standley standing beside a window framing smoke rising from Ground Zero… and a clearly *erect* WTC-7.

5:09 pm: The caption on the bottom of the BBC screen continues to lie:

"The 47-story Salomon Brothers building (WTC-7) has also collapsed."

5:14 pm: The image of Jane Standley begins to break up and the anchor, remarking that they'd "lost the line." The anchor shifts to another report.

Carmella runs to the kitchen, makes a hurried phone call while grabbing clothing under her arm then packs of chips, throws grandpa Carl's jacket at him and shouts, "Fuck! I can see WTC-7 standing with my own eyes. Get dressed. I just called my father on his cell phone." She starts to trickle tears. "Dad's still in WTC-7, right now, in the building that supposedly just collapsed. C-J says there is no collapse. We have to go to New York right now! But first I gotta run home and sort Marise and Tony out."

"This ain't right. My son's inside WTC-7? All our plans spinnin' to nuthin'. WTC-7 just falls down dead. BBC news' always right. I've lost my son? I only see you on

Tuesdays, and never visit the child, or Tony. My only comfort now be watchin foreign TV... and dissin C-J. And now that's gone? What about the plans for the sub?"

"Maybe it's isn't as bad as you think. Anyway, we'll talk on the way to New York. His tin submarine'll probably rust away now. See you in an hour Grandpa."

Carl takes off the gray tie and shirt that he has favored for ten years, and dresses in the yellow tie and mauve shirt that Carmella gave him. He dresses slowly.

Carmella hears the 7pm news broadcast from her bedroom at home: "WCT-7 really did collapse ... but officially at 5.20pm--twenty-three minutes after the first announcements of the collapse were made on BBC World TV News, and later than also announced on one local TV network. One person is known to have died in the basement of WTC-7--Carl Joseph Meeks..."

The police call on Carmella half an hour later to inform the next of kin. Carmella says nothing about the death announcement to Marise--Tony is still playing chess with Marise in the library, away from the TV. He grabs his coffee cup nonchalantly and follows Carmella down the stairs to the kitchen. "Bye Tony. Gotta help Grandpa Carl adjust to this... without upsetting Marise. Thanks Honey. See you tomorrow or the next day. I'll call." Carmella often leaves home for several days at a time.

Grandpa Carl crouches in his corner lounge chair, suffering flashbacks to the cold distance of racially prejudiced DC clerks, and remembers the sour air of Government buildings--with the accumulation of tension from years of arguing for justice across synthetic carpets that crackled and snapped with static electricity. Carl knows the root of his oppression, just as he knows the source of the blinding white light and mushroom cloud that he saw as he crouched behind an embankment at Port Chicago in 1944. Grandpa Carl's memory of cowering beyond the Port Chicago highway is as lifeless as the loose skin on his stomach, which buckles like a washboard when he sits again in his TV chair to pull on his socks. He works hard to remember as close to nothing as possible. Unfortunately his brain is devious. Fifty-seven years later he is still jumping out of his TV chair and running. Carl runs outdoors with stiff knees, across the backyard to the faucet. He looks like an overstuffed scarecrow with bulging shirt and trousers, panic stricken. He is running to the outside faucet to rinse the static electricity and energy-draining radiation from his hands, a frequent panic Carl has suffered since the day he unloaded those two mystery box cars of snapping ordinance into number five hold at Port Chicago.

Grandpa Carl allows the water from the faucet to run over his hands, massaging away the feared radiation. His mind is obsessive about getting every last bit of smacking static off his skin. The rest of his body is too fragile to comfortably touch the fabric of his clothing; he prefers soft double-ply toilet paper against his skin. This is why his clothes are always bulging. He stuffs toilet paper down the legs of his trousers, inside his shirt, and up his sleeves, desperate to separate his delicate skin from the crude and abrasive texture of clothing fabric. It takes him a long time to dress--even the paper can scratch his skin. Carl washes by daubing himself with wet toilet paper. After most of today's dose of radiation is finally washed off his hands, he limps around to the front of his tiny bungalow and collects his shoes.

27

The 7.00 pm BBC World news sounds loud today, even from the front porch. It starts with the story about WTC-7 collapsing and his son, C-J being killed-- And ends with a segment about Hillary:

*... At the unofficial inquiry initiated by Hillary Clinton yesterday, American soldiers said the Pentagon has used the misfortunes of war as a propaganda opportunity to glorify recent military endeavors: Corporal Fletcher, an NHL hockey star who served in the Desert Storm war in Iraq, was actually killed by American "friendly-fire."*

Carmella approaches the porch again, panting, with her dress swaying. "Tony's home with Marise. Good for a few days as usual." Every Tuesday, bar none, Carmella has been busy cleaning Carl's home, a silent visitor--the innocent lamb with whom grandpa Carl made an alliance against the bitterness of her father--his son, Captain Carl Junior... and an alliance to keep her affair with a prominent local politician secret. Both alliances are propelled by their fermenting anger.

"I've washed hands," Carl says.

"OK. Your tie is backwards. Hurry!" She smiles. "How *are* you now... besides miserable?" Carmella laughs and it comes out loose and young.

"Got the static real bad. Even got sparks when I peed in the grass."

Carmella pulls a face as though tasting a bitter medicine. "Too much detail."

"Go on inside," Carl says.

"Porch is fine, Grandpapa. Cool out here... and I'm sick to the stomach from these terrorist attacks. I was sad for the loss of C-J... but no more. I'm cried out already," Carmella says for her grandpa's benefit... she alone knows that her father isn't dead—because she called him again... and arranged to call C-J back with instructions.

Grandpa Carl sits and looks out across the meadow toward Carmella's home, on the other side of the Civil War battlefield. His coffee-colored granddaughter lives in white Emmetsburg—with Tony Chaytor and his surviving great granddaughter, Marise; those two only visit Carl's home in Fredericksburg, a blue-collar town this side of the battlefield, to watch major sporting events.

"Ah baby. You'll miss your father, even though he did you wrong. Christian folk forgive way too easy. Must be why a lyin' cheatin' Bush government got re-elected," Carl says.

"The Pentagon hasn't said an honest thing for the last sixty years," Carmella says.

"The Military lied back in Civil War days too," Carl says. "Huh! George Washington and Abraham Lincoln weren't the heroes they claim. Negro mothers from the past know bout that." Carl knows that the sadness he feels shows in his eyes. He cannot help that. But today he also feels a new energy. "You hear the news about the enquiry into Desert Storm, about the military killin' our peoples with their friendly fire—again?" Carl asks.

"Yes Grandpapa, it's tragic. I telephoned Hillary in New York. The authorities advise that access to New York and the Trade Center is limited. Maybe we wait and travel up there tomorrow."

"Good ho. Always bin sick this country. You just didn't see until now," Carl says.

"My Tony's doin' a script for the *Newton Show*, a docudrama to expose Government lies at Port Chicago, Pearl Harbor, Waco, and the recent building collapses."

28

"Just cause Tony's done a lotta forensic writing bout disasters-n stuff, don't make him no expert on the government."

"He knows all the details about that stuff, and not much about my secrets."

"All that stuff was under Democrats. Git your shoes off, Hon. Let me git you a bowl of water to soak your feet."

"No, uh huh. We got to plan a funeral. And cancel my coffee appointment with Hillary tomorrow."

"D'ya know Hillary's story bout how she and Bill met aint true?" Carl says.

"It can't be. I heard it on the TV. Anyway, how do *you* know?" Carmella asks.

"I know cause her version--that she walk across the Yale Law Library and introduce herself to Bill--*Since you've been staring at me I fink I may as well introduce my self*, that story is a example of Hillary makin' herself more important than she aint."

"Hillary's a politician for God's sake Grandpa. And she's for children, for the poor, and for saving the environment. That's *important*, but she can't let on," Carmella says. "And the Newton PR firm does a lot of research to get our information accurate."

"Program our heads with propaganda, with plastic masks more like... One of Bill Clinton's law-school clansmen wrote, in a magazine *the truth is that it be Bill who made the first pitch, not no Hillary,*" Carl says.

Carmella shakes her head. "Hillary's been a rebel ever since she was young. She's been against war, for health care to the poor, for black people, for the environment, and pro abortion--even without parental consent."

"Too bad girlie! Hillary Clinton's hounds gone signed a contract--with that Newton PR firm--to do her next election biddin. White trash!" Carl says.

"C'mon Grandpa. They're the only media firm that has got the experience and the coverage. Hillary had no choice."

"Why d'ya think she hangs out with you baby? A poor black biddy?" Carl asks.

"You know Hillary and I go way back... and we're on the same wavelength," Carmella says.

"Do she give you money?" Carl asks.

"Used to. But not now, the Navy pays me well enough now. Working on submarines you get higher pay still. And I'm good for Hillary," Carmella says. "She often says that." Carmella turns away to hide her smile.

"Then why you gotta wear all doze fancy clothes to impress her? Or is it someone else you tryin' to impress?"

"Enough! You look good, Grandpapa, for a man that's officially pardoned of mutiny. A co-conspirator to overthrow this Government system. Nice tie. *Boy!*"

"Devil's confusion. He let me look good long as I feel ninety an' bad."

Carmella smiles inwardly. This is the way all those old sailors have been. Spunky. Grandpapa is almost the last of them still alive.

"The Government's secretly keepin' me alive to prove that they aint mistreated us blacks... by doin' nutin.' How can nutin' prove anythin'?"

Except for the nonstop watering in his eyes Carl looks almost as handsome as he did when he returned to Florida after the war: erect posture, straight shoulders. But his skin color is lighter now, a peach stone shade. He shuffles to the bathroom.

Carmella picks up the ringing phone. "...You at a call box?" Carmella looks fierce. "...Lucky you got out before the collapse." She checks that Grandpa Carl is not listening. "They think you're dead. So... you've got to stay out of sight. New York will be in chaos. The military, police, firemen... So, do what I say. You parked your tin submarine down in Fort Pierce last week, right? ...Good. Now's your chance to hide yourself and earn a bit of Catholic redemption! Take the little sub to Puerto Rico. Stay there with Grandma... Or I'll scream bloody rape! ...And keep your phone charged. Catch the Greyhound bus to Fort Pierce, go straight to the sub." Carmella hangs up and smiles at Carl as he returns.

"Why are we doin' a funeral? C-J was bastard to us both. Just for the appearance of bein' a good family?"

For a woman whose dad was supposedly killed by the collapse of WTC-7 three hours ago, it is amazing how ready Carmella is to smile. 'To please me, Grandpa. Tomorrow." Right away, with less than a blink, her face changes from hard to soft. "Pretty please?"

Grandpa Carl grows older, more hunched, as the hours pass through a sleepless night. At dawn Carmella eases up from the sofa and coaxes Carl's stiff bones to the car. "We have to do the funeral thing. Say goodbye to the bastard in the proper way."

Trucks bounce and hiccup along the concrete freeway toward New York. They smell burnt rubber through Carl's open window before they pass an accident. The rough fabric of his shirt is clawing at Carl's neck like a vampire. Carmella refuses to stop.

Carl grimaces, remembering the shame of his only son; Captain C-J Meeks, as Carmella double-parks as close as possible to the Trade Center devastation. On this cold afternoon, days before the official memorial ceremony at ground zero, Carl shudders at the massive blackness. There is no coffin. Carmella has stopped beside where a flag has been draped over the arm of a rusty cruciform. It is too windy for Carl to get out of the car--the wind has ripped the flag--it is all tattered, fluttering on the cross. Carl can see Carmella's eyes reflected in the car window. There are no tears.

C-J will be remembered formerly next week, at the Annapolis Naval Cemetery for fallen warriors, any parts of him they *think* they have recovered, along with a Navy uniform. Those Navy fools would bury road kill wrapped in the flag. Who will get his pension? Grandpa Carl grabs at the place in his belly where the irony strikes him. His son brutalized Carmella's childhood, shamed her and drove her to a whorehouse in Fort Pierce. Dear Jesus! It is amazing that Carmella was strong enough to have a child, yet alone two--and to abort one of them. Grandpa Carl's wife had never been able to have another child after the war.

Carl barks, "America's chickens, they be comin' on home to roost. Mark my words."

"Enough, Grandpa! Get off your pity pot."

"Hillary's PR Company runs the *Newton Show* ... but they aint covered no issues bout radiation or pollution. We'll see if Tony does any better... I ain't holding my breath."

"Enough, Grandpa!"

30

The sun is setting, glaring in their faces. Carl's eyes are devoid of even a flicker of the evening light. They are like two tiny mirrors into which Carmella has trouble gazing. His eyes need to be covered with shades, or marked with some sign to warn people of the emptiness inside.

They are both silent during the return drive. Carmella wakes Carl just before home.

"Hillary was on the radio. Says she'll make things better... one day soon."

"What she says... *exactly?*" Carl asks.

"As best as I can remember: *My promise is to clean up our American Government. I have information that people were severely wronged because of Government mistakes... from Port Chicago, Pearl Harbor, through the Asian wars, to global warming.*"

Back at home Carl turns on the TV. "It'll be BBC now. Shush!"

*A guest on the Hillary Clinton Series, a slain man's younger brother, Kevin Fletcher--said the military knew almost immediately that Corporal Pat Fletcher, an Army Ranger who left a career as a pro hockey player to enlist, had been killed by accidental American fire in Iraq... By fire from his own unit, who had been given incorrect target coordinates--but officials chose to put a "patriotic glow" on his death. Kevin Fletcher said the decision to award his brother a Silver Star and to say that he died heroically fighting the enemy was "utter fiction" that was intended to "exploit Pat's death."*

"Hillary is announcing that Fletcher got killed by friendly fire... Her voice sounds different than in real life, and she looks a lot younger with all that make-up." Carmella then sees the light flash in Carl's eye.

"Sweet Lord! My guess is them Bush people blew-up Trade Center number seven with thermite--while my son was still in there doin' their dirty work. I want Hillary to *clean up* our Government."

"Yes! My Tony says that thermite collapsed WTC-7... says Hillary's got to fire her PR Company first before she can start the clean-up."

"Newton is under the thumb of the CIA," Carl says.

"You're ridiculous Grandpa."

"Yeah. I figure that. Newton Show's been paid off to make Hillary lose. Three things that the Republicans don't want: A woman, a black nigger, or a Democrat... for President."

# PART IV: HILLARY

## CHAPTER 7: 2006

QUESTIONS, always questions. And the media never wait for me to complete my answers. They rush on. Piling question upon question, covering every moment with questions, blocking off every sensation but that relentless clubbing of questions! And if they aren't going to listen to my answers how can I truly express myself? I know better than to say that out loud. Everything in my life that I value has been gained at the cost of not saying what I *really* think, of saying what my minders want me to say. At my therapist's suggestion, I tried writing my Truth in my diary early in the mornings, but invariably some crisis interrupted me, or I simply couldn't bear living the day ahead with fresh memories of the crushing past. So, I now I write my diary in the evenings, and this is more effective therapy:

April 15, 2006:
Dear Diary, What the sensible public part of me chooses to remember reliably about my past is that a calculating will to conquer the world of male sexism was accidentally installed in me by my dad, Hugh Rodham. Dad insisted that a man must be the head of the household. I was his favorite, even though I was a girl-- because I was the eldest and won almost every game at home, thrashing Dad and my two brothers at card games and quiz shows. Maybe that ruthless will to conquer is what it takes to be successful.

I woke up early as usual. One second I was sleeping, the next I was awake, remembering the hell I had just been through while asleep: Bill was lying next to me, on his back. I've never had much patience with other women's fantasies or unhappy love affairs. I hate their weakness. I watch them find a man and go to prenatal classes and have children. The day after the reunion for my old prenatal care-group, I had this particular dream... Bill had suffered a little relapse and I found him rolling around with one of the other happy mothers. In an instant I was then, and am now, uplifted from being the responsible politician, becoming a besieged and staunch feminist.

When I am under siege I rise promptly, dress quickly, and cauterize my emotions. The bubble of anger rising from my gut will remain level. My head must be separated from my heart. My hairstylist is always Isabel when I am in Washington DC. Isabel blows, waxes, and sprays my expensively blonded hair into an unflappable helmet while I study my list of things to do today.

First on the list is the *Newton Show*. This pre-recorded TV series has dominated my schedule every Tuesday morning for the last month. It airs a documentary series about me at 7.30pm Tuesday evenings. Last week's show had a better interview of me than usual, and felt more natural. I rarely read the newspapers, or watch TV-- other than my own series. Why should I want to know more about my husband's acting out of his sex addiction than necessary? If that vixen from Canada knew how

32

his addiction worked she would never put herself out for him. Why won't those sick women leave him alone to straighten himself out with his higher power?

~~~~~~~~~~~~~~~~~~~~~~~~~

April 17, 2006:

I ponder from under the hair dryer, a meditation that has become a routine for me since way back when I became First Lady. I sense the presence of someone who is dead: I am touched by my childhood aspirations and by my connection with Eleanor. She is my angel, the mentor with whom I consult at critical times--Eleanor Roosevelt, the former Democrat First Lady. I know a great deal about Eleanor: Her husband, President Franklin D. Roosevelt, had an affair with Lucy Rutherford from 1918 to 1945, and he fathered Lucy's only child. I wonder how the people will feel about FDR, and his betrayed wife Eleanor, when my future declassification of Government secrets reveals all? The angry feminists who think I should have walked out on Bill after his indiscretions will come to realize that some of our nations greatest heroes have been equally indiscreet. The truth about what happened on FDR's watch at Port Chicago and Pearl Harbor--and the truth about the World Trade Center bombings... is going to disturb many people. I am concerned about the escalation of corruption and about the self-promotion of the rich in American politics. Eleanor Roosevelt was also a socialist, advocating for the poor and minorities. Everyone says to me, "How can you be so calm while Bill is on the rampage?" I tell them that I have been through it so many times before. I have been in the spotlight as a public speaker since I was fifteen years old, when I was president of the Student Government back at Wellesley. Women never attended Princeton, Yale, or Harvard in those days. We gals were restricted to one of seven women colleges, but no campus issue was too large or too small for me. I worked to banish Mandatory Prayer in the dining hall. I pushed to increase the number of black students and black staff. I challenged the rules that decreed girls had to be home from dates by eleven on weeknights, and that stopped male visitors at the door for a virginal kiss goodnight.

~~~~~~~~~~~~~~~~~~~~~~~~~~~~

May 23, 2006:

My family and I are deeply religious. When I was young we talked with God, walked with God, ate, studied, and argued with God. My father came from a long line of Methodists but he left it to Mom and I to do most of the church going at Park Ridge, an affluent professional neighborhood of Chicago. Dad was blue collar, but simulated a professional lifestyle with the nice house and the new car--a lifestyle that mortgaged him to the hilt in order to maintain. Behind closed doors he swore, chewed tobacco, yelled, and shut off the heat in the house every night. He then turned a deaf ear to the complaints of my younger brothers and I during the winter blizzards. *Toughen up* was the message. In the Rodham code any emotional display signaled weakness. Life was seen as combat. My dad prided himself on being a Republican and having trained young Navy recruits for World War II.

Mom never went to college, but secretly harbored more liberal tendencies than Dad, but was loath to offer a dissenting view at a dinner table commanded by the male tyranny of Pop-Pop Rodham. It was a lesson Mom must have learned to survive in her own emotionally starved childhood amidst fifteen siblings. Mom was abandoned by her parents at the age of eight, from where the horror of divorce and broken families was inculcated into me. Behind closed doors there was much yelling from my father's grating voice. Consequently I was determined that no daughter of *mine* would go through the agony of being afraid to speak her mind. I saw that the women of Mom's generation were dominated by men with dreams, men in the civil rights movement and Peace Corps, and men in the space program. I wrote to NASA asking what it took to be an astronaut. I was told, "girls need not apply." Sexism is insidious!

I suffered an identity crisis at Wellesley that went on for four years. I found the process of self-definition to be depressing. At first I diagnosed myself as neither a hippie, nor a jet setter--nor problematic. I saw myself as normal. But it was my luck to live near the *problem* student of my dorm: After analyzing the causes of the girl's confusion I ministered to her out of my understanding of Godly morals and ethics. I was able to maintain my zone of privacy while counseling her--and other gals with broken wings.

During my junior year at college I was leading the revamping of the Republican state organization, step by logical step, and was often photographed by the newspapers speaking to adults at rallies, like a seasoned politician. My favorite photograph shows me pitched forward intently; in my navy pea-jacket, white blouse, and severe ponytail, hands outstretched toward the audience who stand spellbound in the snow. I looked like a modern suffragette, and even made them laugh. But there was a fear behind all my intellectualizing and organizing as I studied political science, a fear that I might discover a void inside myself: *Let's change the subject. Otherwise those damned inevitable questions will keep resurfacing. Why am I so afraid? Am I really not unique after all? Will I live a clichéd life? Is life merely absurd? How do you define happiness--operationally?*

Back then, happiness for me was getting A's, doing good deeds, and running for Office, but I found depression the February following a most successful year in that regard. I had met a new boy, and had embarked on my Christian ministry, a ministry that culminated twenty years later with a talented and beautiful twenty-plus Black-Puerto Rican girl. She called herself Marise Meeks at that time, but changed her name to Carmella shortly after. I promised Carmella back in 1996 that I would share my diary with her in exchange for her writing a diary herself--and sharing it with me. All my 'good deed' efforts to guide Carmella through this most critical stage of her journey as a single mother are starting to show results. Back in *my* college days I had insufficient experience to discern a pathway through the depressing chaos… but I didn't get pregnant like Carmella. I did suffer though: I could hardly get out of bed. I was cutting classes, falling asleep in Bible study, and disappointing my professors. I sat in my room alone and thought. But random thinking without focus on some narrow idea is dangerous for me and leads back to the same frighteningly uncontrollable place: looking inside. And once I slip into self-analysis I find my ego coming out on the short end. The easiest way for me to avoid my rancid mess is to turn my attention to advising others on how to live *their* lives, and thereby halt any thoughts approaching introspection. Introspection is dangerous for me.

~~~~~~~~~~~~~~~~~~~~~~~~

June 24, 2006:

Man is a political animal. He is incapable of the selfless compassion required to make communism work. Nor is he capable of the commitment to self that would make the "I" philosophy of Ayan Rand's ultimate capitalism practical in the real world. Man was born unruly and must be controlled through politics in order to function adequately in the huge bureaucracies of modern society and the complexities of international relations.

The first need that developed from living in a dormitory, aside from the perpetual hunger, was the need for peace. There was no peace in my dormitory, so the desire was suppressed. Instead, it turned into the need for a hiding place, for a secret room. During that year I went through several metamorphoses. I was fully conscious of selecting my preferred personality from a smorgasbord of options: I tried out educational and social reformer, alienated academic, involved pseudo-hippie as a political leader, and compassionate living in withdrawn simplicity. I went so far as to invite a Black male kid to go to my lily-white Sunday church service--and formed a commune of girls in my dorm where we developed what later came to be known as sisterhood. I am incapable of withdrawing from society's needs--because we are all here to help somebody.

~~~~~~~~~~~~~~~~~~~~~~~~~~~~~

September 27, 2006:

My graduation was notable: Firstly for the absence of my parents and brothers--that issue is still a sore point. And secondly, because I was chosen as the first ever student to speak at a college graduation ceremony. That day, as the cheers of jubilation from my speech died down and the last hugs of farewell were exchanged, one friend lingered to tell me that she would have felt lost without me. I could spend my life worrying about other people or the state of the world; sublimating the person inside who I am avoiding. I came to despise my sheltered suburban childhood as I plunged further into depression. I had walked and worked through the slums of Washington DC, Boston, and Chicago to purge my depression.

Every month, from 1996 until now, I have sent copies of the most recent pages from my diary to Carmella--as she struggled with her different reality... parenting from the brothels of Florida back then, and struggles with different but equally debilitating issues now. In spite of all my precocious political activities, I was worried that I might have to settle for the stereotypical marriage to a US congressman or Senator... throw away my fine education. But even as I mocked that sexist picture, I resisted turning that picture entirely to the wall. I was interested in one of the theories proposed by Robert Kennedy: *maximum feasible participation of the poor* in programs designed to help them. The difference between the poor and the rest of us is that we have control over our lives, whereas poor people have always been victims. What will help people rise from poverty and become effective citizens is to empower them. Community action programs, as advocated by Kennedy, can have short-term benefits. But to have any long-term impact on the core problems of negating the shame of poverty we need to have structure, organization, leadership, and a middle class willing to get involved. My professor hoped that I would become the first woman to sit on the Supreme Court after I graduated from Yale law school. Some of my fellow students were thinking of me as the first woman to become President of the United States.

~~~~~~~~~~~~~~~~~~~~~~~

December 1, 2006:

When I am frozen before a blank page of my diary I often turn to reflect upon previous sections. But today I shall write something new:

I am still unpopular with some… with many potential voters according to the latest polls. Obama, my new potential opposition according to those polls, said over dinner that I am too intense, suppressing the feminine--all brain. We are trying a new softly-softly PR image where I try to be different than the old strident Hillary. I get help by consulting with William L. Chaytor, and his clever son, Tony. Tony Chaytor is doing the research for the script of *Hillary;* the next Newton PR series that I hope will turn the 2008 Presidential primaries in my favor. Charismatic performances in the TV studio are rare for me. I have to prime myself for TV by talking to Eleanor Roosevelt!

This morning is another crucial appearance that will either pull my Democrat candidacy out of a nose-dive, or lower my declining ratings further. It is always pressure, and that is what my life has prepared me for, pressure.

Of course Eleanor became a lesbian after that betrayal by her cheating husband! How many times does the author Ed Klein use the word "lesbian" in his book about me? Barack Obama said that the journalist Ed Klein is a friend to me. I don't believe it! If so, why would Klein point out to my voters that I have many friends who are lesbians? Sure, my politics were shaped by the culture of radical feminism and lesbianism at Wellesley College… but the lesbian rumours still circulate about me, and voters are wondering if I am misrepresenting myself as a doting wife to Bill Clinton. "How can I stand his chronic infidelity?" they wonder. That's easy to explain according to Bill: *Forgiveness is a spiritual discipline that I have worked hard at mastering.* That is only half of it! An aide told this to Newt Gingrinch, "The Monica Lewinski bit just reeks of the made-up. Are we talking about the same Monica, the perpetually polished, prim, and proper Monica? The rumor borders on the laughable. In fact, when Newton PR floated this rumor to one State Department official who has worked closely with Monica's family, laughter was the result. It is doubtful that an affair with Bill would float Monica's boat. BBC seems to think Monica is a lesbian. Others lean towards a finding of asexuality. Either way, the notion of her having an affair with her boss strikes me as highly dubious.

~~~~~~~~~~~~~~~~~~~~~~~

January 1, 2007:

Since the sixties I have studied how the media gurus are influencing the American people. A Jesuit professor, Walter Ong, argued back then that the media was creating a global village of instant telecommunication, *which would undermine and reshape our consciousness.* It *has* happened. The Media Bosses are reluctantly working somewhat in my favor at this moment because they are hamstrung in reporting juicy stories about *my* personal life. The media has highlighted Bill's affairs in the past, but avoided any hint of *my* claimed current affair. Carmella says, "Newton PR knows about the source of rumors regarding the Hillary affair… but the predominantly Republican media won't publish it because it might make you *more* popular with the liberals." By contrast, a liberal TV channel reported, "A Mayflower Hotel staffer has confirmed that Hillary Clinton spends one night a week at that hotel, which is four blocks north of the White House—and guarded like an asylum. The Mayflower's official position on the story was that they could *neither confirm nor deny* the identities of their guests. Because of the Mayflower's penchant for security and secrecy, and because two of Hillary's Secret Service guards are sympathetic to her cause, the Mayflower has become a reliable rendezvous for Hillary to escape and enjoy moments of intimacy."

A straight magazine, claiming to have inside information, reported that I have established a habit of meeting someone at the Mayflower Hotel in Washington, DC… visits that started after a fight with Bill. My trysts are said to involve a woman, rumored to be a feminist. But of course, *We The People*, with an insatiable appetite for gossip and power, want to know *how* the fight between Bill and I was resolved.

A prying journalist has apparently seen Carmella and I together and now implies an outrageous conclusion, "Most women have a fantasy of being kissed by the loveliest woman in the world. Hillary's face changed the night that Carmella Meeks kissed her."

My ratings shot up after that kiss was published in a lesbian magazine. So there, you have your answer. My girlfriend has liberated me from the prison of my media image… but that doesn't necessarily mean that I am a lesbian.

~~~~~~~~~~~~~~~~~~~~~~~~~~~~~

March 13, 2007:

For today's interview I have chosen the battle camouflage of a dark suit lightened at the neckline with a twist of seed pearls. A presidential eagle broach is pinned to my chest, like a general's medal. My lips are precisely outlined, as are my thoughts. I am angry and frustrated most of the time these days. The voters are beginning to accept my take-charge confidence. But there is a shadow. I have sacrificed some part of me in order to persuade the people to vote, firstly for my husband Bill, then for fellow Democrats such as Barack Obama from my hometown--and now for myself. I am concerned that corporate America is running amok and subverting bedrock American values. It is outrageous that environmental disasters such as the Three Mile Island nuclear power plant leak, the cancer-producing pollution in Love Canal, and the Iraq war have been *promoted* by American corporations as collaterals necessary to progress, along with the excesses of baby boomer materialism and narcissism that overshadow concern for the public good. We are experiencing a crisis of meaning and spirituality in America today. Much of our society is characterized by hurt, emptiness, confusion, and loss of meaning as a result of corporate America's obsession with short-term profit. This is the major source of the subversion of democratic, family, moral, and spiritual values in America.

# CHAPTER 8: HILLARY, 2007

One second I am sleeping, the next I am awake. "But nothing is as before," as Jesus might have once said. I was with Carmella last night--I rode up in the elevator at the Mayflower. Carmella was waiting in the doorway. I have a ritual: I open my Bible at a random page when I am in doubt as to what to write in my diary, as I am now, to get a sign--a little game between God and me.

"What Biblical passage did you read today," Carmella asked. With someone other than Carmella my ritual might seem like one of the anxiety disorders we Protestants have inherited from the Calvinists and Puritans, subsequently developed further from being rejected, and then mastered from being alone amidst crowds.

"It was the first page of Revelation. *I come with the keys of Heaven...*"

Carmella and I stood their looking at each other.

"How far will you go then?" she asked me.

"Try me," I said. Today I know that I shall go all the way.

~~~~~~~~~~~~~~~~~~~~~~~~~

April 8, 2007:

Dear Diary: Bill was lying next to me this morning, on his stomach with his hands down at his side, asleep. His mouth and nose vibrated gently. I lay quietly and looked at him in a way I haven't been able to before. His hair is graying but it is thick, like the bristles of a broom. There in bed, happiness came over me. Different from when you rediscover an old friend, more like a famous visitor—it was like a breath of fire from God. I let it pass and was able to lie there, grateful for what I have, and wishing for naught. The next moment I knew that I wanted to be President. This is my main chance. This is what I have been working for. This is what I must do, forgoing all else.

My routine is precise: An hour after 4am, after giving Bill a list of tasks to do and taking my meds, I--soft and feminine--enter the make-up studio of Newton PR, hoping to do better than that strident image presented on last week's show. I am all smiles, until Doris, the make-up artist says, "Newt Gingrinch and the Media Bosses are out to get you."

Last night's Newton PR show was the first time the voters saw my battle mouth: My lower lip jutted out while the top one pulled tight, like a boxer with his mouthpiece stuffed in. But a couple of minutes into the interview the director had already taken control: I became the new PR image, the cool Hillary--rather than the strident Hillary of the previous show. The use of my diary as a reference document to obtain spontaneous and rich material resulted in the improvement to my presentation on the show:

"... In 1976, I joined the venerable and influential Rose Law Firm. It was in this role that I first met Dr. William LeMessurier Chaytor, a tall and lean structural engineer, with thick black hair and a sharp intellect. The Rose Law Firm received a simultaneous visit from James Bronner, the head of a multifaceted corporation that in addition to owning the intellectual property rights to volumes of architectural building systems, also owned a practicing architectural corporation that was responsible for the design of Antoin Rezko's high-rise headquarters in Manhattan. Antoin Rezko was a mafia don.

No one could remember the rotund architect, James Bronner, ever going to someone *else's* office before. But there we were, with the senior partners of The Rose Law Firm, who usually didn't work together on the same case. Both partners were present when I was asked to defend Bronner on the Rezko building. Fortunately I relied upon William L. Chaytor to direct the technical aspects of the case.

The Rezko Building was sixty-six stories, on a site that stretched from Forty-ninth to Fiftieth Streets and from Eighth Avenue to Ninth. There had been a fatal accident associated with the building performance. I didn't know at that time that the architect, Bronner, had Chicago mafia connections, and later chose to attend the same church as Barack Obama.

It was anticipated that the case would go to trial because of the insurance money available. Furthermore, another flaw had been found in the design of the Rezko building. The odds were high that we would be defending a multi-million dollar lawsuit on behalf of James Bronner. Bronner insisted that William Chaytor and I visit the Rezko Building."

That was better. But the show still failed to capture the feelings... of the wind surging across the Hudson River, and through the graffiti canyons of Manhattan's West Side. The winds seemed to wail with excitement when they swept through the cleared area that was once the site of Madison Square Garden. Divided by a high-rise building under construction on the Ninth Avenue end of the block, the winds rejoined and raced unopposed across the plaza, creating miniature tornadoes of advertising flyers and MacDonald's wrappers, and playing havoc with Dr. William L. Chaytor's contact lenses.

When the show continued my stronger voice was still with me:

"The Rezko Building swayed so much on a windy day that many companies declined to lease the upper floors, despite the spectacular views. It was a stark, imposing monolith clad in alternating vertical strips of granite and bronze tinted glass. With the exception of small balconies at the second-floor level, the four walls rose unembellished from street level to a pyramidal roof. James Bronner described the building as honest and daringly slender... but he votes Republican!"

There was laughter in the studio, but this last bit was cut... Then I switched to my halting but sexy voice and read further from my diary:

"William L. Chaytor and I stood in a corner office, with Bronner, on the sixtieth floor looking east, on equal terms with the Exxon Building, Rockefeller Center, Trump Tower, and such aging statements of optimism as the Chrysler Building and the Empire State. We swayed closer to the Hudson River... then away. It took almost twenty seconds for the building sway to slowly swing us back to the Hudson proximity.

Maybe that is why we were really there, because the building swayed too much. Rather than to referee a conflict between the dons—Don and Antoin Rezko—regarding Don's wish to maximize the profit, and the wish of Antoin to have tinted glass? Antoin was always looking to impress people with style and generosity... But whatever the reason, an eight feet by six feet sheet of bronze tinted glass had been replaced by a sheet of clear Perspex, screwed to the inside walls. Bronner had arrived at our meeting directly from the funeral of a pedestrian, Joe Battaglia--a prominent Democrat opponent of Tony Rezko's protégée, Barack Obama. Battaglia's torso had been reportedly severed from shoulder to waist by the original bronze tinted window as it scythed it's way earthward from the corner office like a giant Frisbee flashing in the Sun, flashing because the corners of the glass panel rotated like circular saw blades.

As we exited the Rezko Building I said goodbye to William, looked up involuntarily... and shuddered. The next time that I met Dr. Chaytor and James Bronner, the Rezko Building was in an even more desperate plight. Top structural engineers such as William Chaytor and Robert Byrne from Bronner's office, were resigned to its inevitable collapse. The building was demolished soon after."


THAT SHOW WAS BRILLIANT, and helped secure my presidential credentials— just as the Rezko lawsuit established my career as an attorney with the Rose Law Firm. The Rose specialized in intellectual property rights and liability cases, but we also took on child advocacy cases, sometimes pro bono... I preferred the latter work. In 1979 I became the first woman to be made a full partner at Rose. (At that same time President Jimmy Carter appointed me to the board of the Legal Services Corporation.) It has helped my legal career to maintain a lifelong interest in buildings and regional American history... I initiated the *Save America's Treasures* program, to rescue our many iconic historic buildings and heirlooms from deterioration... Unfortunately, the Rezko Building was not one of those buildings saved.

Unfortunately too, Newt Gingrinch was critical of the show... and of my performance. Newt is wrong! It was the advertisements that were boring--about soap and diapers. My presentation was warm and natural, but I must be wary. Bill Clinton and I cannot always be certain about our own veracity--not the *entire* truth and *nothing but* the truth, when speaking about our past. Who can truly recall much of the past with machine-like precision! But we all have different realities--and only the voter's reality counts. Newt's criticism of last night's show has left a sour taste, uneasiness, and Newt has declined to discuss my performance further. My great performances and political successes in the past have resulted from my media friendships, and also from my God-given passion to see justice prevail. But Newt seems to bait me and fluster me. I watch some TV to relax.

I do love the *Sopranos* TV show, about the family of the *fictional* mafia don, Tony Soprano... But I have no mafia connections: the current media attempts to smear myself, (and Barrack Obama, justifiably) with accusations of having Chicago mafia connections, is hurting my ratings in the opinion polls--more than Barrack's polls. I must appear squeaky clean in case I have to use my scandal file to derail Obama's donkey-sized ambitions—Ungrateful bastard--and to think how much I have helped him... and many other young congressmen.

~~~~~~~~~~~~~~~~~~~~~~~~

May 31, 2007:

I blew the whistle on the injustice that Grandpa Carl Meeks suffered at Port Chicago. It was I and not my husband Bill who did the investigating... and then discovered the horrific abuse that Carl's granddaughter, Carmella, lived out in her home, and in the whorehouses of Fort Pierce—My husband got all the credit.

Many of my constituents have suffered like Carmella and Grandpa Carl; some directly in our wars, others from the building failures, due to corruption in the construction industry--elements of which are controlled by mafia dons and other crooks. My constituents have recently suffered indirectly from the tortures at Guantanomo Bay and Abu Ghraib. I am angry that past governments have sacrificed the lives and integrity of our people so easily--along with sacrificing the whole planet to the fate of global warming. It is unfortunate that I have to communicate this uncomfortable information during these TV segments while I am being interviewed by Newt Gingrinch... who is Republican, reportedly gay and carnal... and fastidiously pious.

To have made my face up at home today would have been a waste of precious time... because it is Tuesday again. Dark smudges beneath my eyes, due to anxious evenings pondering the advice of my campaign manager, Mark Penn, contradict my apparent equipoise--Doris has been working for the *Newton* show for years, and is able to make a tense presidential contender look serene. At 6.55 am. Newt Gingrinch dashes up to the make-up room to greet me. Newt's words are fluffy, but hostility glares through his media mask.

It is 7.00 am and I pace around at the rear of the recording studio, alone, preparing for a fight. When the television crew invited me in to inspect the studio earlier, I suggested a revision to the color scheme, and to one of the camera angles--as well as to the height of my chair, and to the selection of which side of me that Newt should sit. I am careful about these things. The boys smile now as I front the studio, anticipating my conflict with Newt. Newt Gingrinch is posing the questions again today. It could seem as if time has stood still, and now maybe a button is pushed so we wake up where we, Newt and I, left off last week. Except for one thing! I have made a decision... am determined now! My face leans into the *Newton Show* cameras, my head bobbing for emphasis on the screen beyond. There she is, me, Bill Clinton's apple-cheeked moon-eyed wife.

"... Hillary. Has your husband told you all you need to know about the shady side of his life?" Newt asks.

"Yes. I have absolutely no doubt about that," I say. On the screen my blue eyes are unblinking beneath the dark hedgerow of my brows. "I don't think I could be sitting here otherwise. For us, over the years, that has been part of our development of trust." I want to have a nervous breakdown, but I don't have the time right now. I need to shift the story line away from my husband: "The great story here for anybody willing to find it, is that a serious confusion exists as to who I really am... What is Hillary Clinton's basic character? Perhaps I can untangle that confusion by revealing my true self through sharing my appreciation of another Bill; another Bill who is also a good role model: William LeMessurier Chaytor.

There are many modern American men with outstanding qualities, such as

William Chaytor and Leslie Robertson: I worked with Bill Chaytor, engineer of record, and Leslie Robertson, the structural engineer responsible for the implementing repairs to the flawed Citicorp Building. Bill's preparedness to be entirely open and admit his shortcomings during design prevented the collapse of this significant architectural monument, *and* probably saved many hundreds of innocent lives. I will talk more about William LeMessurier Chaytor in a later show. He deserves a medal, and is a role model for us all. When my fellow American's come to me with their problems I suggest to them that they read the stories of the great American role models--as well as the Bible of course.

Incidentally, not only was Leslie Robertson involved in the repair of the Citicorp Building; he was also involved in the original design of the World Trade Center in the seventies, and was responsible for strengthening of WTC-7 following the 1993 terrorist bombing... Robertson is a stickler for technical detail and precision, a man fascinated by how things fit together and meticulous to the stage of being anal. That is why Tony Chaytor, (William Chaytor's son), was surprised by the Government's claim after September 11 2001, that WCT-7 collapsed simply due to falling debris; ejected while the 110 story WTC-2 tower fell... Who would design a building to resist the impact of plane crashes, and the associated potential for jet fuel fires? Leslie Robertson and his team of WTC engineers *did*, and had this to say in 1993 when asked if they considered plane crashes in the WTC design: *Yes . . . Our analysis indicated the biggest problem would be the fact that all the fuel would dump into the building."*

~~~~~~~~~~~~~~~~~~~~~~~

July 1, 2007:
Newt Gingrinch wasn't happy with the show--*because you sounded like a sanctimonious bitch!* But he didn't edit it down. I am anxious... because the media often demonizes me. They have pinned my husband Bill under impossible suspicions—and it is all an evil Republican plot to undermine and destroy... both Bill and I.

Last night I watched my show on network TV, in the company of Carmella and Tony. "Great job Hon," said Tony. "You cut Newt off at his knees this time."

"I got some of my old self back."

How things have changed: I first discovered the *Newton Show* when I heard an airing of Grandpa Carl Meeks being interviewed in the mid-nineties--that is what initially prompted me to phone to the Meeks' home down in Florida. That show resulted in my husband Bill, then the President of the United States, acknowledging the good character of men like Grandpa Carl who served at Port Chicago and, then expunging their mutiny convictions.

Meeks and his comrades were more than just victims of fearful racism. They were pawns in the good-old-boy network. Good-old boys indeed! The Republican agenda of global domination required America to nuke Japan and intimidate Russia. To achieve their goal they needed a nuke-test. As I researched the book about Port Chicago by Dr. Robert Allen, I thought, *My God, those black men who served in Port Chicago went through some horrific betrayal. By their own government.*

I am proud that my husband and I took compassionate action for poor Grandpa

Carl and his fellow sailors. Finally, four years later, on 23 December 1999, my husband, President Bill Clinton, officially pardoned Grandpa Carl's brother-in-arms, Freddie Meeks, of Los Angeles, one of the few remaining members of the Port Chicago loading crews. Grandpapa Carl refused to be pardoned publicly. His granddaughter Carmella stated that the family was unable to attend the Pardon Ceremony because Carl was terminally ill, *And still too burdened with the shame of his mutiny conviction to tolerate media exposure.* That 1995 interview with Grandpa Carl was the start of my relationship with Carmella--it began with an exchange of pages from our diaries, progressed to me tutoring her, and then I became her personal counselor and advocate.

Even though Grandpa Carl survived the explosion, the events at Port Chicago virtually destroyed the possibility of any legitimate civilian life for him--irrespective of whether it was an intentional detonation or an accidental nuclear explosion, for the government to continue to deny that it was a nuclear disaster was to deny Grandpa Carl the reality of his suffering at Port Chicago. Of the 328 African-American off-duty ordinance battalion sailors who survived the explosion, 258 subsequently refused to load ammunition because of the unsafe conditions. In the end, 208 of these sailors faced summary courts-martial and were sentenced to bad conduct discharges and the forfeit of three month's pay for disobeying orders. The remaining fifty men were singled out for general court-martial on the grounds of mutiny. The sentence could have been death. Instead, after a subsequent trial that a 1994 review concluded *contained strong racial overtones*, they received between eight and fifteen years of hard labor.

I am dissatisfied with my country's efforts to eliminate racism, even today. I am dissatisfied with its lack of honesty and failure to reveal the truth. How come the BBC and a local network reported WTC-7 had collapsed twenty-three minutes before it had done so? It wasn't an error! That's the point. BBC keeps harping on about what a chaotic day it was. Then why didn't the BBC anchor say, *we're getting unconfirmed reports of another building apparently collapsing... We'll have to check up on this...* No, he had, (23 minutes before hand) the name of the building, the explanation of the collapse--weakened by other collapses. BBC even had graphics made up for the scrolling info at the bottom of the screen. That was precise reporting. And therein lies the key! No doubt the information was just being fed to the anchor and reporter across the wires. So, which agency fed that bit about WTC-7 collapsing? AP? Reuters? VOA? We'll probably never know, but BBC and the local CNN network got the information from some official source more than 23 minutes before it happened. Whoever fed BBC the data got it wrong. Petty conspiracy is beyond the character of the noble BBC. But the BBC was played perfectly by some entity. Who did it? The Republicans!

When I win the Presidency I will be committed to supporting all our administrators and armed forces, but it is essential that our leaders behave within the law. No matter what the real or perceived threats from our enemies, no matter how strong the instinct for self-preservation in the face of impossible odds…the good of the people must come before the individual welfare of our leaders in public service and military. Therefore, I will insist that all classified documents be opened to public scrutiny.

~~~~~~~~~~~~~~~~~~~~~~~~~~

# CHAPTER 9: HILLARY, 2007

October 1, 2007:

Newt Gingrinch's office has a strange smell: not just the paper and book smell, or the carpet glue, but something else that I keep thinking must be onion rings. When he puts down the phone he has that look that means he is really important and has all the answers—and I am someone less. Yet, just this morning, Newt Gingrinch congratulated my performance for the first time in my entire season on the *Newton Show*.

"I have stood for the welfare and support of children, the poor, and the environment my entire career. My childhood, and especially the radical politics of the 1960s, awakened within me not only a sense of obligation to my country, but also a commitment to provide social services to the underprivileged. College, law practice, and marriage, tossed me into the political epicenter of the US. My work with children and mothers has taught me that they need more of our time, energy, and resources. But no experience brought home this lesson as vividly as becoming a mother myself. When Chelsea Hillary Clinton lay in my arms for the first time, I was overwhelmed by the love and responsibility I felt for her. Despite all the books I had read, all the children I had studied and advocated for, I wasn't prepared for the sheer miracle of her being. For the first time, I understood the words of Elizabeth Stone: *Making the decision to have a child. It's wondrous. It is a decision forever to have your heart go walking around outside your body--unless the child is intellectually challenged or unwanted.*

We named Chelsea after the 1969 song by Joni Mitchell, *Chelsea Morning.*"

AFTER VIEWING the show at home I go to the Mayflower--my escape fantasy. I occasionally enjoy the sensual aroma of a cigar. Thank goodness that we women are learning to experience the full range of satisfactions that nature has to offer. Thank goodness that the self-destructive fashion of this era for many women to remain childless is finally coming to an end. It has been difficult for me to serve a community that is anti-child. No wonder that I have to take daily medication.

~~~~~~~~~~~~~~~~~~~~~~~~~~~~~~~

October 2, 2007:

I surprise Carmella at her home the following evening because I was longing for contact with young children. Marise opened the door. Now, I am among the first to admit that a cold weather climate can be formidable, but I'm still momentarily surprised. Outside it's seven o'clock. The first stars have appeared in the navy-blue, cloudless sky. But inside, around Marise, it seems to have been snowing--a fine layer of white powder covers her dark hair, her shoulders, her face, and her bare arms. I follow her into the living room where there is flour everywhere. Another child and Marise continue kneading dough right on the hardwood floor. In the kitchen, Carmella is greasing biscuit tins. On the kitchen table another girl is kneading pastry dough. Now she's trying to knead an egg yolk into it.

"The bottom fell out of the bag of flour," Carmella says.

"I see. The floor will be wonderfully clean."

"Tony is next door," Carmella says.

~~~~~~~~~~~~~~~~~~~~~~~~~~~~

November 30, 2007:

The biggest threat to my presidential election campaign today is the group of radical feminists who remain mad at me because I didn't divorce Bill after the cigar incident with Monica Lewinski... Monica claimed that Bill penetrated her with a cigar. The feminists made the accusation that *Hillary Clinton is riding to the Presidency on the coat tails of her husband.* Envious cows! I hate that. But those charges have been reduced to relative insignificance with my new PR campaign video aimed at the all-important younger voters--where Bill is being chided for eating onion rings instead of the healthy carrot sticks: It's clever, the way the PR show uses the jukebox business from the last episode of the popular *Sopranos* drama show, along with the actors for the fictional mafia don, Tony Soprano, and his wife Carmella, to remind us of my theme song contest. I wonder what *We The People* think of this show?

The NY Times political blogger Kate Phillips proclaimed, "It is the best campaign spot we've seen this season. "

A reviewer said, "We watch Hillary--and later Bill--enter a diner, sit at a table, and discuss the juke box selection from the finalists of the Hillary theme song contest as food is served. Hillary chastises Bill for choosing onion rings from the menu. When we hear him say *No onion rings?* The camera is on her, Bill is off-screen, but at the bottom of the screen we see the carrot/phallus being held between fingers. Oh, yes, I know that Hillary feeding carrots to Bill reminds us that Hillary will provide a better health care, that she's *looking out for us*, but come on, they're carrots! Everyone knows carrots are phallic symbols. But they're cut up into little carrot sticks, you say? Just listen!

This arty Clinton clip, as derived from *The Sopranos*, is perhaps designed to create anxiety that an assassination is about to take place. Having the Tony Soprano actor walk by and glare at Hillary preserves that feeling of threat. It works because with *The Sopranos*, we were waiting to find out how the series would end, but here we are waiting to learn the outcome of Hillary's song contest, but it's pushing the envelope for Mark Penn, Hillary's campaign manager, and Newton PR, to suggest this is a portent for an act of violence toward the candidate Hillary... This is not the only time that the *assassination* word has come into the election campaign. There have been Freudian slips regarding the possible assassination of Obama. Creepy!"

I seriously doubt if many will agree with the assertions from Professor Ann Althouse's blogsite: "That, coming from Bill Clinton, the "O" of an onion ring is a vagina V-J symbol. Hillary says no to that consumption, driving the symbolism home. She's *looking out* all right, vigilant over her husband, denying him the sustenance he craves. What does she have for him? Carrot sticks! Here, Bill, in retaliation for all of your excessive "O" consumption, you may have a large bowl of phallic symbols! When Bill sadly bites into the carrot stick of his own castration, it makes a crunching noise. Ouch! And it's that noise that causes the ominous looking man at the bar, the Tony Soprano actor, to turn and look at him. Tony then walks by and gives Bill a glare. What does that glare mean in the Clinton video? I think it means: *What kind of man are you?*

It's a scary little world when the eerie inference of pending assassination is invoked. But, it's just a bit of fun. Onion rings are Vee-Jay symbols because they're crunchy and rough. Carrots are Pee-Pee symbols because they're orange with lots of green foliage on top. The 'onion rings' gag evokes this nostalgia, and makes Hillary seem like a good, caring wife. But, under-the-surface message and subliminal image is what advertising is all about. And it's very Freudian, full of sex and violence."

~~~~~~~~~~~~~~~~~~~~~~~

March 13, 2008:

I have to improve my relations with the media so I work hard at sweet-talking them, and invite Newt Gingrinch to dinner. The next national TV interview goes even better:

"Bill and I wanted to start a family in 1975, immediately after we married, but we were not having much luck. By 1978, I was starting to wonder if Bill was shooting blanks. In 1979, Bill and I scheduled an appointment to visit a fertility clinic, right after a long-awaited vacation in California--not in Bermuda, and not because of a rape by Bill--as claimed by some Republican media. (This segment was edited out.)

Lo and behold, I got pregnant during that vacation in California. Chelsea's birth transformed our lives, bringing us the greatest gift of joy and humility any parent could hope for. Like every child, Chelsea was her own person from the beginning. She arrived with a look of determination on her face that conveyed a focus and intensity we would come to know well. I prayed that I would be a good enough mother for her.

From the time I was a child myself, I loved being around other children, looking into their faces or listening to their stories. Like many firstborns, I learned to care for children by baby-sitting my siblings… my two younger brothers. As a teenager I baby-sat other children too, and at thirteen I got my first "real" job: supervising children at a park on summer mornings. Through my church, I also helped care for the children of migrant farm workers while their parents labored in the fruit orchards and vegetable fields near my Chicago home.

In college I tutored school-age children, and later, while in law school, I received permission to add an extra year to my regular curriculum to study child development and the effects of abuse. I wondered about children who I passed on the streets, and I worried about their journeys to adulthood. I have seen, first hand, the results of our failure to invest in children at the most crucial stages of their lives: in my work as staff attorney at the Children's Defense Fund, in my private practice, and as a law professor. Too often, individual and national agendas do not seem to make the best interests of children a priority. The consequences of this neglect are there for all of us to see: Children's health lost to spirit-crushing poverty, children's hearts lost in divorce and custody fights, children's futures lost in an overburdened foster care system, and children's lives lost to abuse and violence. Our *society* has become lost to itself as we fail our children and youth. Like many parents, I feel there is so much to worry about when it comes to raising children in America today.

American children are under assault: from the breakdown of family life, the

46

temptations of alcohol, tobacco, sex, drug abuse, greed, materialism, and spiritual emptiness. These problems are not new, but in our time, they have skyrocketed. Against this bleak backdrop, the struggle to raise strong children and to support families, emotionally as well as practically, has become fiercer. It is a struggle that has captured my heart, my mind, and my life…. Because our neglected children are a time bomb that could destroy America. (Newt flips the *Time Up* card.)

My fellow Americans, Barack Obama could also be a time bomb. (Laughter from crew.) Correction, a loose cannon! Still, I am prepared to have him on my team, perhaps as my Vice President; he has great potential to serve this country—if carefully directed. And I have the team to manage all of America.

Thank you and God bless America."

I closed that show off rather well, even if I do say so myself. But I am getting to be a little obsessed with Obama. It is time for some more journaling:

May 8, 2008:

I do not like to fill my diary up with scandal—but Barack Obama has several *major* scandals in his closet. If he decides to continue his run for President, we are going to hear a lot more about Antoin Rezko, the senator's Chicago neighbor. Rezko is the kind of neighbor you want—the absent kind—and he might be absent for a long time—in the federal penitentiary! That possible move upriver could keep Obama from his own ambitious upgrade… to the big White House he has his eye on.

The Chicago Tribune broke the story back in November 2007. But it began in 2004 with Obama's $1.9 million book advance for *The Audacity of Hope*. In June 2005, Obama used the money to purchase a $1.65 million Georgian revival home on Chicago's South Side—paying $300,000 less than the asking price. On the very same day, Rezko, a Democratic Party fund-raiser and developer, bought the adjacent empty lot at the full asking price from the same owner. Rezko, who had raised money for Obama and has known him since the senator attended Harvard Law School, did not develop the empty lot. Rather, six months later, in January 2006, he sold a 1,500-square-foot slice of the vacant lot to Obama for $104,000, a fair sum in that market.

Here's the question: Did Rezko orchestrate his *same-day purchase* of the adjacent lot at full price so that the seller would give Obama a break on the price of the adjacent house? Was Obama in on the deal? And did Rezko never intend to develop his vacant lot? Was his goal to donate Obama a sunny side yard, a favor that he'd call in later?

Obama said that he did talk to Rezko before the purchase, but only because a person who had renovated it for a previous owner had once worked with Rezko--who owns other properties in the South Side of Chicago… He didn't arrange the joint purchase with him. He bought the house at such a good price, Obama told the papers, because it was being unloaded in a fire sale.

When Obama bought his house in 2006, Rezko was not as radioactive as he will become at election time in 2008. Newspaper accounts contain allegations about his business practices, but he was regarded as a typical power broker who cannily cultivated politicians by doing "favors." But by the time that Obama bought the strip of adjacent land, Rezko was glowing toxic. The papers were reporting that he was under investigation by federal prosecutors. In October 2007, he was charged in a 24-count indictment for seeking kickbacks from companies seeking Illinois State business.

Obama presented himself as a squeaky-clean politician, so the dubious association with Rezko causes him more trouble than it would, say, anyone else in the history of Chicago or Illinois politics. To defuse the issue, the junior senator Obama swamped critics with apologies, admissions, and candor. *This is the first time this has happened and I don't like the feeling*, Obama said at a press conference. *It's frustrating to me, and I'm kicking myself about it.* He told the Associated Press: *Purchasing a piece of property from somebody who has been a supporter of yours I think is a bad idea. It's an example of where every once in a while you're going to make a mistake and hopefully you learn from it.*
Obama told the Chicago Sun-Times that he made a mistake and, *I regret it... One of the things you adapt to in public life is that there are going to be a different set of standards, I'm going to make sure from this point that I don't even come close to the line.*

Of course, if Rezko tells a different story to investigators one day, or Obama's statements turn out to be untrue, that's it for him—you can't run for President on your keen judgment and then show a lack of it by lying and covering up. And Barack Obama has been friends with Antoin Rezko since at least 1990. Barack interviewed with Rezko for a job in the early 1990s (offered, but declined), and Rezko raised at least $150,000 for Obama's campaign prior to his running. Prosecutors charged that at least $10,000 of the money Rezko gave Obama was extorted in return for political favors by a different politician. In return, Barack arranged an internship in 2005 for John Aramanda, the son of a Rezko business associate (Joseph Aramanda, who himself gave Barack $11,500.)

There's no evidence that Rezko bought the vacant land for any other reason than to do Obama a favor. The seller would only sell the house if he could *sell the vacant lot on the same day*. And the vacant lot is *only accessible through Obama's yard...* worthless to anyone but Obama. Rezko and his wife sold the lot in 2007 to someone unknown--but to whom Rezko reportedly owed money, and let that naive person keep the small profit Rezko made... to compensate for the dubious property he had foolishly purchased?

Here's the real problem: amidst other situations, Rezko was indicted on a federal government corruption case for demanding kickbacks from companies wanting to do business with Illinois Governor Blagojevich, another politician that Rezko has befriended and donated to. (Rezko was also indicted for shaking down a Hollywood producer for $1.5 million in campaign contributions for Blagojevich. This guy takes care of his political friends.) In fact, Joseph Aramanda is an unindicted co-conspirator in one of the kickback cases.
Obama finally admitted that the Rezko land deal was a mistake, and gave money donated directly by Rezko, to charity. His story changed though: When the land deal was first reported, Obama said his only contact with Rezko was asking him if it was a good deal. In February 2008, one of Obama's staffers admitted that the candidate had

walked around the house and lot with Rezko. Rezko has since said he bought the lot purely to help the Obamas to expand their backyard.

The Republican media has pushed hard to promote Obama ahead of me in the Democrat primaries--so any of Obama's subsequent difficulties and failure will be because he shows in other ways that he lacks experience, can't handle the rigors of campaign life, and because it turns out he only speaks in pleasing generalities. Barack Obama has become a genuine trend without Americans knowing much about him. He started his public career with an unusual move---writing a book where he talks about using cocaine. It's unconventional, but damned if it doesn't look like it just might work.

Long before Obama ever ran for a political office, he wrote a book in 1995 about, well, himself, and his amazing journey from messed up kid to, um, himself. It was quite an epic, considering he was 34 at the time. In that book, called *Dreams From My Father,* he wrote that he used marijuana and cocaine. ("Maybe a little blow.") Oddly enough, he wrote that he didn't try heroin because--wait for it--he didn't like the pusher who was selling it. (Weren't there any other reasons?) In a later interview, he added *Teenage boys are frequently confused.*

Again the media has displayed double standards because in April they were shocked by Scott McClellan's revelation in his book *The Raw Story* where the former press secretary to President G. W. Bush recounted an evening in a hotel suite, somewhere in the Midwest:

"Bush was on the phone with a supporter and motioned for me to have a seat. *The media won't let go of these ridiculous cocaine rumors,* I heard Bush say. *You know, the truth is I honestly don't remember whether I tried it or not. We had some pretty wild parties back in my day, and I just don't remember.*

I remember thinking to myself, *How can that be?* McClellan wrote. *How can someone simply not remember whether or not they used an illegal substance like cocaine?* It didn't make a lot of sense."

McClellan's book is valuable, coming as it does from an insider, someone who was there, who saw it and heard it firsthand. McClellan overheard President Bush telling someone on the phone that he really can't remember whether he ever used cocaine--concluding that Bush convinces himself that unpleasant things haven't really occurred, that the truth is what he wants it to be. Indeed!

Obama has admitted drug use, including cocaine… But the media has selectively ignored this violation of our drug laws.

Fox News ran a story claiming: "Obama had been educated in a Madrassa school in Indonesia--it's a type of fundamentalist Muslim school, often funded by the extremist Wahabi sect of Islam (with Saudi money) and often very anti-American."

There are several other stories about Obama floating around on the Internet… that he has refused to put his hand over his heart when saying the pledge of allegiance, and that he is secretly Muslim and anti-American. Whatever, he certainly was not raised as a traditional Christian, and did not undergo the daily American preparation for citizenship--which begins with the Pledge of Allegiance each morning as school starts, at the age of six.

I have collected a scrapbook of other media references to Obama's mistakes:

"Barack Obama, asked about drug history, admits he inhaled," by Katherine Seelye, International Herald Tribune, October 25, 2006.

"Obama Says He Regrets Land Deal With Fundraiser", by Peter Slevin, Washington Post, December 16, 2006.

"A report that one of the Clintons has an Obama scandal bomb - but won't drop it:" Conservative columnist Robert Novak set off the firefight, writing, "Agents of Clinton are spreading the word in Democratic circles that she has scandalous information about Obama, but has decided not to use it." Novak specified, "The nature of the alleged scandal was not disclosed," then said this, "Word-of-mouth among Democrats makes Obama look vulnerable and Clinton look prudent."

"… Obama quickly pressed Hillary Clinton to disavow the report, saying that; *In the interest of our party, and her own reputation, [she] should either make public any and all information referred to in the item, or concede the truth: that there is none.*"

"It has been suggested that this incident demonstrates that Obama is unprepared to take on the Republican Party. Novak is a Republican-leaning columnist who's trying to set a trap for Democrat candidates, which Barack Obama just walked right into," journalist Carson said. "If you don't know how to avoid that in a primary, you're going to be in a world of hurt in a general election."

"The Obama campaign said it hadn't fallen into a *trap* and would fight any *Swift boat-style attacks*. This is exactly the kind of smear politics Democrats need to fight back on, regardless of the source or the party," spokeswoman Jen Psaki said.

"The scandals surrounding the Obama campaign are growing as new accusations of plagiarism have surfaced: Obama has outright stolen his own campaign slogan. The slogan, *Yes we can,* was lifted directly from Bob the Builder, a British construction worker who coined the phrase in 1999. These allegations of plagiarism come after previous allegations that Obama committed grievous intellectual fraud in taking material originally used by former governor Deval Patrick for his own speeches. So far this week, Mr. Obama has miss-spoke twice. Accused of plagiarizing his dear friend's speeches, he smiled and said, *oops!* Besides allegations of plagiarism, in 2007 Obama's criminal record started to come out: The presidential candidate finally paid off $400 in parking tickets to Harvard University a full 17 years after they were issued."

"What is critical are the outrageous remarks that he and his wife say, such as, "You must vote for me after having a religious experience. We can fix your broken souls.""

"In addition, his friend Reverend Wright, who married Barack Obama and his wife, and has preached to Obama every Sunday for many years--is a radical and a racist: Senator Barack Obama's pastor says Blacks should not sing *God Bless America* but *Goddamn America.* The Rev. Wright, Obama's pastor for the last 20 years, has a long history of what even Obama's campaign aides concede is *inflammatory rhetoric,* including the assertion that the United States brought on the September 11 attacks with its own *terrorism.*

In a campaign appearance earlier this month, Sen. Obama said, *I don't think my church is actually particularly controversial.* He said Rev. Wright *is like an old uncle who says things I don't always agree with,* telling a Jewish group that *everyone has someone like that in their family.*

Rev. Wright not only married Obama and his wife Michelle, but also baptized their two daughters, and is credited by Obama for the title of his book, *The Audacity of Hope*."

"An ABC News review of dozens of Rev. Wright's sermons, offered for sale by the church, found repeated denunciations of the U.S. based on what he described as his reading of the Gospels and the treatment of black Americans: *The government gives them the drugs, builds bigger prisons, passes a three-strike law and then wants us to sing 'God Bless America.' No, no, no, Goddamn America. That's in the Bible for killing innocent people;* he said in a 2003 sermon. *Goddamn America for treating our citizens as less than human. Goddamn America for as long as she acts like she is God and she is supreme.*

In addition to damning America, he told his congregation on the Sunday after September 11, 2001, that the United States had brought on Al Qaeda's attacks because of its own terrorism. *We bombed Hiroshima, we bombed Nagasaki, and we nuked far more than the thousands in New York and the Pentagon, and we never batted an eye,* Rev. Wright said in a sermon on Sept. 16, 2001. *We have supported state terrorism against the Palestinians and black South Africans, and now we are indignant because the stuff we have done overseas is now brought right back to our own front yards. America's chickens are coming home to roost,* he told his congregation."

Obama sought to separate himself from his preacher's remarks... but maybe it is an insidious association. I have heard some of my potential constituents yell at me with the same attitude, virtually a word for word copy of Rev. Wright's sermons. So! We must be suspicious because Obama has the same hidden ideology, which is starting to peek through the cracks in Obama's PR image--following Barack Obama's controversial assertion that voters in some small towns are *bitter*. I am taken aback by the demeaning remarks Senator Obama made about people in small town America. Obama's remarks are elitist and out of touch. They are not reflective of the values and beliefs of Americans, certainly not the Americans I know, not the Americans I grew up with, not the Americans I represent.

Barack Obama reportedly said that People who feel disenfranchised in small town America *cling to guns or religion or antipathy to people who aren't like them, or anti-immigrant sentiment, or anti-trade sentiment, as a way to explain their frustrations.*

Wrong! Most Americans who believe in God do so as a matter of personal belief. Christian people (of faith) I know don't cling to religion because they are *bitter*. People embrace their faith because they are spiritually rich, not because they are materially poor.

People of all walks of life hunt, and they enjoy doing so because it is an important part of their life, not because they are *bitter*.

I don't think it helps to divide our country into one America that is enlightened and one that is not. People don't need a President who looks down on them. They need a President who stands up for them, and that's exactly what I always promised to do.

People have been trying to push me out of the Presidential primary race right from the start. Sometimes you've got to calm people down a little bit. But if you take a look at successful presidential campaigns and; my husband did not get the nomination until June of 1992. I remember too, tragically, when Senator Robert Kennedy won California near the end of his primary process. A retired teacher from New Hampshire put it clearly, *If you look at the exit interviews with the voters, some people have been comparing Obama to JFK, and he was a wonderful leader. He gave us a lot of hope… But he was assassinated.*

I am for responsible socialism: In college I read *Das Kapital by* Karl Marx. It is a book I grew fond of. For its trembling feminine empathy and its potent indignation, that convinced me that I can accomplish liberation if I just have the will to change. Occasionally I have felt that I am taking another huge step toward the light. But then I've also felt some invisible hand push me further along a network of sewer pipes, running beneath an unknown landscape, pushing me until I eat enough sewerage to qualify my need for another breathing hole.

Why do major elements of the media hate me so? And why are they pushing for the success of the inexperienced senator Barack Obama… as he prepares his Presidential primary campaign as a Democrat candidate, running *against* me? Maybe the creator's of Keifer Sutherland's *24* send a subliminal message through the TV, that the color qualifies him to be our next President. I mean, what does Obama know about motherhood and rescuing the next generation? There are so many enemies to a healthy future for our children, and so few friends. But I shall prevail… with the help of God and my small army of loyal followers like Tony Chaytor and Rupert Murdoch, who are functioning alongside the Republican Party's highest ranks.

In addition to suffering stress from battling Obama, I am also emotionally challenged by Carmella's choice to abandon her child, Eleanor, at the steps of an orphanage: I involved myself in Carmella's life because the child is autistic, and the family was poor—pulling on my heartstrings. When people oppose abortion, they must then be prepared to financially support any struggling mothers and the orphanages required to house the unwanted or sick children that may ensue. Tragically, there is little financial support for orphanages or post-natal care for the women.

~~~~~~~~~~~~~~~~~~~~~~~~~~~~~~~~

# PART V: CARMELLA MEEKS

## CHAPTER 10: 2008

May 9, 2008:

My original job with my diary was to record my history accurately, and then to quickly turn the page. As a result I think I have finally decided what sort of life I would like to have. I would like a life with more serenity, security and balance. I know now, after deciding to write a book based on my diary—that that I can only get there by the grace of God--because I have done something wicked. In order to discover the source of my wickedness, I have to back to before I first started writing in it, in 1997:

When I was seven, my father forbade me from playing with a friend. "Why can't I play with her?" I asked.

"Why not? Because I said no. That is why not!"

"That is not an answer." Pow! I got slapped. Why couldn't my parents understand that the best thing for me was to let me be free?

When I was eight years old I heard the expression *son of a bitch* while playing in the street. I asked papa C-J what it meant. My father looked at me with a horrible face and shouted, "Never again in your life will you repeat those words."

"But I only wanted to know what *son of a bitch* means, Father."

Pow! Carl-Junior opened my mouth with a slap.

I now find some understanding of myself by reflecting on my childhood. I can recall being upset because my father wouldn't let me go to the Friday night dance class. At that time, dance class was everything; not being able to go was the end of the world for me. It was a very harsh punishment! My brother was being punished also, but he was allowed to continue playing basketball in the evening. My father was inconsistent. What was the reason for the difference in punishment? Because I was a female, and my brother was a male?

When Captain C-J traveled away from home in his tiny submarine there was always relief, and a dispute to decide which of us children would get to sleep with my mother. My mother is from Puerto Rico, like my grandma, and is a funny and absent-minded woman who insisted that we speak Spanish at home. Mama didn't have to know where her children were all the time, and was relaxed about whether I played with this kid or that.

Carl-Junior needed us children to excel in the professions, such as law and medicine, in order to expunge the shame of his father, Grandpapa Carl, for being convicted of mutiny by the Navy. That shame was even worse for Captain C-J than it was for Grandpapa--and it almost drove Grandpapa Carl to suicide on several occasions. With Papa C-J the shame was meaner and spat at him like those nuclear bombs spat at grandpapa when he was loading them.

Papa C-J had so much venom that he raped me, and then beat me so bad that he had to hide me in the basement for a week.

There was a barrier between my mother and I, a wall that felt cold. Intimacy was not there, not like it is with my daughter. Marise talks with me about all the avenues of her life, and she introduces me proudly to her friends.

With my father it was different again. He didn't kiss me cuddle me, not exactly. When Captain C-J Meeks did kiss me, later in life it was a dark and fast thing... that is why he taught me how to drive his research submarine—for an opportunity to fondle me. Mama said that Carl-Junior accused Grandpapa Carl of being mentally ill... insane--because of Grandpa's bitterness about the war. Mama said that my father got many beatings and much abuse from *his* short-tempered father, Carl. But that is no excuse for the shame that my father put me through. Or the guilt: "Do you want me to tell your mother what you've been doing?" I learned that C-J was the guilty one though, when he said to me a few months later: "I hope this doesn't come back to bite me, after everything I have done for you."

When I first met Tony I was a person who was very closed about sex. In my home it was a secretive thing. The first time that I experienced an orgasm I didn't know that it was an orgasm: Tony and I had walked the streets until dawn. We finally crashed at his friend's house after his friend had gone to work. We had already been dating for several weeks, but we never had sexual contact until that night. We slept, while hugged together in the same bed. It was a tight squeeze in that tiny bed. On the walls hung posters of Michael Jackson, some street signs, and photos of clubs that we had always wanted to go to. Tony has lips like Michael Jackson and I always needed to be with him, all the time. We talked for hours, fell asleep, woke up, and talked again.

At dawn, when we were preparing to back to sleep after a street skate session, he helped take off my clothes, "To admire my apricot colored skin," he said. I let him. I had a certain curiosity also, to know just how far certain things might be going to go. I let him do everything to me that he wanted because it felt good. He put his hand on my breast and it was good. He kissed me for a long time and that was good, and then he descended, and descended, and I let him because it was so good. He did an oral on me! He fucked me with his tongue in my juices! I never dreamed, in my entire life, that a man was going to kiss me like that on my vagina. I was too ignorant. It was inevitable that I had an orgasm, but it was totally unexpected, because I didn't know what was happening to me. I only knew that it was good and that I wanted more.

He said to me, "Now, it's my turn."

"How come?"

He explained to me what I should do, and I was shocked!

"I... no! You want me to put my mouth there on your stick? That's crazy. No way!"

He respected my wish and we slept in a hug, as usual. In the afternoon, after we woke, I wanted more of the kissing and the licking that I had enjoyed before we slept. He did it to me, and afterward, persuaded me to lick and suck him as well. For almost two weeks I was nervous that I would get pregnant from the white stuff he squirted from his stick into my mouth. What a horror!

But from then on, my sexual life went into orbit. There were many attempts by Tony to go all the way. I had to pretend I was a virgin, so I always called out, "Stop, it's hurting." He always stopped. But then, one day, while I resisted with my shouting, he ignored me. He took me even though I slapped his arm. Afterwards I laughed because I was happy! We started to fuck and fuck; it was a crazy thing, the whole time. I had discovered a good thing, and I wanted more. We used preservatives for lubrication, and looked at porno movies to copy their postures. We wrote everything down in a scrapbook. Each position had a symbol. That scrapbook still exists, in the basement of my mother's house.

My family had, at first, been open to Tony, but that changed because I rebelled too much. I was like a little bitch that had been restrained on a collar too long, so that when I got a taste of the freedom of being with Tony, I left home every Friday and didn't come back home until Sunday night. I ate little and roller-skated all weekend so was skinny. Freedom was everything for me.

One morning Tony's condom broke and I got pregnant.

I told my Tony about the pregnancy before I told anyone else. He hugged me, fearing nothing. He would have called his parents if I hadn't stopped him. I knew my father would be furious so I insisted that Tony stay away for two weeks. After that we would declare our intent to keep the baby. I told my sister Donna about the pregnancy next. She hugged me, saying, "I'm sorry. Pedro and I are here for you."

Despite my plans to go to nursing school, we agreed to keep the baby and that everything would come out all right. We had the popular dark red hair, and the smartest roller skates available in Fort Pierce, so we thought everything in life would be easy. Until then that had been the coolest year of my life: I had freedom and had found a boyfriend that was my perfect guy. I did not necessarily want to marry, but I had to leave home.

I told Papa C-J that night that I was pregnant. I was almost eighteen, and he had still been beating me, but this time he did not. No. But the whole night. he punched and punched holes in the wall. I was waiting in my room, dreading the hour he would come up and beat me or rape me. He did not come, but I stayed in my room for a week without going out. He had wanted me to abort my baby from the start, and continued to insist that I should.

I had always idolized women with independent spirits like Hillary Clinton. I love Hillary more than I love myself. But Hillary Clinton needs to pay attention to the survival of her *own* family. She should be plotting revenge because of the Monica Lewinski affair with her husband, and silencing the screams of the feminists: *Liberated women don't put up with cheating and sex addiction like she does, don't put up with humiliation--and don't get over things so quickly.*

Donna, said, "You are lucky with Tony Chaytor. Get married quickly before your tummy gets big, or you'll look disgusting in your wedding dress."

My father overheard my sister say, "It's lucky that Papa C-J isn't the father." That's when Papa C-J suffered his first attack of heart difficulties.

The implications of my pregnancy were deeper than I realized. I had to avoid my classes at nursing school in case they saw my pregnant belly. The rules denied any rights for women to sit exams when pregnant and my baby was due to be born the week after the next. Furthermore, non-attendance was also against the rules.

Tony and I started living in a modest studio in the daytime, but we snuck home and slept in the living room of my parent's house after they went to work because there was a trucking company next to the studio, and trucks came at all hours of the night. Sleep was difficult. Tony worked two jobs, both for minimum wage. We used his first income to pay the rent and bought food with the second.

Tony wanted to marry me. He wanted to be responsible. He loved me.

My family is Catholic, one of only four Black families at our Church. The rest are Hispanic, apart from a few Irish Catholics. My father prohibited me from having a civil marriage because he told the judge that I was under eighteen (I turned eighteen after the fall of 1995). So Tony and I decided to marry secretly, at another Catholic Church. Our local Church had to be bypassed because my father refused to sign the papers to authorize our marriage.

Even though Papa C-J is fucked up emotionally, he has been incredibly successful in his career: When he was in his twenties, he went away to college with a scholarship from the Navy, and when I was thirteen, got command of a small research submarine. Carl Junior is an expert on the hydrodynamic effects of submerged blasts and performed many covert operations. I am sure his exceptional effort to become a success in his career was a reaction to his father's bitter lethargy: a lethargy that resulted from the government deceit around the Port Chicago detonation--a reaction to Grandpapa Carl's dishonorable discharge from the Navy. Captain C-J was aloof to Grandpa's claims of a racist Navy and his aloof denial was justifiable for him, because the Navy was forcibly desegregated after the death of President Delano Roosevelt. My father always wanted discreet and polished children. Unfortunately I did not conform to his expectations.

My belly would be starting to show in a month so I needed a wedding gown now. Grandma Meeks had a beautiful nightdress that she had used on her honeymoon. It was made of satin. Even though my grandma had snuck back to Puerto Rico, the nightdress was still intact. Tony had few clothes: Jeans and a Michael Jackson jacket--those sorts of clothes only. We were fortunate to find some military shoes, a blue-Navy shirt, Navy slacks, and a pea-jacket, in Papa's garage. These were the ideal clothes for Tony to wear to our wedding.

Dressed this way, we walked across the city to marry, in the other church. We passed a florist so I bought a rose, my favorite flower. We invited a skating couple to be Godparents and witnesses; a couple that I had met in pre-natal class. Along with my sister, her man Pedro, and my childhood friend, they were the only witnesses to the ceremony. I was denied the thrill of walking down the aisle to the accompaniment of great organ music, because that cost money. I was just about to begin my silent wedding march when the priest interrupted and requested that both Tony and I go, individually, to the confessional booth, prior to saying our wedding vows.

The priest was shameless. He wanted to know details of my sexual life rather than my last sins. He wanted to know if I fucked every day, and if I liked it. He wanted to know if I enjoyed it the first time, and if I had orgasms. He only asked questions about sex. When he concluded the *confession*, he asked if I had thought about getting an abortion – asked me that in a Catholic Church! I think he had gotten his attention focused on sex from the start because, for a long time, there was absolute silence; he didn't ask me anything. I couldn't remember all the confession prayers by heart, and I didn't know all the rules to follow, but during that time I recited loudly all the parts that I could remember, I think the priest was masturbating himself underneath his cassock... Tony told me that the priest had asked him perverted questions also. We were both totally repulsed. We wanted to be married, to be happy and blessed by God. But when the priest eventually came from the confessional booth, he refused to marry us, saying, "You avoided my questions."

No other priests were available to marry us that day. We had to move in with my parents because the large amount of money required in advance to pay for the use of the Church had used up our cash--cash that would have otherwise paid the rent on the studio. Tony wanted to marry me desperately, but my parents were totally against it. I tried to comfort him, but he wept like a rainy evening, and my heart swelled with grief. We made plans to elope, until my parents found out. They tried to persuade me to have an abortion and marry a local architectural draftsman, a white trash Catholic named Buck, who was an acquaintance of my Father's friend. Tony and I enjoyed that last night on the fold-out-sofa, below my parent's bedroom.

The memory of the sad morning that followed is too painful to dwell upon.

~~~~~~~~~~~~~~~~~~~~~~~~

When I think back to 1995 my eyes well up with tears. It was the beginning of the end for me. The achingly beautiful love that I had for Tony led to the grief that was Eleanor: the daily haunting of her spirit around me, the constant fear and panic at the thought of being found out, being judged and punished for my sins.

I still love Tony. But marriage is probably overrated. I am not capable of falling in love anymore. Just like I don't get the mumps. But of course, anyone can be attacked by love. This last year I have given my mind permission to think more about the early days with Tony--each morning in bed. Then I see how my body yearns for him. I remember the solid core of his original personality, and the force of his desire. When those images radiate too much longing in me I cut them off--at least I try to.

# CHAPTER 11: CARMELLA, 2008

May 30, 2008:

Is there a curse on me, Carmella Meeks? Last night that nightmare came again. And now its afterimage lingers, casting a pall over my day. I dreamed that I was about to be fired. My boss had asked me to find one division within the Navy to which I could contribute. I tried designing, research, nuclear, and as a last resort navigation... which I know nothing about and have no interest in. I spent the first day slaving on the edge of a cliff, (I hate heights) while laying TNT charges to blast a road around the bluff of a mountain. Then... I know I am not into the Navy. I can not see the face of the Navy man who sexually molested me. But I can remember living with chronic fatigue syndrome and having great depression--then I aborted my baby. I woke up exhausted!

It was only a nightmare, but it made me a criminal--without knowing my crime, its time or its victim.

Now that my memories are not suppressed, at least not within my dreams, I have to ask myself: "If I was being born again as a little baby, would I want me, Carmella, to be my parent... Would my inner child trust that I could protect that precious child from sexual predators? Would I abort myself?" The corpse of a fetus would be evidence enough of foul play, even without blood or weapon.

Some days the only way I could get relief from my dark memories was to go fishing, to try to create new memories. Like that day when I yanked in my fishing line, planted, and cast again into the bay. The string sang out, the hook snagged and I damned the rocky bottom. Out on the pond a fish jumped, mocking my embedded hook. "Punishment!" I shouted, pumping my fist at the fortunate fish. An ordinary word about to explode with extraordinary significance: the rare gift of the muse that no aspiring author can afford to squander. I reached for the stroller where my child Eleanor was sleeping. I brushed off any temptation to throw my daughter into the bay, taking out my diary and pencil instead.

*PUNISHMENT*, I wrote on the blank page. I studied the word, a wriggling silver-green worm, daring me to dissect it. My pencil hovered over it like a knife, awaiting the world of insight that would splash fat phrases down the page. I squirmed, starting to sweat, but held my attention on the word, willing its inspiration. The virtually naked paper glared back fiercely in the daylight.

I compensated by hauling an apple from the stroller pocket, allowing myself a generous bite. Through the lazy haze and the insects and frogs singing from the pond, I restudied the written word. Suddenly it did seem to wriggle. I wished to live freely and boldly, to see if I could learn what life had to teach, and not, when I came to die, discover that I had regrets... as my English teacher, Hillary E. Smith, had warned me was a distinct possibility for a lazy wretch like me. I etched a prominent question mark after the single word I had to show for my day's work in my diary. I took another bite from the apple. A fish burped through a cloud mirrored on the pond, some yards out. I tore the sheet from the diary and tossed it into the fishing bag. "I'm going to get you," I swore as I sent the newly baited line singing past my ear. "One fish to go with my one word." The rock under my planted foot slipped. I skidded down the bank and landed in the ooze. I eased my fingers through the oily loam and plastered myself with mud. I scanned the shoreline; nobody was around. Reveling in the impropriety, I stripped and stood, the water up to my thighs, and felt the sun and breeze caress my pregnant belly. A new word, "delight," whistled through my mind. I inched through the shallows, laughing at my tender feet recoiling from the sharp pebbles. Finally, I dove, then stroked, gathering speed, until the yellow-brown water cleared to a crystal green. I shot up. At the leap's apex I arched and gulped, glimpsing the steamy shore, now distant and alien. I yelped, took in the echo, and plunged. Skittish minnow schools darted for cover beneath silt-gray plants as I surged by, intoxicated by my own form flowing through the underworld.

When my lungs began aching for air, I bubbled to the surface, a cork atop a gush of champagne. I floated face up, bobbing in my own wake. Like melting. For an instant, there was that flash of silence--the quiet place, which, as a girl on the shore of the Atlantic, I came to call my personal swimming pool, my true baptismal font, my bath where I could start life afresh after washing my sins away daily—it took an entire ocean to cleanse all of my sins. I lunged after the moment, but it drifted away. The spiritual sensation was replaced with the physical... a swirling nebula of light, heat, and color, its axis in my vagina. A turbulence of sensual images overwhelms: gossamer gowns, golden hair, swollen breasts and flowing limbs, approaching, touching, tantalizing and teasing. I have always had thoughts of the woman's body... Men are attractive to me, very much so--but not the visage of their bodies. When naked, Tony is more attractive than most men, but I still purchased a long nightshirt for him, to improve his appearance at bedtime.

Eleanor's cries disturbed my reverie.

It is interesting how I have adopted the formal style of language that Tony speaks-- acquired during his education at Medbury, Dunedin University, and later, at Cambridge, England. I try not to remember how I got pregnant by Tony with Eleanor. I am forgetting the sound of Tony's voice, and therefore the accent—but I never forget his penis.

When Tony left, neither he nor I knew that I would end up keeping our little girl who I called Eleanor...but I suffer the guilt of abortion anyway. I was working in the local hospital when I was more than two months pregnant, I asked one of the nurses what I had to do to get an abortion. Maybe that was a bad decision, but I felt that I had no choice. If I had shown any further resistance to having an abortion, my father would have taken Mom and I directly to the local butcher. The nurse turned out to be an evangelical Christian who was against the idea of abortions. So instead, I took some pills, but they didn't work. If I had an open relationship with my mother I would have talked to her instead of having to ask a stranger about how to get an abortion. Back then, there was no 'day-after' pill. I searched all over for suitable herbal teas, any known abortion medicines and even made physical attempts to kill the fetus. That was when another nurse talked to me about a medication called *Cytotec*, so I made an appointment with one of the hospital doctors. The medicine was available under approved prescription, but it was also expensive and I didn't have enough money. I finally managed to borrow money from a friend; I swallowed all sixteen capsules. The instructions said to only take four, but to be sure, I took the entire bottle. Soon I was cramping up and lost much blood and I thought I was free of my problem. I was haunted frequently by visions of a tiny corpse floating in the sea.

The following month my period did not resume, so I went back to the doctor, to get a confirming sonogram. When I lay down on the exam table, he looked at my stomach and said he was sure that I was more than three months pregnant now, before he even administered the test.

My sister had gotten pregnant twice by her boyfriend Pedro, and each time they got an abortion in Dodger Town, at the Clinic Catarina. I did not have enough money to go to that clinic, even though Tony had left me all the money he had. I began trying to sell anything I could, to collect more money. When I finally made it to Clinic Catarina and showed the staff how much money I had, they told me that because I was almost four months pregnant and the baby was larger, my money was not enough for that advanced stage. I left, got more money, and went back, assuming a different name. I lay down on the surgery table, the doctor came in, examined me and sent me away because he did not have a enough surgical skill for my more mature fetus.

When I got home and told my parents the news, Papa C-J punched more holes in the wall.

I wanted to keep my baby. I was hoping that everything would turn out alright, even though I knew that my father was close to evicting me from his house, with or without the baby. Buck had already offered to provide a home for the baby and me— but the proposed solution was not ideal. Back when I spent my days roller-skating I thought everything in life was going to be easy. Sure, my dad had raped and beaten me, but I had found Tony Chaytor, my special guy, my soul mate. Those had been the coolest times of my life. I wanted to have my baby with Tony.

Now, because of my fucking father again, Tony was gone. He had flown out of town in tears.

They say that happiness for the poor is short lived. It was like that for me. I had already enjoyed my only earthly months of peace and freedom. I didn't want to do what Papa C.J. had decided. I didn't want Buck. I was still pretty skinny and my bulky winter clothes hid my belly enough, so I though that I could continue to go to nursing school at night. I decided to lie to my parents; I told them I had finally terminated the baby at a back-street brothel, where they put me in a hot bath, forced gin down my throat, applied bromine to my inner plumbing, and trawled my womb with a wire coat hanger. They were horrified, but I had no regret about grossly exaggerating my imagined ordeal. Now that I was *secretly* pregnant I was determined to go through the entry examination for nursing school in the summer, and so wanted to stay at home for a few more weeks at least. But my plan collapsed: My fucking father, Captain C.J. Meeks, kicked me out of house with one week to find a new place.

C-J did not have feelings toward his unborn grandchild, but his behavior became even weirder, doing this blame shifting of his guilt onto me. I had planned to stay for one more week, but putting up with the new attacks on my integrity from my father became unbearable: "You have murdered an innocent baby at a back street abortion clinic. How low can you go?" I didn't have the spite to tell my father that I had not

60

terminated my pregnancy. My father told me that I would have to leave in three days, "Take responsibility and suffer the consequences, alone, for the destruction of my grandchild."

I had no money. I lacked the freedom to steer my life and was pregnant. I could not contact Tony. I didn't even know if he was in England, New Zealand or the US.

Donna told me that I should marry Buck even though she knew I didn't want to--yet she has held out for a decent man—her Pedro.

Before Eleanor was born I suffered greatly in the hospital. They did not want to give me anesthesia because there was nobody to pay the anesthetist. I was getting health care through the county hospital, which was supposedly free, but there were always unexpected items that required money. The government paid only a part of the costs, and I had to pay the rest myself. I experienced severe labor pains from 2pm on the first day until 11am on the following day. I was alone in my hospital room and in so much pain--and was not medicated because I couldn't pay. I yelled at the doctor, "I have no money, and I want no more people examining my vagina! Do a cesarean section now so I don't have to open my legs again." He called for a nurse, who came running with a stethoscope to listen to the baby's heart, but I was in so much pain that I slapped her hand away, hard. She called to the doctor, who saw that I was about to give birth.

Tony and I had wanted to call our baby Marise, after me, but changed our baby's name from Marise to Eleanor because I read in a magazine that a Brazilian porn star named Marise had died tragically. I did not want to be reminded of such a sad fate each time I spoke my child's name.

I was totally alone during Eleanor's birth. Everything was difficult. Right from the start.

I was always going to have to keep Eleanor's birth a secret from my family. Eleanor looked so ugly with the grotesque birthmark on her face and she was black like papa C-J. She was black all over and Tony was not her father.

I had to take Eleanor for her vaccinations when she was only one and a half months old. That was a government rule. She was jabbed with the Pertussa shot, part of the DPT shot.... Eighteen hours afterwards, she threw up, ran a high fever and began to scream, in a high-pitched shrieking sound. I gave her Tempra drops but that didn't help and when I ran her to the hospital, she seemed to be collapsing in my arms. Eleanor was in the hospital for over a week, until her fever finally broke. The doctors said her prognosis ruled out *sepsis*. However, I never gave her a Pertussa shot again after that happened, only DT.

When Eleanor came home from the hospital after that, her behavior had changed. I had to wake her up to feed her. She gave me no smiles back. Before the shot, she was a very alert and happy baby. Now she was either dopey or aggressive.

I was staying in a studio and Buck paid the rent. But he wanted nothing to do with Eleanor. Unfortunately I had to leave them alone together during one of my brief visits home. While I was having lunch at my parents' house, Hillary Clinton telephoned to invite Grandpa Carl to a government ceremony of apology and atonement. Carl refused to take the phone from my shaking hand. My family cannot deal with public exposure--too many ghosts in the closet.

When I got to my home Buck and his buddy were playing toss with baby Eleanor--throwing her like a football over the coffee table loaded with beer bottles.

Fortunately Hillary befriended me--after a few phone calls and letters she became like a counselor. I suffer from chronic depression. I wanted to trust that Hillary could heal me, so that I could become an eco-warrior fighting for survival instead of being a victim of shame. I wrote long letters to Hillary. I told Hillary how I let myself go out of my body, out the window… into Hillary's life instead of my own life. After we became close, years later, I came to realize that Hillary had also traded her freedom--for the shackles of a stupid PR company. Hillary had it all and still sold out in a moment of desperation.

Hillary angered a lot of people with her statement: *I'm not going to stay at home to bake cakes like a housewife.* Damn! She sold out to Newt Gingrinch to buy her popularity back. I know a lot more about that man than she does. I will be a Hillary Clinton supporter as long as I live. But I am frustrated because Hillary is only *beginning* to focus on the pending catastrophe of global warming, on the poison that's killing the planet that the next generation will have to live with. I don't know how serious I am about my Noah's Ark scheme that involves hijacking C-J's submarine. But I am determined to survive the pending environmental disaster so I know I will find a way.

I try not to remember how I foolishly got pregnant for a second time in 1997, pregnant to Buck. He was my father's choice for a man. Faithless Buck! How can I ever fully trust a man again after everything I have been through? Imagine, only a year and a half after Eleanor's birth I was pregnant again. I hoped that maybe being with Buck, the man that my parents preferred for me, would lead to better luck. Eleanor grew violent, and when she was two and a half, she was diagnosed with Autism PDD. I am convinced that my Eleanor's disease was caused by the mercury in her pertussa shot— and other shots… not from the genetic risks of incest. I am sorry that I enjoy sex so much and could not resist Papa C-J. I am sorry that I cannot handle autism. I am sorry that Buck became abusive toward Eleanor, and often failed to pay the rent.

I had no choice but to think about getting help with Eleanor. I took the first opportunity that was offered. I sold my body to an older wealthy man in return for baby-sitting and financial assistance. This Roberto wanted me to leave Buck and move in with him. He had lots of photographs of his own children in his apartment, healthy children who were now grown up. Eleanor stayed in his apartment when I went home for brief visits… and when I went into the maternity hospital again. This time I decided I *would* call my new baby Marise. My luck could only change for the better. Buck came into my hospital room drunk, claiming to be proud to be the father-in-waiting, but immediately left to commemorate the pending birth at the bar.

My second daughter's birth is a clear memory. I was alone. I cleaned my baby, fed her, and put a diaper on her. My life of rock and roll and roller-skating was over. I hoped I could do better with Marise because she seemed normal as far as I could tell. I knew how to be a good mother to Marise when she wanted to nurse from my breast. But I didn't know what to do when Marise cried incessantly.

When Buck came to my hospital room after the birth, he cried because he wanted a baby boy. I also wanted a boy. But when my daughter Marise was born I kissed her all over, and it didn't matter that she was covered in blood and slime. I didn't know how to care for all her needs, but I had a good instinct about protecting her. The nurse asked me if I wanted to donate Marise for adoption. The doctor told me that I was very young and couldn't manage to care for my baby alone. I knew that Marise was my responsibility and never thought of abandoning her or giving her up for adoption. After the conversation with the doctor, I didn't let my baby out of my sight. When they wanted to change Marise's clothes or weigh her, they had to do it in front of me. I read an inspiring article about my First Lady, my friend Hillary Clinton, in a magazine at the hospital. Hillary looks different on TV and in magazine photos. She was quoted as saying that while a mother should have the freedom to choose abortion, once the child was born then the mother must always have the child to raise, no matter how poor, unless there was abuse in the home. Up to that point I had been thinking of adopting out Eleanor because of her health problems… and especially because the birthmark on her face was a constant reminder of the incestuous lust of Papa C-J, of how disgusting I am. It may have been rape at first, and I always resisted him just to make myself feel better later. But I am nothing more than a fucking trollop. Hillary may be a decent woman, but she doesn't know my entire story—not until she reads this. So, her advice about avoiding adoption isn't valid.

Two days after Marise's birth I left the hospital and returned to my studio. Two women came to my home to see the conditions in which baby Marise was living. They wore badges that indicated they were from the government. The two women did not say anything, just looked around my home, examined my baby Marise, and then left. I found their behavior to be strange. They must have worked for the nursing school where I studied. They could have been looking for Eleanor, who was at Roberto's house--that house had grown very smelly. Roberto was not a great choice for a baby sitter… but what other options did I have?

I learned to do everything with my daughter Marise. I carried her in only one arm. I cooked very badly, but at least I tried. With one hand I moved the pan and with the other arm I held Marise. She got used to being carried this way, and it was also the most practical for me. I cleaned the house, cooked, washed the clothes and cared for Marise, all on my own because my father had disowned me. All that Buck wanted to do was to go to the clubs every night and drink. After Marise and I came home from the hospital, Buck quit his job and refused to help with house care. I despair at myself for thinking of Buck as a potential husband. Fortunately, my mother sometimes came to my studio and brought food. Fortunately she always called first so never met Eleanor-her granddaughter. My mother did not greet me or talk with me. She handed me the food, and sometimes took Marise to give me a break. I was glad of this help because I could not rely on Buck for any time of support, for either me or for Marise… and especially not for the bastard Eleanor. He only wanted to know about clubs and bands.

I longed to rock-out at the Michael Jackson Show when it visited Fort Pierce. But I didn't go because my conscience told me that I couldn't waste money on a show when I had bills to pay. But Buck went out that night as usual. I pretended to stay at home, but as soon as Buck was gone I hurried with Marise over to Roberto's house to visit Eleanor--where she stayed in an emergency such as when my Mama was coming over or when Buck was acting weird. The old man kept Eleanor in a pen. He said he had to keep her confined otherwise she would break things and attack him. Eleanor was showing further signs of behavior problems at an age of less than three--behaving like a wild cat: She spat at me, glared, and scratched with wide feral eyes. But I did not recognize those symptoms at that time as being medical rather than the genetic forces of incest. Roberto often wanted sex from me. Fortunately he was generous enough to accept that he was my only source of income now. Buck often came home drunk and I told him that I was disappointed by his behavior, which he found absurd. He became violent at home. We fought often, always about money. He left most evenings and only came home at dawn, so I was alone with baby Marise, a house to care for, and my other secret shame, Eleanor, who was now suffering serious bronchial troubles. Buck and I wrestled and slapped each other. I was at a disadvantage because he was so large. Today I am five-feet-four, a little too short. Anyway, I think now I know why I like small men, and why large men frighten me. My father is enormous, and Buck, while being skinny like my father, also has a large penis, and both my father and Buck had beat me. I discovered that Buck had gone out with one of my girlfriends, and this led to more fights. He would beat me and then show remorse. This cycle repeated and I often had to feed my baby Marise at the same time as he courted my breasts. Sometimes he drank from my breasts. Often I sewed clothes while he tanned under the sun in the yard.

I often opened the refrigerator even though it was empty. But one time I saw four sausages in a plastic bag. Fortunately for Marise she suckled on my breasts. But Eleanor was wasting away. I kept looking at the mystery sausages, and finally stacked them on the sink. Think, brain, and think harder. Find a way to survive. There was this thing that looked like a cockroach antenna protruding from one of the sausages. Buck must have brought the sausages home from the supermarket garbage. This gave me an idea:

I went to the local supermarket where the label on the sausages said they had been packed. The label also indicated that the sausages were on sale. I replaced that label on the sausages, which indicated their reduced price, with a label from the handle of a broom that I had purchased months ago from the same supermarket. I arrived at the supermarket armed with a powerful argument and much hunger. I asked to speak to the manager urgently. When the manager came into the room I simulated a stomachache. "See how sick you have made me. I purchased a big package of sausages that have given me food poisoning. They must have been rancid and so you were selling them cheap!" I used my high voice at the word 'cheap'. He bowed to my baby and me and said, "Let me see how much you paid… OK. Pick any other produce valued at $11 to compensate you for the damages." The broom had a much larger price than four polluted sausages on sale, and that was our salvation on that day. With the largest poker face, I took home a week's free groceries and still brought the four sausages from the garbage can home and ate them. I never knew that cockroaches could taste so good.

I enrolled Marise and Eleanor in a nursery so that I could work. I had to pedal one kilometers to daycare first, with the girls in a buggy behind the bike, then back-track to home and pedal six kilometers to work while Buck rode his motorcycle alone. He could have given me a ride, but did not because he preferred to seize every possible minute to sleep in the morning.

There was no more sex with Buck. I asked myself what I was doing to improve my life because I did not have friends anymore. One day, Marise got very sick. She vomited and I said to Buck that we must take her to the doctor. "You take her," he said. I asked him to hold Marise for me because she was crying and I needed to change her diaper. I placed her in his arms but he let her slide to the ground. He claimed that I was always giving him orders. I dropped Eleanor off to Roberto's pen, gave him a quickie, and then phoned my mother and she accompanied Marise and I to the hospital.

Marise had pneumonia. I lived with her in the hospital for seven days without having any place to sleep. For the entire week I sat in a chair next to Marise's cradle. I only went out in the middle of the night to visit Eleanor. Fortunately, Roberto lived just three blocks away from the hospital. But he wasn't doing well: Eleanor's clothes were always badly soiled and I had to wrestle with her to change her diaper. Eleanor scratched my face and bit my arm. There was plenty of baby food in the refrigerator. Eleanor was unhappy, angry, and violent. I don't know how a toddler could have so much strength, almost like the devil was inside her. Everything about my life hurt. I was worried that Marise might die. During those seven days at the hospital Buck chose to party up large while I tried to sleep sitting in a chair. Buck only appeared at the hospital at lunchtime so that I could go home to take a bath, change clothes, check on Eleanor, and then rush back to the hospital. Marise got better after a week, but Eleanor seemed to be getting worse—slapping away anything I tried to provide her.

The day before my baby Marise was released from the hospital I asked Buck for his motorcycle key and went home for a short break. I took a bath, visited Eleanor, and then I trusted the hospital staff sufficiently to ask them to give Buck a message, telling him that I needed to sleep at home in a proper bed for a little while. I lay down at two pm and didn't wake up until the next day. I didn't realize how tired I was because even when at home Eleanor had woken me every night, and there was always the stress of my secret life. I went to the hospital as soon as I awoke.

When Marise and I got home from the hospital Buck opened the door and bruised my eye with his fist, "You do not care enough for me," he said. "This studio is not mine but yours. I cannot tolerate this anymore."

I emptied my purse, gave Buck all the money that I had, and locked the door behind him. I concluded that I would never again rely on a man. While Marise slept, I hurried over to Roberto's house and collected Eleanor. I wrapped her tightly inside a blanket, placed her at the door of the local church orphanage, rang the doorbell, and ran home.

Four hours later my mother and my father arrived angrily at my door, telling me that they did not understand what madness had caused me to reject Buck. They said that I was irresponsible when I had baby Marise to raise, that I must take the blame, not only for everything that had already happened, but also for everything that would continue to destroy me in the future: "You are a problem without a solution," Papa said. I didn't know what to say and was shivering with cold. Fortunately Buck had not told my parents about Eleanor--he had promised me silence with regard to the birth of Eleanor in return for me not telling the police about him beating me. Suddenly my own mother grabbed Marise off my lap and shouted that my child was not mine anymore. Then Mama and Papa slunk out the door with my baby Marise.

I locked myself in my home, cowering in my armchair, close to a nervous breakdown. I visited my neighbor the next day, but my words were incoherent sentences without structure or meaning. The panic of losing both Eleanor and Marise caused my brain to over-rev with so many ideas that I couldn't communicate. I did not have the mental resources to cope, so I simply broke down, crying desperately.

Fortunately my sister Donna rushed over to sit with me. "Buck told his parents that you are crazy, and claimed that you abandoned your child."

I grew to like my sister during those dark times, and she developed a similar affection for me. After much crying my sister and I came up with a plan: I visited my older friend Vanessa, who was one of the few friends that had remained loyal to me during my problems. I told her everything.

"You can stay here with us, with my sister and nephew, in our tiny studio," Vanessa said. "My sister is a single Mother and will understand what you are going through."

We did not have much food or comforts, but we divided what we did have; it was still better than living at Carl-Junior's house. We ate bread with fried eggs and had lots of good talks. They divided their clothes with me. Hillary Clinton is compassionate like Vanessa and my sister. But she has never been poor--so how can she represent the poor so well? It amazes me.

Vanessa and I slept on the same mattress, and neither of us slept much. Plus, she had to work the next day. After that week I decided that I needed to get a job and make money. I worked hard at trying not to think about Marise at my father's house, or about Eleanor, whom I dreamed had been adopted by a professional couple from up north... and I hoped it was true. I decided to hitchhike by myself over to Dodger Town. I thought it would be easier there to find a job and a permanent place to live. It was a total shot in the dark because I had no money. All I had was the faith that something would come up. When we do not have anywhere to sleep or anywhere to work, life is about survival! I thumbed a ride. After an hour I arrived at the Dodger Town city entrance. The truck driver told me about an old lady who had rooms to rent to students, at Vero Beach beyond the east side of Dodger Town. It was another hitchhike and a long walk, but I made it. The house was two stories and tidy.

The first night in my new place was cold because it was beside an old lighthouse site, exposed to the winds of the sea and I had no coat or blankets. Fortunately, my room was small so it was easy to heat. I got up early. I needed to eat, but what could I do? I remembered that my sister had an account at the corner grocery near her house, and that my father paid her expenses each month--even though her husband Pedro makes good money. I called and asked her to charge some food.

"Okay, I will get what you need," Donna said. "Meet you at the store."

My sister never tried to judge me. She purchased a can of condensed milk, coffee, a pound of sugar, a package of crackers and some mojos... enough food to last for a week. Then I said goodbye to my sister. I gathered fruit from trees in neighborhood yards and stole green oranges. On the way back, with all my purchases and thefts in a

66

sack, I had to thumb a ride back to my home with the old lady. Now I had a home and food, but I still needed a job.

The next day, I started my job search, focusing on shops that might need help carrying bags of fruit and vegetables. I figured that I could take some carrots and bananas home in the process. But I couldn't find such a job. I was also longing for my daughter Marise, and wondering about what had become of Eleanor, wishing for word of her safe adoption. I decided to thumb a ride back home so I could see Marise, and to enquire at the Catholic orphanage about Eleanor's adoption. I was walking along a road with my thumb out when a red Fiat stopped and a woman said, "Hi, I'm Ester. Where are you going??"

"To town, to find a job to support my child." I was foolishly hoping that she was the woman who had adopted Eleanor. She asked if I wanted to work with her, selling books at schools, because she desperately needed help. I agreed to start work the next day. I carried some books home to study in preparation for the new job. At the first school, I enjoyed great success selling books and received my commission that evening. Two days later I gave my landlady a week's rent payment. I was happier than I'd ever been since Tony left. I had a home, food, a job, and nobody controlled me or limited my freedom. The only things I needed were for Marise to be with me, and some sign from God that Eleanor was alive and well.

Ester and I worked frantically, day after day, every day. We sold books in all the city schools. After that we went to neighboring cities. I never had so much money in all my life. If I wanted to eat a chocolate cake I could.

Ester was separated because she had caught her husband with another woman. We talked about sex a lot. Ester said she did not like sex, but I missed it terribly. As our sales increased, we had to hire a sales team--but I was still the best sales girl on the staff. In the mornings we sold these excellent educational books in the streets, and in the afternoon we sold them at the schools. Ester Grossi was brilliant and I loved her, but my landlady did not like me, or the fact that I didn't have a fixed schedule and was evicted from the old lady's house by the beach.

Ester had a wooden hut at the back of her country house. There was no bathroom, only a dirt floor, and an iron roof. But I put my things there and, when we were not traveling, I also slept there. It was very cold at night. Constantly I yearned to see my Marise. But it took three months before I worked up the courage to go to Mother's house and ask for Marise back.

"Why do you think you can do any better this time?" my mama interrupted my father's bluster before he could get a roll on.

"I have a job now, for six months. And a home with my boss."

"How can you work with a baby to care for?"

"My boss has a child also. She's out in the car. Let me introduce you."

Captain C-J sulked but was not opposed to having my noisy daughter reunite with me.

My Mama took a liking to Ester.

~~~~~~~~~~~~~~~~~~~~~~

# CHAPTER 12: CARMELLA, 2008

May 25, 2008:

I had tried writing my truth in my diary in the evenings, but couldn't bear going to bed with fresh memories of the crushing past--so I now begin writing my diary in the mornings:

I make the mistake of getting out of my car when I pick my daughter up from school. I am greeted with a barrage from the mother of a friend of Marise: "How dare you show your face! You're nothing but a whore."

I drive away casually, hoping Marise hasn't heard. Just as well Tony is not here.

"What do you want for your birthday Marise?"

Marise is already bouncing in the back seat. "That depends."

"Depends on what?"

"Marise doesn't answer, and sits still, looking at the fields sliding by the window.

"Depends on what?" I ask again.

"On whether you might be saving up to get me a full-sized horse."

Oh shit. I can imagine what Tony would say to that. "Do you want a horse?" I ask.

"Yes, I do." Her eyes are moist and shining, all that enthusiasm.

"Maybe. Tony and I will talk."

When we get home I am determined to transform my diary to a novel, so I return to the drudgery of re-writing my old diary in more literary language:

June 4, 2008:

Ester and I continued to sell books, but only locally--not traveling. She didn't like staying away from home for long periods of time because of her son. And I, of course, was now living with Marise in the cold hut. Marise and I stayed in Ester's hut for a year. It was too cold in the winter, and impossibly hot in the summer. I got out of bed promptly each morning and took Marise to daycare before going to work. I'd pick Marise up after work, but never late. We did not have television and I did not have a boyfriend, or any sex. But I did not leave for fear of upsetting our good luck.

I don't know how Buck found us but he appeared and started soft talking me, saying that he missed Marise and me. I was very needy, and I succumbed to Buck's seductions. My lifestyle was also very frugal and I hoped that he would help me to care for Marise, now that Eleanor was gone. What a fool I was. He became quickly impossible, and it was obvious that he had not changed his nature. Worse! He had become more aggressive, and was more violent with new resentments. Was it not enough to be beaten and subjugated by my father? No! Now I was being beaten and subjugated by my so-called boyfriend. I wished I could have been more like my sister Donna when subject to violent and abusive men. She didn't get attacked by Captain C-J when she was a child, not like I did, so her tolerance for that type of behavior was much less than mine. Fortunately, she had never grown accustomed to being beaten as a child and found violence and sexual aggression a violation--she has chosen a gentle husband in Pedro. It was different for me. Violent behavior by men was a frequent occurrence. I became permissive in this respect. The beatings I received one day were easily forgotten the next.

My sister took Marise and I home for the Thanksgiving weekend, to visit with Mama. The place had gone backwards--dusty, and broken windows. Mama cried when she saw us. I felt my heart crick and craw.

Hillary Clinton called the next day; what a huge surprise! She was nice, with a creamy voice. We talked about Port Chicago for a while, then she asked if she could call me the following week. I said she should call on the Monday because I was traveling away on Monday evening. My heart took a little leap when Hillary called late on Monday morning. She had read some more stuff about the Port Chicago detonation, and about my life with my babies—and some of my other secrets. Hillary wants us to write every week now. "Everyone should feel good about themselves," Hillary said. But I am not good. My life has depended upon no one finding out what has happened with Captain C-J... about the sex. But Hillary lived in another State so I thought that it would be OK for her to know.

When I received my next pay from Ester I took grandpa Carl to live in an old folks home, so he could get some treatment for his bed sores, and get away from he relentless anger of Papa C-J. Grandpa didn't ask any questions, just meekly climbed into Ester's car, at midday, when no one was at my parent's home. I left a note pinned to the end of his bed. "Gone fishing with Carmella--for a few years." He shared a room with another war veteran, in the Sunset Lodge, but neither of them talked on that first day when I dropped Grandpa off. I planned to move him in with Marise and I, when I found suitable lodgings.

I change my name from Marise to Carmella on the eighteen-month anniversary of the day that I abandoned Eleanor on the steps at the orphanage gates, on December 21, 1998--I can sense that something terrible has happened to baby Eleanor. Tony doesn't know that I finally gave birth to his child. I have confirmed that Eleanor is autistic because of mercury poisoning she suffered from her infant vaccines. That was devastating. The American public has no awareness of what it's like to have a child with autism, no awareness of the epidemic affecting 1 in 150 children. As autism cases soar, what's behind the rise? The government's recent concession that vaccines (not just thimerosal or the MMR shot), have aggravated many of our children's underlying mitochondrial disorders and have led to their diagnosis of autism and seizures.

Eleanor was probably developing normally up until her first vaccination at six weeks. I have been reading in magazines about her mitochondrial disorder. It did not appear until after her vaccinations. Approximately 75% of mitochondrial disorders are caused by medications. I know that the vaccines caused Eleanor's mitochondrial disorder after reading all theses articles. I hope we will have not just a government admission of this terrible tragedy--but also the best minds of medicine working on how to help our children. That would be the greatest correction toward some little justice.

Eleanor probably descended into autism within 48 hours of receiving nine childhood vaccines. Now other people are learning from misfortunes similar to those of Eleanor: Neighbors like Laurie Cunningham decided to vaccinate their 9-month-old daughter with only a few selected shots, to limit the number of shots at each visit to two, and she's decided to decline certain shots: The Hepatitis B shot because she's not at risk as an infant, the Rotavirus [live virus] vaccine because she felt the risks outweighed the benefits. That is what I am doing with Marise, now that I know that I can't trust the government. The rising number of vaccines included in the mandatory schedule--given to babies during the most rapid and critical stage of brain development--has raised additional concerns for we parents.

# PART VI: TONY

## CHAPTER 13: January 2008

I wake, five thousand feet above New Zealand, as the plane banks. Marise smiles. She and I are thrilled to be taking a vacation together--just the two of us. (Carmella is busy, and avoids my mum anyway.) The landscape around Blenheim is like a child's toy set; a quilt of fields dotted with red roofs, white sheep and brown cows. Sparse and winding roads reach out to serve isolated farmhouses. During the approach to landing, when the plane bobbles in the wind just a few feet above the ground, I feel I can save humanity from its corruption. At the small informal Blenheim airport Nana Rita hugs Marise, and kisses me while jostling my hair; "We're coming over to visit you in DC next year, before you return home to the safety of the ranch for good."

"That'll be great Mom. Hillary will be President by then."

"Look at you Marise. Beautiful. Almost a woman now eh?"

"Thank you Nana. Yes, I'm thirteen."

It wasn't long before Marise let everyone in on her secret, "Often, when I came home from school, I was sad. I simply sat in an armchair and I looked out the window. When the silence deafened me, when I heard streams of blood in my hands, when I heard the movement of my eyelashes, during those frequent attacks, my struggle became intolerable." Marise's head bobbed and her face grimaced. "My heart compressed further as my mother fled to the bathroom in tears, praying that her daughter would someday overcome her hearing and speech impediment. Then one day last year my prayers were answered."

Many people would find it hard to believe, that from the time she was 3 1/2 years old, Marise had stuttered severely--and she still can do so on special occasions. While giving her class speech in the school hall, she might have struggled through every sentence, opening her mouth unnaturally wide and clamping it shut in the effort to get out her words... But last time she didn't—she spoke clearly. *As a person who suffered from partial deafness as a young child, I was told I should have a goal, not of achieving verbal fluency... which was thought to be nearly impossible. But rather, of acquiring the coping skills that allow the afflicted like me to stammer openly and to shed the shame and embarrassment that accompanies the speech impediment... That is bullshit! And I am proof that verbal fluency is possible with modern hearing-aid technology.*

"How is Carmella?" Dad asks as we drive home, breaking my proud reflection.

"Good. But a bit tired. She's been working nights on the subs. And busy most days on election campaign work. She'll try and call from Puerto Rico."

"The American style of primaries, that wooing of delegates in elite pre-elections before the presidential election, is crass. Besides, Obama is going to win," Mom says.

"No way," Marise says. "Hillary is the best candidate."

The ranch house has the same style of front gate as the Meeks's front gate, waist high and made of wrought iron with a wooden address plate, *1 Chaytor Rd.* It swings beautifully on its hinges. There is no fence on either side of the gate. This gate looks as strange as the Meeks' gate, standing functionless at the edge of the grass verge. But there is no concrete pathway leading through it, to mark the distance to either the house or the road. Just grass. Even stranger, there isn't a mailbox. (Dad has a PO Box in town.) The gate stands alone, like a tree stump in the middle of a field. Still, I make a point of opening it and walking through. I do this because I find the idea amusing. Mom has already walked around the gate.

Mom insists that Marise goes to school today... *to experience the local culture.* Dad insists that I ride across the ranch with him. The smell of fresh cow shit is as pleasant as I have ever encountered. We ford a stream that tumbles noisily over rocks. There is a painted white cruciform marking the site where the truck rolled over the bank. The road is no longer a muddy bulldozer track, but a strip of hard-packed, short, and bright green grass surrounded by fruit trees. The fragrance of the blossom reminds me of the funeral. It wasn't my idea to mark the spot where Yolanda died. It seems a strange thing to do, to place a white cross in the middle of a hillside that almost no one but family would ever see. But William wanted it. An unopened bottle of *pinot noir* sits at the foot of the cross. The label has faded, bleached by sun and washed by the rain. Written in black on the crossbar are the words *Yolanda Chaytor.* My sister had been twenty-three years old. The carefully framed photograph of her, attached to the cross inside a weatherproof cover, faded like everything else, shows her dressed in a black gown. The photograph was taken on the day of her graduation by our neighbor, Chris Else. Yolanda hadn't wanted to attend the graduation ceremony, of course, being five months pregnant with her twins, Isobel and Sophie. The father is gay, giving my parents great displeasure... I can recall overhearing William yelling down the phone at Yolanda: *You worked hard for that degree and you'll bloody well collect it. And leave the pansy father-to-be at home . . . No, they couldn't post the bloody thing out. You're mother won't hear of it. You'll be there, bun in the oven and all. I'll make sure of it.*

Everything, even pride, sounds aggressive in my dad's voice. After Yolanda's funeral, his grief was almost impossible to detect; he'd been too angry to say anything other than to yell at me, *why in God's name did you let Yolanda drive? What about Yolanda's twins—do ya think Isobel and Sophie will forgive any of us?* he said, eyes still closed. *I could have told you she'd roll the bloody thing. I told you that camber on the road was put in too bloody steep. Christ, if you'd only listened to me none of this would have happened and your mother would have been saved a ton of grief.*

I can remember my mother saying, quietly, *it's not Tony's fault.*

But what stuck in my mind was my father's reply: *Of course it's Tony's bloody fault.*

Dad did his military service with the Americans during WWII... and made a lot of friends, especially in the scientific community. But he also saw too many body bags. New Zealand's population is too small to permit the sacrificing of thousands of soldiers to take a beachhead at Iwo Jima, or any other beach. Dad didn't believe that *any* piece of dirt was worth that much bloodshed. He was further devastated to see the nuclear destruction at Hiroshima and Nagasaki, for which he felt personally responsible--not only because of his nuclear research at Fort Pierce, but also because his mentor, Earnest Rutherford, had been the pioneer who first split the atom and started the field of nuclear physics.

During the eighties the American allies canceled the ANZUS treaty and shunned further imports of our food produce because of the New Zealand nuclear free position. Ranching changed from being an honest family business to a mugs game. Many ranchers had to labor at the local port in order to survive, loading tree trunks to feed Japan's booming economy, and unloading bird shit shipped in from the Pacific Islands to make fertilizer. Dad could have gotten a job as a structural engineer at home, but instead he commuted to DC to work as an engineer, and later started up Lilly-Thomas, Forensic Investigators, and IDS Consultants, Structural Engineering Corporation. Dad was driven to excel all his life. Of course I intend to become even more successful than my father, but to be a family man also--so my work isn't concentrated in a foreign country away from my wife, and doesn't involve sixteen hours of toil every bloody day... a job from which I can take a week off to be with my family, even if they are six thousand miles away.

I try to cheer him up. "Hey Dad. I'm finishing up the forensic job at Fort Pierce--on the EQE building collapse. It's top secret, never did hit the newspapers."

"That job wasn't real--as phony as a Hollywood movie set."

"Hey, Dad. I'm doing a report on the failure of the WTC-7 building on 9/11."

"That building should have been tested after the bombing in 1993. Vanity! It's all bloody vanity," Dad says, "Be careful! There is some funny business going on."

"Hey, Dad. Carmella and I are planning to get married."

Dad turns slowly, "Time for you to take over the ranch, build Carmella a new house, here, where it is safe for kids. Engineering is a flawed profession."

"What about Yolanda?" I ask. "Won't you resent me running the ranch when you think it was my fault that Yolanda crashed the truck?"

"You're the eldest. Besides, Yolanda's dead, and my only nephew has got a hankering to be a gypsy. He doesn't want a home, clean air, and security."

"In that case I just might take you up on that offer, but not until I've saved up a million or two. A rancher's got to have savings to survive these days."

"Do what you've got to do first, but don't forget the ranch... It's the key." Dad blows his nose loudly and folds his handkerchief back into his jacket pocket. "Tell me Son, was oil acquisition Bush's real reason for the Iraq war?"

"My best guess is that oil was *not* the real reason. The Republican mantra, *all roads lead to Baghdad* and *democratization*, were the major ideas behind the war. Bush couldn't have sold "democratization" on it's own, so Weapons of Mass Destruction were *used* as the reason."

"What about the oil then?" Dad asks.

"When the price of oil reaches $140 a barrel, that will be a critical situation threatening real economic decline. If Bush wants to attack Iran, which is pumping about 3.9 million barrels a day now, he's heading for trouble. Iran will scuttle every ship in the Straights of Hormuz and the Malacca Straits in Indonesia. It will take months of dredging and salvaging to approach normalcy. Oil is *not* Bush's top priority because he is just not *behaving* like someone who is managing an oil crisis--he has already been mismanaging oil in Iraq."

"Maybe you are right."

I find Rita in the vegetable garden and tell her about my plans to marry. She doesn't freak, but she wants to know more about Carmella. I tell her about Carmella's tragic relationship with her deceased father, Captain C-J, and how she has been shamed because of her out-of-wedlock pregnancy to me. "We've been living together for six years and have both decided it might be the time to tie the knot."

"You both must have suffered terribly," Rita says. "I'm glad for Marise. Does Carmella have many relatives down in Puerto Rico?"

"Heaps. She's sorry she couldn't come over. Urgent family business on the island."

Mom doesn't need to talk about it any further. But I can see that she is looking into her gypsy world for more information--more reliable information than I can provide. Her face frowns but Mom says nothing. It is that look into the gypsy world, and the frown, that unsettles Carmella—causes her to avoid Rita as often as possible. It's as if Carmella has something to hide from Rita's clairvoyance.

Time idles by while I drink tea with my parents and fish in my dad's boat--it is always moored off School Beach. The best fishing spot this year is out past the Cape, through the mouth of the river and around to the west. I am going fishing alone today because my dad has a sore back, from shearing four hundred sheep last week. He does the shearing in the evenings, after doing engineering reports during the day. He only has one helper: Nana Rita. The thermal currents bring a flow of nutrients to Queen Charlotte Sound during the El Nino season. The green fishing line deviates under the surface of the ocean, bending away; the baited hooks are invested deep in the fertile offshore canyon. A large gull flies low overhead, and then circles. A flock of gulls shriek in the distance, above a school of mullet. I could have made a meager but peaceful living as a fisherman, but then the ranch would have had to be sold... Both Dad and I subsidize it now that sheep prices have crashed.

Back in the house Mom is reclined in her leather lounge chair.

"Where's Marise?" I ask.

"Riding down at School Beach Park. I told her I would come down and help her ride with the hounds when I'm finished sharpening the carving knives."

"I'm not sure about letting a teenage girl go down there on her own."

"Relax Son. This is a different country, no terrorists here."

"I'd feel terrible if anything happened."

"You have to let her be free sometime, Tony. She's not going to get raped at School Beach."

"I'm sorry. I'm being neurotic, I know."

"I'll go down to the park now. Okay?" Mom says.

"No, I can go down."

"I see little enough of my grand-daughters," Mom insists. "Why did Yolanda insist that her kids spend half their time with their homo dad? They were very young babies when Yolanda died... yet Yolanda had already sorted out a custody agreement with him—depriving us of the comfort of our grandchildren. Isobel and Sophie deserve better."

"Fathers sort this custody stuff out from the start these days."

I take Dad's yacht out for some fishing again. There isn't enough wind to sail out, but it might come up later. In the meantime I'll chug out to sea under motor. Marise gets seasick even when it is calm. I wish she wanted to go fishing with me. I'll putter

74

out through the mouth of the harbor and do some twilight fishing beyond the lighthouse, where the ocean currents meet near the Cape. Tramping down the hill toward the mooring at Chaytor Beach, I see Dad's cream-colored boat, buoyant on the flat water just before sunset. Even at this distance I can see that the hull has been scrubbed and is shiny with anti-foul. As I approach the turn in the bay, the deck of the drifting boat is discolored from burd shit. I put my binoculars over my sunburned nose. An army of seagulls is sitting on the freshly painted yacht. And they've definitely been shitting. I tiptoe down to Dad's boathouse where a gun is kept. I wait for a lone bird to take off from the once pristine boat deck, and shoot the bastard in flight. I fire one additional shot into the mass of gulls that are now running for cover in the hostile sky. One dead gull lands on the deck of the boat. The other corpse plunges into the bronze green channel. The sky darkens as a thousand white gulls squawk in from the horizon, on the last rays of the sun, coming on like stars. The gulls congregate in a giant flock above me, gathering to pay their respects to their dead comrades. I can hear a heavy hum below the falsetto squawk. The sound of the massed gulls rises smoothly in volume, to a crescendo, and after an extended chord in unison, the finale ends abruptly. Waves of echoes bounce off the cliff. Then silence.

The sky is empty of sound and gulls. New stars come to life, close, as the full moon rises above the ocean horizon.

On the way home I stop by School Beach. Mom is holding the horses. There is Marise crouched over by the fence, beside Chaytor Road, where the wild rabbits live. It is almost dark. Marise, with her red hair and black blouse over green jeans, is just a shadow. I stroll closer.

"Come on Fluffy, another carrot stick for you--nothing to be scared of. And for you too, Bobtail, don't bite my finger. Maybe Nana will let me have one of the horses, to call my own. And maybe Grandpa will ride with us—and the pretty hounds, so we would come down here and visit you. I hope you won't be afraid of the hounds and my horse. I'll make sure they don't harass you. It'd be so much fun to take care of you all. Its OK, Bobtail, I can be a little girl with you… I don't have to be a responsible teenager all the time."

Marise and I relieve Nana from holding the horses, so she can finish her chores. Marise insists that I stand with her as she grooms the animals. Marise likes to have these long chats in the stables, which is okay as long as there is nothing urgent to do. We are chatting about nothing in particular and then out of the blue she asks me where the sky ends.

"I don't know," I say. "It doesn't really have an end. Just becomes outer space."

I remember my math classes: *A straight line is a segment of a circle that passes through infinity.* Marise is too flighty for that leap.

"What is heaven really then?" she asks.

"It isn't a place at all, not like the library or the chess club, so it doesn't have an address."

After a pause she asks, "Do you think heaven is just a concept, like infinity?"

"Yes," I say, and there is a long pause while she checks hooves.

"It must be peaceful."

"What do you mean?"

"Peaceful isn't a place. It's something that you are. Maybe heaven is a bit like that?"

"Maybe," I say, not sure of myself.

"Maybe heaven's a place that you feel rather than a place where you are."

"That is good," I tell her. Just as well she doesn't go on to explore hell.

"Today has been heaven for me," she says.

"Good. So why are you taking so long?"

"I'm flying again. Down below me the ocean is warm, and there are whales spouting. They are squealing, but I can't understand their whale language. I dive down and swim with them for a while. Then I'm soaring up into the sky again, and the sun is burning my back. Global warming has changed things. I fly over land, and there are green fields with zebras; all the zebras are looking up at me and admiring how well I can fly. Nothing can disturb me up here. The wind is blowing the hairs on my arm... and Mom will find what she's looking for."

"Oh! What is Carmella looking for?"

"She hasn't found it yet so how could I know? ...Peace I guess."


We can hear Nana Rita upstairs now, slamming her hot iron on the ironing board.

"Nana's probably upset again," I explain to Marise. "It is hard when Aunty Yolanda's children are away with their dad... and he smokes. Nana and Mama want all three of you girls to have a safe youth, with no emotional crises or polluted air."

"Doesn't every parent?"

"Yes. But Mama and Nana want a guarantee--for many generations to come."

"Global warming is scary, but not the end of the world... not the way Mama fears."

Marise nods to encourage an affirmation, smiles, hopeful, pushing the loose strands of hair back behind her left right ear in the way I adore. "I'll go help Nana."

Rita yells, "Wait there!" She thumps down the stairs, slowly, glaring at me.

"Did you promise Marise a new horse?"

Rita's voice is calm, too calm. I know it well enough to sense the threat beneath it. Do I fight, or let her have her way? Do I apologize, or agree with her?

"No, I didn't promise a horse." This is about us living in America, not about horses.

"Where did she get the horse idea from then? You say Marise forgets to do her math sometimes. If Marise can't do her math homework how can she possibly take care of a horse? I'd be the one feeding it while you are away."

"Marise asked about a horse in DC. I said we'd discuss it." Why do I feel guilty?

"Marise, is this true?"

"Yes, Nana."

"Okay, Tony. And will you pay for the food and vet bills, and buy the horse?"

"Yes," I say, knowing that this is all a misunderstanding, but I stir anyway.

"Okay. But you'll have to wait until her next birthday, until she's fourteen and has had a chance to read up on the caring."

"No! She's old enough now." My mother has intimidated me long enough.

"If you'll wait another year I'll work with you, share some of the costs. But if you charge in at this, like everything else you do, then I'll have nothing to do with it."

Marise interrupts, "You've got it wrong Nana. I don't want a *new* horse. Just to call one of yours my own. *You* can ride it still, and feed it of course--while I'm in America."

"Of course Dear. Of course. The one you rode today is yours then."

Poor nana Rita. She must feel the hopelessness of ranching more than Dad. And the doom is made worse by the staunch air of being bulletproof, that Dad and his friends pretend, as they share war stories down at the pub. And the pretense that someone will buy the mounting stocks of frozen lamb that the Americans had once been eager to buy.

Marise and I go to her room and play a game of chess. She has grown tall and thin-legged, with tiny wrists and shoulder blades that protrude; yet when she tenses you see that her muscles are well developed. Her speech impediment has been almost eliminated with the help of her therapist and her new high-tech hearing aid. After the game we go down to the kitchen. Rita has gone out and left a note, *Grandpa and I will be home late.*

Marise and I heat up vegetable soup with lamb chops, then spend the evening studying the photo albums while we play another game of chess. It is Marise's turn to play white and I choose a little known version of the Indian defense. Marise finds a picture of her Mama, taken when Carmella was a trainee in the Navy, dressed in her whites.

"Doesn't Mama look like an angel in her Navy uniform?" Marise says.

"She must be an angel, to have a lovely daughter like you."

"And doesn't she look smart, like she could pilot a big submarine all by herself?"

I had never thought of Carmella like that. I suppose she is a *take-charge* person.

"Yes, very smart. I'm glad that you are patient with Nana."

"Yeah. She hasn't been herself . . . You know how I didn't want to be a professional chess player?" Marise says.

"Yes."

"I've changed my mind. It's just that driving a submarine is a lot of physical work, according to Nana--lifting heavy machinery, and taking orders. Not as glamorous as the uniform looks... and it might leak nuclear radiation, and have to stay under the ocean for twenty years if they cannot fix the leak—to prevent more global warming."

"Yes. You have a good head on you. Must get it from your mother's side."

I can sense a constant suffering within Marise, of pain from the family struggles when she was a toddler, living with Carmella's parents... living with Carl-Junior's craziness, and the poverty. Perhaps my parents aren't much better. Rita talks too much about how she resents Yolanda's twins living with a gay father every other week. That resentment coincides with the grief of the ranching business going down the tubes. And now she has grief around Marise living too far away from the fresh air of New Zealand.

The smell of breakfast lifts Rita's kitchen. Morning has always been the time of highest energy in our home. I look out the small window in the sidewall. The postage square of the south Pacific Ocean below is purple and gray, with an arrow of Geese flying north; a sign of winter approaching. Back in DC the spring flowers will be on the trees in the orchards, and the neighbor's horse will not be wearing her cover at night.

Through the picture window I can see a shadow of a cloud breezing across the hill at the head of the valley, then along the top of the cliff over Chaytor Beach, where a new house might be built. Perfect! Except that I plan to stay in DC, despite the pollution. Then I hear the crowing of a rooster, mocking me, and it crows again.

# CHAPTER 14: TONY, January 2008

I am preparing to serve dinner when I her Marise reading something from a magazine to Mom in the living room.

"Julia Roberts is getting married. It's true! Her dress will be a custom-made, two-piece gown--from the Tyler Trafficante salon. At the reception following the ceremony, she'll be able to pull off the train and the long part of the skirt, to dance. The bridesmaids' dresses will be sea-foam green, and their shoes, Manolo Blahnik, will be dyed to match. The bridesmaids will be Julia's two agents, her makeup artist, and an actress. The cake will be four-tiered, with violets and sea-foam ribbons of icing... What I want to know is where's our invitation?" Marise finishes.

"Did it get lost in the mail?" Nana Rita is folding laundry, "And who's her fiancé again?"

Marise is on the floor, reading aloud from the magazine, "Kiefer Sutherland," Marise says. "They met on the set of Flatliners."

"Is he cute?"

"He's okay. Actually, he *is* cute. He has blond stubble and, even better, one blue eye and one green eye."

"Let's see him?" Marise holds up the magazine. "Eh, he's adequate."

Marise and I have now been in New Zealand a week and are celebrating this event with a special dinner. Marise has already prepared the salad and set the table. The lamb chops are almost charred, just the way I like, and are served with home-grown veggies.

"Great salad, dear. You must stay with us longer," Grandpa William says.

"Yes, Marise. You are welcome here whenever you wish," Rita says.

During the early evening chess game William yells from the second-floor bathroom, "Rita, this place is a bloody disaster. Marise will think we're barn animals." He settles down onto his knees and starts scrubbing. Yes, the tub was grimy, but Marise can't believe it. She has never seen her own father wipe a counter, change bedclothes, or unload the dishwasher. And here is my father, William, on the floor after returning from a nine-hour drive to Dunedin. The thing about William doing woman's work is that he's ugly. He's really ugly. His teeth are brownish and angled in all directions, and he has wild eyebrows, long and wiry and as wayward as his teeth, and he has a tiny ponytail. He's too tall and lanky, but his accent is nice—Cambridge English... but still. "If Rita considers Kiefer Sutherland only adequate," Marise must be thinking, "What does her Nana think of her own husband's ugly appearance?"

Grandpa William insists that we all watch TV together after the chess game. I agree because I know that a surprise is in store. The first show is his favorite: The new *Truman Show*--a satirical analysis of the current U.S. Presidential primary election campaign... The TV guide says, *It is an American series addressing the plastic images deviously created for Hillary Clinton by Newton PR. Hillary Rodham Clinton is portrayed by a look-alike who is inadvertently trapped in the prison of a manipulated public media image, disguised as the real Hillary persona.* It seems that almost our entire society is living in a virtual-world of self-indulgence--that is really an environmental and emotional melt down awaiting the death camp of global warming.

*In tonight's finale the actress, Hillary-the-Fake, is making an escape from her virtual world of politics and PR for a rendezvous with her feminist friends on a submarine that is hidden away in a remote part of Puerto Rico--to plot a counter-strategy.*

"Look, there's Mama." Marise says--as Carmella appears on screen in her first effort at acting, dressed in her navy whites, welcomes Hillary-the-Fake aboard a pink submarine decorated with red, white, and blue bunting.

Hillary-the-Fake makes a phony speech on deck, addressing her outrageous petticoat brigade of followers: *To have an authentic chance at winning the Presidency in the current hostile media environment I must distance myself from the false safety of the media culture. I must be willing to live in the world as it really is.*

Grandpa William roars with laughter, "What a load of B.S... but Carmella is great."

Hillary-the-Fake is not finished. "I have been trapped by malevolent simulators and high-tech manipulators who are intent on keeping me inside the fake plastic bubble of my public image."

"What is B.S. Grandpa?"

"B.S. is the phony character the media use to portray Hillary Clinton. Watch!

*All the realms of lifelike fantasy the characters inhabit, whether they are themed stage sets, as in the recent show, Hillary Election Campaign... or virtual realities—they are depictions of the American media culture in which television, internet, video games, magazines, theme parks, and celebrity weddings are surrounding us with simulations that masquerade as something authentic, which is causing us to regress into a new infantilism in which machines and human manipulators feed us fantasies of endless gratification.*

"Nana, what is the show really about?"

"I'll tell you what the TV guide says. *We find ourselves living inside seamless works of theater that we mistake for the real world. Why has Hillary Clinton become such a character of fiction? Is the real Hillary aware of what is going on—of how her campaign manager, Mark Penn, and Newt Gingrinch, are sabotaging her?* Rita reads. "It's a satire on the American election process; suggesting that look-alike actors could portray the candidates and we'd be none the wiser. Might as well do the election campaign as a soap opera on a Hollywood set."

"...Is Mama's acting debut mocking Hillary's campaign then?" Marise asks.

"No. But it must have been Newt Gingrinch who hired her. And it is shocking that Mark Penn and Newton PR have only scheduled campaign events for Hillary up until February 5th. Then the first big bunch of voters, representing more than twenty states, will select their preferred candidate for the Democrat Presidential nominee... Do they think it will be that *easy* to win it all so quickly? Goddamn! The Presidential election isn't until November 4th. Her stupid minders make it possible that Hillary will lose, even though she has been the front-runner until now," I say.

They're fools," Grandpa says. "The Democrats have taken to heart that great line from the old Bonnie Raitt song, *Let's give 'em somethin' to talk about.* They'll be talking about this historic primary battle between Hillary Clinton and Barack Obama forever... The inevitable split decision on February 5th will lead to a long and bloody showdown. How long? "This may not be decided until the convention in August."

"So the ultimate winner won't really be known until much later in the year when one of the two candidates goes over the top in the delegate count. Until then, it's a spin war?" Rita says.

"Yes! Mom, but I'm frustrated. February 5th is supposed to be the day the lethal and inevitable Clinton Machine closes the deal and gets the nomination—according to Hillary's minders. But it will *not* be. And Mark Penn expects that Obama's January surge in the polls will peter out. Wrong! All the Republicans are secretly promoting Obama."

Marise joins in, reading from a newspaper. *In Missouri the polls indicate that the Democrat race is essentially a tie. Polls indicate Hillary Clinton will claim the grand prizes of California, New Jersey and New York... and will win Massachusetts despite Senator Ted Kennedy's much publicized endorsement of Obama. Hillary will end February 5th with only a slender lead in the delegate count-- and that lead only be because women and older voters support Hillary in force. Obama will pick Hillary's pocket in Connecticut, and will handily win his home state of Illinois. He will display strength all over the map from the Deep South to the Midwest and Far West. Well-educated, young and upscale voters will come out for Obama, as will African-Americans. Independent voters will go for Obama by a 58-35 margin according to the polls. But Hispanic voters will stay with Clinton. As for future momentum, well, forget it. This fight is round by round. It always has been and will be to the end...*

Nana Rita looks up from her knitting and interupts, "How come you know so much about it Marise—for a thirteen year old?"

"I am reading from the *Herald,* Nana."

"After tonight, time becomes the ally of Senator Obama," I say, still laughing. "The more exposure Obama gets the stronger his chances become. The compressed primary schedule has been a tremendous opportunity for him."

"Let me read you some more," Marise says. *In the money wars, Obama has the edge. He is expected to raise $32 million in January alone, mostly from his Internet campaigns. Clinton will raise only $13.5 million. This race will be historic because it will produce either the first female or the first black presidential nominee from a major American political party. People will also be talking about this campaign for decades to come for its sheer ferocity, closeness and duration--and its lack of predictability.*

"Attention please. The next show is due to start. Read the TV guide Marise," Grandpa says.

Marise reads again. *10.30pm: A new historical documentary by Newton PR about the first secret nuclear detonation disaster—that was researched by Tony Chaytor.* Wow Dad! That's you."

"Yes Sweetheart. Read on."

"OK. Let me find the page... *A detonation during a Democrat administration in 1944. The concept of the new show is brilliant, but cynically aimed at further covert undermining of Hillary. Newt Gingrinch has bought into the radical concept of this new show because it faults a* Democrat *administration, and HILLARY is the villain. The documentary is called 'The Hillary Bomb.'* Wow!"

"It's Marise's bedtime. Perhaps Daddy will let you stay up to watch, eh Tony?" Nana Rita says.

"OK, I guess it's a special occasion. But no nightmares Marise, OK?"

"Quiet, It's starting," Marise says.

*The government corruption back in 1944 was of a similar scale as that around the adultery of President Bill Clinton—but with no publicity. It is important to demonstrate conclusively, to the American voters, that a devilishly corrupt behavior--by an elected American President, leading a Democrat Administration—who behaved so corruptly that it seems impossible-- has in fact happened... back in 1944 for example:*

*Port Chicago just blew up!*

A man with a voice like Walter Kronkite is doing the narration, with a backdrop of a busy naval base at wartime... Then there is a fade-out to a nuclear detonation—water droplets sensuously migrate up the erect mushroom shaped plume of flame, then the white flash, and finally the sound. Wow! The Kronkite voice continues:

*A massive explosion on July 17, 1944 propelled a small delta port town, located thirty-five miles north of San Francisco, into oblivion. How this global first for nuclear detonation has avoided the national and world spotlight, for so many years, I'll never know.*

*This detonation was part of the Manhattan Project Y, upon which the success of the Pacific war pivoted. This part of Project Y was called HILLARY (Hydride Isotope, Laboratory Los Alamos, Rapid project Y), a rapid or fast track option conceived not only for the development of a nuclear bomb to destroy Japan, but also, importantly, to intimidate Russia aggression in the looming Cold War, victory over which would prove America to be #1. HILLARY provided valuable data for the design of the nuclear bombs dropped on Japan, and was a precursor to nuclear tests RUTH and RAY.*

*Carl Meeks of Fort Pierce, Florida, was unloading ordinance from railway trucks bound for the S. S. E. A. Bryan merchant ship during the evening before this disaster."*

The screen fades to a scene of Carl Meeks' brother, Freddie, being interviewed in a southern TV studio back in the mid-nineties—Freddie looks identical to Carl.

"Look! That's Carl Meeks, my Great grandpa. Eh Grandpa William?" Marise says.

"Yes Honey. Now listen!"

*The last lot of ordinance was so alive it was slappin me,* Carl says. *I ran from the docks ten minutes before the ship exploded, after being alerted by static spitting in the air, by all the stones jumpin off the roadway, and by a hundred dogs barking.*

Kronkite continues: *At 10:18 pm, Monday evening, July 17, 1944, a giant explosion rocked Suisun Bay on the Sacramento River. The blast killed 320 Naval personnel. Mr. Meeks fled for cover behind a highway embankment two miles from the blast. He experienced heat as if the sun had come out at 10 pm, and air turbulence much worse than a Florida hurricane. His hands became transparent. He could see the bones through his flesh. Port Chicago was entirely destroyed within a 1.5 mile radius of the detonation, so the physical area was renamed the Concord Naval Weapons Station.*

*The local news accounts of the blast all focussed on the signature flashing white light and the*

81

presence of a mushroom cloud. Not until the Hiroshima and Nagasaki nuclear detonations, which occurred over a year later, in August 1945, did the world's general population become acquainted with terms such as bright white light and mushroom cloud in reference to a nuclear detonation.

The backdrop behind Kronkite changes from the devastation of Hiroshima to an active railroad dock showing men unloading:

*Records of the contents of two of the sixteen boxcars unloaded at Port Chicago that were all stored at Los Alamos, are missing. A complete list of the contents of all the boxcars is still kept at the famous nuclear laboratory--except for those two boxcars. Did one contain a nuclear bomb? The Navy claims not. The bill of loading provided for only a 1.5-2.0 kiloton equivalent of TNT--insufficient explosive to explain the huge 600-foot diameter blast crater that was created in the bed of the Sacramento River, not to mention the complete annihilation of everything within a 1.5-mile radius of the detonation.*

*A further piece of evidence that contradicts the Navy's official denial is a Los Alamos document, History of 10,000 Ton Gadget, (10 kiloton), describing the 11-step testing procedure of an atomic device and all its parameters. In step 11, the document clearly states, a ball of fire mushrooms out at 18,000 ft. in typical Port Chicago fashion. The fact that this classified document, prepared a short time after the Port Chicago disaster, originated from Los Alamos Laboratory, and specifically refers to Port Chicago by name is evidence of a scientifically observed nuclear detonation. Also, one of the highest rates of cancer in the U. S. has occurred in Contra Costa County, where the Port Chicago explosion took place.*

The backdrop changes to the Fort Pierce Naval base. "Look," Marise says, "That is where Captain C-J works—the other Grandpa we don't talk about."

Kronkite continues: *The Navy Defense Research Centre (NDRC) was housed at the U.S. Naval Base at Fort Pierce, Florida. This critical facility provided data on estimating the magnitude of blasts based upon peripheral damage data and other forensic engineering techniques. The chief of NDRC produced a report entitled Damage Survey at Port Chicago, California, just ten days after the explosion. This rapid response confirms the importance of the damage data from the Port Chicago detonation to the war effort. A similar bomb to HILLARY (but called Mark III rather than Mark II, with modifications resulting from the Port Chicago test results) was dropped on Hiroshima by plane thirteen months later.*

*In autumn of 1980, the Los Alamos National Laboratory Director Donald M. Kerr, challenged author Peter Vogel to prove that the Port Chicago explosion had been a nuclear fission explosion. The Last Wave from Port Chicago is Vogel's response to that challenge: Vogel published, in that book, a signed and handwritten directive from then President, Franklin D. Roosevelt, (a Democrat) to the Secretary of War Henry Stemson, dated July 7, 1944:*

*"By the authority vested in me as Commander-in-Chief of the Armed Forces of the United States of America, and additionally granted to me by the Congressional Declaration of War against the Empire of Japan, I hereby direct you to authorize the Joint Chiefs of Staff and Rear Admiral........... assigned to the Manhattan Project laboratories at Los Alamos, New Mexico, to secretly detonate the prototype Mark II experimental uranium hydride nuclear fission bomb at the Port Chicago Naval Magazine as soon as practicable in order to prove the feasibility of large scale nuclear fission weapons .......... And, moreover, to utilize detailed analyses of the consequences of that proof detonation to be made at the Port Chicago Naval Magazine to establish the anticipated military effects*

82

*that will be realized from the use of the more powerful militarily-decisive nuclear fission bombs now in development by the Manhattan Project, in similar or other circumstances of combat. The exigencies and imperatives of the present War require that the proof detonation of the Mark II prototype atomic bomb here ordered shall be made by the parties without consideration of any physical consequences to property and persons which shall inevitably arise from execution of this order."*
    *Signed, Franklin D. Roosevelt*

    *The explosion at Port Chicago was nuclear, and the weight of the evidence indicates that it was a secret premeditated nuclear detonation. Nations such as New Zealand, and local ports such as Oakland California, have passed ordinances banning nuclear weapons. The US government has countered with trade embargos and lawsuits.*

    *Democrats with the same ideology and allegiances as the power-hungry Hillary Rodham Clinton... perpetrated this massive deceit. Why would Hillary Clinton, another Democrat, behave any differently than her predecessors?"*

During the credits there is a local station announcement: *"The Hillary Bomb* documentary series became so popular for Newton PR that the companion show, *Pearl Harbor*, is scheduled to air on TV New Zealand next month, immediately after this series is completed."

"I've got that *Pearl Harbor* show, on DVD. My son gave it to me hot off the press when I was over in DC. Haven't had time to watch it yet," Bill says.

    A footnote appears with the credits: *You may find further data, in the documentary about this series,data proving that the horrendous Port Chicago detonation was a premeditated nuclear test.*

"Papa. Why don't they like Hillary Clinton?' Marise asks.
"The Republicans are afraid of her because she is a smart and powerful leader--against whom the Republicans have difficulty finding a candidate to match her abilities. The only chance the Republicans have of getting into power, with their own President elected, is for Hillary's teammate, Barack Obama, to knock Hillary out of the competition."
    "So this is just the semi-final—the primaries. The Republican division gets to side against and sabotage that person from the Democrat division they don't want to contest with in the finals?" Marise asks. "They prefer to run against Obama?"
    "Yes. That is the guts of it," I say.

    "Is Great grandpa Carl for or against Hillary?"
    "Carl was an innocent worker in the war... who got a dirty job of loading nuclear weapons in 1944--because he is black. He did nothing wrong." I say.
    "Goodnight Papa. Is that why Great grandpa Carl hates America?"
    "He doesn't hate. But still feels very hurt about the injustice. Goodnight Sweetheart," I say.
    Rita interrupts, "Hey Marise. Before you go to bed... Let's have a party tomorrow?" Rita is holding up two socks, both white but clearly different lengths. She shrugs,

seemingly to herself, then rolls the socks into a ball and tosses them toward the folded pile. "Let's have a party for Julia. With wedding cake and cucumber sandwiches with the crusts cut off. We'll toast to her happiness. Champagne for all."

Marise watches Nana Rita.

"What?" Rita says. "You don't like the idea? I know Julia herself won't show."

"Oh," Marise says. "Okay."

When Nana Rita laughs she opens her mouth so wide that the fillings in her molars are visible. "Marise," she says, "I'm not nuts. I realize a celebrity won't come to my house just because I invited her... or even if Tony invited her—to keep up his delusion of being connected with the rich and famous."

"I don't think like that," Marise says. "But I know what you mean. And actually, Daddy really does work with several celebrities... I've been to meetings with them."

But this is not entirely true; Marise cannot completely read me. Fortunately, Rita has always been a sane presence in Marise's life--to counter my eccentricity... Marise has a memory from age seven, riding in the backseat of Rita's car as Rita sang *You're So Vain* loudly and enthusiastically along with the radio--but for the most part, Rita has been a stable presence. But Marise surely realizes how little she knows about her Nana Rita... or about Carmella's mother. The primary information she has always associated with Rita was acquired so long ago she probably cannot even remember learning it... That once, soon after Rita became a nurse, a patient left her a great deal of money and Rita squandered it on an enormous series of banquets and parties—even though there was no special occasions, not even her birthday. And she's been struggling to make ends meet ever since.

Marise has been surprised to find that Nana Rita always orders takeout, usually Chinese--on the nights William is gone, which is at least half the time. They're not exactly struggling to make ends meet. But it didn't help, financially speaking, that Rita had an affair with a truck driver, Earl--whose brother was a lawyer: the hippie, as William calls him.

Marise asks Nana Rita what *hippie* meant.

Rita says, "A person who is fond of the counterculture."

When Marise asks Grandpa William about *hippie*, he says, "It means Nana Rita's boyfriend doesn't take a shower very often."

"Will we have our party before or after the real wedding?" Marise asks. "Julia gets married on the fourteenth." Then, probably imagining the wording of Julia's invitations, spelled out in swirly writing, she adds, "You are cordially invited to attend..."

"Hey Nana Rita. Let's have a party on the fourteenth? ...This Saturday."

"OK. Curtis can be your date, if he's here, and your Papa can be mine."

Marise feels a stab of disappointment. Of course she doesn't want to date Curtis Sittenfeld--the sixteen-year-old illegitimate son of Earl's sister. Curtis is the final piece in the puzzle of Rita's financial downfall. Curtis is a pyromaniac who burnt down the Chaytor mansion. William said, on the day of Curtis' birth, as he stood in the kitchen after work flipping burgers for Earl and his friends, "Rita's choice to be godmother is a foul trick... we'll be supporting this child all the way to our graves."

But what did Marise think Rita was going to say? *Your date will be the fourteen-year-old son of one of my cowboys. He is very handsome, and he'll like you immediately.* Sure, Marise expects Rita to arrange that. She assumes her blessings will fall from the sky.

"I wish I could find my wedding dress for you to wear at our party," Rita says. "I wouldn't be able to fit my big toe in it at this point, but you'd look real cute. Lord only knows what I did with it though."

How can Rita not know where her wedding dress is? That's not like losing a scarf. Carmella's wedding dress was given to her by her Mama--stored in anticipation, back in DC, stored in the attic in a long padded box that looks like a baby's coffin.

"I gotta put the other load in the dryer," Nana Rita says. "Coming?"

Marise stands, still holding the magazine. "Kiefer bought her a tattoo," she says. "It's a red heart with the Chinese symbol that means *strength of heart.*"

"In other words," Rita says, "As a sign of my love, you get to be poked repeatedly by a needle with ink in it. Do we really trust this Kiefer guy?"

They are on the first floor, cutting through the kitchen to the basement stairs.

"And do I dare ask where the tattoo is located?"

"It's on her left shoulder. Grandpa doesn't have tattoos, does he? Even though tattoos are expected of truck drivers and cowboys? Is this a rude question?"

"None he's told me about," Rita says. She appears not to be offended. "Then again, most cowboys and truck drivers probably don't eat tofu or yoghurt."

"Can you think of a *good-tempered* boy to be my date, please Nana?"

After lunch Nana goes to town to buy supplies for the party, so Grandpa William lets Curtis show Marise the 4x4 farm bike, which William keeps locked in his garage. Curtis shows Marise how to push the red button to find reverse. Then Grandpa points out the woolshed where Nana meditates. During this time, Curtis has a tantrum: "It's my father Earl's bike," he tells Marise several times, gesturing widely at the bike. "Not Grandpa William's." The four-wheel bike is one of Curtis' loony obsessions; the other is his new puppy. Curtis has not actually seen the puppy, but discussion is under way about Rita taking Curtis this weekend to visit the truck drivers sister's puppy--waiting to be bailed out from the pound. I wonder if Marise's tolerance toward her adopted cousin Curtis will continue for much longer. Perhaps the next malicious fire that Curtis sets will finally get him locked away.

After Rita returns she stashes the wet clothes into the dryer,then Rita flings herself onto the couch, sets her feet on the table, and sighs noisily. "So what's our plan for the wedding? I'm taking suggestions."

"We could go for a Merry Olde England style," Marise says. "But... I don't know." She glances out the living room window overlooking the moonlit front yard. The truth is that Marise finds the ranch a bit creepy. Where we live with Carmella, outside Washington DC, the houses are separated by wide lawns, the driveways are long and curved, and the front doors are flanked by Doric columns. Here, there are no neighbors, and no front porches--only stoops flecked with mica and fireflies when you sit outside. The last few nights Marise and Nana Rita have gone out there while Curtis tried to catch fireflies--you can hear the frogs down at the stream. The grass is dry, mongrels bark into the night, and in the afternoon, fantail birds fly in drunken circles.

"Around the pool's not a bad idea," Rita says, "except it's so darned hot."

Then the living room, the whole house actually, is quiet except for the laundry rolling around downstairs in the dryer. Marise can hear the ping of metal buttons against the sides of the machine. And Grandpa rustling through his DVD collection. "I've found it. The *Pearl Harbor* program."

"Oh dear, Marise. Let's get ice cream from the freezer first, before we have to watch Grandpa Williams's DVD about Pearl Harbor," Rita says. "But don't bring that old magazine back into the living room." Rita grins at Marise. "Look at the date: 1999. If Grandpa William knew it was an outdated magazine he wouldn't bankroll our wedding banquet."

"Oops. I'm sorry. Let's watch Grandpa's DVD, keep him happy, and we'll have a full-on wedding banquet here on Saturday evening. OK?"

"OK, Honey. But you must go straight to bed after the DVD, OK. Otherwise you'll get me into trouble."

I `hear the entire conversation. And Mom knows it. I say nothing as I pull a blanket over me in preparation for Dad's documentary. There is the same Kronkite voice, over a backdrop of a massive military funeral scene, then a progressive zoom to a close-up shot of President F. D. Roosevelt.

*"Sixty years later, on the December 7, 2001 anniversary, we honor those 2,403 men, women, and children killed--and 1,178 wounded--in the Japanese attack on Pearl Harbor. However, recently released government documents concerning that "surprise" raid compel us to revisit some troubling issues that question the integrity of the Democrat administration of President Franklin D. Roosevelt:*

*At issue is American foreknowledge of Japanese military plans to attack Hawaii with submarine and carrier forces sixty years ago. There are two questions at the top of the foreknowledge list: (1) whether President Franklin D. Roosevelt and his top military chieftains provoked Japan into an "overt act of war" directed at Hawaii, and (2) whether Japan's military plans were obtained in advance by the United States--but concealed from the Hawaiian military commanders, Admiral Husband E. Kimmel and Lieutenant General Walter Short, so they would not interfere with the overt act.*

After a scene of the Japanese bombing Pearl Harbor, and recriminations against the US admirals, the setting becomes the pomp and ceremony on the White House lawn, where President Bill Clinton and Hillary, wearing a royal blue suit, are shaking hands with several admirals, all before a huge crowd of dignitaries. The voice-over from Kronkite continues.

*The second question has been finally answered in the affirmative: On October 30, 2000, President*

*Bill Clinton signed into law, with the support of a bipartisan Congress, the National Defense Authorization Act. Amidst its omnibus provisions, the Act reverses the findings of nine previous Pearl Harbor investigations and finds that both Kimmel and Short were denied crucial military intelligence that tracked the Japanese forces toward Hawaii . . . information provided to President Roosevelt and his Administration in the weeks before the attack. Congress was specific in its findings against the 1941 White House--that Kimmel and Short were cut off from the intelligence pipeline that located Japanese forces advancing on Hawaii. Then, after the successful Japanese raid, both commanders were relieved of their duties, blamed for failing to ward off the attack, and demoted in rank. Those congressional findings exonerated many years of blame assigned to Kimmel and Short.*

*But one important question remains: Does the blame for the Pearl Harbor disaster revert to the Democrat, President Franklin D. Roosevelt?*

The set changes back to Roosevelt, who is now shown meeting the allied leaders at a WWII airport summit.

*President Roosevelt has been documented as agreeing that provoking Japan into an attack on Hawaii was his best option: Then Germany made a strategic error. She, along with her Axis partner, Italy, signed the mutual assistance treaty with Japan. Ten days later, Naval Intelligence saw an opportunity to counter the U.S. isolationist movement by provoking Japan into a state of war, triggering the mutual assistance provisions of the Tripartite Pact, and bringing America into World War II.*

*Memorialized in McCollum's secret memo dated October 7, 1940, and recently obtained through the Freedom of Information Act, is the Naval Intelligence proposal that called for eight provocations aimed at Japan. Its centerpiece was keeping the might of the U.S. Fleet based in the Territory of Hawaii as a lure for a Japanese attack.*

*Throughout 1941, FDR implemented the remaining seven provocations. He then gauged Japanese reaction through intercepted and decoded communications intelligence originated by Japan's diplomatic and military leaders. Japan's hawk militarists used these provocations to seize control of Japan while organizing their military forces for war against the U.S., Great Britain, and the Netherlands. The centerpiece—the Pearl Harbor attack—was leaked to the U.S. in January 1941. During the next 11 months, the White House followed the Japanese war plans through intercepted and decoded diplomatic and military communications intelligence.*

*Japanese leaders failed in basic security precautions. At least 1,000 Japanese military and diplomatic radio messages per day were intercepted by monitoring stations operated by the U.S. and her Allies. The intercepts were clear: Pearl Harbor would be attacked on December 7, 1941, by Japanese forces advancing through the Central and North Pacific Oceans. On November 27 and 28, Admiral Kimmel and General Short were ordered to remain in a defensive posture for "the United States desires that Japan commit the first overt act." The order came directly from President Roosevelt.*

"Is this true Grandpa?" Marise asks.

"You bet it's true. The attack on Pearl Harbor was similar to hoaxes used to bring about other wars... such as the *Lusitania* attack to spark American involvement in WWI, and was a set-up. The American public wouldn't accept the idea of entering into WWII unprovoked. However, the influential members of the Council on Foreign Relations (CFR) wanted war. CFR members were interested in exploiting the Second World War—as they had the first—ostensibly as a justification for world government.

Once we understand this CFR concept of starting war on purpose, we begin to see how they've used it in the Korean War, Vietnam War, Iraq War, etc."

"Wow. How can I learn more about it?"

"I've got a book, which says *A massive cover-up followed Pearl Harbor*, by noted historical author and Pulitzer Prize winner John Toland in *Infamy*. He wrote, "When the Chief of Staff ordered a lid put on the affair. *Gentlemen*, he told half a dozen officers, *this goes to the grave with us*."

"Bedtime Marise. You can check it out tomorrow."

"OK. I'll take Grandpa's book to bed with me."

I afford myself a smirk while accepting her conditions of retreat. I hope we are not raising her to be a pink communist. Never mind! Better commie than Republican. It costs dearly to raise a child today—but home always does cost, and it's worth it.

# PART VII: HILLARY

## CHAPTER 15: 2008

The first truly dramatic litigation project that I worked on involved William LeMessurier Chaytor. While working on this project in 1994, I developed a passion for reading about the integrity of tall buildings... Some people read astrological signs or tarot cards—I learned to read buildings. This experience lead me to join the Circle, a group of engineers which had begun meeting at the Café Alphar in DC--and I learned to identify the integrity of our engineering designs for these sky scrapers as a reflection of the integrity of our entire society--a microcosm of our modern cultural flaws... systemic flaws which are embedded in personal ethics.

The Citicorp project was top secret until Joe Morgenstern blew the story open in an article for *The New Yorker* of May 29, 1995: "The fifty-nine-story Citicorp Center, which had been constructed in 1977, is, *fortuitously*, still standing on Lexington Avenue between Fifty-third and Fifty-fourth Streets in Manhattan. The case was settled out of court in 1994 and all parties were sworn to silence. Bill Chaytor, the primary defendant, as the project structural engineer, broke the silence imposed by the court."

It wasn't until yesterday, when I found the *New Yorker* article wrapped around a ceramic vase, that I telephoned Bill Chaytor to discuss the inside story. Bill is married, and I know that William Chaytor would not entertain an affair. But he did make a mistake on that project, a mistake that would have resulted in much death and heartache if he hadn't come clean.

I guess I am a sucker for Bills: I still live with the first Bill... Bill Clinton, and adore him. But I can't be a part of his addiction—his disease. How can people accuse me of campaigning to become President of the United States on the coat tails of a man, William Jefferson Clinton--my flawed Bill.

I worked secretly with Bill Chaytor as one of his attorneys in 1994 for the defense on the pending litigation regarding this fifty-nine-story Citicorp Center: My favorite law firm had been selected by the executives of Bethlehem Steel to surreptitiously prepare a defense in the event that Bethlehem were named in the lawsuit as the supplier of steel and fabricator of the steel frame connections--the Asian revolution that has resulted in most US construction using mostly foreign steel.

Bethlehem Steel had foolishly welded the beam-column connections during the construction of the Citicorp Headquarters instead of bolting them, as called for on William LeMessurier Chaytor's structural engineering plans. The construction was completed before Chaytor himself was made aware that the shop drawings prepared by the steel fabricator contained a proposed revision to the fundamental structure of the building... a fundamental revision that Bill Chaytor's joint venture partner on site approved nonchalantly. Bethlehem Steel exited the fabrication business shortly after that near-disaster.

The outcome was that in 1994, William L. Chaytor's liability insurance company paid Citicorp the full policy coverage amount in the sum of $2,000,000.00 toward the cost of repairs of the Citicorp Towers. Bill Chaytor engineered the repairs for free, and Bethlehem Steel was *not* involved in the law suit other than as a very nervous and guilt-ridden bystander. Steel supply and fabrication had both become extremely competitive businesses with the removal of most tariffs on foreign steel. Bethlehem was perceived as being one of the few big American steel companies who had resorted to using sharp pencils to skinny down the new batch of high-rises by reducing the sizes of braces, beams, and columns, and simplifying the connections of these structural members to enable easy fabrication--this was the only way that companies like Bethlehem could make up for the twenty percent efficiency advantage that the new and automated steel companies from places like Taiwan possessed.

What is an engineer's worst nightmare? To realize that the structure he designed for a skyscraper like Citicorp Center in NYC is flawed--and hurricane season is approaching... or to have his professional ignorance exposed before his family?

Bill Chaytor, one of the nation's leading structural engineers, lived out both nightmares. It started when he received a phone call in December 1993 from his son, Tony Chaytor. Tony's professor at post-graduate school in England had mischievously assigned him to write a paper on the Citicorp Tower, the slash-topped silver skyscraper that had become, on its completion in Manhattan more than a decade before, the seventh-tallest building in the world... a building which had been designed by Tony's father.

Bill Chaytor found the opportunity to help his son impossible to resist, even though the call caught him in the middle of a series of meetings. As a structural consultant to the architect Hugh Stubbins, Jr., Bill had designed the twenty-five-thousand-ton steel skeleton beneath the Citicorp tower's sleek aluminum skin. And, in a field where architects usually get all the credit, the engineer had won his own share of praise for the Citicorp tower's technical elegance and singular grace; indeed, he had been elected to the National Academy of Engineering, the highest honor his profession bestows. Excusing himself from the meeting, Bill Chaytor asked his son how he could help.

Tony questioned his father about the four massive column-stilts that supported the building. "According to my professor, you put those stilts in the wrong place."

"Listen, I want you to tell your limey professor that he doesn't know what the hell he's talking about, because he doesn't know the problem that had to be solved."

William L. Chaytor promised to call his son back after his meetings and explain the whole thing...

A church had posed the problem. When planning for Citicorp Center began, in the early nineteen-seventies, the site of choice was on the east side of Lexington Avenue between Fifty-third and Fifty-fourth Streets, directly across the street from Citicorp's headquarters. But the northwest corner of that block was occupied by St. Peter's Church--a decaying Gothic structure built in 1905. St. Peter's owned the corner, but one of the world's biggest banking corporations wanted the whole block. The church was able to strike a deal that seemed heaven-sent: its old building would be demolished and a new one built as a freestanding part of Citicorp Center.

To clear space for the new church, Hugh Stubbins and Bill Chaytor set their fifty-nine-story tower on four massive, nine-story-high stilts, and positioned them at the center of each side, rather than at each corner. This daring scheme allowed the designers to cantilever the building's corners seventy-two feet out over the church, on the northwest, and over a plaza on the southwest. The columnar stilts also produced high visual drama: a nine-hundred-and-fourteen-foot monolith that seemed all but weightless as it hovered above the street.

When Bill Chaytor called his son Tony back in December of 1993, he explained how the peculiar geometry of the building, far from constituting a mistake, put the columns in the strongest position to resist what sailors call quartering winds--those winds which come from a diagonal and, by flowing across two sides of a building at once, increase the forces on both. For further enlightenment on the matter, he referred Tony to a technical article written by Bill Chaytor's partner in New York, an engineer named Stanley Goldstein.

Bill Chaytor said to his son. "Now you really have news for your professor, because you can explain all of this to him yourself."

Later that day, Bill Chaytor, who taught a structural-engineering class to architecture students at Harvard, decided that this information would be of value his own students. "Like sailors, designers of tall buildings must know the wind and respect its power. And the columns were only part of the tower's defense against swaying in severe winds."

Bill's lecture also looked at the tower's unusual system of wind braces, which Bill Chaytor had first sketched out, in a burst of almost ecstatic invention, on a napkin in a Greek restaurant in DC: forty-eight braces, in six tiers of eight, arrayed like giant chevrons behind the building's curtain of aluminum and glass. "I know I am being vain," Bill Chaytor said. "I would have liked my structure to be expressed on the outside of the building, but Stubbins wouldn't have it. In the end, I told myself I didn't give a damn--the structure was there. It would be seen by God."

Bill Chaytor had established the strength of those braces in perpendicular winds during the 1974 design--the only calculation required by New York City's building code. Now, in the spirit of intellectual play, twenty years after he had designed the building, he wanted to see if the braces were just as strong in winds hitting from forty-five degrees. His new calculations surprised him. In four of the eight chevrons in each tier, a quartering wind increased the strain by forty per cent. Under normal circumstances, the wind braces would have absorbed the extra load without so much as a tremor. But the circumstances were not normal. Fortunately, during a 1994 meeting in his office, Bill Chaytor learned of a crucial change in the way the braces were joined.

The meeting was called, during the month of May 1994, to review plans for two new skyscrapers in Pittsburgh, PA. Those towers were also designed by Hugh Stubbins, with William LeMessurier Chaytor as the Structural Consultant--and the plans called for wind braces similar to those used in Citicorp Center, with the same specifications for welded joints. This was top of the line engineering--two structural members joined by a skilled welder become as strong as one. But welded joints, which are labor-intensive and therefore expensive, can be needlessly strong. In many cases, bolted joints are more practical and equally safe. That was the position taken at the May 94 meeting by U.S. Steel, a potential bidder on the contract to erect the Pittsburgh Towers. If welded joints were a condition of Bill's new design, negating the use of bolted joints, the project might be too expensive and his firm might not want to take it on.

While gathering persuasive data to advocate for welded joints, Bill Chaytor put in a call to his joint venture office in New York. I spoke to Stanley Goldstein and said, "Tell me about your success with those welded joints in Citicorp." And Stanley said, "Oh, didn't you know? They were changed--they were never welded at all, because Bethlehem Steel came to us and said, *the welds were stronger than necessary, bolts were the right way to do the job.*"

On August 1, 1974, Stanley Goldstein from Bill Chaytor's New York office had inadvertently accepted Bethlehem's aggressive proposal for a major revision using bolted joints rather than welded, submitted without notice, hidden in the midst of a box full of assumedly routine shop drawings, routinely delivered by the US Postal Service to the engineer's New York office from Bethlehem's steel fabricator.

This news gave Bill Chaytor cause for concern in the days immediately following the 1994 meeting on the Pittsburgh Towers. The choice of bolted joints was probably technically sound, if they were designed correctly. Even the failure of Stanley Goldstein to flag him on the design change, a cost saving change order that was not delivered through official channels because that would entail the contractor being required to return a cash credit to the owner--but as has become common practice among some greedy contractors... the change was simply camouflaged within the shop drawings for steel fabrication. After sleepless nights, the substitution of bolted joints continued to raise a troubling question for Bill: If the bracing system was unusually sensitive to quartering winds, as Bill Chaytor had recently discovered, so were the joints that held it together. The question was whether the Manhattan team had considered such winds when it designed the bolts. "I didn't go into a panic over it," Bill Chaytor said. "But I was haunted by a hunch that I'd better look into it."

Bill Chaytor flew to New York, where his hunch was soon confirmed. His people had taken only perpendicular winds into account. And he discovered another *subtle conceptual error,* as he calls it now--one that threatened to make the situation much worse. In a windblown building, the wind causes tension in the structural members--that is, it tries to blow the building down. At the same time, some of that tension, measured in millions of pounds, is offset by the force of gravity, which, by pressing the members together, tends to hold the building in place. The joints must be strong enough to resist the differential between these forces of wind tension minus the amount of gravity compression.

Within this seemingly simple computation, however, lurks a powerful multiplier. At any given level of the building, the compression figure remains constant; the wind may blow harder, but the structure doesn't get any heavier. Thus, immense leverage can result from higher wind forces. In the Citicorp Tower, the forty-percent increase in tension produced by a quartering wind became a hundred-and-sixty-percent increase in stress on the building's bolts.

Precisely because of that leverage, a margin of safety is built into the standard formulas for calculating how strong a joint must be; these formulas are contained in an American Institute of Steel Construction specification that deals with joints in structural columns. What Bill Chaytor found in New York, however, was that the people on Stan Goldstein's team had disregarded the standard. They had chosen to define the diagonal wind braces not as columns but as trusses, which are exempt from the specified safety factor. As a result, the bolts holding the joints together were perilously few. "By then," Bill Chaytor said, "I was getting pretty shaky."

Bill later detailed these mistakes in a thirty-page document called *Project SERENE*; the acronym, both rueful and apt, stands for *Special Engineering Review of Events Nobody Envisioned.* What emerges from this document, and from interviews with Bill Chaytor and other principals in the events, is not malfeasance, or even negligence, but a series of miscalculations that flowed from a specific mind-set of economic competitiveness, which pervades our culture and can result in a narrow-minded way of thinking. In the case of the Citicorp Tower, the first event that nobody envisioned had taken place when Bill Chaytor sketched, on a restaurant napkin, a bracing system with an inherent sensitivity to quartering winds. None of his associates identified this as a problem, let alone understood that they were compounding it with their fuzzy semantics. In the stiff, angular language of Project SERENE: "Consideration of wind from non-perpendicular directions on ordinary rectangular buildings is generally not discussed in the literature, or in the classroom."

Bill Chaytor never did point the finger at Bethlehem, or at his partner Stanley Goldstein. When asked why the lack of acrimony, Bill Chaytor simply said, "Had every decision on the site in Manhattan waited for approval from my office in DC, the Citicorp building would never have been finished." He then added, "Anyway, modern skyscrapers are considered so strong that catastrophic collapse is not considered a realistic prospect. When engineers seek to limit a building's sway, they do so for the tenants' comfort. The measured period of sway on this building is a good stiff ten seconds."--a lot stiffer than the twenty seconds for the collapsed Rezko building.

Before making a final judgment on how dangerous the bolted joints were, Bill Chaytor turned to a Canadian engineer named Alan Davenport, the director of the Boundary Layer Wind Tunnel Laboratory, at the University of Western Ontario, and a world authority on the behavior of buildings in high winds. During the Citicorp tower's design, Davenport had run extensive tests on scale models of the structure. Now Bill Chaytor asked him and his deputy to retrieve the relevant files and magnetic tapes. "If we were going to think about such things as the possibility of failure," Bill Chaytor said--the word *failure* being a euphemism for the Citicorp Tower's falling down—"We would think about it in terms of the best knowledge that the state of the art can produce, which is what these guys could provide for me."

Bill Chaytor flew to London, Ontario, and met with Davenport. Presenting his new calculations, Bill Chaytor asked the Canadian to evaluate them in the light of the original data. "And you have to tell me the truth," he added. "Don't go easy if it doesn't come out the right way." It didn't, and they didn't. The tale told by the wind-tunnel expert was more alarming than Bill Chaytor had expected. His assumption of a forty-per-cent increase in stress from diagonal winds was theoretically correct, but it could go higher in the real world, when storms lashed at the building and set it vibrating like a tuning fork. "Oh, my God," he thought, "Now we've got that on top of an error from the bolts being under-designed." Refining their data further, the Canadian teased out wind-tunnel forces for each structural member in the building; it remained for Bill Chaytor to interpret the meaning of the numbers.

First, Bill went to DC, where he talked to a trusted associate, and then he called his dear wife at their home in New Zealand, but decided not to inform his son, Tony, who needed to focus entirely upon his studies. "Rita knew what I was up to," he said. "I told her, *I think we've got a problem here, and I'm going to sit down and try to think about it.*" Bill Chaytor drove to the northern shore of a local lake, took an outboard motorboat a quarter of a mile across the water to a rented cabin, and worked through the wind-tunnel numbers, joint-by-joint and floor-by-floor.

The weakest joint was at the building's thirtieth floor; if that one gave way, catastrophic failure of the whole structure would follow. Next, he took New York City weather records provided by Alan Davenport and calculated the probability of a storm severe enough to tear that joint apart. His figures told him that such an event had a statistical probability of occurring as often as once every sixteen years--what meteorologists call a sixteen-year storm.

"That was very low, awesomely low," Bill Chaytor said, his voice hushed as if the horror of discovery were still fresh. "To put it another way, there was one chance in sixteen in any year, including that one." When the steadying influence of the tuned mass damper that Bill had incorporated into the original design was factored in, the probability dwindled to one in fifty-five--a fifty-five-year storm. But the innovative damper required electric current, which might fail as soon as a major storm hit.

As an experienced engineer, Bill Chaytor liked to think he could solve most structural problems, and the Citicorp Tower was no exception. The bolted joints were readily accessible, thanks to Hugh Stubbins' insistence on putting the chevrons inside the building's skin, rather than displaying them outside. The joints could be reinforced by welding heavy steel plates over them, like giant Band-Aids--of both money and materials. But time was short; that was the end of July 1994, and the height of the hurricane season was approaching.

To avert disaster, Bill Chaytor would have to blow the whistle quickly on himself. That meant facing the pain of possible protracted litigation, probable bankruptcy, and professional disgrace. It would mean a burden on his dear wife Rita, and others who loved him. It also meant shock and dismay for Citicorp's officers and shareholders, when they learned that the bank's proud new corporate symbol, built at a cost of a hundred and seventy-five million dollars, was threatened with collapse.

Ensconced at the cabin, Bill Chaytor considered his options. Silence was one of them--only Davenport knew the full implications of what he had found, and he would not disclose them on his own. Suicide was another, if Bill Chaytor drove along the

Beltway at a hundred miles an hour, and he steered into a bridge abutment--that would be that. But keeping silent required betting other people's lives against the odds, while suicide struck him as a coward's way out and--although he was passionate about nineteenth-century classical music--unconvincingly melodramatic. Besides, he could not do that to Rita and Tony, or to the others who loved him. What seized him an instant later was an almost giddy sense of power. "I had information that nobody else in the world had," Bill Chaytor recalled. "I had power in my hands to effect extraordinary events, that only I could initiate."

At his office on the morning of Monday, July 31st 1994, Bill Chaytor tried to reach Hugh Stubbins, whose firm was upstairs in the same building. But Stubbins was in California, and unavailable by phone. Then he called Stubbins' lawyer, Carl Sappers, and outlined the emergency over lunch. Sapers advised him against telling Citicorp until he had consulted with his own company's liability insurers, the Northbrook Insurance Company, in Northbrook, Illinois. When Bill Chaytor called Northbrook, which represented Stanley Goldstein, someone there referred Bill to the company's attorneys in New York, and warned him not to discuss the matter with anyone else.

At 9 am on Tuesday, in New York, Bill Chaytor faced a battery of lawyers who, he says, "Wanted to meet me to find out if I was nutty." Being lawyers, not engineers, they were hard put to reconcile his dispassionate tone with the apocalyptic thrust of his prophecy. They also bridled at his carefully qualified answers to seemingly simple questions. When they asked how big a storm it would take to blow the building down, Bill Chaytor confined himself to statistical probabilities-- storm that might occur once in sixteen years.

When they pressed him for specific wind velocities--would the wind have to be at eighty miles per hour, or ninety, or ninety-five? --He insisted that such figures were not significant in themselves, since every structure was uniquely sensitive to certain winds; an eighty-five-mile-per-hour wind that blew for sixteen minutes from the northwest might pose less of a threat to a particular building than an eighty-mile-per-hour wind that blew for fourteen minutes from the southwest.

But the lawyers certainly understood that the nation had a crisis on our hands, so they sent for an expert adviser they trusted. They sent for Leslie Robertson, an engineer who had, along with John Skillings, been the Structural Consultant for the entire World Trade Center. Robertson explained the difficulties with the building, and everyone, of course, was very concerned. Then they turned to me, *Well?* I said. *Look* they said, *If this is in fact the case, you have a very serious problem."*

The two structural engineers were peers, but not friends: William L. Chaytor was a visionary with a fondness for heroic designs. Leslie Robertson, though he was an energetic manager, he was a stickler for technical detail; a man fascinated by how things fit together. Bill Chaytor, older by two years, was voluble and intense, with a courtly rhetorical style. Robertson was tall, trim, and brisk. He had the manner of a starchy psychotherapist and made no effort to smile for more than an obligatory single second.

In addition to his engineering expertise, Leslie Robertson brought to the table a background in disaster management. He had worked with such groups as the National Science Foundation and the National Research Council on teams that studied the aftermaths of earthquakes, hurricanes, and floods. In 1993, he worked with the FBI on the World Trade Center bombing. For the liability lawyers, this special perspective enhanced his stature, but it unsettled Bill Chaytor from the start. As Bill remembered it, "Leslie Robertson predicted that within hours of the time Citicorp heard about this, the whole building would be evacuated. I almost fainted. I didn't want that to happen." For his part, Robertson recalled making no such dire prediction.

Bill Chaytor didn't think an evacuation would be necessary. He believed that the building was safe for occupancy in all but the most violent weather, thanks to the tuned mass damper, and he insisted that the damper's reliability in a storm could be assured by installing emergency generators. Robertson conceded the importance of keeping the damper running--it had performed flawlessly since it became operational earlier that year---but, because, in his view, its value as a safety device was unproved, he flatly refused to consider it as a mitigating factor.

One point on which everyone agreed was that Bill Chaytor, together with Stubbins, needed to inform Citicorp as soon as possible.

The next morning, August 2nd, Stubbins and Bill Chaytor flew to New York, went to Bill Chaytor's office at 515 Madison Avenue, put in a call to Wriston, but failed to penetrate the layers of secretaries and assistants that insulated Citicorp's chairman from the outside world. They were no more successful in reaching the bank's president, William I. Spencer, but Stubbins finally obtained an appointment with Citicorp's executive vice-president, John S. Reed, the man who has now succeeded Wriston as chairman. Bill Chaytor and Stubbins went to see Reed at the bank's ornate executive offices, in an older building on Lexington Avenue, across the street from Citicorp Center. Bill Chaytor began by saying, "I have a real problem for you, sir."

Reed was well equipped to understand the problem. He had an engineering background, and he had been involved in the design and construction of Citicorp Center--the company had called him in when it was considering the tuned mass damper. Reed listened impassively as Bill Chaytor detailed the structural defect and how he thought it could be fixed. Bill Chaytor said, "We could build a little plywood house around each of the connections that were critical, and a welder could work inside it without damaging the tenants' space. You might have to take up the carpet, take down the sheetrock, and work at night, but all this could be done. But the real message Bill conveyed to him was *I need your help--at once.*"

When Reed asked how much the repairs would cost. Bill Chaytor offered an estimate of one million dollars. At the end of the meeting, which lasted half an hour, Reed thanked the two men courteously, though noncommittally, and told them to go back to their office and await further instructions. They did so, but after waiting for more than an hour they decided to go out to lunch. As they were finishing their meal, a secretary from Bill Chaytor's office called to say that John Reed would be in the office in ten minutes with Walter Wriston.

Wriston was not known for effusiveness in the best of circumstances, and Bill Chaytor expected none now, what with Citicorp Center, and his own career--literally hanging in the balance. But the bank's chairman was genuinely proud of the building, and he offered his support in getting it fixed.

"Wriston was fantastic," Bill Chaytor said. "He said, *I guess my job is to handle the public relations of this, so I'll have to start drafting a press release.*" But he didn't have anything to write on, so someone handed him a yellow pad. That made Wriston laugh. According to Wriston, "All wars are won by generals writing on yellow pads." In fact, Wriston simply took notes; the press release would not go out for six days. But his laughter put the others at ease. Citicorp's general was on their side.

Within hours of Wriston's visit, Bill Chaytor's office arranged for emergency generators for the tower's tuned mass damper. The bank issued beepers to Bill Chaytor and his key engineers, assuring them that Reed and other top managers could be reached by phone at any hour of the day or night. Citicorp also assigned two vice-presidents, Henry DeFord III and Robert Dexter, to manage the repairs; both had overseen the building's construction and knew it well.

The next morning, Thursday, August 3rd, Bill Chaytor and Robertson met with DeFord and Dexter in a conference room on the thirtieth floor of Citicorp Center. Bill Chaytor outlined his plan to fix the wind braces by welding two-inch-thick steel plates over each of more than two hundred bolted joints. The plan was tentatively approved, pending testing of a typical joint. A few hours later, two Koch construction engineers joined the meeting. Bill Chaytor and Robertson took them to an unoccupied floor of the building, where workmen tore apart enough sheetrock of the walls to expose a diagonal connection. Comparing the original drawings of the joints with the nuts-and-bolts reality before their eyes, the engineers concluded that Bill Chaytor's plan was indeed feasible. Koch also happened to have all the necessary steel plate on hand, so Citicorp negotiated a contract for welding to begin as soon as Bill Chaytor's office could issue new drawings.

Two more contracts were drawn up before the end of the following day. One of them went out to MTS Systems Corporation, the Minneapolis firm that had manufactured the tuned mass damper. MTS was asked to provide full-time technical support--in effect, around-the-clock nurses--to keep its machine in perfect health. The company flew one of its technicians to New York that night. Four days later, in a letter of agreement, MTS asked Citicorp to provide a long list of materials and spare parts, which included three buckets, a grease gun, rags, cleaning solvent, and "One Radio with weather band."

The other contract engaged a California firm, also recommended by Leslie Robertson, to fit the building with a number of instruments called strain gauges--pieces of tape with zigzag wires running through them. The gauges would be affixed to individual structural members, and electrical impulses from them would be funneled to an improvised communications center in Robertson's office, eight blocks away, at 230 Park Avenue; like a patient in intensive care, the tower would have every shiver and twitch monitored. But this required new telephone lines, and the phone company refused to budge on its leisurely installation schedule. When Robertson voiced his frustration about this during a late-night meeting in Walter Wriston's office, Wriston picked up the phone on his desk and called his friend Charles Brown, the president and chief operating officer of AT&T. The new lines were installed the next morning.

Robertson took a different problem-solving approach during another nighttime meeting in Citicorp's executive suite. Wriston wanted copies of some documents that Robertson had shown him, but all the secretaries had gone home --and every copying machine was locked. "I'm an engineer," Robertson said, "So I kneeled down, tipped the door off one of the machines, and we made our copies. I looked up at them a little apologetically, but, what the hell--fixing the door was a few hundred bucks, and these guys had a hundred-and-seventy-five-million-dollar building in trouble across the street."

Leslie Robertson also assembled an advisory group of weather experts from academia, and the government's Brookhaven National Laboratory on Long Island; and hired two independent weather forecasters to provide wind predictions four times a day. "What worried us more than hurricanes, which give you hours and days to anticipate, were unpredictable events," Robertson said. "From time to time, we've had small tornadoes in this area, and there was a worry that a much bigger one would come down and take hold." Then Robertson raised an issue that Bill Chaytor had dreaded discussing. In a meeting on Friday that included Bill Chaytor, Robertson told Citicorp's representatives, DeFord and Dexter, that they needed to plan for evacuating Citicorp Center--and a large area around it in the event of a high-wind alert.

During the first week of August 1994, discussions had involved only a small circle of company officials and engineers. But the circle widened on Monday, August 7th, when final drawings for the steel plates went out to Arthur Nusbaum, the veteran project manager of HRH Construction, which was the original contractor for Citicorp Center. Nusbaum, in turn, provided the repair drawings to Koch Erecting. And it would widen again, because work could not go forward, as Robertson reminded the officials, without consulting the city's Department of Buildings. Citicorp faced a public-relations debacle unless it came up with a plausible explanation for why the new skyscraper needed fixing.

That night, DeFord and Dexter, following Robertson's advice, met with Mike Reilly, the American Red Cross's director of disaster services for the New York metropolitan area. "They laid out the dilemma, and it was clearly an ominous event," Reilly recalled. From that first meeting, which was attended by Robertson but not by Bill Chaytor, and from half a dozen subsequent working sessions with other disaster agencies, came plans for joint action by the police and the mayor's Office of Emergency Management, along with the Red Cross. In the event of a wind alert, the police and the mayor's emergency forces would evacuate the building and the surrounding neighborhood, and the Red Cross would mobilize between twelve hundred and two thousand workers to provide food and temporary shelter. "Hal DeFord was the bank's point man for all this," Reilly said. "The anxiety was so heavy on him that we wondered if he was going to make it."

On Tuesday morning, August 8th, the public-affairs department of Citibank,

Citicorp's chief subsidiary, put out the long delayed press release. In language as bland as a loan officer's wardrobe, the three-paragraph document said, "Unnamed engineers who designed the building have recommended that certain of the connections in Citicorp Center's wind bracing system be strengthened through additional welding." The press release added, "The engineers have assured us that there is no danger." When DeFord expanded on the handout in interviews, he portrayed the bank as a corporate citizen of exemplary caution—"We wear both belts and suspenders here," he told a reporter for the News. There was truth in all this: During Bill Chaytor's recent trip to Canada, one of Alan Davenport's assistants had mentioned to him that probable wind velocities might be slightly higher, on a statistical basis, than predicted in 1973, during the original tests for Citicorp Center. At the time, Bill Chaytor viewed this piece of information as one more nail in the coffin of his career, but later, recognizing it as a blessing in disguise, he passed it on to Citicorp as the possible basis of a cover story for the press and for tenants in the building.

On Tuesday-afternoon, at a meeting in Robertson's office, Bill Chaytor told the whole truth to New York City's Acting Building Commissioner and nine other senior city officials. For more than an hour, he spoke about the effect of diagonal winds on the Citicorp tower, about the failure of his own office to perceive and communicate the danger, and about the intended repairs.

Before the city officials left, they commended Bill Chaytor for his courage and candor, and expressed a desire to be kept informed as the repair work progressed. Given the urgency of the situation, that was all they could reasonably do. "It wasn't a case of *We caught you, you skunk*," Nusbaum said. "It started with a guy who stood up and said, *I got a problem, I made the problem, let's fix the problem*. If you're gonna kill a guy like Bill Chaytor, why should anybody ever talk?"

Every reporter in town wanted to know how come all these people were in city hall? The Building Commissioner returned the reporters' calls and reassured them that the structural work was only a prudent response to new meteorological data. As a result, press coverage in New York City the next day was as uninformative as the handout. A short piece in the Wall Street Journal, which raised no questions about the nature of the new data, and one in the News, which dutifully quoted DeFord's remark about belts and suspenders. But when Bill Chaytor went back to his hotel room, at about 5pm on Wednesday, he learned from his wife, Rita, who had come over from New Zealand to join him, that a reporter from the Times had been trying to reach him all afternoon. That worried him greatly; being candid with city officials was one thing, but being interrogated by the Times was another. Before returning the call, Bill Chaytor phoned his friend Carl Sapers, the Boston attorney who represented Hugh Stubbins, and mixed himself a martini. Sapers understood the need for secrecy, but he saw no real choice; talk to them, he said, and do the best you can.

Two minutes after six o'clock, Bill Chaytor called the Times switchboard. As he braced himself for an unpleasant conversation, he heard a recording. The Times, along with all the other major papers in the city, had just been shut down by a strike.

Welders started work almost immediately, their torches dazzled in the night sky. The weather was sticky, as it had been since the beginning of the month--New Jersey's tomato crop was rotting from too much rain, and forecasts called for temperatures in the mid-eighties the next day, with no wind; in other words, a perfect day for Citicorp Center.

Yet tropical storms were already churning the Caribbean. Citicorp pushed for repair work around the clock, but Nusbaum refused to allow welding during office hours, for fear that clouds of acrid smoke would cause panic among the tenants, and set off every smoke detector in the building. Instead, he hired in drywall crews and carpenters to work from 5.00 pm to 8.00 pm, putting up plywood enclosures around the chevrons and tearing down sheetrock; he hired welders to weld from 8pm until 4am, with the building's fire-alarm system shut off; and hired laborers to clean up the epic mess, before the first secretaries arrived.

The welders worked seven days a week. Sometimes they worked on unoccupied floors; sometimes they invaded lavish offices. But decor, or the lack of it, had no bearing on their priorities, which were set by Bill Chaytor. "It was a tense time for the whole month," he says. "I was constantly calculating which joint to fix next, which level of the building was more critical, and I developed charts and graphs of all the consequences: if you fix this, then the rarity of the storm that will cause any trouble lengthens to that."

For most of August, the weather smiled on Citicorp, or at least held its breath, and the welders made steady progress. Bill Chaytor felt confident enough to fly off with his wife for a long weekend. As their return flight was coming in for a landing at LaGuardia Airport Sunday night, they looked out across the East River and saw a pillar of fire on the Manhattan skyline. "The welders were working up and down the building, fixing the joints," Bill Chaytor recalled. "It was an absolutely marvelous thing to see," I said to my wife. "Isn't this wonderful? Nobody knows what's going on, but we know and we can see it right there in the sky."

A great deal of work remained. Robertson was insistent upon a complete reevaluation of the Citicorp tower--not just the sensitivity of the chevron braces to quartering winds but the strength of other structural members, the adequacy of braces that kept the supporting columns in plumb, and the rigidity of the building's corrugated metal-and-concrete floors to function as diaphragms, which Robertson feared might be compromised by trenches carrying electrical connections.

Shortly before dawn on Friday, September 1st 1994, weather services carried the news that everyone had been dreading—a major storm, Hurricane Ella, was off Cape Hatteras and heading for New York. At 6.30am, an emergency-planning group convened at the command center in Robertson's office. "Nobody said, *We're probably going to press the panic button.*" Bill Chaytor recalled. "Nobody dared say that. But everybody was sweating blood."

As the storm bore down on the city, the bank's representatives, DeFord and Dexter, asked Bill Chaytor for a report on the status of repairs. He told them that the most critical joints had already been fixed and that the building, with its tuned mass damper operating, could now withstand a two-hundred-year storm. It didn't have to, however. A few hours later, Hurricane Ella veered from its northwesterly course and began moving out to sea.

Bill Chaytor spent the following night in Manhattan, having canceled plans to spend the weekend with his wife. But the hurricane kept moving eastward, and daybreak dispelled any lingering thoughts of evacuation. "Saturday was the most beautiful day that the world's ever seen," Bill Chaytor said, "With all the humidity drawn away and the skies sunny and crystal clear." Alone in the city, Bill gave himself a treat he'd been thinking about for years--his first visit to the Cloisters, where he basked in an ineffable calm.

The weather watch ended on September 11th. That same day, Robertson recommended terminating the evacuation plans. Welding was completed in October. No further articles about the Citicorp building appeared in the Newspapers because of a labor strike. The building, in fact, was now strong enough to withstand a seven-hundred-year storm even without the damper, which made it one of the safest structures ever built--and rebuilt--by the hand of man.

Throughout the summer, Citicorp's top management team had concentrated on facilitating repairs, while keeping the lawyers on the sidelines. That changed on September 13th 1994, when Citicorp served notice on Bill Chaytor and Hugh Stubbins, whose firm held the primary contract, of its intention to seek indemnification for all costs. Their estimate of the costs, according to Bill Chaytor, amounted to $4.3 million, including management fees... a much higher total was suggested by Arthur Nusbaum--who stated that his firm, HRH Construction, spent eight million dollars on structural repairs alone. Citicorp declined to provide its own estimation of the costs.

Whatever the actual cost, Citicorp's effort to recoup it was remarkably free of the punitive impulse that often poisons such negotiations. When Bill Chaytor on one side, and Deform and Dexter on the other side, first discussed the terms of a settlement--without lawyers, Bill Chaytor spoke of two million dollars, which was the amount that his liability insurer, the Northbrook Insurance Company, had agreed to pay. "DeFord and Dexter said, *Well, we've been deeply wounded here*, and they tried to play hardball, Bill Chaytor observed that they didn't play it with much conviction. After a second meeting, which included a Northbrook lawyer, the bank agreed to hold Stubbins' firm harmless and to accept the two-million-dollar payment from Bill Chaytor and his joint-venture partner.

The crisis at Citicorp Center was noteworthy in another respect. It produced heroes, but no villains; everyone connected with the repairs behaved in exemplary fashion, from Walter Wriston and his Citicorp management team to the officials at the city's Department of Buildings. The most striking hero was Bill Chaytor, who emerged with his reputation not merely unscathed but enhanced. When Robertson speaks of him, he says, "I have a lot of admiration for Bill Chaytor, because he was very forthcoming. While he says that all engineers would behave as he did, I carry in my mind some skepticism about that."

I also am skeptical with regard to the moral fabric—the ethical disposition of many of our business people and professionals... especially our politicians and lawyers.

Now, when William LeMessurier Chaytor talks about the Citicorp Tower repairs to

101

his classes at Harvard--the tale, is by turns painful, self-deprecating, and dramatic--an engineer who did the right thing. But it also speaks to the larger question of how people should behave. *You have a social obligation,* Chaytor reminds his students. *In return for getting a license and being regarded with respect, you're supposed to be self-sacrificing and look beyond the interests of yourself and your client... to society as a whole. And the most wonderful part of my story is that when I did it nothing bad happened.*

The behavior of William LeMessurier Chaytor has inspired me and provided a role model of how far human integrity can reach... a beacon to follow if we could only achieve a critical mass of such refreshingly ethical citizens—who are tempted to avoid the issues, who might even consider suicide briefly, but who will always make the right choice in the end.

One of the honors of being First Lady, and then Senator Clinton representing New York, and soon President Hillary Clinton, is the opportunity I have had to go out into the world and to see what individuals and communities are doing to help themselves, their marriages, their communities, and their children. I have had the privilege of talking with Mothers, Fathers, Grandparents, Civic Clubs, Scout Troops, PTAs, and Churches. From these many conversations, I know there are Americans everywhere who are searching for--and often finding--new ways to support one another.

Even our technology offers us new ways of coming together, through on-line marriage counselling, radio talk shows, e-mail and chat rooms on the Internet. The networks of relationships we form and depend on are our modern-day villages, but they reach well beyond the city limits. Many of them necessarily involve the whole nation or are even global, such as the Truthies who are a global community that earnestly seek a rigorous explanation of what happened at the World Trade Center on 9/11. As a result of the Truthies diligence the government enquiry lead by NIST has now included the *possibility* that WTC-7 (which was not impacted by a plane) was brought down by a detonation of thermite explosives from inside the building—within their scope of study... for lack of any other plausible explanation. The report has been delayed for a further couple of years.

These modern networks of people form the basis for our new *civil society,* a term social scientists have employed to describe the way we work together for common purposes. Whether we harness our human potential for the greater good, or allow ourselves to drift into alienation and divisiveness, depends on the choices we make now.

# PART VIII: TONY

## CHAPTER 16: 2008

It will be more spontaneous than elaborate. Carmella and I have each been to weddings before, and we don't want anyone getting outrageous. No fuss, we just want to get married with only our closest friends and family present with us. Carmella's dad is now officially dead, and Grandpa Carl is becoming senile, so we decided to get married in New Zealand. Neighborhood children are waiting for Carmella and I in front of the Blenheim Anglican church, curious to see the rare occurrence of man marrying woman for a fearless union. Carmella and I are all fresh faced and beaming. There is my father, William, dressed in a kilt and playing the wedding march on the saxophone, real slow, bluesy. Carmella and I glide toward the aisle of the old wooden church. The interior is painted antique green, with contrasting plum color dominant in the leaded windows. The sanctuary is cool, despite the cathedral ceiling that lacks insulation. Marise is sitting in the front row with Rita. A small group of Carmella's girlfriends are behind our daughter, dressed in colorful suits and outrageous hats.

The celebrant, Pastor Michael Riddell, is standing up front, a tall fellow with long hair, and I am happier than any day in my memory. The white robes of the boy's choir reflect a mosaic of red colors as the sun glimpses through the stained-glass windows for just a few seconds. Pungent incense melds with the softer fragrance of cut flowers. Carmella and I stand in front of the celebrant, Father Michael, famous in these parts for his eloqutionary skills.

"The conjunction of eternity and human transience, steeped in the wisdom of the Church... a joining of man and woman, of God and humanity, of purpose and chance, of commitment and love. The binding with ancient symbols, full of mystery and grace: the ring, the cup, the promises, the blessing."

There is a transcending dignity to the ceremony. Carmella holds my hand as we prepare to say our vows. Carmella ignores the prayer book and repeats the vows that she has prepared in advance. "I, Carmella Meeks, do solemnly declare, that I will stay with this man forever, whatever may happen. I acknowledge that Tony is my soul mate, a man I will adore, love, and cherish for the rest of my days. I will always celebrate the soulful purpose of our marriage, to complete the journey of our individual and married souls."

It is my turn. "I commit to enduring whatever obstacles might come our way, to be in love, now and forever."

Carmella grins at me, through joyful tears. We feel as innocent as we have ever been, as uplifted as any couple has ever felt in the history of the planet. On my wedding day my obsessive mind cannot resist a brief reflection...

A will to promote the aristocratic way of life was installed in me by my dad, as the highest priority in life... *and that involves doing the right thing.* William made it clear that our family went back to the noble days of Charlemagne, where we were advisors to English royalty. Later my family owned a fleet of ships and half the province of Marlborough.

Maybe the arrogant assumption of power is what it takes to be successful, but I prefer to make my own way in the world, rather than rely on the family name of Chaytor. Besides, my mother Rita Atis is from a Bulgarian Gypsy family, and she has taught me the merits of embracing Bohemian values of *community before promotion*. I am fortunate to have contrasting parents. Rita told me that she wrote my name on the birth certificate as Tzetzo, but when it came to the baptism, my father insisted that the name be changed to Tony... short for Anthony, a noble name from Chaytor family history.

Rita met my dad when one of the last of the Chaytor ships docked at Antwerp, Belgium, near where Mom was studying to be a concert violinist. Maybe I got my independent spirit, and love of playing the violin, from Mom's gypsy blood. Anyway, I am pleased that Rita requested that I be called *Tzetzo Chaytor* on my birth certificate. All of us kids have Mom's family name of *Atis* included as our middle name... rather than just the traditional *LeMessurier*, to honor an ancient alliance. Dad didn't like it when Rita gathered us around the fire after our weekly bath and told us stories about her ancestors; about how some of the Atis family have had reincarnation experiences, and have been visited by the angel Gaia--the appreciator of the environment of nature. "For goodness sake, don't fill their heads up with that gypsy rubbish," William often muttered.

Although I was born in Fort Pierce, Florida, we moved back to Blenheim in New Zealand at the time of the Cuban Missile crisis--we thought that a nuclear catastrophe was imminent, so we dug bomb shelters in the back yard—a lot of good that would have done. The only real way to survive such a holocaust is to be submerged for years in a nuclear-powered submarine deep below the ocean... or migrate to another planet. Dad is highly respected by the engineering and military communities in the U.S., to which he soon returned after WWII and set up business in DC. During my recent visit with my parents, my dad tried to harness me back to his traditional ethics... *New Zealand is a place where people hold fast to basic values: give an honest day's work for an honest day's wages, don't lie, cheat, or steal, respect others, respect their property, and respect their opinions. New Zealand is a safe place where most people know they can improve their lives, through hard work and education.*

But, what was in short supply in my life as a teenager was intellectual freedom, independence, and a vocation that didn't require conformity to strict timetables and geographic confinement--telecommuting. None of those higher goals are going to matter if we don't, as a global village, cut back our emission levels, at least to the 1990 levels, as proposed in the Kyoto accord.

Not a single light from the civilized world was visible, apart from the occasional satellite crossing overhead. After a fine glass of Marlborough Chardonnay, we had turned off the lights at Alphar Cabin, out beyond Mount Chaytor. The stars were so close now that Carmella reached out to touch them. The Milky Way looked like a lawn fully of daisies, and I was as happy as I have ever been.

# CHAPTER 17: TONY, 2008

Setting up our home in DC has been expensive. But that is what distinguishes us: our enjoyment of home and the land... and all that implies for our descendants. My wife and partner, lovely Carmella, has arranged a sitter for Marise tonight so we can attend Hillary's birthday party. First I must rush to finalize the EQE report because Newt Gingrinch is holding me to my contract to continue with his PR projects despite our conflicts. The script for the TV series, *The Collapse of the EQE Building*, tries to accommodate Newt Gingrinch's specifications--by stating that the collapse of the EQE building *may* have been partially caused by the fire after the gas explosion in the basement. But I have to insert reference to my suspicions, regarding the manner in which that steel high-rise collapsed into its own footprint, and in just six seconds--the ground floor columns failed almost simultaneously.

Such a collapse mechanism is sudden and horrific; to be avoided by engineers at all costs. It should never have happened. The western practice is to avoid such catastrophe by integrating a fuse system into the building beams. This fuse system necessitates that the beams be significantly weaker than the columns. This frugal philosophy is necessary because we in the West cannot financially justify the design of buildings that could resist large earthquakes and forces of nature--without them suffering severe damage. In contrast, high-rise buildings in Japan will generally be built stronger. The Western structural engineering profession has reassured our politicians that, because of their clever *fuse strategy*, occupants will be able to exit our more risk-prone buildings after a major earthquake--despite being more severely damaged than their Japanese counterparts... without fear of a devastating collapse of stairwells or doorways that would otherwise crush the occupants (and the politicians of the day) as they attempted to exit.

That promise by the engineering profession has proven to be false. The EQE building collapse flattened everything within. Fortunately the building was almost vacant. The building had been prefabricated in a factory in Pennsylvania, and shipped to Florida in containers for erection at the sight. The fatal violations occurred, firstly, at the stage of contracting out for steel supply--the engineer couldn't believe his luck when a steel company from Taiwan bid twenty percent lower than his lowest rival... and the contract was guaranteed by the Taiwanese government with a performance bond. The unsettling thing is that the building failed because the beam steel was delivered too strong... and because, secondly, the U.S. fabricator used Lincoln weld rods that were flawed.

The clever fuse strategy appears to have failed to recognize that, in the real world, not all is amenable to the engineer's grand intentions, especially in the face of bullying by building developers to cut costs. But such human errors don't explain this collapse due to a mere explosion and fire. Something doesn't ring true for me! Was the EQE building sabotaged? Why? Was the collapse a dress rehearsal for the World Trade Center collapses on 9/11? Surely not! Impossible?

Bugger. My suit has a lip gloss stain on the lapel, and my favorite tie is at the dry-cleaners. I'll have to wear a sports jacket over polo neck tonight. No biggy! The press won't be there… Hillary's birthday party is bound to be very private.

Barack Obama will be a good host--and his wife is charming. Male politicians have become a liability in these days of political correctness--and suspicion of men as sexual predators. But Barack has bypassed that hazard—is leading the polls at the moment and is expected by many to beat out Hillary at the Democrat convention… and some say that he will subsequently decline to offer Hillary the V.P. position. What a horrid rumor, but one enthusiastically promoted by the Republican media.

Bill will accompany Hillary tonight, of course. And Bill will probably spend much of the evening whispering with that young senator from Canada, Belinda Stronach.

Carmella and I are the first guests to arrive. Our hosts are concerned about the tardiness of the other guests: It is 9 pm… But the beltway is slow, still humming with workaholic commuters finally wrenching their way home.

The doors to all the plantation houses in Emmetsburg are three feet taller than anywhere else in the region. Some locals claim that the ceilings were designed for a household of basketball players… "Didn't you know that they had slaves this far north back in the old days?" I see a lot of confederate flags still flying over the other side of the railway track--a frequently remembered civil war battle was fought opposite the neighbor's pasture.

Barack Obama takes Carmella's coat. He cannot resist a second look at her. The living room is dimly lit so the glow from the fireplace reflects on the walls, and dances across Carmella's apricot face… the whites of her eyes shine. Soon there is a constant influx of tired people working at being jovial. Food service is an all night affair—with self-service from the buffet table.

"Carmella, try these New Zealand oysters," I say. "And the dungeness crab."

"Salt-water fresh," Carmella says in a deep but child-like voice. I like that she goes back to her inner child when she is around powerful and phony people. She would probably rather be eating mango in a shack with legs splayed on the floor and sweat mingling with the juice.

"Hillary's here," Barack Obama whispers to the swollen crowd.

The door chimes trill. Barack Obama turns the lights out. There is a short silence, then another trill. Obama, standing before a dark hallway, opens the door. "Excuse me, *darling*, but I don't recognize you. Is that Bill Clinton? Oh dear! We're *Republicans* in this household. You must have the wrong address." There is a gasp of horror at Obama's gay affectations. He flicks on lights to reveal Hillary's gaping mouth--we all break into the birthday song.

Hillary blushes. Bill's head rocks back in laughter. The Canadian senator, Belinda, rushes over to give Bill a hug, and then to offer Hillary a gift. Hillary is wearing a long beige dress with slits up each side. My God, she is in good shape. I hadn't expected Hillary to wear anything so… spicy. I take another drink. Hillary receives the gift from Bill's new girlfriend with a polite dismissal, then walks over to Barack Obama. Barack and his wife are the only black people present, apart from the apricot-colored Carmella, and of course Condoleezza Rice. Bill has insisted Hillary include Condoleezza in her circle, and possibly as future Secretary of Sate--Condoleezza is rumored to be one of Bill's former squeezes. But I don't believe too many rumors around this town.

I take Carmella to the kitchen to get her a *jolt*. Carmella is a caffeine junkie. The staff is bringing out silver platters with venison and eggplant dishes. The kitchen is located at the pool end of the living room. From the kitchen doorway we can look down upon the sunken living room. Hillary is still talking with Barack Obama and drinking red wine from a monogrammed glass. That will make it easier for someone to spike her drink... nothing too heavy--just a mild aphrodisiac.

Hillary has no anxiety regarding her husband's sexual addiction at this time because, according to an anonymous journalist of the stature of Edward Klein--Bill will always come back to her, and not just because of his deathly fear of public ridicule. Hillary is not a lawyer for nothing. Hillary's terms for staying with Bill, following the publicity of the Lewinsky affair, included a postnuptial marital contract, that provides for Hillary in the event that she chooses to call in her chips... Bill signed the agreement, despite adamant objections from his attorneys. Bill was desperate not to be rejected in a divorce, (or have his medical records exposed,) immediately after his public embarrassment regarding his high-risk sexual proclivities. It has never occurred to Bill that Hillary may have been the person who leaked the Lewinsky affair. For once, Bill was almost innocent, but how thoughtless some journalists can be, foolish enough to believe that a man with as much power and charisma as Bill Clinton, would have a serious affair with a junior intern--an intern like Monica, a desperate nobody. No! The Lewinski affair was really a smokescreen for a much more damaging affair . . . with a *powerful* woman.

I top up Carmella's *jolt* after adding a little "punch." Hillary is still nodding affirmatively as she listens to Barack Obama. Hillary orders another glass of wine. The kitchen door locks from the inside. Perfect! The kitchen has a horseshoe shaped breakfast bar around the gas stove and a solid square breakfast table overlooking the pool. Last night, Carmella and I planned our proposed encounter with Hillary in detail, down to our choice of words—as we romped in our bedroom.

We move the heavy table away from the window--closer to the breakfast bar... and adjust the orientation of the stuffed chairs. Carmella and I further arrange the furniture to conform to a stage setting that might provoke our proposed encounter.

The toasts are completed and most of our crowd is chatting in the living room. A few people are gathered in the rumpus room, probably doing drugs if this turns out like other Washington parties. Senator Biden's wife has just left the rumpus room and is dancing too close with her husband. Bill is standing in the far corner and is in animated conversation with Condoleezza Rice, periodically glancing toward the Canadian senator beside him as Belinda touches Bill's arm for the fourth time. I take a seat in the kitchen where I can rest while observing the party.

Hillary must be a little wasted by now… her glass is half empty again. She will be ready to participate in my plan soon. All the men are glancing at Hillary with increasing frequency… some of the women also. Hillary isn't aware of her intoxication, which adds to her attraction. Barack Obama whispers to me, too loudly, that Hillary might be having an affair with Carmella, *because they spend so much time together at the Mayflower hotel.* "I've never had sexual relations with that woman." Hillary smiles. There she goes again, laughing hilariously. She stands straight when she realizes almost everyone is peeping at her. She spots the only people not watching her now--Bill and Belinda. Bill looks up. Hillary teases a finger at Bill, indicating that she wishes to meet with him in the kitchen. Hillary tosses down the last of her Pinot and sashays toward the kitchen… then makes a sudden turn to the bathroom.

The kitchen counter is stacked with desert trays of pavlova and fruit salad. I stick my spoon into the pavlova, but before I can withdraw I am overcome with drowsiness. I am drunk. Oh dear! Here comes a blurry Hillary… Carmella and I could hide in the pantry—if I could stand straight. Hillary enters and steadies herself against the back of one of the chairs surrounding the kitchen table, and stares out toward the pool. She has only drunk two glasses of wine according to my accounting. But if my woozy head is a measure Hillary feels like she has drunk five. Hillary rises on her toes, as if overtaken by euphoria, as she hears a door open. There is a shuffling of feet as the kitchen lock is sprung. Hillary begins to turn as she hears steps from behind. "Bill!" She can surely feel his warm breathe on the back of her neck… and perhaps she senses Bill's erect stick is in proximity to her butt. Hillary has an aura spining around her fuzzy head. She cannot see Bill, but my fantasy must continue. Hillary flutters her eyes toward Bill to encourage him. And now Bill's left hand is near her breast. It isn't wearing a wedding ring. Bastard! Hillary is perfect. She's in control . . . and likes being the conductor of the nation. Then she feels the calluses on the left hand. "Tony!"

What a give away. Bill has soft hands. I place a party hat upon Hillary.

My fantasy is interrupted by Carmella's desperate voice, "Tony! Tony, are you alright?"

"Yes honey. Do you want to go home now?" I ask.

"No. Not yet, darling."

"OK. But you must kiss me," I say.

"You are such a tease," Carmella says.

Bill arrives at just this moment, "OK. Party hat time!"

Hillary follows, striding in through the kitchen door. The party continues--swells on the inebriated confidence that Hillary and Barrack are somehow both going to be the Democrat candidate for the Presidency…

# CHAPTER 18: TONY, 2008

Newt Gingrinch has invited me to join him on a vacation this summer at the Bohemian Club's retreat at Bohemian Grove on the Russian River, north of San Francisco. I am flown with Newt to San Francisco, transported by submarine to the Russian River, and then driven in another limo through the back roads behind the enclave of Monte Rio. We turn off at the Pink Elephant where a bunch of protestors are wearing pig heads and waving antiwar slogans. We continue on further into the redwood forest and stop at the guarded gate.

The accommodations appear to be modest but rustic, with redwood siding and shake roof tiles--until we are escorted indoors. The interior décor is theatric, with fabric hanging on the walls and covering plush sofas in tropical colors. As Newt's guest I am automatically assigned to his house-group, Cedar, which determines which table we sit at for dinner. We are seated with a group of six Yale graduates, with whom we are required to team up to do an entertaining skit at the variety concert this evening.

Newt takes me aside after the concert, just before the scheduled drinks at the clubhouse across the river, "I've persuaded the Bosses to invest in you. There will be a lot more projects coming up, but not until you're ready. This is a critical time."

"Something big huh?"

"Yes… and no questions? Good. We are all going to have a great time tonight. A hundred of the most attractive escorts are coming up from the city to make intelligent conversation with us, as only professional girls can do."

During the limousine ride back across the river to the bar, Newt and I share a bottle of Absinth—a most intoxicating beverage with hallucinating properties. Newt is familiar with the layout of the Northwood golf club. The bar is full so Newt walks to the enclosure beyond. Here there is no singing or dancing. People sit at the tables like at a regular bar and drink. But at two of the tables women are sprawled on the bodies of men, though one can't make out what exactly is happening. Newt and I sit at the only vacant table. A good-looking woman sashays up to us and whispers, "Gentlemen, do you want to jerk off? $50 now. Or wait till later for a $300 treat?"

"Let's sit outside," I say to Newt. The woman laughs. Newt smiles at her they exit to the first bar.

I wait briefly for his return, but clearly Newt is entirely comfortable with abandoning his guest in favor of a prostitute. So I follow them to the first bar.

"What will you have?" Newt asks.

"I'm not drinking anymore."

"I'll have at least a beer. I hope you don't mind," Newt says.

"I don't mind, but… I would appreciate if you hurry up," I say. "Newt, there's prostitution going on here, openly!"

"No, not openly. But it's true that you can take a girl out for the night. Actually, that's what they want you to do. You don't have to do much. Just fix the price. $200 for a jump. They have a fleet of cars waiting outside. We have the submarine moored near the mouth of the river. The girls will take you there."

"Don't you think this is disgusting?" I whisper.

Newt sips his beer. "This is disgusting for you. You have to understand that it might be very different from your life but it's a daily routine for them."

"But to have this in the midst of a public area like this will corrupt people."

"I can't judge that. Does watching television corrupt the young people? Has the sex or violence in our society gone up because of the movies?" Newt says loudly.

"Yes, but what if the local young men from Guerneville start coming here?"

"You take care, Tony."

"I'm going outside. I can't breath in here."

Next day we have lunch back across the river, at the Northwood golf club, at the patio table where Newt's prostitute, Rachael, had sat the previous night--until they went back to the submarine. Newt can't take his eyes off her now, all six feet of her as she eats at a bust table by the wall. Newt nods to George Shultz and Henry Kissinger as they walk by. There was no acknowledgement from the politician celebrities.

"They don't recognize me in my straw hat and Hawaiian shirt," Newt says. I don't believe Newt, but I don't tell him that he's not as big a fish as he makes out... and his pretense at guiltless whoring last night doesn't fool me. But I have to admit to Newt that the hookers did make intelligent and humorous conversation last night... and yes, they were beautiful.

Both George Shultz and Henry Kissinger look miserably serious as they sit two tables along from us. A woman joins their table... she looked like her child has just been run over by a bus. Something must have gone wrong. I promise myself to cash in my mutual fund investments on Monday.

After lunch, Newt Gingrinch leads me to a sofa in the corner of the lounge. I'm not interested in practicing his politics, but listen to him politely.

"The Saudi Arabians are keen to invest in a certain connected businesswoman. Salem bin Laden and Sheik Khalid bin Mafouz want to invest in a long-term relationship that will keep the oil flowing between our countries, and provide opportunities for their wads to grow. Are you ready to assist with a new project?" Newt asks.

"No. Please, not at this time."

Newt knows that it is time to shut up. He finishes the conversation in a soft supportive voice. "Take your time. I'm always here for you, Tony."

In the morning I fly home and catch up with my research. A journalist on the *Franklin* Cover-up Page has written about the possible killing of a child at the Bohemian Grove. The Nixon Tapes discussed homosexual activity at Bohemian Grove. "The Bohemian Grove, which I attend from time to time... it is the most faggy goddamned thing you could ever imagine," President Nixon said.

Attorney John Decamp was involved in the production of a documentary called *Conspiracy of Silence*. It was to air on the Discovery Channel. This documentary exposed a network of religious leaders and Republican politicians who flew children to Washington DC for sex orgies. At the last minute before the airing, unknown congressmen threatened the TV Cable industry with restrictive legislation if this documentary was aired. The publishing rights to the documentary were purchased by one or more unknown persons--who then ordered that all copies of the videotape be destroyed. However, a copy of this videotape was furnished anonymously to retired FBI. Chief, Ted L. Gunderson. While the video quality was not top grade, this tape was a career breaker with regard to what was revealed about the participants involved.

My head is swimming amidst the whirl-pooling enormity of the extent that corruption has taken over my sense of reality--and over much of America. My equilibrium is restored somewhat when I can finally relax at home with Carmella. We tune into a radio program about Hillary on NPR.

"Hillary Clinton is apparently the *only* viable political candidate for the Presidency this year who accepts that we have a national emergency: The climate centers around the world have reported on the Earth's changing physical condition, and the climate specialists see it as seriously ill, and soon to pass into a morbid fever that may last as long as 100,000 years.

Our planet has kept itself healthy and fit, just like an animal does, for most of the more than three billion years of its existence. It was ill luck that we started major polluting at a time when the sun is too hot for comfort. We have given Planet Earth a fever and soon her condition will worsen to a state like a coma. She has been there before and recovered, but it took more than 100,000 years. We are responsible and will suffer the consequences: as the century progresses, it is estimated that the temperature will rise 8 degrees centigrade (14.4 degrees F) in temperate regions and 5 degrees centigrade in the tropics... according to an article written by James Lovelock and published in *The Independent of Britain.*

Much of the tropical land mass will become scrub and desert; this adds to the 40 percent of the Earth's surface we have already depleted to feed ourselves. Curiously, aerosol pollution of the northern hemisphere reduces global warming by reflecting sunlight back to space. This *global dimming* is transient and could disappear shortly like the smoke that it is, leaving us fully exposed to the heat of the global greenhouse. We are in a fool's climate, accidentally kept cool by smoke, but before this century is over billions of us will die, and the few breeding pairs of humans that survive will be in the Arctic poles--where the climate might become tolerable.

By acting as if *we* are in charge of the Earth, rather than God, we have condemned ourselves to the worst form of slavery. When *we* chose to be the stewards of the Earth, we became responsible for keeping the atmosphere, the ocean, and the land surface, healthy for all of God's creatures and plants. A task we have failed at. We have treated Planet Earth badly and have been ungrateful, even though Mother Earth, Gaia, has provided for us perfectly well.

Hillary Clinton attended the forum today, and listened intently--she was the only Washington politician present at this well-publicized event, brokered by top scientists from around the world, and sponsored by the United Nations. When asked to comment, she said she was *committed to our survival.*"

# CHAPTER 19: TONY, 2008

According to a poll conducted by Scripps News Service, one-third of Americans think the Bush administration had foreknowledge of the 9/11 attacks, and allowed them to happen--in order to provide a pretext for war in the Middle East, and thus prevent China, the main threat to the US #1 power position, from obtaining access to further oil reserves. This is both alarming and unsurprising.

Alarming, because tens of millions of Americans believe the US government was complicit in the murder of 3,000 of our fellow citizens.

Unsurprising, because there is a history of deception by the U.S. government-- such as foreknowledge of Pearl Harbor, and of the 1944 Port Chicago nuclear disaster--the US sacrificing her own people to provoke a desired military outcome-- to achieve a military goal that the American people were too moral to support democratically. Therefore the Bush administration is more easily suspected of complicity in 9/11 now, and more so because of the corruption around the Iraq war and the Asian wars... but it remains difficult to accept, deep down, that such a massive violation of morality and law, should be performed by our own US administration. Or is that why we have all those law-and-order TV shows—to herd us, the unruly mob of citizens, into an unnatural lawful behavior.

Another one-third of the population probably dismisses the suspicions of government malfeasance as a delusion promoted by the suffering of the paranoid, or as a destructive bent of conspiracy nuts. Lots of conspiracy theories are bogus, but rejecting them all, just because of how they're framed, is not rational. The way it is today, a gang of conspirators could get away with almost anything illegal. The gang just need to start an Internet rumor, about what they just did that was illegal, framing an accusation against them as a conspiracy theory, and anyone who tries to talk about it, or prosecute the conspirators, will be dismissed as suffering from the paranoia and destructive bent of a conspiracy nut.

Hillary Clinton should be the person for the Presidential job of cleaning up the corruption among the good-old boys—the men who run the political, military, energy, media, and construction industries. But she must adapt to the reality that Newt is holding me to my contractual obligations with Newton PR in his attempt to sabotage Hillary... and that Obama is ahead of her in the delegate count and popularity polls.

I am legally obligated to research the new script that attempts to vilify Hillary, by exploring her integrity in an even more cunningly didactic way--but I intend to expose Newton PR as a dirty-tricks expert—a villain that supported the corruption of my naïve and befuddled friend George Bush--by planting an administration around him that was luke-warm to Christianity, and under the thumb of Vice-president Dick Cheney and his Carlyle Group cohorts.

The patterns of current government deceit have evolved from Pearl Harbor and Port Chicago. This deceit has not only fed diverse public cynicism, but has provided an opening for alternate theories of 9/11 to flourish. As these theories-- propounded by the so-called 9/11 Truth Movement--seep toward the edges of the mainstream, they have raised the specter of the return of what Richard Hofstadter describes as *the paranoid style in American politics*. But the real danger posed by the Truth Movement isn't paranoia, Rather, the danger is that it will discredit the healthy skepticism that many Americans increasingly show toward their leaders.

The Truth Movement's recent growth can be attributed to Internet journalism, burgeoning the portions of the Internet users devoted to the cause of the *Truthers*. A variety of sympathetic groups have chapters across the country that organize various conferences: Prior to the last Bush election, in 2004, the website 911truth.org produced a questionnaire with pointed inquiries for candidates, just like the US Chamber of Commerce or the Sierra Club. Truth activists often maintain they are simply *raising questions*, and as such tend to focus with dogged persistence on physical minutiae. *The lampposts near the Pentagon that should have been knocked down by Flight 77, the altitude in Pennsylvania at which cell phones on Flight 93 should have stopped working, the temperature at which jet fuel burns and at which steel melts.* They then use these perceived inconsistencies to argue that the central events of 9/11 --the plane hitting the Pentagon, the towers collapsing--were not what they appeared to be. So, the eyewitness accounts of those who heard explosions in the World Trade Center, combined with the facts that jet fuel burns at only 1,500 degrees Fahrenheit while steel doesn't become molten until at least 2,500 degrees, indicating to some Truthies that the World Trade Center was saboutaged with controlled explosions-- now shown by tests to almost certainly be thermite... in the case of WTC-7. Why?

If the official story is possibly misleading, then what did happen? There is disagreement on this, even among my Circle Group from the Café Alphar. Like any movement, the Truth Movement is beset by internecine fights between different factions: those who subscribe to what are termed LIHOP theories, (that the government *Let It Happen On Purpose*) and the more radical MIHOP contingent, (*Made It Happen On Purpose*). Even within these groups, there are divisions: Some know that WTC-7 was detonated with thermite explosives well after the planes hit. My Circle Group have identified as possible motivation the *acrid emotional state* that would have devolved around the status of the otherwise blackened skeletons of the former WTC buildings, standing wobbly, like giant black crows, to become an ugly reminder, and possibly a premonition of further disaster.

Would the Bush government have had scruples about letting 3000 Americans be murdered in their quest for oil domination? --a la Pearl Harbor? Of course! But politics requires tough decisions. Regardless of the status of the balance of world power, and therefore the temptation for governments to create events such as Port Chicago, Pearl Harbor, and 9/11, we need to know more.

113

But now we are told that we are unpatriotic to even consider the possibility that the 9/11 attacks were engineered to provoke wars, and thus potentially create an opportunity to seize control of Iraq, Afghanistan, Central Asia and world oil leverage…undermining the global rise of China-that threatens to take over the #1 position from America in the world power hierarchy.

Who decides where responsibility lies? The US press, including parts of the alternate media like *The Nation*, desperately want to be respectable so they can get in on White House and Pentagon press briefings and can participate in pundit talk shows like Katrina Vanden Heuvel and David Corn do. Sidney Blumenthal, the alleged "independent" voice of the Left, is but a devious mouthpiece for the traitorous Newton PR firm and its duplicitous campaign manager, the immoral Mike Penn. Thank God that no one in Hillary's potential administration has an oil agenda or war plans—but that is why she is the vilified target of the Right, and why the ultra-conservative Carlyle Group have promoted a media campaign that employs a team of investigators trained by the same intelligence community as that which has a program to undermine China—the Carlyle group followers have been arranging a barrage of press releases, media events, and anti-China protests… with the two pronged goal of destroying Hillary's Presidential bid—now in danger of succeeding, and of undermining global trade with China on account of their poisonous exports.

My Circle Group are supporters of the premise that the US has an important role in promoting global peace and justice, and has served a valuable purpose in this regard from a position of world #1 since WWII. But, the current zealots in power who insist that we must maintain our #1 power position in the world at all costs-- they undermine the values that led the US to our privileged position.

A major component of the "inside job" thesis is that 9/11 was a "Pearl Harbor"-- an attack anticipated by our government but not resisted--or worse, a "false flag" operation, staged by the US government posing as Arabs, to discredit its opponents in the Middle East, in order to provide the pretext to seize the oil fields, and impose the *Homeland Security* police state at home. It would be naive not to assume that some *inside job* conspirators were not also conducting false flag operations, as saboteurs amidst the media, to con the public that 9/11 skeptics were easily debunked because of their *planted* outrageous conspiracy assertions, in order to hide the actual evidence for complicity.

The problem with the conclusions of the 9/11 Commission Report is that there is no plausible explanation, for any possible heat source of temperatures anywhere near high enough (2850 deg. F), to account for the pools of molten steel found at the basements of WTC, other than with the use of thermite demolition explosives--meaning there is compelling evidence that it had to be an inside job.

But why? Does this mean that the official explanation is wrong--that 9/11 was more than a job performed with some inside foreknowledge--and that our own government has sanctioned the crime as well as its cover-up?

How does, *weakened steel from melting at local hot spots*, induced by thermite incendiary detonations, translate to *three unprecedented fire-induced instantaneous collapses?*

How much explosive would it take to disconnect the beams from the columns at several floors, simultaneously, so the beams fell onto the floors below to fail those beams in turn, and thus to sequentially unzip the entire building?

It would only take a small amount of professionally placed explosive to separate the beams from the critical columns--an airplane impact could do it if sufficient coordination of several aircraft was employed to hit the critical columns at the same time. But then the collapse would have occurred almost immediately after impact, and the challenge to the viability of this unzipping theory--this domino concept of failure--would be to conceive of preventing the steel beams from falling *au naturale*, at fractionally different times. The challenge would be to prevent the beams from interacting, creating a log jam at one floor or another, rather than falling in unison--in formation--with a single impact, untangled, on the floor below with sufficient momentum to shear the bolts and welds, designed to resist massive earthquake and wind forces in an unyielding manner, at these most critical elements of the building.

Such an unlikely hypothesis would have to be instigated at the beam to column connections at upper stories. But there was not enough loose debris, located at the source-of-impact story, to constitute a source of concentrated momentum, so as to be able to crash--unimpeded to the ground--unzipping, due to an improbable orderly falling of debris--with beams and trusses falling neatly in coordinated unison without a log jam. The only other conceivable collapse mechanism then is that WTC-7, and possibly the Twin Towers, collapsed because of a professionally designed array of simultaneously triggered thermite incendiary ignitions.

# CHAPTER 20: TONY, 2008

Carmella hurries to gather leaves as they rustle and scatter over the lawn. Carmella's long hair falls down in front of her eyes as she bends. She must sense me watching. She lifts her head and looks toward me on the veranda. She smiles, holding a bundle of dried leaves. I motion to her. Her face is dirty from leaves and garden soil. Carmella makes a questioning gesture with her shoulders: "What is it?"

"Where are the kids? Aren't they supposed to be home by now?" I ask.
"What? A new terrorist alert?"
"No. I didn't mean to panic you, Honey. I'm a little jittery."
Carmella nods toward me and I continue, "Will you take a look at where the kids are, please?"
Carmella has this ESP-like ability to sense the kids. Maybe she's momentarily forgotten about her gift, because of her garden work, because of the terrorist bombings in Europe. She closes her eyes. I wait patiently. I know by now that the look on her face means that she is homing in on the children's location. Less than half a minute passes and she begins to speak. "Marise has detention, is still at school. And Yolanda's twins--I see Isobel and Sophie both well," she says, eyes still closed. "They're walking down the little street. There's nothing wrong, they got sidetracked and had a chat with one of the neighborhood kids..."

Maybe I am getting paranoid, but Carmella can be so casual... and the twins are only visitors, for a semester, from New Zealand because their dad is sick. What do they know about American street life! I want the children to understand about life, time, and their responsibilities within the family. After a few minutes the twins rush through the door, as young ladies will do. The bags on their backs are heavy. The weight of the bags and the tiredness disappears the moment they find themselves in the sight of Carmella and I. They tackle Carmella, throw themselves into her arms and shrill in unison: "How are you Aunty?" Carmella holds them tight. After a few seconds of hugs they pull away from Carmella's arms. Now it is my turn. They skip over to where I am working at my laptop. "Good day Uncle." We hug and I ask them, "How was your day? Everything as we anticipated?"

The girls know what I mean and their demeanor changes immediately, but it takes a few seconds to get a reply. Isobel, who is half an hour older than Sophie, looks at her fairer twin sister and they say in unison, "It was fun after school but it wasn't like we had planned. We're sorry Uncle."
"Sorry? But what do you have to be sorry about? Has something happened that I should know about?"
Isobel speaks up, "Well, after school, we were playing and forgot about the time. And that you worry about us. Sorry."
Sophie nods in agreement, and despite being younger than Isobel she knows her responsibility.

I smile, look at them both calmly and say, "You know that to me the best apology is if you learn from your mistake. I want you to become even happier, but with a new sense of responsibility about being conscious of the time. You remember that I have told you that this life is comprised of four facets – time, energy, space and matter, and if you want to achieve something in life you must master these facets. Learn to create opportunity in this world. If you don't do this, life will control you, which doesn't lead to further happiness. I want you to be happy."

Isobel and Sophie agree with me, of course. Marise arrives and is even chirpier than the twins, despite her detention for being late back to school after lunch. So I give Marise the same speech as the twins, almost. Afterward the girls chat for a while and then skip through to the kitchen from where a pleasant food aroma is wafting. Their eyes dilate with anticipation of eating whatever the delicious smell is from. Before Carmella can warn them that the food is hot, Sophie almost burns her nose when she opens the pot of boiling soup.

The table is soon set and ready. The three girls sit and begin to discuss with one another what kind of soup it is. This continues until Carmella serves them the soup and their curiosity is settled with a mouthful. "Wooowww…haricot beans…" Then there is silence broken only by clanging spoons.

As they begin to fill up the chat resumes, "Mama, today it was tense at school because of the terrorist bombings in Europe." Marise says. "And that nasty boy Jacko who is…."

I interrupt. "Jacko is a strong character of a young man who loves to play chess, the same as you women do."

"I don't like him."

I have to persist. "Marise, you know you cannot speak about someone like this. Even if you have the right to say that he is odious. Remember—never speak negative things about someone when he isn't present, except in the case when you want advice or help. Even then you shouldn't criticize."

"I knoooow, I knooww…you are right," sighs Marise, "Speak only positive things when the person in question isn't around. But I get angry. Those idiots will just drive me fucking crazy… oh… excuse me."

Carmella and the twins laugh. This helps Marise to calm down. They change the subject.

Having listened to them talk about what excites them, Carmella then asks, "Was it tasty?"

"Yes," the girls reply.

"Then put your dishes in the washer, clear the table, and attack your homework please."

It seems that the homework part of the family treaty is not the girl's favorite activity, but Carmella insists that they learn to be disciplined. I often tell them that love for work and order is one of the most important things in life. Even if something is not popular, it is important to do their best and work with passion.

While cleaning the table, Isobel and Sophie hear their favorite old song playing on the radio. It is The Trons' "Sister Robot." They both run over to the radio to turn it up. They are singing, out of tune but with so much enthusiasm…tam…tam…Tara dam… After a few seconds, Marise and Carmella make the duo a quartet. Carmella holds a broom in her hands, with Marise, Isobel, and Sophie following. Each of them is holding either a towel or a dish and is dancing one after the other, like a train. Then they turn around and continue in the opposite direction. They are like four happy sisters. The fun continues and every time someone makes a mistake in the "broom dance" they all burst out laughing. Finally Carmella trips over Sophie's bag and falls to the ground. Of course the teenage darlings have been waiting for a moment like this and they jump on Carmella and begin tickling and playfully attacking her with whatever they can grab – sofa covers, pillows… Soon they wear down. Exhausted from laughing, they lay on the floor near each other, panting until their hearts calm.

Isobel seizes her opportunity, "Aunty," she says. "Tomorrow evening is our classmate Kathryn's birthday party. There will be lots of other girls there. Can I go and take Sophie?"

"Will you and Marise come with us?" Sophie asks.

"It would be great if you'd come," Isobel explains. "There will be a lot of students that do not know you and we can tell them you are our older sister." Everyone bursts out laughing again.

Isobel continues the plea, "You know Sophie, there is no point in asking Kathryn to come here, don't you? Because she wouldn't come because they think Uncle Tony is weird. You know that don't you Carmella. So, can we go to Kathryn's house after school?"

Carmella looks at them and while getting up from the ground she says, "Yes you can go with Marise, if you finish your homework--and all of your other responsibilities… before bedtime. Also, you will have to come home before dark, which means around… 9.30pm."

"Why is that? 9.30pm is too early. The other students…" the girls begin to whine.

"9.30 it is!" Carmella knows when it is time to have fun but is careful that they stay on a healthy schedule befitting young ladies in high school.

The girls often try with their best acting to convince Carmella with different explanations. Now they want to sleep at their friend's house tomorrow. Carmella obviously does not like the idea. She is looking in those six eyes and it seems that she can see exactly what they are planning. Since they cannot reach an agreement they walk quickly towards me on the veranda. Before I have a chance to clarify what is going on, the kids bombard me with their side of the story. I listen patiently as usual. Then I ask them a few questions. Whatever their wish, I am most interested in how the experience will affect their growth.

"I understand that you want to go and sleep there, right?"

"Yeeeeeeeessssss!"

"Well, why do you think Carmella cannot agree with this?"

A solemn silence settles on the girls. They reconsider. The answer becomes clear to them.

Isobel feebly attempts to avoid the question. "Okay. I understand. You don't have to look at me like that."

I turn to Sophie. "Why don't you answer?"

"Well it is clear why Aunty cannot agree," Sophie says. " Because as usual she cares about us and our security. And she has that bad habit, or that wonderful ability, to see everything inside of our heads. She can even see things that *might* happen… This is our Aunty."

They all rush into each other's arms. The teenagers themselves have resolved the issue. I helped them to look deeper into Carmella's reasoning. I wanted them to remember how Carmella has an extra sensory gift, and can use it to foresee trouble. The night before the Twin Towers a bird crashed into the living room window and Carmella said, "Something terrible is going to happen. Oh my God! Look at the huge red moon!"

The girls' talk is like a dance: sound meets sound, curtsies, shimmies, and retires. Another sound enters but is upstaged by still another. The two circle each other and stop… and all of it is punctuated with the heartthrob of laughter. The teenagers ask if we can all go out this evening to a restaurant for a late dinner, "Being with the whole family will be fun."

The answer is "Yes," if they can finish their homework. They have no morning classes the next day and Carmella likes the idea of going out to eat. One of the greatest pleasures the kids enjoy is dinner with the family. Whether at the table at home, or together at a restaurant, these are the moments when there are so many jokes. Most of all these are the moments when new interests, new knowledge, and the wisdom of the whole family interact.

Carmella and I never preach at the girls now. We attempt to guide them towards an understanding of life, environmental issues, and of themselves, with love and responsibility. Of course this is not always easy and funny…but tonight everything works out and is settled due to our careful conversation.

A few hours later almost everyone is ready. Marise is late coming downstairs from her room again, but soon even she is ready to go. It is the usual trip out; Sophie and Isobel argue about who is not going to sit in the middle over the drive shaft. After a few minutes everyone is ready for the restaurant. I turn to the back seat and ask, "Are we all ready to go?"

"Yeeeeeeeeessssss."

"And where will we be going this evening?"

"To the Cafe Alphar."

It is Marise's favorite place to eat out because everyone knows us there, and it is open almost all night.

The car rumbles along and the girls start with a song by the Trons. "Life is a place for flying dreams, for weird and wonderful dreams." I am driving the car slowly. I have to be careful with the cats and dogs running around in our neighborhood at night. The streets in our outer suburb of DC are small, but neat, and filled with plantation houses whose yards are peppered with flowers. Looking at these carefully arranged yards, fields with horses and fruit trees; I cannot believe that our countryside is situated only an hour away from the Nation's capitol. Here, it seems that time is not moving and no matter what the season, it is always covered with greenery.

There is excited chatter in the back seat. When we stare in the distance at one of the turns in the road, we can see our house in the midst of this wonderful big garden. I slow down, as much as I can, and say, "Can you imagine if one day I can have a house like this in a place like this… and even a woman like Carmella, a teenage daughter, and nieces?"

Everyone laughs. Carmella continues in the same manner. "The people that are living there have arranged their things--have made it in life--they've succeeded and… " Everyone is laughing because quite often we people dream about things that we do not possess. And when we finally obtain them, we begin to crave for the next thing we do not have. If nothing else, we can at least be aware of this truth. We can admit what we have fallen short, and we can even laugh about it. We think about the unachieved more than enough. Our family is thankful for our achievements and blessings.

Carmella's mobile phone rings. While she answers the kids continue their humorous conversation in a whisper.

Carmella's telephone conversation sounds urgent, "Hello…Yes…Oh Hillary, is that you at last? I'm so glad to hear from you."

Hillary replies and Carmella continues, "Of course you are welcome. You know where the key is and if we are out, you unlock and go in. How are you doing with all the fuss?"

Carmella's face is focused and her eyes intense. She looks as if she is concerned, but wants to conceal that from the kids.

"I will wait for you on Saturday, and I'll take care that everyone is home so that we can have a wonderful time together… Of course I will hug the girls for you… All right, yes, Tony as well… Ok, we love you."

The conversation is over and the girls and I are waiting to know why Hillary called.

Carmella explains that Hillary will drive over on Saturday to spend the weekend with us. "A new terrorist alert has just been posted by the Pentagon."

"What does Hillary say?"

"No need to create alarm about our government until we have a solution."

I interrupt Carmella, "Hillary doesn't want us to worry about all the difficulties she is facing… losing out to Obama. *I will continue to fight until I go crazy*, she said."

The children do not seem concerned. Carmella turns to them, "Eh girls, do not forget that the world is complicated. Love and pray for Hillary. Without love, all this togetherness would not be possible."

Sophie whispers, "I don't understand how Hillary can care so much. Doesn't she remember the bad things that people have said about her?"

"No Sophie. You see, to her, bad things are like a pair of dreams. The first one lives deep in our soul and sleeps. The other haunts the air around us. As soon as you make a mistake it bursts in and wakes up the sleeping nightmare inside of our soul. Then it is like we are not ourselves anymore. To Hillary, everything bad we lived through with the Republicans was not the real Republicans…and everything wonderful... is because of the freedom we have in the United States."

The girls kiss Carmella from behind and they talk about boys and music. Fifteen minutes have passed unnoticed. We are almost at the Cafe Alphar. Carmella is snoozing. A few more busy traffic signals and we will be there.

"Look Papa, Mama is so beautiful. She is very calm--and it seems to me like she is happy," Marise says.

"Yes, at last she's calm as well as beautiful. Generally, when a woman doesn't speak everyone is calm." The kids laugh but nudge my head with a half-kidding unappreciative frankness. They are future women as well after all.

Carmella yawns and stretches as she sits up. She opens the mirror in front of her seat and arranges her hair. "Now if you'll excuse me, I would like to put myself in order so as not to scare the people in the Cafe Alphar."

I turn right and here we are. "Alright, we've even got a place to park. Wonderful. Thank you to God."

Isobel asks, "OK Uncle. But tell us Aunty--about the Creator, about Gaia, the Creator?" The girls are looking at Carmella with expectation.

Carmella answers as I park the car: "As I see it, we humans are all lost because we separated rebelliously from our Creator and our deeper purpose, a long time ago. This means that now we are totally confused people who are afraid from our birth to our death of how to survive meaningfully. Americans have mostly come to worship their greatest powers on the planet; that is money and sex. Everyone justifies their selfish priorities in their own way according to their culture, faith, and social level. But we have ignored the pollution of the air. We must regain our survival instincts or become extinct."

"It's amazing you have this knowledge Aunty Carmella."

"I don't have ESP. I only pretend sometimes, to counter Papa's delusions of granduer. Now, which restaurant do you prefer – upper or lower?"

"The upper...the upper...it is always great there because we can look from above on the buildings and people below!"

"Carmella does have ESP. But she doesn't know it," I say.

Our family loves both little restaurants because they have no limits on the time for arriving or leaving. They work the whole day and night, the service is good, and everyone knew them personally. We feel at home. The girls climb first to the second floor where they find their favorite table. Having greeted the boss, the bar tender and the waiter on the ground floor, Carmella and I find the girls seated at the table with a view of the hills, and the bright park and streets around us. They call the waiter who greets them with a smile, and asks how they are doing before taking our orders. The girls notice that I am looking at them flopped on the comfortable sofa. They ask me, "Why are you looking at us Tony? What are you thinking?"

"This evening is a gift for Carmella and I, because you are all here with us."

The girls laugh, "We are simply the best!"

"Tell us more about what you are thinking Tony?"

"This moment was once the future, and now like a breeze it has passed. Once I dreamed about the way things would be, and now I'm living the reality of it. Life builds up from many successive "present" moments. It is lived best when we can be alert and focused in our present time... not in the past or the future."

The girls look astonished with this simple truth that is so hard to implement.

After a while Marise says, "Sometimes I think that the more we grow up the more we lose everything wonderful we had as children--our innocence. On the other hand I would like to be grown up in order to be able to do things. To be honest, I don't know what we are going to do as adults without you living with us." Marise continues to debate the issue with herself until her words unravel into her thoughts.

I understand that Marise is an old soul, "Look Marise. Carmella and I have no such concerns. Our concerns are for the future time when this world will try and deceive you in its trap of lies, wrong sex, and later, money and exploiting the planet for short-term comforts. We must try to teach you everything we know about life."

Marise sits next to me, and as a sign of her agreement and love she rests her head on my shoulder. Then she sits next to Carmella, together with Isobel. Both of them cannot fit in that sofa because it is so small, but still they find a way.

Carmella laughs, "Hey, young ladies, don't you think you are a little bit to big to squeeze up like this."

"Noooooo," Isobel and Marise answer together. "Uncle Tony... how come you found Carmella?"

"What is it with you girls tonight?" I say. "I feel like I'm on an interview."

The children explain how important it was for them to hear the whole story again. They had heard it when they were younger, but never from beginning to end at one time.

I smile. "It all happened according to the options before us... when we met, Carmella was very frank and direct. She told me that what was happening to her was not normal. That safe and normal things never happened to her in her life. That she was afraid. She even thought she was being possessed by the devil!"

"The devil," the girls gasp." "Why the devil?"

"She was influenced by a religious sect which has its own interpretations of life—where men had many wives, some only sixteen years old. If you follow the story with me you'll understand why."

"All right...go ahead," the girls say.

"Carmella asked me not to laugh at her and then told me that strong feelings for me had developed within. She couldn't sleep, she saw my face everywhere all of the time. She felt a strong desire to touch me. From that moment on, I knew we would be together forever. Inside, I was certain of the truth. I even shared it with Nana Rita when I got back home."

"So you met Carmella just before you finished at college. And then what happened?"

"We kept meeting together. Her mother visited and told me that Carmella was not feeling well and wanted to speak with me... I hurried to her room. Carmella tried to say something but there were only tears, nothing could be understood. I asked her mother to call the doctor. I ended up having to take her in my arms and carry her to the hospital. She was pregnant, with Marise. And you know the rest of the story now."

# CHAPTER 21: TONY, 2008

I am in love with Carmella. It is nothing as easy as simple happiness, but an aching inter-dependence with another person... a woman who compliments my own broad-brush approach to life. What, with Carmella's attention to the details, and my unbearable awareness of the simultaneous power and transience of now—will my abundant talents lead me to fame, or will I shipwreck on my singular obsession with collapsed buildings.

Asked if the vertical support columns of the Twin Towers gave way before the connections between the floor trusses and the columns, Ron Hamburger, a structural engineer with the FEMA assessment team said, "That's the $64,000 question."

Ron Hamburger's answer reveals that the NIST federal experts have identified a key question --but they haven't yet resolved the answer to the question.

A structural engineering report by IDS Consultants and Lilly-Thomas says that the columns failed because there was a serious lack of restraint to buckling that should have been provided by the floor diaphragm. The report goes on to say: "The U.S. Building Code only requires that the floors of an office building be designed for relatively low contents loading--and certainly doesn't allow for the accumulation of loading from debris falling through from floors above. Therefore any overloading of the connections supporting the floor trusses is not surprising--but the failure of the steel columns indicates another building-code flaw. Furthermore, the earthquake loading specified in the U.S. Building Code is but a fraction of the real maximum earthquake inertial forces or hurricane forces--this cost saving measure is justified on the grounds that code attempts to ensure that the beams will yield before the columns." Geez! The floor trusses installed in the WTC Towers would have prevented collapse if they had even just 1% post-elastic strength.

George W. Bush's administration became distracted from investigating the 9/11 collapses at WTC further because of the convergence of other crises. In the summer of 2007 the administration arranged for Public Law 109-364 to be signed, as part of The Patriot Act, by the commander in chief--it allows George Bush, as President, to declare a *public emergency*, station troops anywhere in America, and take control of state-based National Guard units without the consent of the governor or local authorities--in order to *suppress public disorder*. But there is a hesitancy toward applying this extreme legislation, perhaps because of the scandals reported in the new *Hillary Series* on the Truman Show. The latest program purports to investigate corruption within President Bill Clinton's administration, particularly the lobbying work of Leon Panetta. But the corruption revealed within the building industry by today's *Hillary Series* show is much more damning to the Federal Administration:

"When the Northridge quake awakened Los Angeles on January 17, 1994, it was measured as 6.7 magnitude, a moderate sized earthquake. However, because of its location--it was the first true seismic test for many of the USA's tall steel-frame buildings—1500 of which are located in LA. At first glance, most of these LA tall steel buidings seemed to fare well and occupancy continued, but a disturbing trend has surfaced. Many of the interior beam-to-column connections had cracked, in some cases splitting all the way through. This problem first came to light in structures still under construction, like the Getty Center, which was then just completing construction of the steel frame. Engineers found a series of cracked weld connections--and decided to replace all of the original welds. Owners of completed steel-frame buildings in LA thus learned of the threat, but it would require breaking through concrete just to get a look at the status of the covered welds of completed buildings—so the owners decided to avoid action. Still, the damage had been done--the long-standing myth of the seismic invincibility of steel buildings has been exposed as a false assumption.

Shortly after the Northridge quake, the Federal Emergency Management Agency (FEMA) joined several independent firms in conducting tests on the flawed connections. The examinations determined that the typical Lincoln weld metal was too brittle to withstand severe seismic activity. By the end of 1994, the city of L.A. Issued construction guidelines that effectively banned the use of this Lincoln weld electrode, called a self-shielded flux cored wire E70T-4.

In 2001, at the beginning of the presidency of George W. Bush, and six years after the realization of this fundamental engineering flaw, even as geologists discovered new and potentially catastrophic seismic fault lines across the nation, a rather ominous question persisted: What about those Lincoln self shielded flux cored welds? Nearly all of the nation's steel-frame buildings constructed prior to Northridge were built with the flawed Lincoln weld connections. Shouldn't they be repaired? Some say that the Cleveland-based Lincoln Electric Co, which has produced and supplied the self-shielded E70T-4 weld wires to contractors and builders for the previous 30 years, should be held responsible for the flawed welds. Executives at Lincoln had another idea: According to a Greg Brouwer of *LA Weekly News*… Lincoln has spent more than $1 million on a quiet, sophisticated lobbying campaign designed to press the Federal Government to step in and pay the enormous cost involved in retrofitting hundreds of thousands of welded steel connections in thousands of buildings throughout the quake-prone regions of the USA… and perhaps the hurricane prone East.

Lincoln launched, via the attorneys at Cassidy & Associates, a high-priced Washington lobbying firm, the "Seismic Safety Coalition," (SSC) which purports to be "a broad-based, non-partisan organization" and a "national coalition"-- but in fact claims a single dues-paying member-- Lincoln Electric. The chair of the SSC commission was Leon Panetta, former congressman from California, former chief of staff at the Bill Clinton White House, and long-time associate of the FEMA director for President Bush--James Lee Witt. In his capacity as SSC chair, Panetta had registered for the first time as a congressional lobbyist. As described in it's mission statement, the Seismic Safety Coalition seeks to--*improve public health and safety by encouraging more vigorous pre-disaster hazard-mitigation efforts with respect to earthquakes*. But then came the punch line: *Specifically, we want to see new developments in earthquake-resistant design and construction practices incorporated in a responsible and effective retrofitting program*--**with the federal government picking up the tab**. Government commitment to this policy would save Lincoln

124

millions in liability arising from inadequate welds in Southern California alone.

The Lincoln E70T-4 weld wire had been touted as enabling a very high weld deposition rate, and that was a key justification for its use. Steel building joints were in the past welded with SMAW stick electrodes that typically provided approx. 2 to 3 lbs/hr. The change to the E70T-4 wires enabled mechanized welds of 25 to 30 lbs an hour—but these wires did not deliver welds that could pass minimal cyclic load requirements, and resulted in excess weld heat and extended grain growth in the weld's heat affected zones.

John Hall, a structural engineering professor at Caltech, was hired by FEMA to determine why the pre-Northridge connections were cracking. In a lecture later published under the title *Tall Buildings, Bad Welds, Large Earthquakes--Big Problems*, Hall explained that engineers had been designing buildings in L.A. on the assumption that, in the event of an earthquake, the building joints would reach an elastic limit, and then yield *like chewing gum*. What happened with E70T- 4, Hall points out, is that many welds failed well within the elastic range. The self-shielded weld joints didn't bend; they simply broke.

The Northridge Earthquake raised serious questions about the design and construction of steel high-rise buildings. It was revealed that an astonishing 99% of the brittle weld failures occurred with the Lincoln self-shielded flux-core weld metal. Almost all of the failures from the Northridge event, observed by those interviewed, were a brittle form of failure in the welded joint area between beam and column flanges. Only two or three joints in the thousands surveyed were observed to be capable of enduring specified forces.

Retrofit strengthening generally consists of adding plates or tees to the bottom and top flanges of the beam at the column joint--to increase the connection capacity. There is little attempt to balance the design out by adding similar stiffness and strength to the undamaged connections of the building. However, there is widespread concern is the engineering community that such an unbalance in stiffness and strength could result in less favorable performance in future earthquakes. Few owners are going beyond the cheapest repair process of putting the damaged connection back as it was before the Northridge earthquake.

Only where FEMA or some other agency is picking up the cost of repair and retrofits are the owners initiating seismic upgrades. Proper repair costs for damaged connections in typical commercial buildings range from $3,000 to $20,000 per connection. The typical costs are in the $5,000 to $8,000 range. In residential and institutional construction these costs may double or triple to $15,000 to $30,000 per connection, and cost $15,000 to $60,000 per connection if lost rental income is included.

The fact that the lobbyists for Lincoln, such as Leon Panetta, were included by FEMA in the retrofit decision making process, was a brilliant legal move to escape liability for the failures. That's a beneficial lesson for those other global corporations who want to avoid large liability consequences when they make mistakes that cost life. Its interesting that Lincoln choose Jones Day Reavis & Pogue, the legal firm that represented R.J. Reynolds in the Great American Tobacco Wars, to defend them against lawsuits."

# PART IX: HILLARY

## CHAPTER 22: 2008

Invariably some crisis interrupts me, and I simply can't bear living the rest of the day ahead until I have solved the problem of *How do I, Hillary Cinton, become President... when my party has apparently chosen Obama as their Democrat candidate?* Thank God that I have sensitive and intelligent friends, such as Carmella and Tony, who listen to my dilemma. There is so much good to be done for the cause of social justice, yet many focus on gossip mongering and throwing punches and filth at their leaders, especially at we Democrats. And all the while I have to endure the vast right wing conspiracy—the Republican plots to smear me and undermine my sanity with lies and leaked vitriol.

Most of our network mass media outlets are now owned and operated by Republicans-and increasingly rely upon government subsidy. I know that the Republican right wing hired Tony Chaytor to do research for a certain *Hillary* documentary, for *The Newton Series*. The goal of the script is to disparage my skills and reputation with lies and innuendo. Fortunately, Tony is a decent and a clever man, so their devious plan will backfire. I must likewise bring some justice to the lives of my detractors. I have made a list of those people whom I cannot trust to behave responsibly:

1. Newt Gingrinch. Connie Chung broadcast Newt Gingrinch's opinion of Hillary Clinton: "Bitch." We suspect it's merely a case of the pot calling the kettle black, and you can include Connie Chung in that.

2. Rush Limbaugh. He deems it worthy to share his unsubstantiated claim with his audience, "OK, folks, I think I got enough information here to tell you about the contents of this fax that I got. Brace yourselves. This fax contains information that I have just been told will appear in a newsletter to Morgan Stanley sales personnel this afternoon. It is a bit of news that says, *There's a Washington consulting firm that has scheduled the release of a report that claims that Vince Foster was murdered in an apartment owned by Hillary Clinton, and the body was then taken to Fort Marcy Park.*" No such report was ever issued.

3. Bob Woodward. On 23 Jun 1996, a story by Watergate reporter Bob Woodward in the Washington Post reveals to the world "First Lady Hillary Clinton employed psychic Jean Houston to help her get in touch with her inner Eleanor Roosevelt. We elect freaks, people."

4. Tom Bauerle. On 19 Jan 2000, Buffalo radio personality Tom Bauerle needled me about rumoured infidelities--of Hillary Clinton:

BAUERLE: Mrs. Clinton, you're going to hate me, you were on television last night talking about your relationship with Bill Clinton. Have you ever been sexually unfaithful to him and specifically the stories about you and Vince Foster? Any truth in those?

CLINTON: I do hate you for that, because you know, those questions I think are really out of bounds, and everybody who knows me knows the answers to those questions.

BAUERLE: Is the answer "no?"

CLINTON: Well, yes. Of course it's "no," but it's an inappropriate question.

5. Bill O'Reilly. On 31 May 2001, on his television show *The O'Reilly Factor*, O'Reilly accused me of being a tax-mongering socialist and declared, "Sixty percent of poor kids can't read in the fourth grade. Where's that child-care expert Hillary Clinton on this one? Oh, yeah. It takes a village to educate a kid, not a public school, right, Mrs. Clinton? She wouldn't dare say a word because she needs the teachers' unions to prop her up, and the unions simply want more money, not more performance accountability."

6. Edward Klein's attack book, *The Truth About Hillary*, infers many times that I am sexually frigid and a lesbian.

7. The negative reviewers of my book, *Living History*, including political scientist Bruce Miroff, who wrote, "While most of the lessons Hillary learned throughout her tenure as First Lady were decidedly positive, there is another side to the coin. Mrs. Clinton has also become a master at blurring the lines between campaigning and governance. She has become more media savvy, and it shows. Hillary knows that the American public views the Presidency as a combination of politics and entertainment." Miroff went on to describe the contemporary Presidential leadership as a titillating "spectacle" that numbs and awes its audience, and declared my Christophe haircuts, Oscar de la Rente dresses, and Twisted Fabric gowns as signs of my increased concern about my feminine appearance.

Miroff also attacked me when he said, "By writing her own book, *Living History*, Mrs. Clinton has embraced the spectacle of American public leadership, but in a way in which she controls her present and future political scripts. From her traditional midwestern upbringing as a devout Methodist, Girl Scout, and Goldwater Girl, to her adult roles as attorney, wife, mother, First Lady, and Senator; Hillary has adapted to her environment, and redefined roles with a mixture of tradition and progressivism. One common theme is *running for office*. Hillary ran for president in high school in Illinois (she lost), and at Wellesley College (she was president of the College Republicans and the Student Body), assisted Bill in many campaigns from Attorney General to Governor to President, and most recently won election as Senator. In each of these episodes of public service, controversy surely followed. But Hillary faced her greatest organized opposition when she took on Healthcare--as First Lady."

Miroff goes on to imply that I am delusional and crazy: "Hillary was a different First Lady than her predecessors. In her book *Living History*, she describes many contacts with previous First Ladies, including Jacqueline Kennedy Oasis (advice about protecting Chelsea), Lady Bird Johnson (appreciation for mobilizing Democrats who supported Bill), and even Eleanor Roosevelt... if you count her visualization and conversations with Eleanor Roosevelt in the White House, an exercise from Jean Houston who helped console and motivate Hillary after healthcare reform was killed by insurance money. Hillary was the first First Lady to enter office expecting to share power--with the President, and have the public acknowledge her importance. Hillary often displayed more stereotypical masculine traits of being a protector, competitor, economic provider, and private person. Bill displayed the more traditional feminine traits of empathy, cooperation, financial dependence, emotional expression, and public revelations of his private behaviours. These reversed characteristics may be particularly jarring and annoying to traditionalists, but point to a new era toward the extinguishments of sexism and gender bias.

The revelations about Bill's affair with Monica Lewinsky drove the First Couple to marital counselling. She resisted divorce for a variety of reasons: her mother's experience as a child of divorce and the desire to protect Chelsea from that same outcome, her sense that Bill is the man who understands her, and her opportunities at that time to exert political power as Bill's wife. She already has the support of Democratic, college-educated women, and racial minorities. The key to her continued political success is to expand her coalition. First, she must win back the full support of feminists, who are wary of her after her decision to remain married to her husband Bill. And, most importantly, she needs to appeal to moderate voters of both sexes, who may have traditional values and concerns. By emphasizing her religious beliefs, her intergenerational connection with her mother, her strong relationship with Chelsea, and her willingness to stick it out with Bill, Hillary aims to tap into this vast reservoir of the electorate. It is clear from *Living History* that Hillary understands that Presidential politics is about knowing how to produce results like a workhorse, and play to the cameras like a show pony. Several knowledgeable Democrats have warned that Hillary Clinton cannot be trusted with National Security--she suspects the cause of the collapses of the WTC buildings around 9/11 has not been fully revealed, and she is going to muckrake. Hillary looks weak on terror. We ought not let women run everything."

Outside it is hot and dry, and I must squint against the glitter of all the parked cars. The people walking on the sidewalk are difficult to see--dark blots against the shimmer of the light, until my eyes adjust. I am walking too fast. I know that not just from the firm smack of my shoes on the pavement, but because the people walking toward me have their faces bunched up in the way that I think means they're worried. Why? Because they know that after years of systematically trying to destroy my reputation and derail my political career, Republican operatives and surrogates again have me in their crosshairs, and are throwing barbed slander at me. While they haven't succeeded in stopping me, they have managed to drive up my negatives, and turn a significant portion of the electorate against me.

During my first run for the senate from New York State in 2000 the Washington, DC-based National Conservative Campaign Fund issued a "Special Report: Campaign Strategy to Stop Hillary Clinton." By mid-year, veteran conservative activist Morton C. Blackwell organized the "Emergency Committee to Stop Hillary Rodham Clinton." In another effort on behalf of the American Conservative Unions--the Hillary Rodham Clinton Voter Alert Campaign--former New York Republican Party Congressman Gerald Solomon sent out a 92 page paperback book titled "Hillary Rodham Clinton: What Every American Should Know."

The National Conservative Campaign Fund (NCCF) provided a detailed strategy aimed at stopping me by: 1) Driving up my unfavorable poll numbers by "attacking her pro-big government liberal record;" 2) Setting up a "Defeat Hillary Clinton" website to recruit supporters; 3) Distributing scads of targeted anti-Hillary materials; 4) Running anti-Hillary newspaper and radio advertisements; and 5) Start early and strike often. The NCCF made it clear that its ultimate goal was to stop my senate election in 2000, and therefore "destroy any hope she has of being elected President in the future."

The American Conservative Union--whose goal was to distribute some six million copies of its book--claimed that the book was an "abbreviated yet clear snapshot of the words, deeds, and misdeeds of the most self-absorbed and power-struck First Lady in our nation's history."

In February 2005, longtime GOP public relations maven and campaign consultant Arthur Finkelstein, the head of Arthur J. Finkelstein & Associates, launched what he hoped would be the deathblow to my political aspirations. His "Stop Her Now" website aimed to raise $10 million to help defeat me in the 2006 New York senatorial race. For Finkelstein, "Stop Her Now" would be the mother of all gathering places for Hillary-bashers. However, "Stop Her Now" failed to live up to expectations and I won the Senate election.

"Stop Her Now," according to its website, is "an organization of concerned citizens that is dedicated to "spreading the TRUTH about Hillary Clinton and my dangerous ideas and plans for our country. STOP HER NOW is out to expose me as a confirmed left-wing radical and life-long liberal who long ago sold her soul to the divisive, radical, and ultra-liberal special interest groups--who see everyone as *victims* and want to use tax dollars and the power of the state to make things right."

People on Republican mailing lists recently received an appeal for funds from Dick Morris, President Bill Clinton's political strategist in 1995-1996, asking for a contribution of between $25 and $100 or more to finance a film documentary *critical of Senator Hillary Clinton*... Signing the letter as "Former Clinton Adviser."

Who wouldn't get a little paranoid when surrounded by all this betrayal and character assassination?

The irresponsible journalists also disturb me. I am haunted by a sense that we don't yet know fully what happened on 9/11. Tony and William Chaytor have undertaken an engineering investigation on high-rise buildings, an investigation that has serious implications for the safety of our urban dwelling population. I think that Tony's suspicion that thermite was used to demolish WTC-7 is well founded, but not proven beyond reasonable doubt. What I find most sinister is the denial of flaw and responsibility that has become rabid in our culture. When did it start? Port Chicago? Yes! That was the first covert government operation that not only defied morality, but also became the breeding ground for the corruption derived from America's passion to become the world's *only* superpower. And yet, the media is blindly obsessed with the possibility that I am frigid... and drove poor Bill into the arms of other women—or that I am lesbian, having an affair with Carmella Meeks to vent my bleeding liberal heart and recapture the feminist vote.

My godmother smoked a pipe, and she never told a lie. But if there were some truth she wanted to conceal she would scrape out the pipe, put the scrapings in her mouth, say "lovely," and then pretend to be unable to speak. Keeping silent is also an art. But I cannot keep quiet any longer. However, it is difficult to keep the music going sometimes when my opponents resort to telling lies. On the way back to work, I let my I-Pod ease me through intersections, traffic lights, and then the Whitehouse... Oops, I have absently walked into the wrong office. I am supposed to be seeing my psychiatrist.

# CHAPTER 23: HILLARY, 2008

Many people who work at the White House know me well—but the staff behind the wrong door don't—yet don't give me that go away look, even though I have never been to the cigar shop before. We know much more now than we did even a few years ago about how the human brain develops, and about what children and underprivileged people need from their environment to develop character, empathy, and intelligence. When I put this knowledge into practice—when I finally become President, the results will be astonishing. When I read, travel, and talk with people around the world, it is increasingly clear to me that nearly every problem children face today has been solved somewhere, by someone. I also sense a new willingness on the part of many parents and citizens to turn down the decibel level on our political conflicts, and start paying attention to what works.

Oh my God! There is Rupert Murdoch and Newt Villain coming from the oval office of President Bush. At the age of seventy-six, Rupert Murdoch has finally proven to me that he is willing to pay attention and change. But I used to think Rupert was the enemy. It started with Newt's book scandal: When Newt was first offered $2.5 million, then $4.5 million was offered by Harper Collins--a publishing company owned by Rupert Murdoch, (who also owns the Fox TV network and newspapers and TV stations around the world)--and Newt was merely the Republican Speaker of the House of Congress… and of small literary interest. But, Murdoch has been having problems with a complaint by NBC that Fox is a foreign owned TV network--which is against US law. In the past, Murdoch's publishing company, Harper Collins, has offered million dollar book contracts to several conservative politicians--in countries where Murdoch was having regulatory trouble, including England (Margaret Thatcher, Jeffrey Archer) and China (Deng Xiaoping's daughter). A week after the initial offer, Newt met with the mogul Rupert Murdoch and his legislative lobbyist--to discuss politics, including the NBC complaint. As facts about the deal were made public, and even Republicans criticized him, Gingrinch decided to give up the $4.5 million advance for a still-lucrative deal based on royalties.

Gingrinch's story kept changing throughout the controversy. First, Newt's spokesman said that Murdoch knew nothing about Gingrinch and the book deal. On Friday January 13, Newt's spokesman admitted that Murdoch actually met Newt on a park bench the week before the deal was made, but claimed he didn't talk about it. He also said he knew nothing about Murdoch's lobbyist being at their meeting. The next day, he admitted the lobbyist was there, but claimed he didn't say so because no one asked. Newt also said repeatedly that the Harper Collins book wasn't his idea; that a literary agent named Lynn Chu had sought him and proposed it. After Ms. Chu proposed that, Gingrinch's associate, Jeff Eisenach, called her first on Newt's behalf, Eisenach and Newt's spokesman admitted that was true.

Rupert Murdoch has grown his giant mammoth of a media company, *The News*

*Corporation,* into one of the largest and most influential media groups in the world--from a small town newspaper in Australia. Murdoch wields considerable power with his global media company and is often wooed by politicians to persuade him to favorably cover their campaigns. His empire covers television, filmed entertainment, cable network programming, book publishing, direct broadcast satellite television, magazines and newspapers operating in the United States, Australia, Continental Europe, the United Kingdom, Asia and the Pacific Basin. President Roger Ailes of Murdoch affiliate, Fox News, has claimed in a *Wall Street Journal* article, that his boss is a Republican-hater, and lists all the books that Harper Collins has published that are severely critical of Republican leaders: "Murdoch published a book that says, *The G. W. Bush takeover of the world economy is designed to benefit such corporations as Bechtel, Lockheed Martin, Chevron, Texaco, Halliburton, and many others.* Murdoch loves Jesus because he purchased Zondervan, the Christian publishing house. It could also be that Murdoch is a closet liberal. Murdoch-the-media-mogul has released an ambitious plan to tackle the problems of global warming by making his global corporation carbon neutral. He told 47,000 employees that they must not only cut their energy use, but that the word on climate change will also be put out through his many media outlets.

There's an old saying I like--*you can't roll up your sleeves and get to work if you're still wringing your hands.* So if you, like me, are worrying about our kids; about what they read in books and smutty magazines, hear on acidic and parochial radio talk shows, watch on TV, the movies, see in sex scenes--and on porn sites… hear on the street and in the school yard, and what they smell in the back rooms at parties—we had better match our actions to our words?

*It Takes A Village to Raise a Child* was my first book. I chose that old African proverb for the title because it offers a timeless reminder that children will thrive only if their families thrive, and if the whole of society cares enough to provide an encouraging environment for them. The sage who first offered that proverb would undoubtedly be bewildered by what constitutes the modern village. In earlier times and places--and until recently in our own culture--the concept of *village* meant an actual geographic place where individuals and families lived and worked together.

For most of us, though, the village doesn't look like that anymore. In fact, it's difficult to paint a picture of the modern transnational village; so frantic and fragmented has much of our culture become. Extended families rarely live in the same town, let alone the same house. In many communities, crime and fear keep us behind locked doors. Where we used to chat with neighbors on stoops and porches, now we watch TV while isolated in our darkened living rooms.

We can't turn away from this new world however. The horizons of the contemporary village extend well beyond the town line. From the moment we are born, we are exposed to vast numbers of diverse people and influences through the media. Technology connects us to the impersonal global village it has created. I am still trying to measure the social consequences of the proposed new legislation to make telecommuting compulsory at work places, in order to reduce carbon emissions and thereby to start mitigating global warming.

To many, this new world seems dehumanizing and inhospitable. It is not surprising, then, that there is a yearning for the *good old days*--as a refuge from the global problems of the present. But by turning away, we blind ourselves to the continuing, evolving presence of the village in our lives, and its critical importance for how we live together. The village can no longer be defined as a place on a map, or as a list of people or organizations, but its essence remains the same: it is the network of values and relationships that support and affect our lives.

We cannot move forward by simply looking back to the past for easy solutions. Even if a golden age had existed, we could not merely graft it onto today's busier, more impersonal and complicated world. Instead, our challenge is to arrive at a consensus of values and a common vision of what we can do, individually and collectively, to save the environment and build strong families and communities. Creating that consensus in a democracy depends on seriously considering other points of view, resisting the lure of extremist rhetoric, and balancing individual rights and freedoms with personal responsibility and mutual obligations.

The true test of the consensus we build is how well we care for our children. For a child, the village must remain personal. Talking to a baby while changing a diaper, playing airplane to entice a toddler to accept a spoonful of food, tossing a ball back and forth with a teenager, are tasks that cannot be carried out in cyberspace. They require the presence of caring adults who are dedicated to children's growth, nurturing, and well-being. Telecommuting will allow parents to stay at home with their children, so new opportunities can arise from environmental constraints.

What we do to participate in and support the responsible network of American adults--from the way we care for our own children to the jobs we do, the causes we join, and the kinds of legislation we support--is mirrored every day in the experiences of America's children. We can read our national character most plainly in the children that are raised by our system. How we care for our own and other people's children isn't only a question of morality; our self-interest is at stake too. No family is immune to the influences of the larger society. No matter what my husband and I do to protect and prepare our daughter, her future will be affected by how other children are being raised. I don't want her to grow up in an America sharply divided by income, race, or religion. I would like to minimize the odds of her suffering at the hands of someone who didn't have enough love or discipline, opportunity or responsibility, as a child. I want her to believe, as her father and I do, that the American Dream is within reach of any individual, or any community, willing to work hard and take responsibility. I want her to live in an America community that is part of a global village, that is gaining strength and promise for its members as a village of hope and opportunity… and enjoy the protection of the constitution of the United States, and the services that can be most efficiently provided by a large coordinated federal organization such as environmental protection, social services, postal services, justice, and defense.

# CHAPTER 24: HILLARY, 2008

Now that I am ready to liberate myself from the shackles of Newton PR, from the corruption of Newt Gingrinch, and from the duplicity of my campaign manager, Mark Penn--I can admit that my presidential aspirations really started back in the summer of 1975, back when I married Bill. It wasn't long before the next statewide elections in Arkansas, and I had developed the taste for winning elections. One of my election-winning assets is a gift for reading people. But my election campaign with Newton PR has become manipulated and counterproductive. There are *surely* other PR firms out there available to address the issues that truly demand our full focus--such as the pollution of our environment, health care, global trading practices, and the education of our children.

I thought that I was about finished with Newt Gingrinch back in April. But, unfortunately we were linked again—linked in another scandal on the six o'clock news. At that point, Gingrinch's mission was clearly different from that stated in our contract--*to promote me as the most qualified presidential candidate.* Lord have mercy! Newt Gingrinch got *me* painted in the six o'clock news as anti-labor and pro-tobacco. And that may have turned the election tide against me...

Several of the union officials who are pledged to support me have expressed concern that my Democratic Presidential Campaign Committee used Newton PR as my publicist. The problem is that Newton PR has a subsidiary, the global PR firm Burson-Marsteller (B-M), and Newton PR appointed Mark Penn, CEO of B-M and president of the polling firm Penn, Schoen and Berland Associates, (PSB) as my official campaign manager. For God's sake! Newton PR try to cover up by stating that they appointed the new villain, Mark Penn, merely as a "strategic adviser," in my presidential election campaign.

Mark Penn and I were in the news again--initially because B-M has a specialist unit that advises clients on defeating union campaigns. Mark Penn is also implicated in promoting tobacco, and most recently as the PR person for the government of Colombia—"Hillary Clinton's chief campaign strategist met with Colombia's ambassador to the U.S. on Monday to discuss a bilateral free-trade agreement, a pact the Presidential candidate, Hillary Clinton opposes. Two Colombian officials confirmed attendance by the adviser, Mark Penn. He wasn't there in his campaign role, but in his separate job as chief executive of Burson-Marsteller Worldwide, an international communications and lobbying firm. The firm has a contract with the South American nation to promote congressional approval of the trade deal, among other things, according to filings with the Justice Department."

I have little problem with Mark Penn holding down two jobs, or privately disagreeing with his boss on certain issues. But when you're the outspoken chief strategist of a Presidential campaign that was targeting blue-collar voters wouldn't you want to avoid the appearance of hypocrisy? Wouldn't that be a good strategy?

Not surprisingly, Newton PR merely shrugged off the criticism, insisting that *Mark Penn is a vital member of our team and will continue to manage the Hillary campaign.* In an email to Atlantic Online, Penn wrote that that he had "never personally done such anti-labor work" and insisted that he has "strong personal sympathies with the labor movement." The reason why someone who proclaims their pro-labor sympathies would ever be employed by a PR firm that runs an anti-labor unit went unexplained. Even if one accepts Penn's explanation at face value, it left me wondering whom he really works for?

A little digging now reveals that, for well over two decades, both Penn and his opinion polling company PSB have advised the tobacco industry on how to counter the campaigns of the tobacco control movement. Based on internal tobacco industry documents, it is clear that Penn and his colleagues have little personal sympathy for those of us promoting policies that put public health ahead of the interests of the tobacco industry. What sort of anti-labor pro-tobacco monster would seek to run a democratic Presidential election campaign with such a conflict of interest?

Amazingly, all that bad press worked to improve my declining opinion poll ratings, although not enough to win... The voters evidently liked that I had conflicts in my campaign team. "We shall hopefully win the primaries – despite Penn," I said back at that time. Now that I have failed, the liberal press, and the Truman Show, now describe Newton PR and Mark Penn as "foxes in the Hillary hen house."

When Penn's Columbia deal was revealed I fired Mark Penn--another media leach had been levered from the chain that was dragging my Presidential campaign down—but too late.

Kneeling before the hotel refrigerator, I am alarmed by the two suede shoes beside me on the merino carpet. Bill is back. For a girl who could have damaged her first boyfriend at school... when I punched his nose--to love anything as much as Bill is dangerous, especially when it is a politician, and especially when it is the duality of Bill Clinton, the charming man who is addicted to sex—the man who I have settled on to love. The best thing I know is to love just a little bit, so when one Bill or the other breaks my hope, and he shoves his latest love letter into my in-tray, well, maybe I'll have a little love left over for myself.

My heart finally stops bouncing from the excitement of being so close to Bill.

"No Bill," I say, "I can't see why you would imagine I had it any easier than you." Long lashes make my eyes seem busier than they are, deceptively--even when I hold a steady gaze as I do now.

"I never said that you did," Bill says.

"But you think that sometimes."

Carmella and Tony join us for a late dinner to pretend-celebrate my victory in the last primary—the night before I will have to concede to Obama... I know that Bill will not get anywhere with regards to practicing his sex addiction around Carmella so I am able to relax at dinner and start planning for a possible refurbishing of the White House in 2012...even though I do not yet have a strategy to achieve this impossible but essential task. It is recommended that I request Barack Obama to be my running mate then. I am not sure about that!

In his 1995 memoir, "Dreams From My Father," written before Mr. Obama entered politics, Obama provides a revealing, introspective account of his efforts to trace his family's tangled roots and his attempts to come to terms with his absent father, who left home when he was still a toddler. (That adds up to three men: Bill Clinton, Newt, and Barack Obama who are fatherless and power hungry.) That book did an evocative job of conjuring the author's multicultural childhood: his absent father was from Kenya, his mother was from Kansas, and the young Mr. Obama grew up in Hawaii and Indonesia.

And the book was equally candid about his youthful struggles: pot, booze and "maybe a little blow," he wrote, could "push questions of who I was out of my mind," flatten "out the landscape of my heart, blur the edges of my memory." Most memorably, the book gave the reader a heartfelt sense of what it was like to grow up in the 1960's and 70's, straddling America's color lines: the sense of knowing two worlds and belonging to neither, the sense of having to forge an identity of his own.

Mr. Obama's second book, "The Audacity of Hope"—the phrase comes from his 2004 Democratic Convention keynote address, which made him the party's rising young hope—is much more of a political document. Portions of the volume read like out-takes from a stump speech, and the bulk of it is devoted to laying out Mr. Obama's policy positions on a host of issues--from education to health care to the war in Iraq.

While Mr. Obama occasionally slips into the flabby platitudes favored by politicians in his second book, enough of the narrative voice in this volume is recognizably similar to the one in "Dreams From My Father," an elastic, personable voice that is capable of accommodating everything from dense discussions of foreign policy to streetwise reminiscences, incisive comments on constitutional law to new-age personal asides. The reader comes away with a feeling that Mr. Obama has not reinvented himself as he has moved from job to job—from community organizer in Chicago, editor of The Harvard Law Review, professor of constitutional law, civil rights lawyer, and most recently to State Senator--but has instead internalized all those roles, stuffing down, rather than working out, whatever internal contradictions they might have produced.

Reporters and politicians continually use the word authenticity to describe Mr. Obama, pointing to his ability to come across to voters as a regular person, not a pre-packaged poll. And in the book he often speaks to the reader as if he were an old friend from back in the old days, salting policy recommendations with colorful asides about the absurdities of political life.

Obama recalls a meet-and-greet encounter at the White House with George W. Bush, who warmly shook his hand, then "turned to an aide nearby, who squirted a big dollop of hand sanitizer in the president's hand."

"Good stuff," he quotes the President as saying, as he offered his guest some. "Keeps you from getting colds."

And he recounts a trip he took through Illinois with an aide, who scolded him for asking for Dijon mustard at a dinner event, worried the Senator would come across as an elitist. The confused waitress simply said: "We got Dijon if you want it."

In his 2004 keynote address, Mr. Obama spoke of the common ground Americans share: "There is not a Black America and White America and Latino America and Asian America--there's the United States of America." And the same message--rooted in his youthful efforts to grapple with racial stereotypes, racial loyalty and class resentments--threads its way through the pages of this book. Despite the red state versus blue state divide, despite racial, religious and economic divisions, Mr. Obama writes, "We are becoming more, not less, alike beneath the surface: Most Republican strongholds are 40 percent Democrat, and vice versa. The political labels of liberal and conservative rarely track people's personal attributes."

Mr. Obama eschews the couched language that has come part of political discourse, and he rejects what he sees as the either-or formulations of his elders who came of age in the 60's: "In the back-and-forth between Bill Clinton and Newt Gingrinch, and in the elections of 2000 and 2004," he writes, "I sometimes felt as if I were watching the psychodrama of the Baby Boom generation-- a tale rooted in old grudges and revenge plots hatched on a handful of college campuses long ago--played out on the national stage. The victories that the 60's generation brought about--the admission of minorities and women into full citizenship, the strengthening of individual liberties and the healthy willingness to question authority-- have made America a far better place for all its citizens. But what has been lost in the process, and has yet to be replaced, are those shared assumptions, that quality of trust and fellow feeling, that bring us together as Americans."

His thoughts on domestic and foreign policy try to hew to this consensus-building line. Some of his recommendations devolve into little more than fuzzy statements of the obvious: I.e., that America's "addiction to oil" is affecting the economy and undermining national security, or that the education system needs to be revamped and improved. Others echo Bill Clinton's "third way," methodically triangulating between traditionally conservative and traditionally liberal ideas.

Mr. Obama writes that "Conservatives--and Bill Clinton--were right about welfare as it was previously structured. By detaching income from work and by making no demands on welfare recipients other than a tolerance for intrusive bureaucracy and an assurance that no man lived in the same house as the mother of his children, the old A.F.D.C. program sapped people of their initiative and eroded their self respect."

He uses the Bush administration's tough language to talk about national security in the age of terrorism. "If we have to go it alone, the American people stand ready to pay any price and bear any burden to protect our country." But adds, crucially, "Once we get beyond matters of self-defense... I am convinced that it will almost always be in our strategic interest to act multilaterally rather than unilaterally when we use force around the world."

He assails President Bush for waging an unnecessary and misguided war in Iraq, and for promoting an "Ownership Society that magnifies the uneven risks and rewards of today's winner-take-all economy." Yet he also takes the Democrats to task for becoming *the party of reaction*. "In reaction to a war that is ill-conceived, we appear suspicious of all military action. In reaction to those who proclaim the market can cure all ills, we resist efforts to use market principles to tackle pressing problems. In reaction to religious overreach, we equate tolerance with secularism. and forfeit the moral language that would help infuse our policies with a larger meaning. We lose elections and hope for the courts to foil Republican plans. We lose the courts and wait for a White House scandal."

The second book does not possess the searching candor of Obama's first book. But Mr. Obama strives in those pages to ground his policy thinking in simple common sense--be it, "Growing the size of our armed forces to maintain reasonable rotation schedules," or reining in spending and rethinking tax policy to bring down the nation's huge deficit--while articulating these ideas in level-headed, non-partisan prose. That, in itself, is something unusual, not only in these venomous pre-election days, but also in these increasingly polarized and polarizing times.

*My advisors argued at the start of the year that I should invite Obama to join the Hillary ticket before he snowballs in popularity.* Were they serious?

In contrast to Obama, the liberation of children has been a major platform in my political career, and will continue so, especially during my anticipated Presidency in 2012. It is more than coincidence that I have involved myself with poor Yolanda's orphaned children: Isobel and Sophie Chaytor. The presence of children is soothing, but I will have difficult weeks ahead when dealing with the Republicans and Barack Obama. On my better days I have tried to view it all as part of the ebb and flow of the rich tapestry of the electoral cycle, akin to a political market correction. Other times the veins on the inside of my wrist throb because my blood has become cold due to the heartache of electoral rejection.

On not-so-bad days, I merely fault myself for botching health care reform back in the nineties--coming on too strong and galvanizing our opponents. There are still plenty of people inside and outside the White House who are ready to point fingers when some government program misfires. It is hard to ignore the grumbling. I have to develop a new strategy for repairing the environment, and the Republicans won't like what I have in mind--ratifying the Kyoto agreement and introducing a carbon tax on industry and wealthy individuals.

One dreary November morning, I stopped by the Whitehouse after a meeting with Tony Chaytor, and glanced at the framed photograph of Eleanor Roosevelt displayed on the library wall. I am a huge fan of Eleanor Roosevelt, and I have long collected portraits and mementos from her career. Seeing her calm, determined visage brought to mind some of her wise words: "A woman is like a teabag. She never knows how strong she is until she's in hot water."

I go home and watch a rerun of the final of the *Hillary series* put out by Newton PR-- now that some influential Democrats are starting to get suspicious that I was railroaded, and want a little justice. Perhaps as a consolation for all my suffered injustices, ironically, Newt Gingrinch received an Alphar Journalism Excellence Award for his show that played in April… but it was Tony Chaytor, who developed the script as part of his ongoing efforts to educate the public to the history of deceit by US administrations… but Newt had the gall to accept.

I have often joked in my speeches that I have had imaginary conversations with Eleanor Roosevelt to solicit her advice on a range of subjects. Eleanor is an ideal person with whom to help analyze problems. I have been tracking her career as one of America's most controversial First Ladies, sometimes quite literally. Wherever I venture, Eleanor has been there before me. I have visited dust bowl towns, poor neighborhoods in New York City, and outposts as remote as Uzbekistan, where Eleanor had already blazed a trail. She championed many causes that are important to me: Civil rights, child labor laws, refugees and human rights. She drew harsh criticism from the media and some in government for daring to define the role of First Lady in her own terms.

Eleanor was called everything from a communist agitator to a homely old meddler. She rankled members of her husband's administration--Interior Secretary Harold Ickes Sr., (Father of Bill's Deputy Chief of Staff and my friend,) complained that Eleanor should stop interfering and "stick to knitting,"--and complained that she drove FBI Director J. Edgar Hoover crazy. Her spirit and commitment were powerful, and she never let her critics slow her down.

So, what would Eleanor have to say about my present predicament? Not much. In her view there is no point in agonizing over day-to-day setbacks. You have to press on and do the best you can. Controversy can be terribly isolating, but Eleanor Roosevelt had good friends, who she relied upon for support when she felt unsafe or besieged in the world of politics. FDR's trusted advisor, Louis Howe, was her confidante, as were her Associated Press reporter and lover, Lorena Hickok, and her personal secretary, Malvina Thompson. I am fortunate to have a loyal staff, and a good circle of friends. Although I have trouble imagining Eleanor blowing off steam with her confidants-- that's what I have done ever since my days as First Lady. Arkansas friends, Diane Blair and Anne Henry, who visited me during Bill's post-election hangover, know me well, and they were kind enough to offer their support, as well as perspectives on politics and history.

I am proud of my achievements. For example, on my final visit, as attorney for the plaintiff, to the Rezko building before it collapsed: I was with a senior journalist from the Elsinore Times, who pointed out a pair of window cleaners riding an electrically powered scaffold up the face of the building. The scaffold acted as a plumb bob and measured that the Rezko building had a substantial lean. I called William Chaytor to get his take. His response: "Yes. I just ordered the building evacuated. It's in imminent danger of collapse. The average wind speed in Lower Manhattan is almost five miles per hour greater than in Chicago, and they call Chicago the windy city."

Then William broke down, anxious, speaking rapidly, rambling about cracks in the foundation that opened and closed as the building swayed in the wind, aghast that an engineer could have designed such a flawed building.

Old Grandpa Chaytor and I had lunch that day, sitting on one of the benches at the south side of the plaza facing the Rezko building. William needed to talk. "After spending the weekend sleeping with the plans and specs," William said, "that building seems like an old friend. I feel sympathy for it."

I laughed in surprise, "That's an odd thing to feel for a building. Concern, maybe, but sympathy?"

William's answer kept me thinking: "Not odd if you think of it as alive. Once you know how the beams and girders and columns carry the loads to the ground, how the whole thing twists and flexes in the wind, how it settles and changes with time, it takes on a personality of it's own. It's constantly moving, stretching, and straining, like an animal. In this case a sick animal."

William and I were there, trying to make the right diagnosis for the sickness.

William looked to the horizon: "Maybe I can push the owner into doing some repairs. Usually I get called in when the patient has already died. Then I'm the coroner picking through the remains and guessing the cause of death. And somewhere, there's a panic-stricken engineer who wonders if he miscalculated, and how he'll face his family if he did." Then, after a moment's thought, William Chaytor turned back to me and smiled with a trace of embarrassment, "That's why I feel sympathy."

William called me two days later to say he had discovered the fundamental problem. "The steel supplier shaved so much steel off the original design that the building doesn't have enough ballast from it's own weight to stop the wind from heaving it. One day soon a strong wind will topple the entire Rezko tower over."

The Rezko building was demolished with thermite that afternoon – soon after the NYC building department was shown William Chaytor's calculations."

My ratings drop another three points after that show airs. Newt Gingrinch affords himself a smirk while accepting his Excellence Award at the gala dinner... until the host poses a mischievous question: "Is it necessary to understand the *surprise attack* on Pearl Harbor in order to comprehend the nature of the *surprise attack* on September 11?

I enjoy another surprise when Barack Obam calls upon me and asks me to be Secrtary of State in his new administration.

Of course, I accept. It's my duty to serve—but I shall also run for the Presidency in 2012... Obama promised me that he will only serve one term.

Oops! That is top secret.

# PART X: CARMELLA

## CHAPTER 25: 2010

July 12, 2010:

I only joined the Navy to learn how to drive a nuclear-powered submarine. I enjoy my real career, as a hooker—but a call girl like me could never stand even the thought of the job as a shop attendant or President of the United States. But Hillary is different, so now that her dream of the Presidency is virtually over she seems to have lost her spark--and her mind. Tony says that she may have to be institutionalized because all the rejections and smear campaigns have been too much for her. She has become delusional, thinking a right wing conspiracy is going to steal her opportunity to become President. Poor girl. I wish I could help her.

We had a good evening at the Bohemian club tonight. I had three clients, and Rachael had four. Rachael and I are the last ones to go to bed, and we are the only girls sleeping in the captain's quarters on the submarine--with silk sheets, satellite television, and a huge bed. The toilet makes a strange noise when you flush it. After Newt and his friends finished their drinks and drove back to the Bohemian Grove, we poured ourselves some cranberry juice and went to our cabin. Many of the girls are alcoholics, so we lock up all the freezers on the submarine before we sleep. But it wouldn't be necessary to do that because of Rachael and me. She is not too fond of drinking now. The difference between the two of us is that Rachael always knew how to drink. She could handle a shot or two of whiskey, if a client wanted her to drink. I drank too many of those energy drinks earlier tonight; it feels like I'll never be able to fall asleep... So we start to chat, and Rachael tells me one of her stories:

Once upon a time she went to a room with this client, at a club in Vero Beach. He took his underwear off and asked her to use it as a blindfold on him. Then he asked her to hand him her panties. When she argued that she didn't use any, he asked for her bra instead, and wanted her to tie up his hands with it.

After he was tied up, and the blindfold was in place, he asked her to talk dirty. Rachael has a vast repertoire of that, on account of her years of experience in the business, and started off: "Picture two girls with their legs spread, licking each other and blah, blah, blah... I talked dirty like that for half an hour, while the client touched himself with his free hand." Rachael started to get fed up with that because the guy wouldn't cum. So she decided to get really wild: "How do you like two fat guys fucking each other good?" The guy moaned with lust, so she continued: "You know, I have fantasies about getting fucked by a horse. I'd love to feel it's hard dick and all that warm cum." She's a real pro; I've got to say it. She got so low she was embarrassed to tell me the exact words she had used. He sensed she was so open-minded about it that he felt free to let all his demons out.

Rachael was all ears, and he ended up telling her about this so called church that he was part of back in Texas... telling her about the other members, the kids they kept at their headquarters and the horrible things they did there. He still had the blindfold and couldn't see Rachael's tears. Children are everything to her, and she wanted to kill the guy after hearing the things he told her. I guess that if she had a gun she'd have shot him right then and there.

~~~~~~~~~~~~~~~~~~

July 14:

I despise perverts and pedophiles. What can I do to protect the children? The perverts force girls and young women to fondle each other's genitals. Rachael didn't know that client's real name, and even if she knew it, she wouldn't be able to do much about it now. I guess some of the girls that go missing end up at phony churches like the one he described.

That story makes me hate such men even more. I really loathe those pigs! I don't want to stay tied to shore one more day than I have to. Life on shore would be impossible now if I didn't have a secret life… and Marise. I wonder where my daughter is right now? Is she OK? I start to get paranoid. She is a beautiful young woman. What if they kidnap her? Our holiday with Nana Rita last winter went well. Rita suspects that there is something up with me, so I keep my plans secret, even from Tony and Marise.

I telephone and ask Marise's math tutor to stay with her until I pick her up. I have to spend another hour with Newt. What if perverts kidnapped Marise while she was waiting for me to arrive--because I was with Newt? Losing Eleanor was bad enough!

The sun disappears behind a cloud. I am getting more and more paranoid these days--afraid that Tony will find me out sooner rather than later. I can't stand to be thirty miles away from Marise; Rachael's pedophile story scares me… Scares me more that my worst times back in the Magic Touch days I was worried a lot the last year at the Magic Touch. Finally I packed up my stuff in preparation for leaving there. Vanessa told me I was out of my mind to consider leaving. I was too mad at men to act like my normal self. Arrogant men make me furious. But there was hardly any money left because I had formed an attraction to cocaine. Hillary advised me to seek help from a professional therapist; Hillary and I had become friends, *so it's not right for me to counsel you in depth*. The therapist, Elisa, gave me a free session. I promised to pay for it when I made more money. Elisa raised an eyebrow. "But I don't know when it will happen." All I had was about $150. I hoped I would find a way to pay my energy bill. It would be too hard for Marise if the company cut our electricity. She had just got back from her vacation with my mom in Fort Pierce, so we were together almost all of the time.

I hadn't been working at the Magic Touch for several weeks because classes had started at college, and also because I was fragile and weary, like I was about to break up from myself. I only felt better when I fell asleep, or received a letter from Hillary. Hillary hardly ever talked long on the phone--she always sounded nervous and hurried, sort of cold. I slept a lot, or just lay there. I suffered from some kind of mental exhaustion. Mondays were bad. I only felt good up until six seconds after I opened my eyes in the morning, or after I snorted cocaine. The moment I realized I was awake I resented it. I figured out that I was getting stale at the Magic Touch. That's why I do the drugs--to numb those stale feelings. But when I didn't go to work I still wanted to do the drugs. The anguish was unbearable until I got high. I worried about how to make ends meet. I needed money. Newt was trying to change our scene, becoming weird and domesticated. Elisa tried to encourage me at therapy. She told me that I'd gone through a lot, and couldn't give up now. I cried from the moment I got to her office. The main thing I talked about was how would I ever manage to make any money again, how could I go to work like that, after what had happened with Newt. I don't have the strength to stay up late every single night at the Magic Touch--and absorb the smoky air. Elisa said I would find an answer, and that I just needed to calm down.

My sister left a note on my door back in February 2001, saying that Tony had been down to Fort Pierce, visiting with my father and looking for me.

Grandpa Carl was losing his mind in the old folks home. An idea occurred to me. I tracked down Tony in Washington DC, and gathered Grandpa… I wonder. Did Newt arrange the EQE job for Tony? I bet he did--to get me hooked on Tony again and to get me back to DC. Cunning bastard!

~~~~~~~~~~~~~~~~~~~

August 11:

I've had some setbacks recently. When I was in the shower I started crying and caught myself praying. Sometimes I even get down on my knees repeating "Our Fathers" and "Hail Mary's" over and over. I recovered by learning some relaxation techniques, by enrolling in that belly dancing class in Emmetsburg that I had wanted, and by going to Reiki sessions… I was able to pay for these classes with the extra money I got from Newt, from a whoring job at the Skulls Mansion near the White House.

When I got home from the Skulls mansion, I prepared dinner for Tony and the children, cleaned up the house, did the laundry, and cooked some rare steak for myself. The kitchen cupboards were always full of cockroaches. I don't like them. I should have got rid of those creatures rather than leave poor Tony to deal with them.

~~~~~~~~~~~~~~~~~~~~~~~~~

August 28:

Last week in DC, I was with a guy who works at the local electricity company. I went to meet him at the Hotel Grande, and made $140, plus 20 bucks for the receptionist. I was especially devoted to it, and we had sex three times. The guy was real gentle, and I was in the mood for it. Sometimes I need sex, and sometimes I need it a lot. We talked and I gave him a massage. He complained about his wife and told me she was too cold and strict.

In my view, every girl should be allowed to be with various partners before she chooses to hook up with anyone, and after she's married too. There are people who remain a virgin until marriage--my mom, for instance--I know she was a virgin when she got married. But what if my father was a disaster in bed? I pitied her, really… Dad posed virginity as his requirement of Mom before he would marry her--the day before the wedding. They had never discussed the matter until then, and I guess he would have called the whole thing off if he found out his wife didn't have her hymen intact. It doesn't make any sense, for Christ's sake! Luckily for me no one gives a damn about hymens nowadays.

142

This new boy was a sales representative from Gaithersburg MD, on the road all the time, and didn't have much money to spend. He called me because he really needed me. After being on the road and alone for two weeks, he started to hear lustful moans from the next room in his hotel. The Hotel Grande is considered almost one of the best in town, but they don't have cable TV, and some of the rooms are interconnected--with just a hollow wooden door separating them.

After hearing the suspicious sounds, he peeked through a crack in the door and caught a glimpse of a naked woman. The sight drove him mad. He told the receptionist he needed a hooker for a hundred bucks, *cause that was all the money he had with him.*

I gave him a massage with the lotion I had purchased. I like to do some things that are not purely mechanical and straight to the point. Sometimes I chat a little bit, and I try to show some affection, although most of the clients lack the sensitivity to return any of it. But fortunately I'm not the kind of girl who attracts psycho killers. I said goodbye to the boy, and he said that he liked me a lot. I said he should tell that to the receptionists so they'd call me more often.

You need to know how to market yourself. The boy called the receptionist right away, and I was on my way out when the man in the lobby told me he had another client waiting for me, and had negotiated a higher price. "The last one was *just* fascinated. What did you do to him?" I decided not to answer. A certain aura of mystery tends to make things better.

I keep questioning myself about men's attitudes, about the choices I've made in life, and about the way people tend to act rather than behave. And, above all, I question my own character... I question whether the burden of all my deceit is worth it. It may sound weird, but during those times in the face of life's challenges, when we find ourselves most fragile--such as when Eleanor was discovered to be autistic, there's a kind of supernatural force that takes hold of us and shows us we are able to go ahead and surpass it all. At those times life is not about following the law, or being moral, or having integrity. Sometimes you have to kill in self-defense! I wonder where the psychological boundaries are between those things we see as difficult to accomplish, like denying your own father--and the ones we might consider impossible, like abandoning your child at the gate of an adoption agency... or abandoning your husband--in order to survive.

~~~~~~~~~~~~~~~~~~~~~~~~~~~~~~~~~~

# CHAPTER 26: CARMELLA, 2012

April 5:

One of the things I hate is spilling coffee on my diary, and another is morning time. I look out my kitchen window over the dank fields while drinking a cup of acrid coffee. Hillary's private phone is calling me again. I avoid her now that she is crazy. Anyway, Hillary knows me so well that she would pick up on my anxiety about pulling my devious plan off. The carbon dioxide levels are no longer published in order to avoid panic. I overheard a scientist tell Newt, during a recent orgy at the Skulls Mansion, that carbon dioxide levels have increased 10 percent already this year. Despite the blackout on news, I have discovered that the biospheres that FEMA constructed have all been taken over by armed thugs who look like Hell's Angels--who are probably Republicans gone butch. Thugs will even invade backyard fallout shelters, so a submarine is the only sure way to survive.

I suffered from conflicted sadness like this once before, when I was on the verge of suicide after abandoning my baby Eleanor at the orphanage gate--sadness and anger that insisted Eleanor had no future with me, that she would never be able to enjoy any life that I might have, and that I would always be with the same problems of poverty, sadness, and disease--problems that seemed to have no solution. It is the small things in life that are difficult--like not feeling the soft spring breeze blowing the hairs on the back of my neck, or the nail from that board in the garage that has pierced my numb foot, or the unnoticed burn on my hand that occurred because I was shaking too much to pour the tea into my cup. The big things are not so difficult--like raising children and facing death--because my soul travels to all the different worlds. But why does God test me with this wicked pain? Is it because I am too bad, or am I too good? I really don't know! But I can imagine how cool a razor blade would feel against my wrist. Jesus promised me that I would never have to endure pain that is more than I can handle. Geez, You are coming unbearably close to my limit... driving me fucking crazy. In the name of Jesus, I beg you to explain--even half of what I am going through? Am I supposed to go insane? Am I the devil being punished, or a saint being trained for judgment day? I don't believe in judgment... because who knows the suffering that another has endured.

I am going to survive--while virtually everyone else on the planet will die from the poisoned environment. There is only one solution to global warming... escape in a submarine. How could anyone invade a nuclear powered submarine while it is sitting deep on the ocean floor under Antarctica? Newt and I, and my descendants, will wait there for maybe twenty years, until the pollution has subsided.

Today I do not cry. I have learnt to control myself, and I never talk to Tony about what I am feeling or planning--but when the end finally comes I will leave him a note telling him that I love him, and telling him how to find my tin fish and me. I do not talk to anyone now that the last days are approaching--except for my friend, Linda, who is going with me, to the Russian River initially, to do tricks for Newt and the Bohemians next week. Linda often tells me about the beauty of Santa Augustine down in Florida, where she will live one day. More and more I keep imagining the future of Linda and I, together in a nuclear submarine, under Antarctica. That plan keeps me from sleeping. Linda has beautiful children; Vanessa will mind our children at the Russian River Motels.

~~~~~~~~~~~~~~~~~~~~~~~

April 6:

We have again been invited to live aboard the official cathouse of Newt Gingrinch and the Bosses, for the weeklong duration of their Bohemian Grove power lunches and evening whoring. We will take Marise, Vanessa and the children aboard just before we are ready to cast-off. We don't even have to kill anyone... Club rules require that all the members of the exclusive Bohemian club sleep at the Grove during the ten days of session—so we will sleep on the submarine alone and unmolested.

What a contrast this excitement is to the hopelessness of my early adult years, which was mostly about by despair of finding an end to my vicious cycles of depression. When it first started I left Fort Pierce in search of happiness in Vero Beach! I got up at 6am and said to myself: "It's today that I start a new life!" Buck slept. I arranged two backpacks, lifted Marise, put the suitcases outside. Buck awoke, thinking I was arranging our girl for kindergarten. I left on my bicycle; I put a backpack on each side of the handlebars, and a smaller backpack on the rear. I had a hundred dollars, with which I would pay the kindergarten fees owed. I left to go live at Vero Beach.

I passed by my friend's house and hit her window. Vanessa opened the shutter, asking the time.

"I'm fed up. I'm going to live in Vero Beach. I can't stand my life here!"

Vanessa said that if I was keen we could go together. I waited outside, with Marise in my lap. Vanessa left a note for her boyfriend, saying that we were going go to Dodger Town (Vero Beach is near Dodger Town) and she would stay a week with me to help me with some things. Vanessa had freedom. We traced our plan. First, we would sell my bicycle at Terri's sale. Terri would drive us, in her car to the nearest city, to avoid being seen by any friends of Buck on the bus or hitchhiking. But Terri's car was so noisy and dangerous that the Police check point would not let us travel further. We hitched a ride in a truck for the rest of the distance to Vero Beach. and thus started our future. A little more than a year before I'd had gone to Vanessa for help because of money problems, and she told me, in a very practical way, that I should go to the Magic Touch. "It's near here, in Vero Beach," she said. "I've worked there for sometime, it's a good place for call girls. When you arrive at the bus terminal find a cab driver and ask him to take you to the finest brothel in town. Then you pray to God and ask Him to give you a not too hard first time. If you have the stomach, you'll do it forever. After the first one, things get easier."

When I got to the freeway off ramp, a cab driver took us to the Magic Touch. The facilities were nice and the girls—or at least most of them— looked either Black, or Hispanic like me. First I stood in the corner, just watching, but pretty soon I'd made friends with an older blonde girl who was different. Eventually, two guys approached and sat at our table. I watched her every move and tried to imitate her. She set the price for both of us, after realizing I was new to the business. As I followed the guy upstairs, I quietly prayed and asked God to make things easy. It turned out to be the easiest hundred dollars I'd ever made in my life. And I never stopped doing it after that day.

It was cold in room no. 2 of Magic Touch. We wrapped ourselves in blankets against the unusual cold caused by an Atlantic storm, and lay there, watching the rain outside. Vanessa and I were close like we have known each other forever. We'd been friends for a long time and, come to think of it, our story is one of those that make you think that there's really no such thing as luck, but rather, there is fate.

Vanessa is a sister of Rejane, the religious lady from Fort Pierce who used to baby-sit my daughter. Vanessa was already 53 when I met her, but still very active. Although she didn't have the freshness of youth, that woman sure was a cunning lady. No one beats Vanessa in her ability to charm clients and get what she wants from them. She did it with everyone. She personally duped me several times. The first time I met Vanessa there was this Texan guy called Michael, who was seriously in love with Vanessa's daughter, Rachael. Michael sent Rachel $2,500 every month so Rachael wouldn't need to take any other clients. He said he would marry her and take her to Texas. This was the period when we all lived in the so-called House of Eleven Women. Rachael also works as a call girl now, with the alias of Bruno. She loves to surf. Rachael got pregnant with Maysa… who is now being raised by Vanessa. Michael was so in love that he wanted to take care of Vanessa, and Rachael, and Maysa, which shows just how crazy love can make us act. No man in his right mind would ever undertake that kind of responsibility. It just doesn't make any sense to the male's logic. But anyway, we were right there on the bed, chatting, and I asked Rachael, "But what did you do to Michael that made the guy fall so crazily in love with you?" "Well, girl, I have this rubber dildo and put it in his ass very gently every time we did it." I couldn't believe it. So the guy came to Florida four times a year, sent money to the woman every month, and wanted to marry her, all because of a rubber dong? Rachael's looks and her expertise as a hooker might lead you into thinking she is the hottest of all women, always ready to set the bed on fire. But she confessed to me that she always fakes it, that she doesn't give a damn about peckers because they can never make her cum. Yeah, she must have had a tough life then. I at least can enjoy most of my "dates." It's not that I have orgasms with every client, but let's say I don't have to fake it a lot either. I really like Rachael, and her mother: Vanessa told me a lot about Rachael that day. Gosh, it was so cold in room No. 2! We had to find more blankets to warm us up, and only left the room for a brief snack. But mother and daughter didn't get along, and were always fighting for the custody of Rachael's daughter. Rachael mistreated Maysa but wouldn't agree to give her away to Vanessa. One day Vanessa decided to take Maysa and run away. God, what a mess that was! Later Rachael told me she'd never forgive Vanessa because of that.

I think Rachael only ended up working as a hooker to hurt her mom. She found out what Vanessa did for a living in her early teenage years, and it was a harsh blow to Rachael. Things got even worse: Rachael always knew the name of her father. Then, around this time, she finally got the nerve to go look for him. She found out where the guy lived and went there. The man was alive and fine, but wouldn't help her. And worse than that, he confessed he wasn't her true father and only stood by the pregnant hooker, then known as Tania. as a favor to her. The truth is that not even Vanessa herself knows who the father is.

Back at room no. 2, I asked Rachael why she didn't marry Michael after all. She told me she would never stand his kisses or that "hard vicious dick" on a daily basis, and confessed that the guy gave her the creeps. But I wonder... could any guy be worse than wandering from brothel to brothel, trying to make ends meet and raise a daughter in the process? I can understand Rachael's point of view though, as I myself would never marry for money either. Fortunately I was still young and capable of avoiding that sad fate. But what about Vanessa? How long will she manage to keep working like this? Vanessa had eight true loves in her life. I have one, and would think that loving eight times was too much for one woman. But not for Vanessa, of course. I have good stories to tell myself, but the things she went through in her life are really amazing. Eight true loves, she told me, and only one of them was not a client. Strangely, things never worked out right in Rachael's life. Rachael has made a lot of money, but spent it all on clothes and other petty things.

Prostitution is against the law in most States. But the cops look the other way mostly. Rachael had to stop working for a few days because of bruises on her face. A client has never beaten me that bad. Men who have said they loved me were the ones who hit me. I never trust them when they say, "I love you." And I hope I never go through a situation like that. Except for one crazy freak that wanted me to piss on him and drank my piss, no client has ever offended me in any way. As to this guy Rachael got, I think he was deranged, or maybe on some kind of drug. I get frightened when I think about that kind of guy. I wonder if they act like that with all women, or do it just because we're prostitutes. Do their wives know about it? Why do they lead double lives? Why are some men such perverts? I don't see anything like that with women; none of my female friends is half as weird in bed. The kinkiest I've heard of is a girl named Adriana, who talks dirty throughout the whole session with a client. I've learned some good smuttiness from her. There are plenty of men who suffer from sexual deviations, but not as many women. I've never heard of a female rapist. Come to think of it, there was this maid who abused a little boy from the family she used to work for. But, statistically, the difference is huge. And most of the pedophiles are male. I've never heard of one woman who gets turned on when she sees two men having sex. I bet there are some, because we see all kinds of weird things in this world. But men like it better... many just love to see two women together.

As I sit here I wonder what would the clients think if they could hear the things we say. At breakfast, all the girls gossip about the clients they saw the night before. "The guy was a freak, you wouldn't believe what he did..." or, "Let me tell you what he had the nerve to do to himself." Almost all the girls at the club were hookers because they needed the money badly, or because they have nowhere else to go. Fights were frequent at the club, but most of the times the "family" there was much better than the broken homes we girls left behind.

I think a lot about it, and realize that all prostitutes come from dysfunctional families. We are all marked by the lack of the most basic support structure. No one is here for the sex itself (although there are some exceptions to the rule). All a girl wants from a client is that he pays her, does what he has to do quickly and leaves her free for the next one that hopefully they'll be able to find on the same night.

The guys usually feel like supermen when they finish. My friend Gena, the other day, faked it three times, and afterwards she heard the client boast to his friends that he had made her come three times in a row. But what about the men? How do they see us? How would they really like things to be? I bet the average guy's dream is to find a hooker that would flirt with them for hours without asking for any drinks, that would let them feel her all up, and then give them her phone number so they could call on the next day that he had a mind for her, and she'd go with him free of charge, just because the man is so hot. But girls who do things this way are not hookers. They're air-headed Barbie girl types who choose their boyfriends because of the cars they drive; girls that have big crushes on the hottest guy in town but pretend they're too pure to even think about that, or those who say they'd rather die than have sex for money, but are capable of worse just to ride in a luxury car. And this kind of attitude is nothing but prostitution as well, under the guise of social hypocrisy. That's why I like the call girls better, cause they are more real than the plastic Barbie girls who live in the suburbs. We hookers are hard-working girls that just want better lives for our children and ourselves.

Our life on the submarine will not be grand, but it will be better than that for the billions left behind to die from environmental poisoning. Maybe we didn't choose the perfect way to achieve it, but we girls are all going to survive global warming, armed with a sperm bank we have collected for ourselves over the years from the more intelligent clients. We anticipate that remote green countries like New Zealand will be inhabitable again in twenty years, and certainly within fifty years, provided the military powers of the aggressive nations don't nuke each other too severely. I am proud that we girls have such a strong instinct for survival, which is more than I can say for those idiots who live in the suburbs. It seems that humanity in general lost its survival instinct about the same time that men lost their sexual drive... even the young men take Viagra now. For many older men they only have sex with us prostitutes because they have lost all desire for their wives and girlfriends... A sign of these apocalyptic times. Sometimes prostitution is a woman's only option for sex. For some girls, prostitution has been a big miscalculation. For others of us, it is proving to be the best thing we ever did... in that it enables us to survive poverty.

Rachael is working with me now, for the Navy. Operating a nuclear sub isn't going to be much different that driving my father's tin fish... I called C-J just now and the submarine is still in operational order--but my father cut his finger badly while pruning grandma's roses. Rachael's daughter, Maysa, is the same age as my Marise, and she told me she wants to be just like me when she graduates from college. I love Maysa. She's a very mature girl on account of all the things she's gone through in life. Rachael used to take her when she'd see a client, and left the girl with her scrapbook and crayons in the other room while she was with her client.

~~~~~~~~~~~~~~~~~~~~~~~~~~~

# PART XI: TONY CHAYTOR

## CHAPTER 27: 2012

The naked sky is boasting, and hot air wraps lazily around DC this afternoon. Carmella and I have been instructed to take good care of Fluffy while Marise is away on a college trip. I hoist the shade umbrella. Fluffy jumps from under the table onto Carmella's knee. Carmella is working night shifts with the Navy now because there are some urgent modifications that need to be done to the entire Astute class of submarine--amazing nuclear powered submarines that can stay under water indefinitely. The more Carmella denied me in bed this morning the more I wanted sex. She slides her hand around Fluffy's ribcage, lifts Fluffy to her face, and buries her nose into the soft fur behind the cat's ear. Fluffy gives a twitch, wriggles, and then lies in Carmella's shaded lap. Carmella reaches for her coffee but Fluffy extends her claws. Carmella strokes her and Fluffy settles.

When it is time for me to go to my class Carmella walks me to my vehicle and reaches up to kiss me goodbye. "Tony! You must take Marise with you when you fly to New Zealand. It will be great for her." Carmella eyeballs me until I nod in agreement. "I'm visiting Hillary tomorrow," she says.

"Good. May I join you two?" I ask.

"No. Girl talk," she says.

"My class is not for an hour," I say, lifting Carmella's skirt.

"I love you so much," she whispers. "I love you Tony, I love you."

I slip my warm hand inside her panties and stroke her wetness. "I love you, and love you." My thumbs slip her black panties from her thighs; I kiss them as I go down. I push her onto the back seat of my SUV. She falls across sideways, letting herself bounce on the cool leather upholstery.

"Hold on," I say. I loosen my zipper and kick off my trousers and shoes. I kneel beside her. She reaches her hand out for revenge, cupping me, taunting me. I grab the small of her back and pulled her close to me, our lips and tongues dance with the waves. I force myself inside her. She makes a token protest.

"Wait a minute," she says.

I move slowly. Then waves of pleasure pulse from her even before she begins to thrust back at me, as I angle myself inside her deeper, the tip of my sex stroking her white hot spot. My rhythm comes faster and more furious, sending the silver lines of ecstasy running up to her nipples and down to her thighs, as I reach behind her to grab her butt, stroking it, toying with it, using it to pull her deeper against me, until all she can do is to gasp *Tony*, and clutch me, and the bright wall of pressure inside her explodes, and everything except *Tony*, falls away.

"Shall we talk now?" Carmella says to me when I get home.

"What about?"

"About what we did after lunchtime," Carmella says.

"Let's go out for dinner and talk?" I say.

Carmella estimates it will take an hour for her to bath and get dressed.

149

I gave a lecture to a class of engineers at the local university earlier this afternoon, starting with slides of damage from the 1993 WTC terrorist bombing two decades ago, when terrorists set off a bomb in the Trade Center's lower parking levels. My students' perceptions of the 1993 and 2001 terrorist attacks on WTC, and the ensuing collapses, have come entirely from replays of Newton PR archive footage--and footage from a few other network channels. How could I have taught them that there is a different reality than what they see on network television?

I started the lecture by projecting slides of mangled I-beams, twisted columns, and quantities of molten steel that must have been heated to at least 2800 degrees.

I asked, "How could the burning buildings possibly have created such unusual heat?" Jet fuel burns at less than half of this temperature. Structural steel beams were specified in the drawings as ASTM A36-Grade 36K psi, and the columns were specified as ASTM A572-Grade 50K psi – the same as for the EQE building, and virtually all US steel buildings. The actual strength of the column steel has not yet been measured because the structural steel was cut up and shipped to Asia for recycling, with undue haste... but Lilly-Thomas have taken samples from some rusty steel cruciforms that were erected as monuments in a vacant lot--nearby to ground zero.

I refer my students to the old government report sponsored by National Institute of Standards and Technology, Gaithersburg, MD, which documents the strengthening modifications that were made to the structural systems of World Trade Centers 1, 2, and 7 after the 1993 terrorist bombing.

WTC-7 (the Salomon Brothers' building) was designed in 1987 by Leslie Robertson and his team of structural engineers. The building was damaged in the 1993 terrorist bombing, subsequently repaired according to designs by Robertson, and then collapsed eight hours after the 9/11 attacks on the adjacent WTC-1 and WTC-2 towers in 2001.

The bomb that damaged WTC-7 on February 26, 1993, was set off in the second basement-level parking garage under the north end of the hotel, adjacent to WTC-1. The explosion caused a major collapse of the slab at level B2 (approximately 130 feet by 130 feet in dimension) and a major, but smaller, slab collapse at Level B1 (approximately 50 feet by 80 feet). Following the 1993 terrorist bombing, extensive renovations to the hotel required additional transfer girders at the fifth to seventh floor levels. These new transfers were designed by Leslie E. Robertson Associates.

After the 9/11 terrorist attacks on WTC-1 and then WTC-2, the following preliminary account of coincidental damage to WTC-7 was developed by NIST through interviews with occupants: "Only small fires were ignited as a result of projectiles entering WTC-7 after the collapse of WCT-1 several hours following aircraft impact. All of the WTC-7 building occupants were safely evacuated, except that two members of the management team re-entered the building to check on the safety of guests and firefighters, and incurred fatal injuries form flying debris upon the collapse of the closer WTC-2... almost seven hours prior to the collapse of WTC-7." But, WTC-2, even though it was struck second by an aircraft, collapsed less than an hour later, long before the collapse of WTC-1.

The structural response of WTC to the September 11 events of 2001 is complex and noteworthy... and is still unresolved more than ten years later. WTC-7 was subjected to two unusual loading events. The more critical event involved the earlier collapse of the south tower WTC-2, which stood approximately 350 feet away from WTC-7." Because of its 350 feet distance from WTC-2, (closer than WTC-1) only small items of debris could have fallen directly on the roof of WTC-7. However, larger debris from WTC-2 *reportedly* struck the center of the face of the building with sufficient force to *noticeably damage* the building at 10.30am. (WTC-2 collapsed at 9.59am.)

In spite of this allegedly extensive damage to WTC-7, the *noticeable damage* did not continue down to the foundations or extend horizontally to the edges of the structure. In fact, the two northern-most bays remained intact all the way to the roof. A similar, but lesser damage condition existed in the southern bays. Even in the center of the building, the damage stopped above the seventh floor." It is also reported, "This arrested damage implies that the structure was sufficiently strong and robust to absorb the energy of the falling debris, and the consequential local damage to the floors... The connections between the damaged framing and the adjacent undamaged framing were able to break apart without pulling down the building.

This complex behavior resulted in the survival of large portions of the WTC-7 building following the collapse of WTC-2. Indeed, some exterior columns from WTC-2 reportedly collapsed onto the southern face of WTC-7." But this could be a dubious claim from a government spokesman because of the 350 feet building separation— although WTC-2 columns were originally about thirteen hundred fifty feet tall, but unlikely to have remained in one length during a fall, and the fall was almost entirely vertical according to many observers.

The second unusual loading event was the collapse of WTC-1. Debris from WTC-1 is claimed to have fallen along the entire length (height) of WTC-7. An FDNY fire company was in the building during the collapses of both WTC-2 and WTC-1--and they survived. "The firefighters were near the top of the building, in the process of making sure that there were no civilians present in the building, when the closer south WTC-2 tower collapsed. Firefighter Heinz Kothe is quoted as saying, "We had no idea what had happened. It just rocked the building. It blew the door to the stairwell open, and it blew the guys up near the door halfway down a flight of stairs. I got knocked down to the landing. The building shook like buildings just don't shake." The firefighters were in the lower portion of the southwest corner of the WTC-7 building when the north WTC-1 tower collapsed. They survived the collapse and were able to leave the WTC-7 building, uninjured.

WTC-7 was thus reportedly subjected to extraordinary loading from the impact and weight of debris from the two adjacent 110-story towers. It is noteworthy that the building resisted both horizontal and vertical progressive collapse when subjected to debris from WTC-2. The overloaded portions were able to break away from the rest of the structure without pulling it down, and the remaining structural system was able to remain stable and support the debris load. The structure was even capable of protecting occupants on lower floors after the collapse of WTC-1.

I told my students that it is a mystery as to why WTC-7 suffered sudden column failures at 5.20pm on 9/11, about six hours after the collapse of the Towers--I and other scientists and engineers suspect that thermite explosives must have been the cause of the collapse, that it was a planned detonation. BYU physics Professor Steven Jones was sent samples of steel taken from the WTC site memorial icons, such as steel cruciforms, for analysis in his physics laboratory... the remainder of the evidence has been destroyed unfortunately.

I can hear Carmella upstairs, opening drawers in her dresser. I throw the remains of my coffee in the sink... My students were disinterested again today, too tired to question my information, not interested in the denials by officials regarding the use of thermite explosives. So I tried to stir then up:

"WTC-7 should be studied further to understand what really happened," I said. "Other failure possibilities should be investigated: including the foundation slurry walls, the design of the column support system, and the performance of the beam-column welds and the floor system.

Who stood to gain from a premeditated thermite detonation of WTC-7? Thermite detonation involves extreme temperatures of more than 2500 degrees, and is the only feasible explanation to date for the large volumes of molten steel found in the basements. There had to be a good reason for this building to be rigged for demolition. Did Silverstein, the World Trade Center owner, who wisely invested in insurance against terrorism immediately prior to 9/11, have prior knowledge of the attacks? One thing is for sure; any decision to "pull" WTC-7 would have delighted many people:

WTC-7 contained offices of the FBI, Department of Defense, IRS (which contained prodigious amounts of corporate tax fraud, including Enron's), US Secret Service, Securities & Exchange Commission (with more stock fraud records), and Citibank's Salomon Smith Barney, the Mayor's Office of Emergency Management and many other financial institutions. The SEC has not quantified the number of active cases in which substantial files were destroyed by the collapse of WTC-7. Reuters news service and the Los Angeles Times published reports estimating that 3,000 to 4,000 files were destroyed. They include the agency's major inquiry into the manner in which investment banks divvied up hot shares of initial public offerings during the high-tech boom. ...*Ongoing investigations at the New York SEC will be dramatically affected because so much of their work is paper-intensive,* said Max Berger of New York's Bernstein Litowitz Berger & Grossmann. *This is a disaster for these cases.*

Citigroup says some information that the committee is seeking, (about WorldCom), was destroyed in the September 11 terror attack on the World Trade Center. Salomon had voluminous files in WTC-7. The bank says that back-up tapes of corporate emails from September 1998 through December 2000 were stored at the building and destroyed in the attack, [The Street]. The US Secret Service's largest field office with more than 200 employees was inside WTC-7--*All the evidence that we stored at 7 World Trade, in all our cases, went down with the building,* according to US Secret Service Special Agent David Curran.

The collapse of WTC-7 also profited Silverstein Properties to the tune of approximately $500 million through insurance payments.

Any questions?" I asked my fourth year engineering students when my presentation was complete.

"Thank you. Can we go now?" a student asked from the rear.

I tried to provoke further discussion, but the students walked out. "I know this is hard to comprehend. We'll talk more about it when the new lab results come back from professor Jones."

My students were tired, so I referred them to my research paper that demonstrates why fire is an implausible explanation for the collapse of WTC-7. This fire hypothesis involves an improbable sequence of coincidences. So, it was probably a demolition job? Why has it taken ten years to learn nothing?

The kitchen clock has been ticking loudly for the last twenty minutes.

Finally Carmella descends the stairs. She is wearing a string of pearls over a dark suit with diamond earrings that flash when she laughs.

I drive and she smokes.

The French waiter gives the impression to the Tuesday evening crowd that we might be celebrities. Our table is located in a soft corner away from the turning heads. Our waiter's presentation is impeccable, as is the escargot.

"What do you want to happen with us?" she asks.

"I wish to remain in love forever."

"With me?"

"There will never be anyone but you."

She smiles stiffly. "I really do believe that you mean what you say." When Carmella is nervous, which is rare, I also get nervous.

"Of course I do. You are magnificent."

Carmella leans forward, her elbows on the table.

I let the pause lengthen. I can smell her Musk perfume--and feel her uncertainty, her discouragement beneath the mask of her social confidence.

"I'm hopeful," she says, "that we can work through my painful past."

"Whatever it takes. OK?" I say.

We go home. I cannot sleep. I go downstairs to my office. Carmella is my almost-perfect lover, whose pleasures include erotic and uninhibited sex that must start slowly and build to a frenzy, until she insists upon a more aggressive approach: a type of sex that maybe was a by-product of her molestation during her teenage years. While we dined out this evening she behaved like a loose kid. Maybe that was a by-product of the molestation also. I was in the company of a dirty-eyed motor mouth of a sex kitten. "When a woman who really likes sex walks into a room, a man knows it?" She said. "And the same thing happens the other way round. With certain men, no matter how outwardly proper, all women instinctively know what delights that a certain type of man is capable of enchanting them with."

Carmella had another glass of wine and told me that she fantasizes about having sex in the White House, tied up with four of my silk ties to the President's desk. I am still haunted by the puzzle regarding the collapse of the WTC buildings, especially WTC-7: It is difficult for me to believe that our government could have been so deceitful as to have detonated the building--and then deny it.

# CHAPTER 28: TONY, 2012

I can't give Newt Gingrinch my file of regurgitated dirt on Barack Obama: He is too cautious to say anything new. Therefore I shall try to arouse his interest in Hillary again... she is desperately in need of some attention as she tries to restore some purpose to her shattered life. I send Newt a copy of a funny press release published on the White House website a while ago--with the hope that it will appease his demand for anti-Democrat material.

"Remarks by Laura Bush to the Washington Wives Book Club--Congratulating Hillary Rodham Clinton on the Publication of her Memoirs:
Washington Wives Book Club Breakfast
The Ritz Carlton Ballroom
LAURA BUSH: Good morning, gals. I hope you're all enjoying your breakfasts. I promise to be brief, so we can all get back to those punchbowls of Ritz Carlton Hollandaise sauce that help fill out our control-top JC Penny under things so splendidly.
(Laughter.)
You know, as a former librarian and teacher who talks ad nausea about loving to read, I understand the importance of pretending to value literature – so much of which is nothing but the boring, written-down blah-blah of America-hating intellectuals. Which brings me to the matter at hand. This morning, I want to congratulate Senator and former First Lady Hillary Rodham Sometimes-Clinton--whom I'm sorry to say isn't welcome at our events--for neglecting her duties as a mother, wife and public servant long enough to churn out all those chapters of liberal fiction which make up her memoir, *Living History*.

I just don't know where she got the energy to write so many pages! Personally, after I finish the *USA Today* crossword puzzle, have a few ciggies, then endure my daily 90-minute call from Barbara, it's nearly all I can do to wrestle the safety cap off my Xanax bottle, take a six hour nap, then be refreshed enough by 5:02 to greet George in the family quarters lobby with a frosty mug of tequila.
(Applause.)
To me, it's just so impressive that Ms. Rodham – it is "Ms.," isn't it? And "Rodham?" How confusing! That's why I flushed my old name down the toilet, and just go by "Mrs. George Walker Bush." Anyway, it's so impressive to me that whatserface had the courage to slap an $8 Million price tag on dredging up the lurid details of her humiliation so that America's high-minded news anchors and Matt Drudge can breathlessly revisit the salaciously yummy comings and goings of her hubby's horse-like pee-pee. Why, just imagine the crushing shame and dishonor by association that poor woman felt knowing that her husband had gushed mansnot all over some chunky little Jewess. In comparison, I thank Jesus every day that George's only faults have been minor little peccadilloes--like a running a string of failed businesses, dabbling in insider trading, and reducing his septum to a Peruvian blue

flake-flavored strip of Knox gelatin!

And so again I say, congratulations Senator Hillary. I'm sure your book will be a big hit--one that will serve to humanize you, yet whose lurid details will fade from the popular consciousness just in time for your failed Presidential bid. Against my brother-in-law, Jeb Bush. That's right... His wife Columba and I are already choosing fabrics for the East Wing renovation; so don't even think about it, sister.

In closing, let me just assure you Washington Wives that you won't ever catch this lady writing a messy book on politics or something mean-spirited like Neil Bush's horrible wife almost did. We had a little saying at our White House: dungarees and typewriters are for cowboys and lesbians. That said; I have been considering writing a book with the help of my friends at the Austin Women's Flower and Garden Club. It's a simple tale about a woman who befriends a Mexican girl named Consuela, (or is it a Puerto Rican beauty named Carmella) then teaches her that beauty can be found pulling weeds shoulder-to-shoulder with her cancer-ravaged daddy in a finely manicured country club flowerbed (or kneeling in the rubble of WTC-7 where her beloved, Carmella, pretends to grieve for her fallen papa C-J, kneeling before a rusty cruciform of steel structure, that she manipulates in her mind to represent the cruciform of the martyred American dream, draped with a tattered stars and stripes).
(Applause.)

Of course, I'm going to have the good graces to not publish until I'm long back at home in Crawford, Texas, and all my enemies and naysayers are dead.
(Applause.)

Thank you all for coming and have a wonderful day."

That will have to take care of my assignment deadline for Newton PR. But what should I do with the damning material I have gathered on Newt Gingrinch.

Former House Speaker and prospective presidential candidate Newt Gingrinch, at a public discussion, admitted to having an affair while cheerleading the assault on Bill Clinton during the Monica Lewinsky scandal. Hypocrisy is nothing new to Newt, who extolled family values after serving divorce papers on his wife while she lay dying of cancer. And people are worried about Hillary and Barack's electability!

"The honest answer is yes," Gingrinch, formerly a possible 2008 Republican presidential candidate, said in an interview with *Focus on the Family* founder, James Dobson, according to a transcript provided to the *Associated Press*. "There are times that I have fallen short of my own standards. There are certainly times when I've fallen short of God's standards."

Gingrinch argued in the interview, however, that he should not be viewed as a hypocrite for punishing Bill Clinton's infidelity. "The President of the United States got in trouble for committing a felony in front of a sitting federal judge," the former Georgia congressman said of Clinton's 1998 House impeachment on perjury and obstruction of justice charges. "I drew a line in my mind that said, 'Even though I run the risk of being deeply embarrassed, and even though at a purely personal level I am not rendering judgment on another human being, as a leader of the government trying to uphold the rule of law, I had no choice except to move forward and say that you cannot accept perjury in your highest officials."

A summary of Newt Gingrinch's family life is revealing.

1) Gingrinch marries his high school teacher, Jackie, who was seven years his senior.

2) Jackie puts Gingrinch through college and she works hard to get him elected to the House in 1978. Gingrinch won partly because his campaign claimed that his Democratic opponent would neglect her family if elected--at that time it was common knowledge that Gingrinch was straying.

3) Shortly after being elected, Gingrinch separated from his wife, announcing the separation in the hospital room where Jackie was recovering from cancer surgery, (the divorce was final in 1981). Jackie Gingrinch and her children had to depend on alms from her church because Gingrinch didn't pay any child support. Six months after the divorce, Gingrinch, then 38, married Marianne Ginther, 30.

4) "In May 1999, however, Gingrinch [55] called Marianne [48] at her mother's home. After wishing the 84-year-old matriarch happy birthday, he told Marianne that he wanted a divorce." This was eight months after Marianne was diagnosed with multiple sclerosis.

5) In 2000, Gingrinch, 57, married ex-congressional aide Callista Bisek, 34, with whom he was having a relationship while married to Marianne."

Mr. Family Values, Newt Gingrinch, is amazingly similar to Bill Clinton--both are pot smoking, draft-dodging adulterers from poor Southern families. Gingrinch is reported to have committed adultery with Callista Bisek, and Anne Manning--the unnamed "young volunteer." Are we missing anyone? His campaign scheduler said, "We would have won in 1974 if we could have kept Newt from screwing a young volunteer on the office desk."

Newt Gingrinch said to author Gail Sheehy, "I think you can write a psychological profile of me that says I found a way to immerse my insecurities in a cause large enough to justify whatever I wanted it to."

"She isn't young enough or pretty enough to be the President's wife." – Newt said of his first wife.

# CHAPTER 29: TONY, 2012

After reading the first page again I am satisfied that the new company brochure is an improvement over the last… but why have there been no reported building collapses over the last decade?

Across the top of the page is bold-typed the header:

**Lilly-Thomas, forensic division of IDS Consultants, Structural Engineers.**

What do these disasters have in common?

1   1978, Rezko building collapse, NYC.
2   1981, Harbor City Condominiums collapse. Cocoa Beach, Florida.
3   1989, Hyatt Hotel collapse and 9 other buildings, Baquio City, Philippines.
4   1993, WTC severe damage x 2, NYC.
5   1994 Citicorp Headquarters saved. NYC.
6   1995, Federal Building collapse, Oklahoma City.
7   2001, EQE Building collapse, Fort Pierce, Florida.
8   2001 WTC collapses x 3, NYC.
9   2001 Pentagon partial collapse, Washington DC.

I bound into Dad's room and slap the draft on the bed. "OK," I ask, sitting on the edge of a chair to await the verdict from my founding partner. Dad makes no sudden movement. His hair has become white as he nears the age of seventy. Mom is constantly after him to diet, claiming that his chin is starting to sag so he will have to take Viagra soon.

William sighs and picks up the paper. The window behind him faces south, giving me a view of the orchards around the colonial architecture of the FEMA training office in Emmetsburg. The buildings are a crème color, with the window trim painted two shades darker. The campus is surrounded by the gently rolling meadows that encouraged the Civil War generals to face off their troops. Dad once taught earthquake engineering here; he often walks the campus trails before breakfast when he's in town for a visit. William and I occasionally teach a course together now, but only once this year; we've been too busy.

After several minutes of reading, William puts down the draft brochure. "At the top, you call the collapses disasters. But in every case there was a loss of life. I'd call them catastrophes. But it's up to you."

"Right, Dad. No problem."

"The lack of consultations over the last decade may infer that we are out of favor. Many buildings have collapsed… secretly. But no investigations have been called for— or are being done by someone else. Does Hillary have clout anymore?"

In order to protect his shirt from the points and clips of pens and pencils, Dad still wears a nerd pack in his pocket. He fumbles with it and says, "What about those high-rises in Los Angeles that suffered weld failures and beam-over strength consequences after a small earthquake in '94, or was it… And put in the month that the catastrophe occurred."

"Right, Dad. This is just a rough draft. I didn't have the months handy."

I pluck a pencil from William's shirt pocket and scribble, "add months" in the margin of the paper.

"Son. It may seem that I get too picky, but this brochure is going to be read by some of the most fastidious people on the planet. So list the casualties because that shows that when a lot is at stake, the lawyers and insurance companies turn to us. When people have been killed you want the best investigators you can get."

"Do you want to stay with the old brochure?"

William sighs and rubs his eyes. "All this emphasis on catastrophe analysis . . . well, it's not what I had in mind when I started the company."

"The new materials, the new design theories about ductility and fuses, the push for cost cutting, planned obsolescence, explosives, the decline in inspections from building departments because of liability issues . . . there are bound to be more failures."

"Maybe so, but . . ."

"More people are willing to go to trial over them, too, because of the money involved. And the rate of building collapse has skyrocketed over the last fifteen years. Juries are throwing insurance money around by the billions. And we're the best."

"If that is the work you want—why don't you lean on Hillary?"

"OK Dad. Worth a try. How many engineering firms can do first-rate investigations? How many know liability law? We have an opportunity-to make up for the decline in the economics of ranching."

Dad turns and gazes toward the FEMA campus. "I've got to tell you, Son," he says, "I worry that someone is going to bump you off. This afternoon while you were out, a man named Ross Higgins called. He wants you to look at the dusty old WTC-7 file again. The insurance company doesn't want to pay out on the building collapse. That'll piss a lot of people off... They've been waiting ten years."

"I know Higgins. He worked on the Oklahoma City bombing."

"As long as he has an interesting puzzle to solve, he's happy. I don't think Higgins cares much about money."

"Don't be too sure."

"I never make that mistake anymore," William says. "I've seen the wreckage of so many lives lately that I'll never be sure of anything again."

"Let's take a drive to New York City... Take a look together, before you have to fly back to the ranch. I'll get Davey to meet us on site. He's in New York on another job."

Dad climbs into the passenger seat. On the central console he lays out some of the tools of the trade, which he slips into various pockets of his jacket: a magnifying glass, a small folding telescope, a six-inch depth gage, a collapsible measuring rod, a tape measure, electronic calipers, a pocket knife, screwdrivers, and a tiny digital camera.

We park the company car at Hillary's vacant house and stay the night there before catching the train into Manhattan in the morning.

I cling to a metal strap on a squealing lurching subway car, crowded on all sides by people I don't know. The train jolts to a stop. "Is this Church Street?" William asks, lowering his head into a woman's newspaper and squinting through the dingy windows.

"Yes," the woman says, yanking the paper away from his chin. "If you're blind, where's your cane?"

The herd pushes us across the platform, through the exit gates and up the concrete steps. We push our way across Church Street into a stiff westerly breeze.

We arrive at Barclay Street at precisely 9.00 am.

"What I need on this job is a stomach pump," I say.

"Davey!" William says in surprise when he sees him at the site of the former wreckage of WTC-7. "What the hell have you been doing? You look like you've been working in a bakery." Davey looks down at his clothes as the security guard takes our ID's into his trailer--and talks on the phone. Davey's windbreaker, corduroy pants, and shoes are covered with a fine white powder, despite the powerful wind gusts that cause us to lean periodically. This area of Manhattan is renown for the intensity of wind loads that are funneled by the neighboring high-rise buildings. "Cement dust," he says. "I've been at the Ready-Mix plant."

"Till midnight?"

"Well, no. Till midnight I've been drinking beer at the sleaziest bar I've ever seen in my life. It's where the local teamsters hang out—had a photo of Hillary on the wall... drinking whiskey with the boys. I kept asking myself, 'What am I doing here?' I hate bars. I hate sleaze. I'm not even that crazy about beer. I hung in there hoping those truck drivers would eventually tell me something useful, and finally they did. But my God, at what expense to my stomach and my head!"

"I don't believe it," William says. "Davey with a hang over. What'd you find out?"

"Hoppy Boone confirmed my suspicion. He drove on the concrete trucks that delivered the mix for the repair of the connection of the new foundation of WTC to the old... back when he first started driving. I can't believe they built a forty seven-story building on top of an existing fuel station. Bloody nuts. They had to rely on the foundations of that old hunk of lime and gravel to hold up a section of the new building."

"So what *did* you find?" I ask impatiently.

"First let me tell you what I learned from the archive videos of the WTC-7 collapse, and the fire department," Davey says. "The fires weren't too bad, but there was some damage on the south side due to falling debris from the adjacent collapse of WTC-2. Some debris took a gash out of a few columns. The NIST had a witness who said that ten to fifteen stories of columns were taken out in the middle third of the south face. Gotta have been on wacky backy. Not enough large debris could travel hundreds of feet from the Twin Towers. There's no question that the south face is a frame structure. Should have had sufficient ductility and redundancy to resist way more load than was apparently thrown at WTC-7. Something doesn't add up. Could be that rebars at the foundations of columns 65 thru 72 were so closely spaced the concrete didn't penetrate."

"Happens all the time," William says, his eyes almost closed against the wind. "We need to get a sample of the steel to the lab to see if the yield is up to code. The only sample available is from that rusty steel cruciform, the tall one constructed as a flimsy memorial near ground zero. Take it."

"You're generation has no scruples William. There's a rumor that a load of cheap beam steel came in from Taiwan. The developer of the World Trade Center beat the steel bids down by almost fifty percent from the initial bid… Took the job off the big US steel supplier, Bethlehem Steel, and then subdivided it out to a bunch of little guys scattered all over the world, from Texas to Taiwan," Davey says.

"And what did the truck driver say?" I ask.

Davey dons a pair of sunglasses and zips his jacket against the gusts of cold wind. "Ready-Mix has a modern set up, deliveries are all computerized. On the day they were pouring the foundations of columns 81 thru 97, four of the trucks must have added water to the drums after they left the plant. It turns out that the trucks left the bridge at noon and didn't return until quarter to two. Boone didn't admit to it until our table was swimming in beer. We're great pals now."

"Wow. Do you mean they stopped for lunch with their trucks full of concrete and the drums turning?"

Davey nods. "The greasy spoon by the interchange. They parked behind, out of sight. After lunch they took a hose and added water to the loads until it looked as wet as when they pulled in."

"Of course he knew extra water would cut the strength?" I ask.

"Not a clue. I'm too nice for this kind of work. You need a heavy drinker like William on this duty," Davey says.

"Well done David," William says, "Take the rest of the day off."

"Geez," I say. "We spent all last night studying the plans of WTC-7 while Davey was drinking beer, and what he comes up with might be the key to the whole mystery as to why a building that never got hit by a plane and only had light to moderate fires-- suddenly collapses."

"No!" says William. "That information was planted to sabotage our efforts. I've just checked out the records. Somebody has been a master at information manipulation throughout the September 11 tragedy."

"I know, but shit…"

"All this time—more than a decade after the 9/11 terrorist attack on the WTC, we still don't have an official reason as to why WTC-7 collapsed. However, there is strong evidence as to the causes: The strength of the beam steel and the welds, the huge offsets in the columns above the lobby, the adequacy of the foundations (partially caused by constructing WTC-7 over and around an existing emergency fuel depot), and the adequacy of repairs to the steel connections or fireproofing after the 1993 terrorist bombing," William says.

"I still have not completed our final report. But we aren't the only ones. NIST has stalled and finally given up and sublet their investigation out to a private firm--so the project can be managed by one of their own investigators."

"That's not right! According to the National Institute of Standards and Technology, on March 31, 2006, under solicitation number SB1341-06-Q-0186, the Federal Government awarded a fixed price purchase order to Applied Research Associates, Inc. (ARA) of Albuquerque, New Mexico to research and provide WTC-7 structural analysis and collapse hypotheses. Specifically, the U.S. government has contracted with ARA to: *Create detailed floor analyses to determine likely modes of failure for Floors 8 to 46 due to failure of supporting columns (at one or more locations) in WTC-7,*" Dad says.

"The Bush government's hiring of ARA was a conflict of interest. NIST reports that Dr. Steven W. Kirkpatrick, who is employed by Applied Research Associates, Inc., will be the Program Manager for the WTC-7 collapse analysis. Can Dr. Kirkpatrick be objective in his research or is his opinion already skewed?"

"It is highly unlikely that Kirkpatrick will contradict the government's official *pancake theory* of an unzipping floor collapse for the Twin Towers by reporting the truth about WTC-7, which is that it might have collapsed as the result of a denied controlled demolition," Dad says.

"Kirkpatrick was a NIST Contractor through his employer, ARA, during the NIST investigation into the cause of the collapse of WTC-1 and WTC-2. With Kirkpatrick leading the team that will provide the research and findings for WTC-7, the integrity of the government's investigation into how WTC-7 collapsed is already compromised."

"Beyond the fact that Kirkpatrick is a safe bet for the government, and an obstacle to honest analysis, NIST has taken further measures to assure that no rogue scientist emerges from the inside and starts talking about *controlled demolition* in regard to the collapse of WTC-7. How did the government create this truth guard? Contractually, of course, that's how." Dad kicks his foot at an empty coke can.

"As of today, the US government has yet to provide an official, public explanation of how WTC-7 suddenly collapsed at freefall speed onto its footprint at 5.20pm EST on September 11, 2001. This was a forty-seven story steel tower that was not struck by an airplane, was the furthest distance from the Twin Towers of all seven buildings on the WTC site, experienced only moderate debris damage when the towers collapsed, and only had moderate office fires burning between the 6th and 12th floors. The reason why the government has not yet released an official account of how WTC-7 collapsed is because there are few if any plausible explanations--other than controlled demolition."

"Yes!" says Dad. "And I need to know the answers to these questions."

"And so do I. Not just because of professional responsibility, but because my wife's father, Carl-Junior, died in there."

"The 9/11 Commission failed to mention the collapse of WTC-7 in its 9/11 Commission Report. Not one word about WTC-7 is found in the government's first official account of 9/11. What followed the 9/11 Commission Report was the research conducted by the National Institute of Standards and Technology. It should be noted that NIST was directed to provide a report that explained how, from a structural perspective, WTC-1, WTC-2, and WTC-7 collapsed. The research and findings on how all three of these buildings collapsed was supposed to be included in a single report. NIST started its investigation in August 2002. However, when the draft of its final report came out in December 2004, there was no mention of WTC-7. According to NIST, it was decided to research WTC-7 separately. Why? The reason is simple. NIST is delaying a public account of the WTC-7 collapse because it cannot explain it," Dad says.

"I know. And Professor Jones, the physicist from BYU has got the forensic results from his steel tests. The spectral analysis demonstrates compelling evidence for the presence of thermite detonation at the WTC-7 collapse site, and possibly the other collapse sites. The case for thermite is damn close to being conclusive."

"But why? What is the motive behind the deception?"

# PART XII: CARMELLA

## CHAPTER 30: CARMELLA, 2012

June 28, 2012:

A permanent lifestyle on board a submarine could get claustrophobic—it is demanding enough just doing a weekly reality TV show for Newt. I try to keep my professional and acting life separate from Marise and Tony. Too bad that Marise doesn't like my acting career. At least she hasn't found out about my other profession… and I pray to God that she never does. But now I have a nice surprise: After that encounter at the Magic Touch in Fort Pierce, I didn't know Rachael and I would meet again on the set of the Newton Show. When I first met Rachael she wore a short, tight dress, high heels and heavy make-up. Some time after that, we lived together at the House of 1ElevenWomen; the group that I hope will make up the core of my submarine crew.

Rachael is what you'd call an "all-purpose" hooker--and is now trained as a Submarine navigator. She took eight clients at the same time one night. "How was it?" I asked afterwards.

"Eight guys in me, 800 bucks in my pocket. Not bad."

I was shocked!

People become prostitutes because of freedom. Not sexual freedom, but the kind of freedom money can give you. It gives you the power to buy the things you want, to stay in bed and sleep the whole day if you feel like it, to take a day off when you're fed up with having sex. You don't need to worry about how society will judge your actions. You are free to wear what you want, to speak your mind. There's a true freedom of soul. Hookers are the most authentic people you'll ever meet.

Politicians could learn a great deal from us hookers about integrity, about speaking your mind—rather than hiring a PR person to create an image of the ideal composite person with the values and policies that the polls indicate could win the election. I'm not speaking about being right. But even when we hookers are wrong we are not afraid of expressing our true selves. There are those of us who are exceptions, of course, but the vast majority of us are real.

We develop integrity because our naked exposure somehow pulls the masks down as our panties come down.

My cellular phone rings, but it isn't Hillary. Now I am sad again. I need her advice… I remember the last time I had this feeling--waiting for someone to call on the phone. It was my father, Carl-Junior. He finally called though: "There is someone here," he said. "They've sent me into WTC-7. Just like at Fort Pierce… they always sent me in for the final check before they blow the charge. But someone else is here. Something is wrong."

Officially no one was killed when WTC-7 collapsed ten years ago. They told me that C-J was on a secret mission, so his name would not feature on the WTC memorial. Stupid bastards! The Navy thinks they have recovered unidentifiable parts of his body from the basement, but under WTC-1, not WTC-7... *He must have been clobbered by falling debris. That'd be the noise you heard. It's one giant parking garage under the WTC complex. Your dad must have been confused as to just where he was.*

Bullshit! They didn't bury C-J... he's down in Puerto Rico, at Grandma's house.

~~~~~~~~~~~~~~~~~~~~~~~~~

July 6, 2012

It was a fractious family dinner, just Tony and I because Marise is at school camp. I'm beginning to feel better now but I was struggling for a while back there, pinned back by the force of Tony's irritation over our daughter's minor alcohol infractions--tame events that briefly visit all adolescents at some stage of being a teenager. I jump into the conversation now, "Tony, I can see that you want to humiliate us all. How could I have forgotten that this is always what happens with zealots?"

Tony drums his fingers on the table and thinks furiously. "No, I'm sorry, you're right. It *is* outrageous. I've overstepped the mark. Please forgive me."

I want to destroy Tony's whole save-the-world campaign, but I want to do it using his engineering logic. And of course it's not possible because Tony is fluent in his style. I am doomed to frustration--unless I am prepared to provoke him by using the tools of sexuality.

We are in bed at 9pm, and we've just made love for the first time in donkey's years--and I ask Tony if the prospect of having sex with me and no one else but me for the rest of his life disturbs him. Tony is uncharacteristically reflective about it.

"It does get me down occasionally, but I know that I would never be able to tolerate anything other than monogamy from you Sweetheart."

"Are you sure?"

"I couldn't tolerate you having sex with another man," Tony says.

"Really?"

"Really, So I could hardly expect indulgence for myself," Tony says.

I ask him whether there are any circumstances in which he would forgive me an infidelity--a drugged one-night stand of sexual intercourse, followed the morning after by shameful remorse.

Tony points out that I never got very horny when I did drugs. He says, "If you were unfaithful, it would be for another reason, it would be because you were rebellious... And that would spell trouble." -- Trouble he doesn't want to think about.

I very rarely credit Tony with any intuition, but I take my hat off to him now. I wasn't drugged. But I have been sleeping with his enemy for all sorts of other reasons, every one of which spells trouble. Geez Tony. Did you think you could keep the weapon of betrayal exclusively for yourself, hidden forever?

~~~~~~~~~~~~~~~~~~~~~~~~~

## CHAPTER 31: TONY, August 3, 2012

Fuck the media! The critics of the media have been revealing to *We The People* some of those falsehoods that we have recently been indoctrinated with on TV. I can see that Hillary was highjacked by a hostile media, and is now suffering from nervous exhaustion. She has been hospitalized in New Zealand, with a media blackout. The willingness of the TV viewer to exploit an endless parade of victims on the "Reality TV" is an addictive public desire to experience an easier and more exciting substitute for real life, which is what fuels the media machine and its virtual world.

I am going to give the media and voters something to talk about--a new *virtual* Hillary, an actress performing under a great director (me, Tony Chaytor) who has learned much from the movie *Simone*... Where Simone was created digitally by movie director Victor Taransky, who has just blown his last movie after falling out with his demanding lead actress. That is, until he discovers Simone, a digitally created beautiful talented leading lady without ego, and totally committed to the director.

My new surrogate Hillary-the-Fake will look and talk like the real Hillary. I shall call the surrogate *Simtwo*, a digital creation that has the benefit over *Simone* of reverse engineering--and psychological profiling--based upon poll results... and a personality and policy package that truly resonates with the public heartstrings. I will be satisfied with a human-like digital facemask and voice box, supported on a robotic body of the appropriate womanly proportions. Simtwo will have the same face as Hillary, but a brain that is more conducive to control.

The message of the Internet and underground journalists is that today's society has become a controlled environment. The media and advanced technology have become the exclusive tools of those in power. In the case of Simtwo, my Hillary surrogate will be irresistibly electable because Simtwo will speak wisely, unencumbered by a strident personality, gross ambitions, and cautious ethics:

"What we thought was the beautiful world outside is beginning to look like a poisonous cage--on our rare excursions outdoors. What we thought was a life is beginning to look like a lie. We are in a culture that is controlled, inauthentic, regressive, and full of illusion--stuck before sensory simulations and psychological illusions. Malevolent simulators have the ability to immerse us in lifelike *virtual* realities, through mind control, and trap us. I, Hillary Clinton will bring back healthy reality."

I start watching TV again to learn how the networks are reaching people these days. There is the same popular show running on four major channels: The *Newton* show has started a new season and features my Carmella in a reality show--she is out-of-town but called last night to tell me that her show is being piloted now, so I have to watch. But first I read the TV guide: "This is a twenty-four hour reality TV show that stars Carmella Meeks, and is getting rave reviews: It is about a coven of prostitutes who escape their sordid and shameful environment in a stolen nuclear submarine. What will the media Bosses think of next?"

There is Carmella on TV. I don't like her playing the part of a prostitute—we have a teenager daughter and nieces to think about! There seem to be only three cameras mounted in the submarine... there is one in Carmella's bunkroom—thank God that Marise isn't watching this.

The next shot is taken in the mess--with paper drinking cups, jars of vitamin pills, and plants growing under lights. I see in the background of the camera shot that there is a TV set on board the submarine that is picking up this same signal as I--tuned to the same "Reality" show that I am watching. Weird—this must be live!

An audiotape, pre-recorded by the show narrator, plays repeatedly over the live visual: "I repeat. What we do not know is just where the pirated submarine is located. Tall Rachael, the navigator, says they are headed for Antarctica when their navigation system mysteriously failed at a depth of five hundred feet. The vessel is of the Astute class and was on standby for a covert naval operation known only to a few high ranking members of the Navy command. The CIA is assembling a dossier on the prostitute pirates.

And now an ongoing development:

The submarine is understood to be unable to surface due to a malfunction. The sub is stuck on the floor of the ocean. We can see a shot of the pirate leader, Carmella Meeks, lying on her bed and reading the Navy's repair manual. Stay tuned and listen in on the pending B-team summit meeting--perhaps to discuss the next step, including the possibility of mutiny.

Will Carmella be able to manage the panic that must be visiting this crew of prostitutes now? How will they perform under this new stress? Will they be pardoned if it can be proved that Newt Gingrinch set them up, as they claim? Or will the Navy attempt the dangerous task of rescuing these prostitutes?

Use your remote to vote. Indicate if you wish for these disease-ridden harlots to be the subject of a high-risk naval rescue mission during this extreme hurricane season? Whatever you decide, please do not leave your set. Newton PR is the lifeline to your emotional security."

The narrator does a voice-over as the camera focuses upon Carmella's eyes blinking:

"On the TV news yesterday a family of Americans reportedly attempted to leave their TV sets to go shopping at an old-fashioned retail store. They died... of insanity.

Do you want to risk a painful death by leaving the security of your living room? Remember, it is illegal to turn your TV set off. Please relocate both your bed and your vitamin supply to your living room," the drone said. Then the camera merges back to the prostitutes eating in the submarine mess. The camera bobbles, as if a wave had disturbed the submarine--supposedly parked on the floor of the Atlantic Ocean."

The submarine show is going off with the public opinion. That show gives me an idea that just might get Hillary the Presidency... I am going to video a series of smart promos for airing in September and October, using my obedient Simtwo.

## CHAPTER 32: TONY, August 1, 2012

Today is the deadline to get Hillary's name in for the write-in ballot. But Detective Snipes from Fort Pierce called, demanding a meeting in my office. That was half an hour ago. And here he is with his hand extended. I cannot get enthusiastic over white shoes and Panama hat.... Nor the deodorant.

"We suspect your girlfriend, Carmella Meeks, of abandoning your daughter, Eleanor Meeks." Inspector Snipes paces around my office.

"You've got the wrong person. My only daughter's name is Marise."

"I'm sorry Sir. Marise may not be your daughter."

"Fuck off."

"Eleanor is your daughter--according to our DNA tests. Eleanor was abandoned on the steps of an orphanage by a young woman. The police found Eleanor... in a sex den run by a religious cult of perverted bigamists in Eldorado, Texas," Snipes says.

I cannot speak.

"It has taken a lot of therapy before we could get any sense out of Eleanor."

"So what I am supposed to do?"

"Get revenge first, then forgive... but not until after the bastards are executed."

What am I to do about Carmella for lying to me, and for abandoning my daughter Eleanor? Do I turn her in? Or try to save her? In the movie *The Interpreter*, Nicole Kidman grows up among the Ku, in the fictional nation of Matobo. When someone commits a heinous crime such as rape or murder among the Ku, they are allowed to live for a year. Then they are dumped in a lake with their hands tied. The victim's family members must decide whether to plunge into the water and save the criminal, or let him drown. Those families who save the criminal, in effect *forgiving* the criminal... releasing themselves from resentment--are better off for it. But does Carmella want forgiveness? Doesn't *forgiveness* fly in the face of natural justice?

Whatever, Right now I have to think of Hillary--because she has dropped the coy pretense of indecision, and has told me that she wants to run again for President. Therefore I must register her name as a write-in candidate today. However, Hillary's personality is not right for the job, and she's hospitalized in New Zealand due to a breakdown. I have perfected the technology for Simtwo to stand in for Hillary during the election campaign. But, ultimately, after we have won the election, I need to be able to seamlessly revert to the real Hillary, in time for her Inauguration... hopefully she will be healed by then. In the meantime, I need to develop Simtwo so the robot will only say what I calculate that it should say to win votes—a perfect puppet. I know it is risky to put Hillary's name forward, but she desperately needs some success in her depressed life... and that is what good friends do—help out.

There are journalists calling on the phone, calling about Eleanor. It is time for me to use the media! My job is to record promotions with Simtwo--promotions to be played on the network TV channels and the Internet--pre-recorded. Live interviews or debates are out of the question. I must have predictable behavior and total loyalty.

# CHAPTER 33: CARMELLA, 2012

July 27, 2012

What sort of a terrible mother have I been for Eleanor? I finally know where she is… But do I want the police telling Eleanor where I am? Do I want the police talking to me? About Eleanor, or my father C-J? Detective Snipes referred me to a press release about what has happened to Eleanor:

Eldorado, Texas - The 18-year-old girl, whose call triggered the police raid on a polygamist sect's Texas compound, said that her husband beat her, according to court documents. The San Angelo Standard-Times newspaper cited court documents that said the girl was the seventh wife of a sect member who is named in an arrest warrant on possible abuse charges. The young woman told authorities at a family violence shelter that her husband hit her in the chest and choked her, while another woman held her infant child at the sect's *Yearn for Zion* ranch. Child welfare officials say they took 416 children from the ranch last week, and 136 women left on their own accord.

Officials continued searching the polygamist sect's compound on Tuesday. Until the raid on their compound, the women and girls spent their days caring for its many children, tilling gardens and quilting, dressed in pioneer-style dresses sewn by their own hands. It was a world difficult to leave, but it was no nostalgic recreation of 19th-century prairie life. Five miles off the highway, beyond a double gate, the group's members lived lives that were isolated, even for the scruffy West Texas prairie. Their 1,700-acre ranch is like its own city, with a gleaming temple, doctor's office, school, and even factories.

"Once you go into the compound, you don't ever leave it," said Carolyn Jessop, who was one of the wives of the alleged leader of the Eldorado complex, but who left the sect before it began moving to Texas in 2004. Jessop alleges the sect practices a form of pedophilia--hiding behind a religion as a protection. "There's just a desire to control and manipulate and torture people, and religion is just used as the cover."

Authorities were looking for evidence that another girl, who allegedly gave birth at age fifteen and called authorities about alleged abuse, was married to a 50-year-old. Texas law forbids girls younger than sixteen to marry.

Merrill Jessop, who oversees the ranch, and is a presiding elder in the Fundamentalist Church of Jesus Christ of Latter Day Saints, told the Salt Lake Tribune that officers conducting the search were collecting cell phones "as fast as they can find them." Members believe the apocalypse is near, and they will have to start over when the world is destroyed. They were not allowed to wear red—the color that Jeffs said belonged to Jesus, and were not allowed to cut their hair.

Detective Snipes says that custody of Eleanor has temporarily been awarded to the father, Tony Chaytor--because the mother is missing or dead. Eleanor will be kept in a hospital for therapeutic purposes for the next while.

~~~~~~~~~~~~~~~~~~~~~~~~~~~~~~~~

# CHAPTER 34: CARMELLA, 2012

August 7 2012:

I live suspended between my desire to survive the plague of global warming, and an emotional paralysis that makes each breath a burden. My last hope is this Astute submarine, safely moored in a bay on a remote movie set off the Florida coast while we do another reality TV show for Newton PR. It is a hot night. I rest up on the deck before the next scene. My cellular phone is ringing... The man's voice says, "Carmella Meeks, this is Detective Snipes from the Fort Pierce Police Department."

"Fuck off," I say.

"We have confirmed the identity of a teenager discovered at the cult den in Eldorado, Texas, identified as Eleanor Meeks," Detective Snipes says. "We have proved that you are related--traced the DNA through hospital records. The DNA records indicate that you are related to the young woman."

Snipes sounds gay. "No way." I say.

"It has taken us a long time to unravel the history of Eleanor. We'll fry the pedophiles," Snipes says.

My throat is dry. "I'm stoned. Why don't you call back tomorrow?"

"This is *important,*" Detective Snipes persists. "It's a pedophile case."

"Bullshit. I never did anything wrong in my life," I say.

"No. It's your sister Marise that we are after." Snipes says.

"My sister doesn't have a child."

"First Marise tried to abort her daughter Eleanor. Then..."

"But Mr. Snipes, abortion is *legal* in America. Hillary Clinton will be President soon. It's a woman's right to choose."

"The child was three years old lady--at the time she was abandoned," the cop says.

"Eleanor was adopted out at that age," I say.

"Your sister is going to jail, for a long time lady."

"Bullshit. Marise died in the EQE building collapse at Fort Pierce. Check it out!"

"Costody has been awarded to the child's father, Tony Chaytor... do you know him?"

"I had nothing to do with the death of that girl, Marise, under the EQE building collapse... I suspect that Newt Gingrinch did that to set Tony up--made sure that Tony went looking for his real Marise so he could use us both, blackmail Tony and I to conform to his plan—to control Hillary... knowing that her bleeding heart has a soft spot for me. Oh shit! I sound weird. And what does Tony have to hide?"

I don't know if Detective Snipes says anything after that. The phone falls out of my hand. I am not ready for such terrible news. Guilt taints my blood, requiring my heart to pump harder. My blood is a leaden poison, a guilt mire that sears my wrists with it's terrible cold. I do know that I am lost, lost, fucking lost! What I did not know is that I love Eleanor very much. But I have forgotten something: The Newton PR show is on a break and I am due back on the set. Fuck!

# PART XIV: THE DIARY

## CHAPTER 35: CARMELLA, 2012

August 17, 2012:

I try to live in the present, but on this hot August day my past continues to prey upon me, even though I have filled two diaries--designed to exorcise me of that haunting shame:

I couldn't contact Tony for several years after we first met--well I didn't even try because Eleanor was black and autistic, and I didn't want to burden myself with explaining the blackness--and Tony thought that Eleanor had been aborted. It seemed like fate back then, fate that Tony and I would be apart for a while, until I sorted out the child problem. But sometimes I had wished that he could hear my prayers, and wished that Tony would show up unexpectedly and find me with both Marise and Eleanor--and ruin my deceit.

The very day my father got a letter from Tony, Captain C-J wrote back. My father told him that I had a child, Marise.

Tony never enquired who the father was because we had intended to call our love child by the name Marise--I didn't change her name to Eleanor until after Tony had left, five months before Eleanor was born. Therefore he didn't want to know the truth--that he was not the father of my second daughter Marise. I wonder if I am more immoral than most people? No! Tony chose to deny the evidence--in the same way the American people deep down know they have been lied to about Port Chicago, Pearl Harbor, 9/11, and the Iraq war. The American people don't want to know that thermite was used to detonate WTC-7, or that Father Christmas and Hillary Clinton are not real. We have all become accustomed to swallowing white lies, and have developed the psychological techniques required to deny the truth.

I never did abort Eleanor! Who could do such a thing when it comes down to it? Eleanor was born with autism, and she seemed to know my entire history because she often glared at me and scratched me. It was horrible. When I got pregnant to Marise's father, Buck, I thought about letting Eleanor out for adoption. That is, until I read that magazine article about Hillary Clinton. It said that abortion is OK when all else is impossible, but that once a child is born the child's parents must keep the child at all costs, unless there is abuse or beating of the child in the home. Only then should an institutional adoption be considered.

It has turned out fortunate for me that I changed the name of my first baby from Marise to Eleanor just before the birth--leaving the name Marise vacant for the next child... in the same way that Hillary Clinton has gone to New Zealand and left the media identity of Hillary vacant. Hillary is rather vacant herself at the moment, has been overcome by too much disappointment and needs bed rest. This will enable Tony and I to create Simtwo to take advantage of her history but run a more effective election campaign than that which resulted in her unfortunate rejections of 2008—we have already built a digital 3D model, the voice is synthesized, and the wardrobe purchased... Bill, and hopefully an alert Hillary, will be excited when we score high in the polls.

That Snipes detective calls me again--says that I can see Eleanor when the bruises from her beatings go down. There was no beating of Eleanor by me. But Buck could have been a different story. I took good care of Eleanor despite the fact that she had the devil in her, often hurting me with her claws. Her autism was not my fault, as I had assumed. I heard on TV that autism is caused by the Federal Government! They put too much mercury in the compulsory vaccines for polio, measles, tetanus, and all the other diseases that the government is afraid our children will inherit. I was so ashamed that I kept Eleanor hidden away from the world. Buck knew that Eleanor existed, but Tony and my parents didn't.

~~~~~~~~~~~~~~~~~~~~~~~

November 9, 2012:

It was great that Hillary won the Presidency; I am so pleased for her. It sure has been keeping Tony busy—he's hardly ever home. But, I rush ahead too fast. Often I have to stop and go back to digest just how the terrible evil came into my life.

I was with my older friend, Vanessa, side by side on the bed in room no. 2, as we chatted about our lives. We both had started working at the Magic Touch Night Club in Fort Pierce three weeks before, and decided to share the same room while there. I had to drop out of my nursing course. There was no alternative. I had paid part of my college tuition, but there was no money left over. So that's why I was back in Fort Pierce, trying to get some more cash. It was the only thing I could do. Vanessa and I still had plenty of time before the club opened. It would be a long day, and we didn't have anything to do. The previous nights had been good. I was always amazed by Vanessa's willingness to work after so much time in the business.

That evening it did not take long before two customers arrived. One of them was a pretty cat, about 30 years old, well dressed, wonderful smile, shaved, tidy short hair, and in good shape. Everything was a perfect. It is logical for my personality that I did not give attention to him, but to his friend who was an older guy--gray, short, chubby, and a little tense... and may be sexually less active. But before I went with him I asked the program girl for information about this older man, and she told me that he had a smallish penis and enjoyed fast sex. "This man belongs to me!" I said.

I approached, smiling, a little meek. I did my angel trick on the little guy. Both men looked at me. I asked the older man, "What is your name?" He looked me over from head to feet, with a superior look. What an ass that guy was.

He frowned and asked, "Why do you want to know?"

I didn't react. He didn't have the presence to know what to say now that there was a long silence. Finally his mouth opened and talked the first thing that came to him: "You are an interesting person." It got worse. He turned to his friend, said nothing, and left as if I never existed.

He came back an hour later. I understood why he wasn't comfortable there. I tried to be more hospitable this time and stretched the talk: "You always come here?"

"No."

"Newt's your name?" My question was polite but he was shocked that his friend had told me his name. We finally talked. He said he was a salesman in Washington DC. I kissed him. We went to the little corner table; I ordered my whiskey with an energy drink added. I had only drunk half when he propositioned me; "We go to the room now?"

He paid only $80. I didn't argue. I didn't have the personality to argue about money.

I did him at once.

The next time he came we went to room no. 2 immediately. This time he was cooler. He was even affectionate. I was calm and kept listening to wave after wave of self-pitying bullshit, and telling him that, today, I would do anal sex with him, without preservative, only for him because he is special. After much joking I proposed that we put on the condom. I was mad at that man. He was too fast, but, as there was a prior agreement to enjoy ourselves for two hours, I told myself that I had to pretend. Newt gasped, perspired, and then trembled all over.

He lay down by my side, finished. We talked about life and drank the single beer left in the hallway fridge. I drank, sucked it into my mouth, and passed the beer from my lips to his. We then took a close bath and went back to the bar. I asked for one more energy drink with a whiskey dose. Red seven they called it. That kept me dancing. After I drank my thoughts changed to Buck. Newt talked but I hardly heard him. I did hear him say he was married. "Newt, what did your wife do to make you unfaithful to her?"

He answered, "Nothing, she's great."

I was Petrified. This is a man's instinct! I felt a profound sadness. How was I going to find any man who always wants to be with me? Does such a domesticated man exist? Does this feeling that I imagine should occur between a man and a woman ever happen: Love, fidelity, respect, dedication and friendship? Everything gathered and tempered with sex and chemical attraction? Is it too much to ask from life?

I took Newt outside for fresh air. I forgot about the time limit and was almost at the door of his car. Wilson shrilled at me. "Come back, Carmella, remember the time limit."

"Sorry Wilson, I forgot again." And it was true. I was such an airhead, fighting against my reflections and against the memories of all the torments of my relationship with Buck.

Two days later I got a call from Wilson--the escort manager at the gate. They had an outcall client for me. I had almost forgot about Newt. Wilson picked me up in a limo and told me Newt Gingrinch, the former congressman from DC, was waiting at the Sheraton hotel. The Magic Touch charged him $500. I'd get four hundred bucks from it.

The limo pulled into the hotel parking lot. Wilson dropped me off at the room and wished me luck. "You should play with his ass hole. It drives guys crazy!" "And what the hell is that?" I thought to myself. But I put my best smile when I got to the room. Newt wanted to know what my name was. "Carmella. And you?" Oops. It was my first blunder. He told me his name was Newt, and when he asked what I did for a living I blushed so badly I practically had to confess that I was a nursing major instead of a prostitute. He told me that it really didn't make any difference what I did. That Newt guy was in his fifties, the former speaker of the house of Congress, and was going through a divorce again. He was now a regular at the Magic Touch when he was in Florida because he went there whenever he felt depressed, and it happened almost every day.

Newt had some privileges on account of being a regular client and so had upgraded to the presidential suite at our client hotel--located just two blocks from the Magic Touch. "You are worth of it," He told me, and I felt flattered. The Sheraton is the best hotel in the region. The rooms are equipped with Jacuzzis. We chatted while he ate his dinner and then enjoyed a nice bath. It was a cool session, with nothing out of the ordinary. I even forgot all about that ass play stuff. We spent most of the night talking about family, future, life's setbacks, and money. Soon the receptionist called to tell us that our time was up and the Magic Touch had sent someone to pick me up.

I wondered why people talked about "Magic Touch" so pompously--as if it was some big important entertainment corporation. But it was time to say goodbye. Newt wanted my cell phone number, but I explained that I was not allowed to give him that information and he had to contact Magic Touch if he wanted to see me again. Newt assured me that he most certainly would, talking as if he should be obligated toward me—the attitude of a man who lacks fidelity. I said goodnight hurriedly.

Wilson asked me how had the client liked it. "I guess he was happy," I said. "So you must be an expert in ass hole play." I just nodded with a smile and quickly changed the subject. I asked if he could get me some more clients, "Cause I really needed the money."

"Sure. If you promise you'll be a nice girl and behave, I'll get you all the clients you can handle."

Now I just had to find someone to explain to me what ass play was.

I was spending little time studying. I still felt exhausted due to my new position. Hillary and I wrote every week, but she never knew about my prostitution job, not until she started reading my diary.

The out-call deal was doing it. I made $935 that week. It wasn't bad, but it wasn't the best I could accomplish either. Newt wanted to see me at the Sheraton again. He was a man in crisis, looking for some great orgasm that could help him untangle his soul from his ex wife's life. Therapy was just what the guy needed, and soon. I asked what he meant by untangling his soul.

He just said: "Well, that's a good question."

We had a nice time together. He is an easygoing type of guy who knows how to respect privacy. In bed, he finished it off quickly, and so quietly I barely noticed it. And he's always concerned about making me feel good. They made an excellent chocolate mousse at the Sheraton, and it always made me feel great--the mousse and the Jacuzzi. The only problem is I couldn't linger in there alone for as much time as I'd like to. I'd have stayed in the Jacuzzi all night long if I could.

That night, after our sex session, I was about to get in the Jacuzzi when he asked me to leave his suite. I pretended to feel hurt and rejected. But the truth is, I wasn't hurt. On the contrary, not even the nicest client in the world would make me feel like staying with him longer than was necessary. But Newt threw a tantrum because of my rush for the Jacuzzi. Then I could see his wife had plenty of reasons to leave him. He said he was fed up with the call girls he'd been hiring for months--and now he wanted a real girlfriend. He told me that I could keep seeing him if I wanted to, but it would require that I spend the week with him in Washington DC.

"How much?"

"Three thousand plus expenses!"

"Maybe."

I went to the pharmacy, to buy lubricating gel and moisturizing cream for massaging him. With Buck I did not have time to understand: I was required to perform immediately when he wanted me. Love blinded me so that I lost my identity. But I was the guilty one; I was guilty of not having had the courage to take care of myself.

Buck was five years older than me and was a nymphomaniac. At the beginning, I did not identify that problem because he hid his addiction to sex. We had a normal sex relationship, as does any couple that starts out. I was to discover major problems later. The separation was very difficult and painful, but, when something goes wrong, you have to remove the problem. He was quiet, introspective, seemed to like to have a lot of me, very often. But he had the habit of suddenly leaving the house and coming back an hour later. As usual, when he came back we finished fucking. I never imagined that the reason he suddenly left was to go fuck another woman. After a while, Buck was leaving the other women and depositing in me all his needs, and his sickness. At the beginning, there was sex three times a day, but that proceeded to becoming seven, eight, and nine. I did not do anything else and, in a way, was annulling myself as a person. I lived for Buck. My life shrank little by little, in a very subtle way. And that fissure for sex started to tire me.

I had to regulate our sex relations, and it became worse then. He revolted and left. He stayed out for an hour or a night, and came back calm. From then onwards we did not always live in the same house, but we were definitely boyfriend and girlfriend, including having sex. We ate meals together, and, generally, I slept in his bed, or he slept in mine. I had stopped working until then and studied full-time. Buck worked well and helped me. That happened naturally between us, because he liked spending a lot of time with me. However, it inconvenienced him that I started working on Saturdays in the realtor business because he wanted us to stay together all day Saturday also, fucking. We use to fuck so much that I learnt to do many things. such as Karma sutra positions, front and reverse.

One night when I slept at his house the same fight started as always. Already we had fucked five times in that day and he wanted more. I was tired and wanted to sleep more. I had advised him to consult a psychologist, but he gave up after his therapy session the previous Friday. I was convinced that I was also diseased with an STD because of his irresponsible sluttish behavior. He beat the door and left. I lost sleep because I knew that he would come back in little more than one hour. I

173

started to think that perhaps he had a steady girlfriend elsewhere.

I went to his home office where he had a computer and files. He worked as an architect's assistant. There were so many papers and plans. I searched through every paper, looking for anything. When I was ready to give up and thinking I was crazy, I found a book with his handwriting and the title, *VOL. II.* I opened it, without expectations--because what I suspected would be in a love letter... in a note with a phone number. That is the way of secret lovers.

I opened the book out of pure curiosity and because it was hidden, in the bottom drawer. I respected his privacy and he believed that I would not inspect his things. I almost fainted! "No! No! No! It cannot be. That cannot be true!" The book contained a list of women's names with which he had relations, as well as an explanatory text of what they had done. I searched for me, in *VOL. II.* Found! The date of our first encounter, the ways we did it. I was the girl number 991 of his life. After me, there were more than 200 others. By the dates, I could tell that he had done several other women on the same day as me. The world, for me, was finished. I could not believe that I had been so betrayed. I felt used: A sexual slave. It meant that the relationship did not exist, except in my mind.

I came back from the pharmacy with my massage oil, lubricating gel, and these memories of how everything had started and ended with Buck, thinking: "Today it is Tuesday. Soon, there will be few customers." I became happier after I returned to the Magic Touch; I only had that job to keep my mind occupied. An empty mind is the devil's workshop. I must concentrate on my work and my friendship with the girls. I went into the salon. The girls and I started to dance, as if just we were there. We were happy. Someone burst a lot of popcorn on the floor.

At 11pm, Wilson called out to me: "Phone for you." It was Newt Gingrinch. He could not manage to come over and was in bed in his hotel room. He asked if I would go there. I went to the Sheraton. It was good for me and great for him. Newt again invited me to go to Washington DC with him, to stay with him for a week. "Three thousand dollars if you will do everything I want."

"OK."

We kissed and hugged for a long time. The problem was that his penis was small, and I almost did not feel anything. I had to put my fingers into action. We kept talking. I massaged him and then asked to take another bath. I started to masturbate him with my foot. I learnt that men stay crazy when I jerk them off with their penis between my toes. Then we did what merely passed for a 69. At least his tongue worked. He invited me to sleep there, and we caught a plane in the morning.

I enjoyed Christmas shopping in Washington DC, alone with Newt's credit card. I received a call on his cell phone just when I was about to return to our hotel. I was not far from the White House so put up the hood of my cape so the President would not recognize me should he glance through his window in the oval office... Newt was a little agitated. He arranged to take me for a walk in a private section of the White House gardens to talk out his bad behavior. Newt apologized to me for abruptly leaving the restaurant at lunchtime; he explained that he felt jealous about me being in love with Tony Chaytor. Afterwards we took a stroll in the garden, and sat on the edge of a garden bench. I noticed at one corner beyond the garden, at the street, a honking Cadillac, that because of its yellow color it resembled a taxi.

"Come on. Let's go," Newt said.

I got in. It was fall, and coming up to dusk. I was dressed in high heels, a dark suit with a pleated skirt, a silk blouse, and a sleeveless black cape. My leather gloves were the only new item. In my leather handbag I had my identification papers, my compact, and my new lipstick.

The car moved off slowly. Newt hadn't said a word to the driver, who was separated from the two of us by a sliding partition. Newt pulled down the shades of the windows on both sides of the car, and the shades of the back window, and the partition. I took off my gloves, thinking that Newt would want to kiss me or that he would want me to caress him. But instead he said:

"Your handbag is in my way. Let me have it."

I gave it to him. He put it out of my reach and said, "You also have too many clothes on. Unfasten your stockings and roll them down to above your knees. Here are some garters."

By now the car had picked up speed, and I has some trouble managing the maneuver. Newt wasn't afraid that the driver might turn around. Finally the stockings were rolled down, and I was embarrassed to feel my legs naked and free beneath my silk slip. Besides, the loose garter-belt suspenders were slipping back and forth.

"Unfasten your garter belt, and take off your panties," Newt said. That was easy enough, all I had to do was to slip my hands behind my back and raise myself slightly. Newt took the garter belt and panties from me, opened my bag and put them in. "You shouldn't sit on your slip and skirt. Put them behind you and sit directly on the seat."

The seat was made of some kind of calf leather that felt cold. It was sticking to my thighs.

"Now put your gloves back on," Newt said. It is uncanny that I couldn't resist Newt's commands, but I was not drugged in any way.

The car was still moving along at a good clip, and Newt just sat there without moving or saying another word, nor could I guess what all this meant to Newt-- having me here motionless, silent, so stripped and exposed, so thoroughly gloved, in a yellow Cadillac. I had no idea where we were going. Newt hadn't told me what to do or what not to do, but I was afraid either to cross my legs or press them together. I sat with gloved hands braced on either side of my seat.

"Here we are," Newt said suddenly. The car stopped on a lovely avenue, beneath a tree, in front of a three-story Victorian mansion painted a beige color with a darker trim and a sign saying *Skulls Chateau*. The street lamps were some distance away, and it was still fairly dark inside the car. Outside it was now raining.

"Don't move," Newt said. "Sit perfectly still."

He reached for the collar of my blouse. I leaned forward slightly, thinking he wanted to fondle my breasts. No. He was merely groping for the shoulder straps of my brassiere, which he snipped with a tiny pocketknife. Then he took it off. Now, beneath my blouse, which he had buttoned back up. My breasts were naked and free, as was the rest of my body, from waist to knee.

Then he asked me to sit on his lap, to straddle him. This was my father's favorite position on a Sunday morning, after dropping Mama off at church. He wouldn't allow me to go to church. He called traditional organized religion a mind-fuck. My father and Newt both wore trousers from the best fabric, pleasantly rough on my bare skin. Newt stroked me gently for a time then lifted me back onto the seat and knelt down to kiss my juice. I lifted my knees and welcomed him. Newt had changed since I told him about my past, changed a lot.

"Listen," Newt said. "Now you're ready, nice and juicy. This is where I leave you. Follow whoever opens the door to the Skulls mansion for you, and do whatever you're told. You will be safe, and in no way disrespected."

"My bag?"

"No. You have no further need for your bag. I wish for you to be entirely unencumbered by morality, cultural conditioning, or material baggage. Yes, of course I'll be there. Now enjoy yourself Sweetheart."

A man with short hair and thick neck had been driving the Cadillac and he explained that I would be turned over to the men from the Skulls Chateau, where in due course I would be instructed as to what I should do. The car door was opened by two young and handsome men dressed in the garb of sixteenth century courtiers: wigs, wide-shouldered colorful satin jackets with ruffles, tapering to narrow hips, with full length scarlet tights which sharply accentuate their bulging sticks. The two doormen helped me to alight from the car, guided me up a few steps and through several doors.

As I walked this guided path my curiosity was rising. I looked at myself in the mirror that hung before me at the end of the hallway. My hair bounced around my shoulders and my green eyes looked clear and wide. I was dressed in red high heels, a sleeveless black cape, and a dark suit with a pleated skirt, a silk blouse, and a silk slip. My legs were naked and my breasts and hips felt cool as silk slid loosely across my skin.

They left me alone in a warm but dark Skulls Chateau reception room, lit only by a giant fluorescent fish tank. A plate of finger food was the first thing I observed as my eyes accustomed to the dim. I helped myself to an excellent guacamole dip. After what seemed like ten minutes duration the door was opened and the light turned on, I could see that I had been waiting in an unusual room. There was a thick rug on the floor, but not a stick of furniture, and all four walls were lined with closets.

The boyish doormen returned and walked me again, accidentally brushing my buttocks as we turned corners in another hallway. We arrived at an empty beauty salon that was warm and softly lit. The boys told me to get undressed, and informed me that they were going to bathe me and make me up. It was obvious that I was forbidden territory for their youthful lusts and that sexual touching was subject to some form of embarrassing admonishment. I encouraged them to strip my silk blouse and slip until I hadn't a stitch of clothing on. Their hands were nervous as they fumbled around my breasts and inner thighs. They put my clothes away neatly in one of the closets. I was not permitted to bathe myself. The boys tried to behave professionally--but they shoved each other in competition for access to my orifices.

After massaging me all over they made me sit in one of those large chairs, which tilted back while they washed my hair. They massaged my head as proficiently as any hairdresser, and they straightened me back up after my hair had been set and I was ready for the dryer. The boys joked and flirted more maturely as they waited for my hair to dry. This took another hour so we had drinks, and since the wall in front of me was covered from floor to ceiling with a large mirror, which was unbroken by any shelving, I could see myself, thus open, each time my gaze strayed to the mirror.

When I was properly made up and prepared--my eyelids penciled lightly; my lips bright red; the tip and halo of my breasts highlighted with pink; the edges of my nether lips rouged; my armpits and pubis generously perfumed, and perfume was applied to the furrow between my thighs, the furrow between my breasts, and to the hollows of my hands--I was led into another warm room where a three-sided mirror, and another mirror behind, enabled me to examine myself closely.

I was told to sit down on an ottoman, which was set between the mirrors, and to wait. The ottoman was covered with black fur, which prickled me slightly; the rug was black, the walls red. I was wearing red mules. Set in one of the walls of the small bedroom was a large window, which looked out onto a floodlit park. The rain had stopped, but the trees were swaying in the wind, and the moon raced high among the clouds.

I had no idea how long I remained in the red bedroom, or whether I was really alone, or whether someone was watching me through a peephole camouflaged in the wall. All I knew was that when the two men returned, one was carrying a dressmaker's tape measure and the other a basket. With them came a masked man dressed in a long purple robe, the sleeves of which were gathered at the wrists and full at the shoulders. When he walked the robe flared open, from the waist down. Beneath the robe he had on some sort of tights that covered his legs and thighs but left his donkey sized stick exposed. Then I saw the two-headed vibrator that he had slung in his belt. Then I saw that a black hood did not only mask the man, but that even his eyes were concealed. But behind the mask there was a network of black gauze. And, finally, that he was also wearing fine black kid gloves--which were reaching for his huge stick.

He led me to a bedroom and massaged my feet with his tongue, and gradually spread his stimulation to other erogenous places, until I had several orgasms under the intensity of his fine tongue work, followed up by the expanding world of his vibrator. My orgasms spread to the far reaches of my pelvic center… I was left to recover alone. Then an invisible hand passed a plate of steaming hors d'oeuvres through a small window in the door.

When my appetizers were consumed the first two men come into the bedroom and covered me with a long red cape. It covered me completely, but opened when I walked, and, being fully aroused, I had no desire to close it. One man walked in front, opening the doors. The other man followed, closing the doors. They crossed a vestibule, a living room, and a billiard room, and entered a library where four men were having coffee—in front of a fire, around an ottoman. They were wearing Zorro masks, and the same long purple robes as the other man. I didn't have an opportunity to see if their faces were also covered with a network of black gauze, or to ascertain whether Newt was among them. Everyone remained stock still, the two men flanking me, and the men in front, studying me. Then they walked forward, took me by the arm and led me until I was standing in front of the fire, standing on a huge bearskin rug. I could feel the heat and in the silence, could hear the quiet crackling of the burning logs. I was facing the fire.

Two hands lifted my cape from me. Two other hands descended the length of my back and buttocks. The hands were not gloved, and were warm, smooth with oil. They invited me to sit on the ottoman.

They turned me around, and the heat of the fire was against my back. A hand grazed one of my breasts; a tongue licked on the tip of the other. I was gently lifted and laid out on the bearskin rug. (Supported by whose arms? Was Newt there?) Then they opened my legs and gently spread my lips. Hair grazed the inside of my thighs.

"She's so lovely?"

"Yes, a pleasure."

"And never to be mistreated?"

"No, never. But as a matter of fact..."

Is that you speaking Newt?

"As a matter of fact," the other voice went on, "If she gets so turned on that she demands penis penetration, then we shall pause, partake of our excellent wine and cheese, and discuss where to go from there."

"We must surely get her past the pleasure stage, to the stage of ecstasy."

"Is that you Newt?" I ask.

"Yes," says a voice I recognize. "Do you feel safe?"

"Am I safe, tomorrow?"

"Yes. These are my friends, leading us on an erotic journey."

While the men were circling my body and circling my sex with their tongues, one of the men cupped my breasts up high, bit my nipple sharply, and then kissed the back of my neck. The first vibrator approached me slowly, whirring softly. I was overwhelmed with a sense of inner warmth, passionate pleasure that took on new dimensions as all my orifices were filled—with a texture of primal as well as aristocratic knowledge.

When I came down from the next extended orgasm I could hear glasses being filled, the sound of men laughing, and the scraping of chairs. One man touched my inner thigh with his tongue, then my pubic mound, and my juice. That set me off again. It went on like this again and again, through many fantasies and pleasures... until I pleaded, "No more Sweetheart. That was perfect."

The men put wood on the fire and talked about a submarine project. Newt said it was ready, fully stocked, and docked beyond the mouth of the Russian River, near the Bohemian Grove.

"So when do we leave?" another asked.

"When the carbon dioxide levels climb a further fifty percent," Newt said.

"What about fresh water? We can't carry enough to stay submerged for two years?" another man said.

Flaming hell! They were planning to survive global warming. This may be a better plan than my scheme to survive in C-J's tin fish… but I shall try to keep both options open.

"We have a desalinator," Newt said.

"Won't the Navy get suspicious?" the other man asked.

"No. It's on a secret mission, and the Admiral is coming with us," Newt said.

Could this be true? I listened furtively for a further five minutes then stood. They passed me a glass of wine and invited me to sit in their circle. They talked about the latest literature, music, art--and the state of the environment. This serious talk was soon replaced with wit and sexual jousting. I enjoyed the warmth of their company, and my only wish was that Tony could become so free spirited, a sexual beast.

~~~~~~~~~~~~~~~~~~~~~~~~~~

December 2, 2012:

Following Hillary's suggestion, I have been patient in recreating my truth. My job with this diary has been to record my history accurately, and then to quickly turn the page. As a result I think I have finally decided what sort of life that I would like to have. I would like a life with more serenity, security and energy. I can only get there by the grace of God because often I am lethargic and depressed.

"…Time is short. From now those who have husbands should live as if they had none; those who mourn as if they did not…. those who use the things of the world, as if not engrossed in them. For this world in its present form is passing away." The Holy Bible, I Corinthians 7: 29-31. So, I have my Noah's ark plan to survive the end times in a submarine --as the curtain is about to fall on America.

~~~~~~~~~~~~~~~~~~~~~~~~~~~~~

December 3, 2012:

I, Carmella Meeks, have lived a fast life but am still young. It is difficult for me to keep clear about all the details, some days. But I have been patient in recreating my truth: Papa C-J chose to serve the Navy, and I chose to fuck white guys…. It's all of it inevitable: The madness brought on by the victimization of the child, Pecola, raped by her father, frightens others, causes them to shun her because of her uncanny staring eyes, and her chronic fatigue. Her madness spooks everyone… As does my wandering like an animal indulging in useless, repetitive sexual adventures--reenacting the original sexual encounters with my father… Fucking psychobabble!

There are very interesting events in my past. There are things I prefer not to

179

remember. My job has been to quickly forget. Sometimes, I ask myself if there is a point in time after which I would prefer to rewrite my history. Or, in other words, if I started again, would I do everything different after that horrid turning point in my life of being born black? Of course, there are many turning points since--but my self-esteem problem started with my father, and his with his father--the shame of the court martial resulting from the Port Chicago nuclear detonation. I call papa C-J in Puerto Rico to tell him to have the tin fish ready to sail in the New Year... There is no answer.

~~~~~~~~~~~~~~~~~~~~~~~~~~~~~~

I was due at the hairdresser ten minutes ago. I rush from my bedroom and down the stairs. My hairdresser jokes about me wearing my slippers to his salon. I decide to use the same subtle reddish hair color as last month. I have to wait forty minutes for the color to take. My magazine drops. I am falling asleep in the chair.

I hate that drugged feeling of waking from a deep sleep. I drive home in a fog, not pleased with my new hairstyle. I know Tony doesn't like me wearing my hair up. And today my hair swirls like a massive rope on top of my head. My home is an old wooden villa with high ceilings. My hair is so high I cannot see the top of it in my bedroom mirror without dipping my knees. I can hear the wind lifting and rattling the open window. A lone gull is surfing the wind gusts beyond the oak tree as the sun peaks. Was that a shadow crossing behind me? What is wrong? Oh my God! I left my diary on the bed when I went to the hairdressers. There is a note beside it!

*Carmella, I read the diaries that you left out on our bed... Tony.*

Damn! He will be home any minute. Fuck! I can hear him now, parking his car in the garage. The diaries were Hillary Clinton's idea--for us to share and examine our lives openly and truthfully. I am holding my breath, waiting for Tony to open my bedroom door--he is walking slowly up the stairs. I am waiting on the bed.

Tony looks gray and worn.

"Why did you read my private diary?" I scream at him.

"The diaries were sitting on the bed... You wanted me to read them. I have always respected your privacy. But clearly you wanted me to..."

"You bastard!"

"No! It cannot be. Your diary cannot be true. Say it's fiction," Tony begs.

"What? You want me to lie *now*?" I say.

"No. But I can help you?"

"OK. You are white and I am black. Change that!"

Tony stampedes down the stairs. The front door slams. He is walking across the civil war field. He stops half way, his back to me. His body is convulsing, wretched.

I am abandoned. I feel panic accelerating, then my circuits break down. I am numb. My therapist wants me to remember the rapes by my father, to recover the reality of that traumatic experience from the silence and repression. But I can't remember that. And the diary idea has caused me to lose my husband. To hell with counselors and therapists... I *will* go for counseling only when Tony and Hillary insist, but for no longer than necessary.

Damn! Mr. Newt Gingrinch, the epitome of the corrupt modern man, has been entrusted with the passions of my wife. Am I doomed because of my Calvinistic shadows? Dig Lazarus dig. …. But how can I dig my way out of this… this threat to my marriage? Not only am I not the father of my daughter Marise, or either of Carmella's daughters according to the diary, (but Detective Snipes and I know different)… and my wife is fucking my boss—Newt, and his ass-licking friends. It is disturbing how treacherous life can be.

A breeze lifts and a fat cloud darkens the sun. The gloom is interrupted by the ringing of the dinner bell. Surprise! Carmella is calling me in to the kitchen… and early.

"Would you like a hot drink?" Carmella asks. I step through the kitchen door into the aroma of coffee and fresh scones.

"Thank you." The kitchen counter has fresh fruit and damp trails from being wiped clean. The picture windows have trails of detergent as I look over the fields with shadows of racing clouds to the left, and the bruised lake to the right. The new kitchen table is freshly polished. I sit beside the larger plate of scones with raspberry jam.

There are three bowls; one with guacamole, another with corn chips, and the other with bean dip. Carmella's bean dip! I dip a scoop of chip into the reddish paste of beans and coriander, then lifting to my mouth; I experience the scrunch, the cold, the texture of pinto beans, the scent of garlic, the sharpness of lime juice. Then another taste, maybe the musty flick of oregano on the end of a sweet bite of diced onion.

"Don't eat it all. It's for Marise's birthday party," Carmella says.

"Thank you… and for the cleaning. Did you have a siesta?"

"Strange dreams. I'm sorry about what I've put you through… I have been slow to recognize my problems."

"I take it you're volunteering to turn a new leaf?"

She blinks, three times, quickly, "Yes, I'm punished by my dreams. I intend to make it up to you."

"I've had a dream also. About you apologizing and seeing a proper therapist," I say.

She sits on the chair adjacent to mine, not opposite, and doesn't sit all the way back. She perches on the front edge, leaning forward, with her hands flat on the table. Her legs are bent at the knee and crossed at the ankle. Her boots are shiny black with small heels and chisel toes. I do not like her new haircut. "Is that really what you want to happen? Or are you setting me up?" she asks.

"Maybe understanding it, or trying to, is a means of working through it," I say.

Carmella nods, maybe agreeing with me, or perhaps just allowing the moment. Then she smiles stiffly. Carmella moves, leaning forward, drawing her feet back towards the chair, and then her ankles entwine the chair legs, her forearms are on the table, and her hands flat, facing upwards.

I let the pause lengthen. I can feel her uncertainty, her discouragement beneath the mask of her social competence.

"I'm here to try," she says, "to see if we can work through our past."

Maybe this is the right time to confront her. "You used and abused me," I say after a long silence.

"And you used me." Carmella sips from her coffee. "And, that's what people do in relationships. Use each other, kindly in good relationships. Right?"

"No! There's another level where there is trust."

She looks directly at me, takes another sip of her coffee, and looks down.

"In what way did I use you?" she asks softly.

I look out the window again. The garden shrubs form a shield but they are not impenetrable. Like a painting, they draw you in and invite you to a space where strange things can happen. I watch her; see the uplifted nose, a pained grimace to her mouth, and the shame, the inevitable shame.

"Where to start?" she asks. "We were under great pressure, almost beyond our ability to endure. But this happened that we may not rely upon ourselves, but on God, who raises the dead. he has delivered us from such a deadly peril, and he has delivered us. On him we have set our hope that he will continue to deliver us. II Corinthians, 1:8-12"

"Here's the deal. You cheated on me. Think about it," I say.

"How can you possibly know what my motives were?"

"For a start, when you were out fucking around you obviously weren't considering me--or our family."

"What *are* you doing?"

"Our marriage has been a lie!"

Carmella takes another sip of coffee and slowly stands up. She looks as if she might hit me. Suddenly her expression is twisting up, the tears threatening. "You are wrong. My father raped me, and I haven't dealt with it well. I'm sorry. I fucked up. But for God's sake, have some compassion."

The phone rings. I ignore it. I don't understand what is going on here. "Forgiveness is something we have to earn."

"Maybe I am sick, and need help."

She gives a little sigh while she is conquering her emotions. Seeing her do it, watching her fight back the tears is almost as guilt provoking as the tears themselves. But I have to finish the confrontation now that I've started it.

"Manipulation and bullshit are your tools of trade."

And now she tries tears again. "I figured that I had to screw Newt to get our freedom. You and Hillary are slaves to him. I have a secret plan to save our family."

"Tell me about it?"

"I had a long term plan, but that will seem crazy now. I really want to design a new relationship where monogamy is the goal."

"Damn it Carmella, you cheated on me, abandoned my daughter Eleanor, deceived me about who Marise's birth father is... and have never tried to make amends, all these years later. I call that out-of-control behavior."

"You are vicious," she spits her words. "And it wasn't an abandonment. It was an adoption. You don't like my new haircut do you?"

I look her down in exasperation. She grins, knowing that I cannot rebuke that.

"Keep your voice down, Marise will be coming home from school soon," I say.

"Oh shit! Carmella's hands cover her mouth as her head bows. She peers between her fingers. I've got a confession--The cat got Marise's pet lizard." Carmella stands suddenly, breathing fast through her nostrils, pacing beside me.

The word confession grabs at me. "Where was the lizard?"

"In her room. She was playing with it on her bed. Then I opened the door to her room and the cat pounced in."

"How'd Marise take it?"

"I don't know that an eighteen year old should be talking to me like that: *I've told you before to knock before you come into my room! Why does life always have to be tragic around you?*"

"Oh dear--she's really seventeen--then what?"

"I apologized. It was one of those moments when you're walking in a kind of dream. I just walked into her room without even knocking, seeking out her company."

Marise isn't quite an adult yet, but I know what it is like to observe my almost-adult daughter learn to move through the world intelligently, to achieve success with the peace she exudes in her better moments.

Marise might go to my old university for her postgraduate degree--and have a career. She'll marry. Will she really? Perhaps. Perhaps she'll have a child, the start of family traditions, like lamb for Christmas dinner and gifts at midnight. Boys are a different prospect; they grow up and go their own way, but daughters grow up and call their dad's on the phone, talk for ages.

"Your behavior sounds a little desperate," I say.

"Let's get on with it and finish the fight before Marise comes home."

I had thought that Carmella was trying to divert me from the confrontation, evidently not. "I assume this is an acknowledgement that you have lied, lied through your fucking teeth, and that Eleanor really is my daughter—not your father's... and she's smarter than you might think."

"Smart enough to be your puppet fan eh? Disgusting! It's not just about you, Tony. I have an appointment to see Chris Else, a renowned therapist. Get off your high horse and give me a break." Carmella dashes out of the house, slamming the door. I hear her car start. She squeals down the road.

Desperate for something to do I wrap the uneaten food in plastic, and then sink back into my chair. The birds outdoors are singing an irritating trill. There is a bang on the outside wall and the cooking utensils hanging on the kitchen wall move and rattle. Marise's bike has landed. It is more than good fortune that caused them to open a college here—it was Newt who smiled upon us on this occasion.

The door is opening. Marise's thin flushed face moons around the door, framed by a creation of straight, mostly reddish hair. Class is out all ready. Her hair's done differently these days, parted slightly left of middle, and longer on the right side so that it drapes down to her neck. She's dyed the front of this drape a grayish blonde, causing her to look much older than eighteen... seventeen.

"Hi," Marise says, shuffling to the kitchen table.

"Hullo Sweetheart, how's it going?" I look at her, the way she has changed, the way she moves to the refrigerator now, skinny limbs becoming graceful, and I'm overwhelmed. I try to take comfort in the things that haven't changed, like study, horseback riding, and driving her to meet her friends at the library on Saturday mornings... although she would rather ride her bike.

"Is Mama home?"

"No, we're having a fight. She'll be back later."

"It's my fault; I upset her this morning, yelled at her. Why is Mama always wandering into my room wanting hugs? Your cat got in and ate my lizard," she says.

"No. The fight isn't your fault. We're just clearing the air."

"Sometimes I want to push Mama away."

"Give her time. She and I have a lot to work out."

"Good luck with that job. You should feed your cat better."

"How was class?' I ask.

"OK."

Marise is sitting at the kitchen table in her navy-blue jacket with a cream blouse. She is eating cereal, her bony wrist shoveling. Head bowed, not looking at me.

I look out the kitchen window. The heat shimmers off the brow of Lincoln Road. A woman is walking toward my house. Is it Carmella? I wish it were Hillary—I need some advice. It is still three weeks until we fly to New Zealand to bring Hillary back and settle her into the White House after the successful completion of her treatment back in New Zealand—at the New Year. Simtwo has provided the mouthpiece for my pre-recorded interviews, her digital Hillary mask and the voice module have worked perfectly... I specify the carefully chosen words that appear to come from her automatically synchronized mouth and gorgeous lips.

Tonight's birthday party for Marise will be small, time to unwind a little... and Eleanor will not be coming—is still in a psychiatric hospital. But how can Carmella and I possibly unwind from our shit and reach a healthy reconciliation?

# CHAPTER 37, CARMELLA: December 29, 2012

At thirty minutes before midnight on December 29 Tony and I settle into first-class seat 5A of Air New Zealand Flight 5 from Los Angeles to Auckland--where we will arrive at 10.00am on December 31. The jetsetters have booked out this flight, known as the *Cocaine Train* because a primary goal is to party through New Years Eve in New Zealand, and then fly back for another New Year party in Los Angeles... Forty-eight hours of intensive partying. For Tony this trip will be a mixture of work, and partying before and after the gig. In fifteen minutes or so the next leg of the flight will be airborne. I remember thinking earlier, as our flight from DC was about to land, that LAX must be the most dangerous airport in America. Tony was asleep and I heard him talking, and it really is like this . . . As if some stranger was using his mouth as a loudspeaker, "Is Carmella with another man?"

It occurs to me that he has hardly thought about me for the last week. During the first days after the discovery of my sex addiction I was all he thought about, it seemed . . . *Is she going out to bars, with her tits showing, and of course, who is she seeing and who is the father of the kid?*

When his own healing finally began last week, it must have happened very fast . . . as if he had been injected with some antibiotic... or another woman. But there has been no *other woman* for Tony -- not a single date. He has simply . . . healed.

Tony watches his fellow passengers come aboard, mostly partygoers with popping eyes and rapid speech. He watches a gangly Chinese boy with a tennis bag over his shoulder walk down the aisle of the Boeing. Tony stops him and invites him to join us in first class. Xiu Zhou is twenty-five and looks both nervous and excited, his eyes full of the future. Tony envies him. He is flying to a tennis tournament in Dunedin so maybe Xiu and I can hang out when Tony is busy.

There is a lot of wariness between Tony and I now. The relationship has just crutched along for the last two months, but it come to a crisis in that moment when Tony took the phone off the hook two weeks ago... and hope almost died when Tony saw me with Newt out front of the White House back in DC.

As the last passengers begin to trickle on board, Tony is talking, almost obsessively, about the perfume I wore at the one meeting we had with a divorce lawyer, Muleskinner... a friend of Hillary, who was able to talk sense into Tony. Tony can recall its fragrance, exactly, but not the name. "What had it been? Lisome? Lithsome? Lithium, for God's sake?" It dances just beyond his grasp. "It is maddening," he says dully. "Now that she's with another man I miss her. Isn't that amazing the way we men think?"

"Lawnboy? Something stupid like that?"

"No."

"Don't tell me."

"OK," his mind agrees. "No problem, I can quit. I can quit anytime I want. Was the perfume maybe Lifebuoy? No – that's soap. Sorry. Love bite? Lovelorn?"

Tony snaps his seatbelt shut, leans back, closes his eyes, and smells again a four hundred dollar perfume that he can't quite name. (Newt paid for it.)

This is when the flight attendant speaks to him. "Pardon me . . . " she begins, and then stops. Her eyes go from the name on Tony's sweater, *The Trons*, and then turn to the rowdy noise from the rest of the band seated in the back of the economy cabin, to Xiu Zhou asleep on the other side of Tony.

The attendant rethinks herself and starts again.

"Pardon me sir, would you like coffee or orange juice? Tony is amused to see he has flustered her a little. She gestures toward the table at the front of his first class compartment, just below the small movie screen. There are two ice buckets on the table. The slender green neck of a wine bottle pokes out of each. "Of course, I also have champagne."

Tony considers

"Love Boy that's it, no, close but no cigar."

The attendanr offers the champagne again, but only briefly. "No thanks," he says. "And no in-flight service. I think I'll sleep all the way to Auckland. How's the weather look?"

"Some turbulence near Hawaii. Otherwise smooth sailing. Tail wind so we'll be half an hour early. You should be able to see Venus on the horizon?"

"Someone's been taking too many uppers, or coke," Tony says. She laughs. "I think I'll just snooze, thanks."

Tony wakes up flying away from Los Angeles International Airport, on schedule for our appointment to bring back Hillary from New Zealand, and install her in her office in the White House... after the inauguration in February. Tony handles Simtwo as an actor does a prop--for the articulation of character, for support of a role he frequently imagines might become his, the Presidency. Simtwo hides behind the clever lip-syncing software Tony has purchased from the campaign funds. Concealed, veiled, seldom peeping out from behind the shroud, and then only to yearn for the return of her beguiling mask, Simtwo has become part of the family. Tony just wakes up briefly...

During the landing in Dunedin, when the plane bobbles in the wind just a few feet above the ground, Tony feels he can save America from her lack of spiritual clarity. This moment defines his hope. This Moment cures his fear of being insignificant, and feeds his hope of mastering an endeavor and proving something to his dad. It is OK to be incompetent at parking a car, dancing, or listening to boring people, as long as he can master engineering and Hillary's campaign.

Tomorrow Tony and I will spend a foreign New Years Eve in New Zealand, partying and him playing a gig at *Alphar Ranch*, a new Dunedin club, partying with Hillary and Bill now that she is healed, and the next day we all wake up at Los Angeles International Airport, at 10am on New Years Eve, Pacific Standard Time, preparing for the New Year celebrations at the *Alphar Ranch* in DC.

Tony works part-time as a back-up drummer for a rock n' roll band called *The Trons*. He formed the band in August and has become notorious because Tony doesn't play the drums in reality, or sing. He just plays air shots with his drumsticks, and lip-syncs the vocals--throughout the entirety of every gig, relying on the sound tracks from the latest album. He learned that unique skill at a Gospel revival meeting that time at the White House Crusade in DC, when they booked a rap band by mistake. (Never trust politicians to organize anything.) Tony's band has come a long way--they now have a new line-up and play under the coaching of Greg Locke.

Tony is a day person. But he's a surrogate drummer in the Trons. I prefer to stay out and dance all night. Some people are night people. Other people are day people. Tony could only work a day job because he prefers to go to bed at 9pm. He tried playing as a real drummer in a blues band a few years ago, but before 4am he always fell asleep on a sofa or in a closet while waiting for the other band members to finally chill out enough to go home and sleep.

Tomorrow is New Years Eve in New Zealand, and later that night the band will play both forty-minute sets nonstop. While Tony and Bill are rehearsing, Xiu Zhou and I will go and pick up Hillary from Dr. Moon's asylum on the far side of Dunedin. Then, in two days time Tony and I, and the Clintons, will wake up above Washington DC International Airport on New Years Eve, after a New Year Eve concert gig in Dunedin.

This flight is fully booked with party animals on the coke train… but first class is almost vacant. Tony has folded the armrests down before stretching out, zigzag, knees bent, bent across three seats. It can be a handicap having long legs. He sets his watch one day later.

This is Tony's life, and it's ending, one hour at a time. Nothing pleases Tony much these days, after his election success with Simtwo, apart from the prospect of a date with me, for which I am eternally grateful to  Muleskinner, the divorce lawyer.

It is almost a twelve-hour flight from New Zealand to the U.S. Tony melts and swells at the moment of landing when one wheel thuds on the runway and the plane leans on one side and slews. For this moment, nothing matters. If the pilot looks up into the stars for a split second we're all gone. I will never have to go to jail, suffer another hangover, beg another line of coke, or clean up in a whorehouse bathroom. Tony will never have to lose to his dad again at golf.

A thud, and the second wheel hit the tarmac. The chorus of a hundred seat belt buckles reverberates, and the white-knuckled Xiu Zhou, the neighbor Tony almost died sitting next to says, "Good luck with your life."

"Yeah, you too." Tony sounds sincere and earnest, but he doesn't plan upon using that gift indiscreetly again, not in the New Year, the year of Hillary according to Xiu Zhou's fortune cookie.

And this is how long his moment lasts… that day of the year when even an average band can command triple pay for playing at any old dive. And life goes on, and Tony is confronted with a new vision of rescuing a godless and polluted

America.

Bill meets us at the airport and insists upon taking Tony to the club immediately, because he wants to rehearse and play saxophone with the band at the Alphar Ranch. Tony rides an electric bus with Bill straight from the airport to the gig. Tony is tired and hung-over, so I am glad to say *bye* and take Xiu Zhou with me to pick up Hillary. There is a petroleum shortage so the taxis are not running. We take an electric bus out to the seaside on the far side of town where Hillary has been attending an eighty-day spiritual retreat to prepare her for the Presidency. She said on the news that if Jesus needed forty days of solitude in the desert to prepare for his ministry then she surely needed eighty days in New Zealand.

By the time we finally get to the bus terminus a nasty February storm tries to blow my fancy-dress costume off-- Xiu Zhou has done a few lines of coke with me, and has dressed up for the occasion. Then I see Hillary at the terminus, wearing a ten-gallon hat while purchasing a snickers bar from the vending machine. Hillary must have been snorting coke to look like that... white! What a surprise—I thought she would have a limousine. "Hullo President Hillary. I've been stalking you."

Xiu Zhou is wearing a dark suit and a white shirt and shuffles beside this Arab-looking chick... that's me.

"Good to see you two. Thanks for coming." Hillary says.

"This could be your last day on the planet Madam President," I say. " May I offer you this opportunity to repent?" I held a religious tract a few inches from her nose.

"I'm already saved thank you." She pushes the flyer away.

Geez, Hillary was getting heavy, and we were a little high. What fun.

"You must be waiting for the central Dunedin bus to catch up with Bill and Tony?" Xiu Zhou asks.

"None of your business."

"Come on Sweetheart, I can tell by the shameful look on your face that you don't even know what salvation is. I'll ride with you and explain."

"Go back to your husband," Hillary snaps.

"I am a good girl now, Hillary--Xiu is gay, a priest. We know about your war plans for China. Get down on your knees now or Allah will strike you down before the day is over," I say.

Hillary swings a punch.

I back off. Xiu Zhou and I assist Hillary onto the bus... she is behaving strangely— seems to have snorted too much.

"Come on, Hillary! You're a lame duck otherwise. Read our tract and change your life. Support the Progressive Youth Movement."

Hillary remains silent and motionless, refusing to look at anything but the puddle of water covering the hard gray pavement where the bus will arrive.

"I'm rather impressed with your sudden ability to have a rational discussion," Xiu Zhou says.

"Your baby boomer generation has sold the young people of America out. You lost the power of prayer, have no real communication with the Father, your Higher Power, and then your lot raped and pillaged the Earth. Sucked its oil dry. Wrecked the climate. Shame on your generation! Please try to understand dear, sweet Hillary."

"The future belongs to my China... Your America must acknowledge this. I must

188

commend your brand new Administration, for that appears to be the tact you are employing with China."

"Is it?" Hillary grins, "My husband always says I am smarter than I seem."

The bus pulls up to the curb. Hillary jerks her torso away from me, and steps toward the bus. Her legs topple in the sudden motion and her feet slipped off the curb. As she falls, she tosses her bag with the flowers and the bottle of wine, in a misguided attempt to save them. Her naked, unguarded face slaps down onto the pavement.

"Jesus freaking nut cases," She mumbles as I giggle and step over her body. I deposit my banana peel in the recycling bin.

Avoiding the stare of the bus driver Hillary retrieves her bag, leaves the broken bottle on the curb, climbs onto the bus, and sits down on a seat behind the driver. It was one of those seats which had its back pressed up against the side of the bus, forcing her to ride sideways. Hillary locked her eyes onto the floor, miserably content to be staring at the dirty grime covering the black rubber mat that ran down the center of the aisle. Xiu Zhou and I stomped aboard and sat either side of her. The bus pulls out of the terminus and silently steers away from the ocean toward central Dunedin.

"Are you happy now Hillary?" I ask.

"I am healed from my little breakdown. Of course. I am a happy servant of the people."

"What about my husband Tony, the one to be in charge of the Treasury?"

"Your husband is proud of his achievements. He knows that God will make him the Treasury Secretary in order to heal America."

" Listen up Hillary. This is no coincidence. And get your hand off my leg or I'll give you some scrotum-tightening insights into the hollowness of male desire. My husband is Tony Chaytor and I'm on a mission to save us all from Global Warming," I say.

"Of course Carmella. I was at your wedding… Tony and you." She must be afraid that we are going to blackmail her?

"Your husband Bill broke Monica's heart with his simpleton mind," I say. "I'll teach you about saving the environment, and how to behave at our fancy dress party at tonight's New Year's celebration."

"Really?"

"It's alright for the privileged, climbing over the backs of poor people. I'm glad to see my China is screwing you. My country will erase your arrogant, cold-blooded, war-mongering kingdom from the face of the earth!" Xiu Zhou says.

I jump in, "And the headlines are a further indictment of your policies: *The President will nationalize the Nation.* What do you say to that Hillary?"

"Nationalization is just one of Tony's suggestions. For goodness sake, I haven't even had my Inauguration yet. My head is spinning."

"I want to change that Hillary, to liberate you from your do-gooder burdens." I take her cold hand, "God loves you. Goodness breeds goodness Hillary."

A tear trickles down Hillary's face, "I'm sorry Carmella, and I didn't realize that you are a Christian. Please forgive me. I'm more comfortable with *Speaking in Tongues* than talking about my feelings. This was my first gift from the Holy Spirit, *Tongues*: My compensation for my husband's infidelity. I'm good at understanding victims of infidelity, like you with your father, because I have also suffered. It was so hard to suffer that rejection from my husband. I love Bill deeply. I will tell him that tonight."

I lecture her over the hum of the bus engine as we accelerated before a steep hill, "You and I can repair America by applying the Gaia spiritual concept -- that says we, all humanity, are the Earth becoming aware of it's Self. We also affirm the Great Spirit of Oneness found at the heart of Christianity, and all the world's spiritual traditions. What is most important may not be what we believe, but what we find we all share when we put our thoughts aside to go into meditation and prayer together... work closely just like mother and daughter. How about it Hillary?"

"I would like that Carmella. I would like that very much. Do you know the purpose for your New-Age rituals?"

"Healing. And a sense of Global Community. What is threatened is the biosphere on which present and future generations depend. Let us start the planetary gardening job now Hillary…"

"OK Carmella. I like gardening very much. And want you to heal."

I reach for the *stop* bell. "You don't think I've healed yet?"

"Healing is demonstrated by our fruits—the same as the fruits of the Holy Spirit… serenity, harmony, love. And that doesn't mean fucking every man in town."

"I am born again Hillary, and therefore surely free of my addictions. Here's our stop. The party is being held just around the corner, at the Alphar Ranch. But first, the costume store… to get you a funky outfit in which Bill will not recognize you. Your big hat's good." I trip as I step down from the bus.

Now it is really New Year's Eve in New Zealand. One minute the band is playing *Two Times Reality* in the key of E, and they are going to do a smooth changeover to the next song on the play sheet, *Black Hearted Bitch* in the key of love, "F". You have two songs in your mind and one song is running.

The next song was recorded with a slap bass and a saxophone track. They reproduce this sound from a disc in the second keyboard. Bill cannot possibly play two keyboards, plus guitar and sax, (while also singing). Tony's job is to kick the yellow foot pedal at the first note of the second bar of *B. H. Bitch*.

The band has two W-30 workstation keyboards stacked center stage. They are now playing the old standard, *Two Time Reality*. The top workstation is running. At the end of the song Tony will push a foot pedal to stop the top machine. The lower machine is not running. Not yet, because the band hasn't finished *Two Time Reality*.

Things are about to change, change to a faster tempo.

Much later, twenty four hours later, it will be New Years Eve in DC.

Tony kicks with his right foot at the same time as the real drummer hits a snare crack, and starts the tom roll. *B. H. Bitch* is started: *Born to be Burned.* boom ba bom boom, *Oil black and slick,* KICK with right foot and the lower W-30 kicks in. It is Muleskinner--the real drummer, that hold the band in sync with the recording. Music has got to be Bill and Muleskinner's other addiction. We all have two! Why else would Muleskinner sell his herd of mules off Mount Shasta and work so hard day after day, country after country, all New Year's Eve, all week long. I'm here because Tony understands that time can be bent, and that bad girls like me can be fun.

I call C-J in Puerto Rico again to check on the tin fish. . . Still no answer.

# CHAPTER 38: HILLARY, December 31, 2012

The crowd at the Alphar Ranch in DC cannot tell if Tony is a split second late changing over the background track for the next song because he can bend time and perception to suit his purpose. Tony peers at the orange dots on his teleprompter. This is his warning for a tempo change. Watch the screen and you'll see two green dots just before Tony kicks the yellow pedal. Tony is a fake drummer, but a good puppet master, and is focused on the teleprompter after the change over. He is a traditional musician who relies on instinct and his own heart beat.

The fourth orange dot flashes. Tony has picked up on the tempo and is playing air-shots with his sticks. On the count of four the band will change. At the same time the first green dot should come up. Two more, then kick the yellow pedal and the air shots are now hitting skin, bouncing, but no sound. There is a mean motherfucker snare crack from the real drummer, and the audience cheers. They remember this song; it brings back another time. This is how Tony has learned to understand how the space of the media is curved and convoluted... and how to run an election campaign from the virtual world.

It is New Year's Eve again, but this time it is slightly different: Tony has a meeting with me tomorrow--to discuss who is to be the new Treasury Secretary... our first scheduled meeting for a long time. Tony is to meet me at the bottom of the cliff, by the lake, down below the steps, on the sand. Thank God that Muleskinner and Seal have been up all night and so can wake Tony in time. They do some powerful drugs those two. But not Tony! I can imagine how Tony woke up on New Year in a hotel room on top of a cliff, over the small lake in DC. I watch from a distance as Tony squeezes into a restaurant booth with Muleskinner and his girlfriend Seal. Breakfast arrives, corned beef hash with huevos rancheros. Carmella is not there, probably in bed with a hangover. The egg yolks are bound to be flat, and the salsa is probably dull.

Nobody but Tony would choose this little lake in winter. But it is a pretty day, and Tony is surely able to appreciate the scent of the manicured gardens beside the architectural steps to the beach. A few candy wrappers twinkle in the sand but there is no dog shit on the beach, because there are no dogs. There are rows of staircases from a scatter of cliff-top mansions down to the lake. Tony probably studies the personalized retaining walls and landings behind the row of iron gates. I am not down there... a No-Show!

I am a No-Show because I am sick: The two days since my release from Dr. Moon's asylum have been horrific. I do not take recreational drugs, but the atmosphere in the Alphar Ranch last night was pungent and contagious. Today I have been suffering from delusions... delusions that Bill and Carmella are emotionally illiterate, and devoid of any spiritual component. I shall beg Tony to return me to Dr. Moon's asylum in New Zealand. Then my mobile phone rings. Why do I have Carmella's phone in my pocket? "Hi Baby. This is C-J. The tin fish is all ready, but I am being transferred to New Zealand." I hang up, with the certain knowledge that I am going nuts.

# CHAPTER 39: TONY, January 2, 2013

I am sitting in Hillary's office reading a book titled *Sexual Terrorists*, about two women who look like Patty Hearst--and who are abducted by a gang of terrorists that look like Hells Angels. The women are kept in bondage in the mountains near Waco, and gradually acclimatized to their captivity. The terrorists do all the cooking and cleaning. The women have no drudgery or responsibility, and when released, just before the cops arrive, these educated sophisticated women chose to stay in the terrorist den. The cops therefore are not able to prosecute the terrorists. This is my worst fear... and it gets worse when I receive a phone call on my mobile from the police... The police have found Carmella—loaded... in some dive at the back of the Skulls Mansion downtown DC.

The small white room smells of ram stink and Carmella. I stumble into the corner, clenching my stomach, and stare at the floor. Hillary nudges me.

I keep my eyes locked onto the floor, but stumble and fall next to a soiled bucket. I try to control my breathing and force my eyes up off the floor.

Carmella is sitting on a torn mattress. The mattress is covered with orange and brown stains. She sits naked, her legs spread open. Around her neck is a thick, black dog collar. A chain is connected to the collar, shackling her to the bed head. Her glazed eyes are caked with eye shadow. Her lips are smeared with pink lipstick. Her body is covered in bruises and blood. There is a green bruise around her mouth that has an inner ring of yellow.

*Oh Geez, what am I doing?*

Carmella stares up at the ceiling.

*I can't do this.*

"Which hole?" Carmella asks in a lifeless voice.

I crawl across the sticky floor and grab the side of the mattress.

"Carmella. It's me Carmella. It's Tony."

She drops her head down and stares at me with dead eyes.

"I know who you are, Tony. Which hole do you want?"

I lead Carmella to a cleaner room along the hallway, near the kitchen, so she can sleep. She closes the door behind her. I am spinning from the cold way that the detective talked about Carmella. "Get it to bed to sleep it off. We've done our exam. No use talking to it until she has straightened up."

It is warmer in the hallway. I spit out my chewing gum, realizing that somewhere down the line it has become too bitter.

"You have to talk to her," Hillary repeats for the tenth time.

"I can't Hillary."

"You have to."

"I . . ." I shake my head.

"Tony," Hillary pleads, "I have to take off to talk with the cops. You have to talk to her and explain the need to tell the cops everything and get her into a rehab program."

"I can't."

"Why? Jesus, Tony, isn't this what it's all about. Catching Carmella after she hits bottom. Saving her?"

"I can't! What if it hits the media. It'd ruin my career . . . I can't think. Carmella needs to take the initiative. Marise will be coming home soon, and my plane leaves tomorrow." I walk to the corner of the kitchen. My body feels tired and empty, my head heavy and cluttered. No matter how hard I try, I can't focus my wrestling emotions.

"What's left to think about? Just get your ass in there and do what you came here to do."

"I can't." I push my fingers through my hair. "I can't, I can't. I . . . This is wrong, this is arrogant and wrong!"

"What's wrong?"

"I . . . Carmella needs time alone, or with a therapist, to choose her own response. She's got to be respected and supported, not directed and cajoled.

"What does that mean Tony? What in hell are you talking about?"

"I don't want to go in Hillary. It just feels wrong. Jesus Christ, it feels like I will prop her up and interfere with her opportunity to experience her bottom. I think if I go in there I'm going to . . . to . . . ."

"Sanctimonious prick." I turn away from Hillary and see Carmella standing in the doorway."

"Anyone got chewing gum?" she asks.

Her eyes are freed from the heavy make-up and she has brushed her hair. Her left eye is puffy and discolored, but her jeans and T-shirt cover the rest of her cuts and bruises, except she still has green and yellow bruises around her mouth.

"Carmella . . . Hi."

She turns towards me and gives me the exact look I have always feared she would give me, a look of indifference, a look that wonders why this ridiculous boy is wasting her time.

"How are you feeling, Carmella?" Hillary asks from behind a white face mask.

"I'd feel better if I had some gum."

"Carmella," Hillary says, her voice sounding strong and confident, "I have to leave for a bit, but it's very important that you talk to the police tomorrow. Tony will explain, all right?"

Her expression remains stony as she turns back toward me. I try to smile, but can only produce an awkward looking grimace.

"A piece of gum?" Carmella asks, what do I have to do to get gum around here?"

"Perhaps you could start explaining to her Hillary?'

"I have to go," says Hillary. I stare at the door, knowing that she will leave soon. "Tony."

I turn to Carmella, scratching a bad itch on my head

"Gum?"

"What? Oh."

I give her my last piece of gum.

"Carmella," Hillary says, "Would you mind stepping back into the bedroom?"

She shrugs and does as Hillary asks her.

Hillary drags me in behind her, pushes me and I stumble to the floor.

Carmella laughs.

"OK," Hillary says, pulling off the hospital mask, "I'm leaving. And we need you *straight*, Carmella, so you are going into a rehab program tomorrow."

"I don't even know who you people are," Carmella says, turning around and staring out the window at the darkness of DC. "Who are you?"

"Carmella . . ."

Hillary gestures for me to talk, and then leaves, banging doors.

"Carmella?" I ask with contrived hesitation.

The room is dark and I flick on the lights.

Carmella winces.

"Sorry." I return the room to darkness, closing the door and walking over to the window. I stare up at the sliver of moon, patiently waiting for Carmella to speak.

"What are you doing here, Tony?" she finally asks.

I turn around.

"I've been brought here to save you," I say.

Carmella laughs angrily and grabs for another piece of gum from my shirt pocket. Right now Hillary is downstairs talking to the police. She is arranging a rehab program for you."

"Fuck off," she yells.

"In six months we can move to the ranch in New Zealand, for good, if you cooperate with the cops."

"Yeah, huh? Who the hell *are* you?"

"You know who I am, Carmella."

"No. No I don't. You're just a memory, Tony, a vague memory too stupid to stay that way. It strikes me that I've heard all of this shit before. *I'll protect you. I'll save you.* Grow up."

"Are you ready to take care of yourself?" I ask.

"Geez." She blows a bubble at me. "When are you going to get over yourself? Well, there's nothing clean about me anymore, so why don't you just go home."

"No one's forcing you to be here, Carmella. Leave if you want."

"What, you mean like the Skulls Mansion has been my free choice?"

"I'd say I'm sorry, but I don't think you'd believe me."

"Try me."

"I'm sorry," I say.

"Fuck you. I don't care if you're sorry or not. You don't mean anything to me anymore."

"I *am* sorry, Carmella."

"I don't care."

"I'm sorry anyway." I sit down on the edge of the bed and soften my voice. "Leaving that day was a huge mistake."

"I doubt it. And if it was, get over it."

"I have tried so hard." I drop my face into my hands and try to look sad. "I loved you so much, Carmella, and I wanted it to work. I was stupid."

"You failed."

"It never left me." I coax a crack into my voice and put on a faraway look. "I kept waiting for the feelings and the memories to leave, but they never did. I look at you now, with this violation all over you and it's like we're back at home. It's like when I'd

195

get up in the morning and you were still sleeping. I'd look at you before closing the door. The sunlight would be slipping through the corner of the shade, draping across your body. You never pulled the sheets up past your waist and you looked so awesomely beautiful. Your skin was tanned and you were perfect."

"Let it go."

"Don't you think I would if I could? All the fear and hurt, and all I could feel was your love, and the untroubled face of God. All I could remember was you laughing at me because I was afraid to cum in your mouth."

She covers a smile with her fingers.

"On New Year I was at the Alphar Ranch, mainly to play that phony music with Bill Clinton. I was enjoying myself. And I hated it, because I wasn't dancing with you. You couldn't stay there alone, you had to search for something more intimate," I say.

"Tony . . ."

"I was stupid. What we had was the most important thing in the world. I'm sorry Carmella. I never should have left you alone... flirted with the devil."

Carmella edged closer. "It was . . . I might be a different person now."

"I'm so sorry, Carmella." I sob. "This is all my fault. Everything. I loved you so much and I let you down. I know you hate me, but . . ."

"I don't hate you," she whispers, more to herself than to me.

"I screwed up so bad."

"It wasn't just you." Her fingers brush across my shoulder. "It was . . . It wasn't your fault Tony." Her hand presses down onto my shoulder and I touch the skin on her wrist, hesitantly, almost as if I am afraid of her. She slides close to me and I push my face into her shoulder and begin crying. She wraps her hand around my shoulders and rocks me back and forth. I raise my face towards Carmella and she looks down at me, her breath pressing warm against my face.

The smile disappears and her face becomes frozen as she leans over and kisses me. She pulls her hand away from my face and slides it down my chest, undoing shirt buttons on the way, finally resting it on my groin.

"Carmella . . ." I pull away from her mouth.

"Tony," she whispers, and bites into my nipple.

"Carmella, don't . . ."

She tugs at my belt, skillfully yanking it open.

"Carmella . . ."

The buckle flips open and she unzips my fly.

"Carmella, don't" I grab her wrist.

"I want to suck your cock, Tony," she whispers in a throaty voice before sliding her tongue into my ear.

I pull her hand away.

"Please, Tony, please let me suck your cock. I want you to cum in my mouth."

"No. Not like this, Carmella."

"Please Tony."

She tries pulling my hand free. "Please. I *need* to suck your cock. She shifts her body and drops her free hand onto my lap.

"No Carmella, no!" I grab her shoulder and push her away.

"Well to hell with you then!" She pulls out of my grasp and slaps me across the face before standing up. "I bet you let Hillary. What do you *want* from me?"

"I want to save you."

"Fuck you!" She slaps me again. Where were you when there was still something left to save?"

"I'm sorry."

"Sorry don't change anything!"

"I know. But I'm still sorry. I love you."

"I hate you!" she curls her open hand into a fist and punches me hard in the face. I fall back onto the floor.

"I still love you," I say, and wipe the blood away from my split lip.

"You fucking asshole!" She runs towards me.

"I wrap my arms around her and she falls down on top of me.

"It's too late! There's nothing left! She spits in my face. "There's nothing left!" She stops fighting my hold and begins sobbing. "There's nothing left, Tony. Where were you when they were raping me, raping me the first time and raping me the second time?

"I'm sorry."

"I hate you," she cries and falls onto my chest, wrapping her arms around me.

"It's OK, baby."

"No it's not." She rubs her face back and forth across my chest. "It's not OK. They did things to me, they . . . they made me do things. They . . . Oh my God, Tony, they hurt me so much." She claws at my chest as though she is trying to climb inside me.

"Why did they do those things? Why would they do that? I never . . . they did things Tony. There's . . . there's nothing left. It's all gone. I'm lost. God save me, please."

"They hurt you. But they didn't kill your spirit, they didn't beat you down."

"I'm so dirty, Tony."

"Carmella, you're the cleanest person on this whole miserable polluted planet." I carefully place her underneath the blankets and smile. "It doesn't matter what they did to your body, you never let them get near the place that really matters. You're spirit's good and beautiful and clean and perfect. They couldn't touch that. You didn't let them.

"I love you Tony," she says, so quietly that I barely hear it.

"I love you too, Carmella." I press my lips to her cheek.

"Tony, will you . . . will you please fuck me?"

"No. But I'll crawl under the covers with you and snuggle your butt. How about that? I'll wrap my arms around you and we'll close our eyes and pretend that we're back at home."

"You always . . . you always used to tell me that you liked snuggling with me more that you liked fucking."

"Yeah."

"I always thought you were lying."

"I wasn't."

"I know."

Hillary is interned again, under the watchful curiosity of Dr. Moon, but tonight she is alone in her white room at the asylum. It is close to bedtime, but I stay because Dr. Moon got called out on an emergency. Hillary gets up from her bed, picks out her jacket from the closet, and strolls across the asylum yard toward the ocean, smokes a homegrown cigarette… and returns to the asylum. Smoking marijuana is illegal in New Zealand, but it grows well, especially around Blenheim.

The dining room is completely empty. There isn't even Hillary's husband: Bill is in Canada--and Carmella is in a recovery center. I have brought Simtwo with me, in my luggage, and seat her by the dining table. The freshly polished table has been moved to the center of the room. Now I draw out a chair for Hillary, as though I'm the butler, breathing noisily behind her. Hillary grabs an edge of the chair in either hand and pulls the seat tight to the back of her knees before she sits.

Only when we are seated opposite each other do I notice that Hillary is dressed in the same clothes as Simtwo: the same long sleeved version of a yellow Macy's casual shirt, the same pleated navy trousers with the wide cuffs, the apricot colored jacket--a duplication of the convenient uniform that Simtwo has used since the election campaign started back in August. This duplicate identity reeks of the duplicity of the political world. I recall, when Carmella and I dressed Simtwo as the Hillary-look-alike for the first interview It was then that I saw that Simtwo was due for a new outfit--and so too now is Hillary. Her jacket is threadbare at the left cuff where her oversized watch has separated the lining, and there is a length of loose silk thread… I notice because for some time now Simtwo has been suffering from similar damage to her left cuff due to the same oversized watch… Did Hillary just ask Simtwo a question? "You have chosen to go about as a duplicate?"

There is no reply.

"Like to order dinner?" I ask.

There is still no sign of Dr. Moon or a nurse, and it occurs to me that this dining room is not set with condiments or water jar. This is not a dream, however moronic this happens to feel at this moment? I am afraid of the American people not liking Hillary when she reverts from Simtwo and becomes real. Therefore her return to the asylum is a relief for me—as long as she is discharged before the inauguration on February 14th.

"I'm talking to you," Hillary says to Simtwo.

"And I'm talking to you. And not just in my head," comes the echoless reply.

"I mean I would like a serious answer from you." Hillary says.

There is a long pause, then I have to translate Simtwo's response, "OK, I'll be blunt. You've tried to be too good and became stuffy, using words that are too big."

"Ah, so you are the breed of lady that claims to have all the fun?" Hillary asks.

I cringe, feeling morally inadequate for the divine purpose that I have been assigned to on this planet. I deflate and pack Simtwo into her case.

Unfortunately Dr. Moon enters the room just at that precise moment and listens to every ensuing word that Hillary has to say.

I visit Hillary the next day with two-dozen red roses. She is heavily sedated so I return to DC and pray for a speedy recovery.

## CHAPTER 41: CARMELLA, January 21, 2013

Noon is a lonely hour for Carmella: Baked beans on toast for lunch again... There is still no answer from papa C-J's phone, and Greg is in New Zealand. Carmella has now survived in the recovery program for the mandatory forty-eight hours, but needs a fix... She calls Newt from her shiny new mobile; persuades him to sail his submarine to a fabulous party in Puerto Rico.

Carmella has ignored papa C-J and Newt recently. Her husband insists that therapy alone will cure her sex addiction, but unfortunately Carmella has this pesky cocaine problem, and the Navy has mandatory drug testing. She knows that Judgment Day is brewing, so now is the time to escape ... During the cruise down the Atlantic coast Carmella tells Newt that she is taking happy pills, and so has lost her sexual appetite—Happy pills are like Valium and can have that effect... Newt and the other men had demanded some explanation for her change of sexual appetite.

The maternal grandma's family home is a wooden bungalow with a garden of flowers, weeds, vegetables, and neatly pruned vines. Grandma is dead, so certainly won't be into gardening--therefore papa C-J must have been here recently to maintain this garden. Carmella turns the key in the front door of grandma's house and calls out, "Anybody home?" There is no answer so she walks to the kitchen. Carmella lights a reefer and switches on the TV--to the cartoons. She tries some stronger dope and flips channels. Then the phone rings. "Newt here. I know where C-J's tin fish is hidden. We're waiting for you with an offer that you can't refuse-- the big sub is ready to go... to Antarctica." Carmella barely recognizes Newt's slurred voice from the bar by the fisherman's dock—they were there an hour ago. Carmella is also smashed, and she can still smell ram stink on her hands. Newt interrupts, "Lady, I have a submarine ready to go to Antarctica... We have an Astute class nuclear powered submarine designed to stay under water indefinitely."

Carmella sniffs the ram stink again. "Where's papa C-J?"

"Papa C-J is not on the island. If he's gone maybe he's not for you... not a serious contender is your father. Your father doesn't like you so you'd be better off an orphan. Come on down to Antarctica with us Carmella?" Newt begs.

There's nobody else around to comfort Carmella. She drinks a carton of milk and drives to the dock. What has she got to lose?

There are the same three Arabian men standing by the gray Astute submarine, moored beyond the rusting fishing boats. She's got nothing to lose--except Carmella is afraid that she might lose Tony and Marise forever. The Captain opens the conning tower on the deck of the sub. Carmella recognizes the cherubic face of Newt from their last encounter at the bar. Carmella smells her hands and offers the Captain a toke from her reefer. Carmella has forgotten his name. The Captain smokes, passes the joint to the other three--who were all at the Skulls Mansion the other night, and are now crammed on the ladder leading down from the tower into the submarine. Newt turns back to Carmella, "What you have to understand, is that your father was your model for God." Behind the smoke, Carmella's Navy grades at DC and her memories of Tony and Marise, of Hillary, and of her father—of Captain C-J, are smaller, smaller, smaller, gone.

Carmella smells ram stink on her hands.

The Captain says, "Call me Captain Newt. If you're female and you're Christian and living in America, your father is your model for God. And if you never truly knew your father, if your father bailed out, or cheated at family games, or was never at home, what do you believe about God?"

Carmella wants to say, *what in hell are you talking about,* but it's too much effort to move her tongue. How come Newt seems to know what is inside Carmella's head? This is supposed to be a secret.

"What you probably end up doing," Newt says, "is you spend your life searching for a father and a god."

Carmella is thirsty.

"What you have to consider," Newt says, "is the possibility that God doesn't like you. Could be that God hates you. That is not the worst thing that can happen."

Carmella knows that getting God's attention for being bad is better than getting no attention at all, maybe because God's disappointment is better than His indifference.

"If you could be either God's worst enemy or nothing, which would you choose?"

It's important that Carmella shape up because unless she get God's riveted attention she has no hope of escaping the desires of the men at Skulls, and therefore no hope of a glorious survival of the End of The World. Carmella suspects that she and her husband are instruments for God and America's greatness… But she could be pregnant because Newt didn't use a condom that last time.

*Which is worse, hell or nothing?*

*Only if we're caught and punished can we be saved!*

"Burn the Pope," Newt says, "wipe your ass with a portrait of Pope Gracious. This way at least, God will know your name. Besides, I hear that the Pope is not a true Christian, not a believer in Christ's second coming. Just a fuckin greeny environmentalist -- *Pollution of air and water threaten more and more the delicate balance of the planet… Ours is the generation that must shift gears if there is to be a civilization of any quality left for future generations…The first step towards the well being of our planet is not political but spiritual.* Horse shit! "

Carmella is clairvoyant and knows better. The Pope's wrong about the future. There will be an awesome war, leading to the Rapture--before the second coming. But it's not Carmella's job to educate the Pope… or Newt. *The lower you fall, the higher you fly.* The further you run, the more God wants you back.

"If the prodigal son had never left home," Newt says, "the fatted calf would still be alive."

*Bullshit,* Carmella says to herself, mouthing the words at her reflection in the instrument panels on the bridge. It *is* enough to be numb and numbered by God, along with the individual grains of sand on the beach, and the stars in the sky.

Newt turns the sub into the east channel, jumping the line, and already a line of fishing boats strings together behind the Astute, which is taxiing at the legal speed limit of 5mph.

"Carmella, my information is that you and your husband are going to become co-Presidents of the US. This must be scary for you... your turn in the sun. It's simple. Just keep your mouth shut. Watch the movie *Being There*. Be like Chauncy Gardener... say as little as possible and pretend you understand what the questions mean. Just smile a lot, keep stoned, and crack jokes. You'll be fine."

Newt introduces Carmella to the rest of the crew, "These are people selected by the Bosses for you to make acquaintance with in preparation for your successful co-Presidency. First in the reception line--this is Prince Turki Al-Faisal."

"Pleased to meet you sir. Life is a state of mind," Carmella says.

Because of her inbred survival instincts, Carmella immediately senses the prince as a man of character, of strong resoluteness--and because of Faisal's job as director of general intelligence for Saudi Arabia, a person who understood the opportunities of networking.

Newt continues, "It was under Faisal's leadership, and after the terrible confusion of the Israeli wars, that our intelligence communities began to work more closely together. These changes have helped the Bosses to fight our common enemy: fundamentalist Islamists and fundamentalist Christians!"

"I know about his secrets. I have been to his bed," Carmella says.

"Then let me tell you this Carmella. Faisal was educated in this country. He's a founding member of the King Faisal Foundation."

"All part of the rich tapestry of life," Carmella says.

"Ah, you are a simple woman Carmella, daughter of the distinguished Captain Carl-Junior Meeks," Faisel says.

"Yes, that's me. Carmella with a C."

"In that case you shall be distinguished. We shall call you Carmella with a C, just like the man at the gas station said when I asked him how to spell C-a-s-h."

Carmella laughs. "You know about harems, injecting drugs, sleep deprivation, and extreme temperatures."

"Of course Carmella, that is my business too."

"We're in the same business," Carmella says, "A girlfriend gave me an injection of an hallucinating drug once. And she promised me the injection wouldn't hurt. But it did."

Faisal and Newt laugh.

"You know, I've never met anyone like you in America before," another Arab says from the rear.

"Yes, I've been here all my life," Carmella says.

The submarine fills with noise as Newt downs periscope and submerges.

"A criminal always serves time unless the Bosses have a higher purpose for him. Then God will save her, and her marriage," Newt says.

Carmella is thinking about the British song: *God Save the Queen*. What does this say about aunty Liz, the Queen of England and the grand poobah of a church? She's a helpless victim of history. Carmella prefers to be like Winston Churchill, who didn't rely on academic grades or church attendance to qualify himself as an instrument of God.

"This is just like television, only you can see much further. I've never been at the controls while submerging before." Carmella says.

"But you are in the Navy, a submarine pilot in the Navy for god's sake."

"Yes I am. And I keep my mouth shut and smile."

Newt introduces Carmella to their second guest who is wearing a pink headscarf. He paws Carmella's hand.

"Good afternoon. I am honored to welcome Sheik Khalid bin Mahfouz to my country. America has a strong relationship with Saudi Arabia," Carmella says.

"You ask us Saudis for more oil anytime, yes?" Sheik Khalid says.

"Yes," Carmella agrees.

"Ah, tell me, Carmella... have you ever had sex with a woman?" Khalid asks.

"No. I don't think so," Carmella replies.

"We could go to the bow right now," Khalid says.

"Is there a TV in the bow? I like to watch," Carmella says.

"Like a colonoscopy... You like to uh, watch, do you?" Khalid asks.

"Yes."

"You meet my friend, then we go."

Newt grips the controls, does a U-turn, and dives--down to a thousand feet, without a word. Carmella is jammed back into her seat, and is frightened when Newt suddenly pulls the nose up and deliberately stalls the sub. "Are you afraid of this thing?" Newt asks as they dive further.

Carmella's will to live dissolves at this moment. Nothing matters. Not even her husband. Nothing matters. Not even her daughter's autism. Not even Marise's lousy grades. Death is not unwelcome.

"You will never have to play nurse with your father again, or cut his toenails. Quick," Newt says. "Because if you're afraid of this sub you'll never be a pilot."

The sub stalls again.

"What," Newt says, "What will you wish you'd done before you died?"

Newt is so cool he even looks away from the controls to look at Carmella beside him in the front seat.

"My father," Carmella says. "I wish I'd killed my father. I have a resentment package for him, undelivered." These are revelations given to Carmella by Satan. Her horny priest doesn't have the same depth of relationship with Satan that Carmella has.

The AC screams until the sub climbs again.

Lights are coming just ahead, and Newt yells to the three Arabs behind him, "Hey, you see how the game is played. Fess up now or we're all dead."

The three Arabs are alternately chanting prayers in the back and laughing. The cigarette lighter in the control panel pops out hot, and Newt tells Carmella, "Light us a cigar."

Carmella lights two cigars, and the bridge dims under a shroud of smoke.

"What's your game?" Carmella asks Newt.

"Newt. My name is Newt. I am a project manager at the CIA, on the Middle East project. But I am more interested in the China issue and their threat to invade Antarctica. What will you wish you'd done before you die?"

There is a silence. Newt introduces Carmella to the third Saudi sitting behind them, "Carmella, meet Salem bin Laden. He has more than fifty siblings."

"Tell me about yourself?" Carmella asks.

"I'm here to establish a business relationship with your husband Tony.

"I know about Tony's business, managing Hillary. But why you?" Carmella asks.

"My father is dead, and was famous, with many wives. He owned a construction company, wealthy, with a favorite younger son, Osama bin Laden. Osama has big plans. There is a plan to invest in American business. We shall become your benefactors."

The bridge of the sub is tiny and close, forcing economy of motion. Carmella is distracted by the pretty colors of the instruments.

"This is a very small room," Carmella says.

"Would you like a turn at navigating?" Newt asks.

"I like to watch," Carmella says.

Newt tosses a bottle of whiskey to Carmella.

"Make your wish quick," Newt says to the three Saudi guests strapped behind him. "We've got five seconds to oblivion."

"One," he says.

"Two."

The sub is diving toward a lighted submersible in front of them, and the AC is roaring.

"Three."

"Ride an oil gusher in Manhattan," comes from the back.

"Build an oilrig in the White House," comes another voice.

"Reinvent myself . . . as a virgin," Carmella says.

"Give me a hit on the whisky," Newt says as he pulls out of the dive.

Newt blathers about the problems he is having with China pushing their fleet further south toward Antarctica while another Middle East War distracts him, "I am, however, better off than the *director* of the CIA."

"Fascinating," Carmella says mechanically.

Newt continues, "I'm more focused on the psychological aspects of intelligence, such as personality profiling of leaders and terrorists."

"Why are you in a better position than the director of the CIA?" Carmella asks.

"Because the CIA depends on secrecy to develop its contacts."

"I have heard that the CIA won't recruit potential agents who are religious. How do you know who is religious and who is not?"

Newt laughs, "Certain CIA agents have identity confusion. Given the plots and counterplots, double agents and moles at ambiguous stations.

"Nice for them," Carmella says.

"Where is the root of identity in modern hedonistic man? In such a dark lifestyle the personality divides. The CIA is a tomb of shuffled identities, and America's history may indeed be unknowable, and the same with the identity of the director, or shortly, the true identity of the President of the United States."

"That is fascinating. Spiritual integrity, and therefore allegiance, is arbitrary and confused. So why all the anxiety about China?" Carmella asks.

"The Chinese military upset our country in Korea, to the stage that our guys had to mock up a phony attack on one of our own destroyers as an excuse to attack North Korea... Or was it North Vietnam? We might have to pretend that China is attacking this sub soon."

Newt is obsessed with China. "The Chinese goal was never independence for Malaysia, Korea or Vietnam, but to extend China's control to new territory such as the Far East and Antarctica." Newt raises his eyebrow toward Carmella, "Right?"

Newt pauses until Carmella makes eye contact. "Will you agree with me that it is essential to secure the spiritual integrity of America?"

Carmella replies with a crisp "Yes sir," and follows up by nodding affirmatively as Newt prompts Carmella with his wagging head.

"Then will you entertain the possibility that some of us are dedicated to installing a reliable puppet into the Presidency in order to maintain continuity of policy... and to prevent China from beating us in the economic and survival conflict?"

Carmella can't argue with that because her throat dries. Newt goes on drunkenly, oblivious to Carmella's spinning head. "I'm sharing this with you because I want to recruit you into our camp. Your husband doesn't have the stomach for intelligence work anymore. That's why he's being groomed for puppet master of the President -- Your husband doesn't ask silly questions."

"So, Hillary became President because Tony doesn't ask silly questions?" Carmella grins.

Newt takes Carmella seriously, "Keep your opinions to yourself and you'll soon be serving the planet by exploring the options in the biggest global game of spiritual poker that civilization has ever seen. The Chinese are smart, very damn smart. They fully intend to set up a colony under Antarctica."

Carmella doesn't mind that Newt is a little crazy. "What's the crux of the problem?"

"Capitalism and democracy! We are committed to it, but the concept has a flaw. A highly centralized government, like China, which controls their exchange rate artificially, and who doesn't give a shit about the environment or God--will beat us head to head at the game. We have to find a way to tilt the table further in our favor."

"And what do you want me to do?" Carmella asks.

Newt smiles at last. His shiny skin is sweating out as fast as he is drinking in. "I want you to control Tony, the puppet master of the President. You are a relaxed young woman, and your native intelligence isn't muddled by reading newspapers or books. I want you as our front woman. Are you in?"

"How much?" Carmella asks.

"We'll pay you generously enough."

"That's the standard compensation package?"

"There's a retirement package, after one years service. Done deal?"

Carmella nods and smiles. "Sounds like an easy job."

"Our anti-China unit is called The Knittings Club. You keep your mouth shut and don't ask questions. OK?" Newt asks.

"OK," Carmella says again. "What goes on tour stays on tour."

"Are you excited Carmella?"

"It's all part of the rich tapestry of life sir. Want me to cook some burgers?"

"I thought we might drop you into the place where your father lives, for a visit. What d'ya say Carmella girl?"

"I want to go to Antarctica and watch television."

"If you insist. But you are addicted to TV. The Bosses will prevent you from watching TV when you become grand Presidential puppet master. They will put you in a twelve-step program. What's the matter Carmella?"

"Nothing." But Carmella feels stupid. All she does is want and need things: to hide the evil truth about her father, to improve her little shit lot in life. And to go back to Newt's sleazy frat house, to Skulls and Bones, to relax in his Newtonian symmetry. She never told anyone this, but ever since Carmella met Newt she's been planning a grand finale.

"This is how good life can get when you find your soul mate, Carmella. But your father doesn't like you, so your mom had to dump you Carmella!" Newt says.

"I don't want to lose Tony. My father thinks that I am stupid. Kill me," Carmella says as she grabs the wheel and cranks the sub.

A stranger speaks, "Carmella, you're feeling very sleepy, Mr. G is here and talking to you."

"Who said that," Newt asks. "Forget about fears of losing your relationship. Otherwise you'll make Tony a widower. Pretty women like you always end up getting screwed violently if you don't behave. Focus on saving yourself."

Carmella drums her fingers on the bridge bulkhead and tries to think clearly. God speaks again; *You are humanly perfect, despite the rotten behavior.* God has a voice like Moses.

"Nobody is talking to you Carmella. Sober up or you'll screw our crew," Newt says.

Carmella smells ram stink and pulls away. Her seat belt feels twisted like a straight jacket around her, and when she tries to sit up, she hits her head against the wheel. This hurts more than it should.

"I really love Tony. What a fool I've been," Carmella says.

"I look forward to working with you," Newt says, and brings the submarine to the surface to test the air quality. "We are going to change the world--our little Knitting Club is going to make the planet a truly Christian community and market place."

"Agreed. But first take me to captain C-J. How do you know where he is?"

"I hacked the Pentagon computer system. He's hiding out in New Zealand, running our satellite surveillance station up by Tekapo."

"Take me there. It's on the way to Antarctica, right?"

"Yeah. But they've got gasoline rationing in New Zealand and their airline is only doing one flight a week."

"No worry, I know where Tekapo is. I'll walk there, while you and the boys take some R. and R."

# CHAPTER 42: CARMELLA, January 31, 2013

The hair on the back of my neck rises, bristles. I strap on my shoulder holster and a belt of ammunition. I am fully alive, and pumped for action. Hells teeth! I start walking… hiking with a dog, Phillip, that I have seconded from in front of the Port Temple Library, hiking through the rolling tussock land that has the pungent aroma of sage and thyme. Papa C-J is sure as hell going to be surprised when I show up.

I hold my hand over my eyes to shade the bright sun, stride through the next damper gully, and then pause atop the next mound. Thank God it's summer, and there's been some rain. My dog Phillip and I gradually climb. The colors are still dark brown and golden. Even the sheep in these parts are dark brown, although the wool will wash back to its natural white when freed from dust and sunburn.

The colorless flowers of cottonwood and leatherwood trees that grow around the bogs mock the relentless sun. Further ahead I can see the turquoise of this lake and the blue of that lake, and further still the high edges of the black mountains.

I have a tape recorder but I am not planning to produce a tape of a confession from C-J as evidence for a court of law. Justice shall perform much more rapidly than even a bush court. I must do this solo… then reconcile with Tony. That is my way. Tony will be back in New Zealand by now, trying to get Hillary released from the asylum in time for her Inauguration. But the tape might be useful to demonstrate to Captain C-J that I have an iron will. It also may help to convince them that they will be better to let me free during any possible court hearing than having the military aspirations of global cover-up exposed.

At the climax of the day the wind lifts dust clouds from the riverbeds at the foot of the mountains, and the heat-haze mixes with the wind-shaken tussocks so that the near horizon moves. Captain C-J's perverted crime has damaged my family and me. In so doing he has wounded my entire village.

The slopes of great mountains swing up on either side, broken by black bluffs or the gentler planes of terrace that might have been carved by bulldozers a thousand years ago. The summits of the flanking ranges and the mountains at the head of the valley are hidden by cloud so the valley seems like a hall of cloud and rock with no end. It rains heavily for half an hour and then clears.

Beneath me the hillside slopes down two miles to the braided shingle of the Last Stand River, a tributary to the Custer River, flowing from a wider valley on my left hand where there are dark trees in sheltered bays; there are none in the eroded distances of the Liberty Range and the Freedom range. (I make up the names of rivers and mountains so I can maybe feel at home in Tony's country.) Two other rivers join and filter through the swampy head of the large turquoise lake, revealed entirely now, filling the west and north; and between the junction of the rivers there is a hill, smooth and separate from the first high range, and on the terrace at its foot there is a cabin, large, 'vee' shaped, with a roof of thatched tussock. This will be the base camp serving as the delivery drop-off point for the Tekapo Observatory. I hike up the two valleys, to the mountains in the clouds that descend towards me. Far ahead the observatory has been laid down on the end of a terrace that runs for miles, until a bluff hides its curve up the valley. There is a cliff face two hundred feet above the observation station, on the south side, where there are boulders almost as large as the south wing of the station. Now I see a larger building around the corner, above the cliff—huge, with a massive dome. Who but the CIA would want to build a massive observatory at the mouth of one of the most beautiful natural hanging valleys in the world? I stroke the gun in my holster, warm against my shoulder.

"Stay close Phillip." The wind is stronger now and cools as the sun drops. My eyes water so the cabin becomes a small blur in the expanse of rock and sky and the tussocks dulled brown by the failing light. I sneak over the stony flats toward the station. What in hell! There's no need to be cautious. Captain C-J hasn't any reason to suspect that I mean desperate business. So I stand up tall, sing to Phillip, and as bold as can be, march up and knock on the door. There is no answer so I enter the unlocked door.

Inside the dim kitchen I take off my backpack and gun. There is a photo of me in a swimsuit, pinned to the wall, and my name is carved into one of the rough sawn planks that make up the tabletop. There is a scratched heart on the tabletop. And the obligatory arrow. Shit! "C-J loves Carmella." Oh my God! He's worse than a nut case. It turns my stomach to think about having sexual intercourse with him, with that faggot . . . I hold the gun at the ready and search every room. Then I sit outside, watching, watching for any movement in the hills and valley… Nothing! I am relieved. The observatory is huge, and is entirely vacant, mine for the night. There is firewood resting on a hearth of clay and boulders, and a clean brown pot and lid. I light the fire and will soon have a hunk of mutton boiling in the pot, simmering to a stew. I come back from a daydream and breathe in the fumes of stew, then stand up again, eager to rediscover.

There is a pair of lanterns in the rafters beneath the tussock thatch, cleaning soap behind the door, a spade and an axe beside the hearth.

I check outdoors. No sign of Captain C-J. Phillip is quiet, exhausted, on guard duty under the entrance deck. I will leave at dawn and travel quickly, further into the mountains valleys and foothills where Captain C-J is likely to be stalking food at this time, no more than a day's ride by horseback, perhaps two days by foot.

I wake quickly, feel cold across my forehead like a scoffed margarita. I pull the blanket so I might see the sky to the east. There is no light, but from the silence of the cold that quells even the noise of the river, I know there is a sprinkle of first snow on the tops, and it is close to dawn. I do not linger because I know the temptation if I compare too long the comfort of dry woolen blankets with cold boots. I pull them on and stamp to warm my feet before slithering into my coat.

I recover my drying sleeping bag from the back of a chair in front of the dead fire and load my pack. Captain C-J has a pistol stashed under the corner of his lumpy bed mattress. I will not take any risk so I pack his pistol and his 0.22 long nose ammunition with me, in addition to my shoulder holster. I am on the move again, almost happy, despite the delay in finding C-J.

The warmth of the sun comes between the mountains behind me, warming us, and a spattering of a few hundred sheep below, searching for a green leaf in the shade of the dry tussock. C-J won't be hard to find. I sit on a rock outcrop and wait until my eyes can focus on the smallest details. He is probably camping on the broadening valley floor. I see a trickle of dust, like smoke from a cigar. Then it is gone. Do I hear the galloping of a horse in this silent valley, devoid even of birds? I search for another dust trail in the distance, patiently methodically. Finally I see a puff rise from a knoll... pointing me like an arrow. There are few things for me to consider in my plan: It is all straight forward, a result of my good instinct for the functioning of the perverted mind.

Finally a track becomes more distinct, mountains move apart, and I have the sight of a long turquoise lake in the setting sun, and of Captain C-J's horse tethered outside the observatory. I rest and think, then walk straight for the observatory with my plan intact. I will behave casually, like nothing is going on, just finding the place by accident, on my way out... not coming in.

I call, "Anyone home?"

Captain C-J comes out from the station. He offers help with my pack. "We smelled your dog, Phillip Temple, an hour before you made the brow. Captain C-J laughs in his newly hoarse throat, a grayish beard covering his mouth and cheeks, his coat collar is turned up as he moves closer to pat my dog. He smells of sweat and alcohol.

"In which direction is Dunedin?" I ask.

Captain C-J peers up at my face, his face different in this clear place. He runs stubby fingers through his long hair. He grins stupidly so his teeth show faintly, and I see the grease glisten along the edges of his beard. Captain C-J chuckles and chews at the hair from his moustache. "Hard question." He offers me a drink of whisky. I explain that I've quit drinking. Then I have second thoughts and pour enough to almost fill a tin cup, and pretend to drink it around the fire. Of course Captain C-J hasn't changed—he makes a move, he would have to; it's still his instinct to try to fuck a drunken woman.

It was not hard to control him, and his military roughness was a badge of his neutered existence, a curse of the military lifestyle of killer training. I feigned a preference for angry verbose foreplay from the start. Out there in the mountains is an emptiness that might be called freedom. I could perhaps have stopped Captain C-J before he exposed the slack barrel of his perverted lusts, but decide to be cautious this once, to play to the tape, encouraging from Captain C-J words of passion and violence, his response to my initial and unrecorded seductions. Now that I have pushed the record button, and toyed with him, I cry Stop! and Rape! In a cycle of ascending volumes and urgencies, and laugh quietly to myself as the bugger sags further.

I pull out my pistol, produce the recorded tape, and feel powerful. I offer the now trembling Captain C-J an opportunity he cannot refuse. This conception of an opportunity might be tinged with desperation, but my determination will make my plan work. I will take over his job and destroy his identity, another step forward with my ever-adapting plan for survival.

Captain C-J pleads, "I'm sorry."

"You'll surely go away for life. But first, just fucking listen or I'll cut you."

Beneath us the hillside slopes down, slopes two miles to the braided shingle of the Tekapo River.

"Please, no. Anything but mutiny! I'm not going to shoot Newt."

"I can still smell your ram stink. Don't worry—Newt will shoot back."


Two days later I get a whispered call from Newt, "Captain C-J has snuck onto the sub and has just shot the other guys. Do you know what he's up to?"

"Yeah. I sent him to kill you. It's the only way he can avoid me calling the police."

"What if I shoot him first?"

"You will. But he is so drugged up that he will still shoot you too. Time to start saying your prayers. Try asking God for forgiveness… and see what answer you get."

# CHAPTER 43: CARMELLA, February 2, 2013

I call Hillary with the news, "Papa C-J died yesterday."
Hillary seems to understand: "He had to die... to release you."

Hillary has researched how child sexual abuse affects victims physically and mentally with regard to forgiving or not forgiving the offender--following a study of fifty-five traumatized females, who have been tracked for over ten years, by Professor Jennie Knoll. Hillary has been asking me to read this book by Knoll, that I have now borrowed from the Tekapo library, about the implications of various steps of forgiveness:
1. Giving up the desire for revenge.
2. Letting go of anger.
3. Victim moving on with her life.
4. Reconciliation with the offender.

If forgiveness is taken to include only the first three steps, the results of such clinical forgiveness are positive for the lives of the forgiving victim. Jennie found that abused girls who had let go of both anger, and the desire for revenge--had higher self-esteem, less anxiety, fewer symptoms of post-traumatic stress disorder (PTSD), and better relationships with their mothers. Reconciliation is a different matter: When the abused girls wanted to reconcile with their offenders--who were sometimes their fathers, they were more anxious, had more symptoms of PTSD and dissociation, and were more likely to have bad relationships."

Professor Noll advises clinical therapists: "Do some work with the victims that lets them get over their anger, gets them over wanting to hurt the abuser, but don't encourage a renewal of that relationship. It could put the victim at risk and make them feel powerless again."
I am certainly over wanting to hurt my abusers... C-J is dead! As is Newt: I heard Newt over the phone, "Put the gun down or I'll shoot." C-J's answer surprised me, "I came here to die, to save my baby from you. Please shoot me fucker, shoot!" Then there were two sets of gunfire.
I still have some decisions to make. Firstly, I have to decide whether to stay on longer at the Tekapo Observatory--stay in New Zealand, because there is no known danger of the Chinese invading here... or hike back to Port Temple and hide the submarine before going back to DC to collect my family—to save them for the Judgment Day, save them under Antarctica.
My intention today is to move on, seeking forgiveness and reconciliation with my family and friends. But I also have to confess that my *self-destructive instinct*--which is reportedly the nature of the disease that often afflicts the raped... as is the instinctive compulsive desire to resume with the offender. The desire to resume can be so powerful that it takes more than a *Thou shalt not* from an authority figure such as a therapist to convince the victim of the merits of disassociation from perpetrators.

My father died yesterday so I don't have to ever worry again about my compulsive instinct to resume with the offender. But how do I get to forgiveness and reconciliation? Subsequent to my rape, I have done terrible things and betrayed Tony. Fuck! I am so sorry.

I call my therapist from the Tekapo Satellite Tracking Station. She tells me that my health-insurance company, Kaiser Permanente, does not provide treatment for childhood sexual abuse... "Too complex and expensive to treat." Fortunately a local therapist, Chris Else, agrees to treat me for sexual addiction and chronic fatigue—by phone. He says that treating the symptoms is almost as good as treating the problem. What is the difference I ask? "Simple," he says. "Symptomatically, I just give you happy pills (like valium) that dull your natural sexual drive by changing your hormone chemistry, and relieve anxiety in the same chemical way that an anti-depressant does."

"And if you treated me for the rape?"

"If you prefer me to treat your sexual abuse then we would open up your repressed memories, process your anger and your self-blame, and then graduate to the sophisticated art of forgiveness of responsible parties: Your God who did not intervene, you for not asking God to intervene, your sick father, depraved Newt, and all the responsible adults who might have protected you from the offender ... Then we would affirm your inner child that also got hurt, your goodness, and your love. Carmella, you are a special and wonderful person."

"Don't lie to me. I hate lies. I could shoot you for that. You know I arranged for my father and Newt to meet up... to shoot each other? You could be next if you don't save me in the next five minutes."

"Carmella, listen to me. Firstly; I will try. Do you comprehend that almost one quarter of all girls are sexually assaulted before reaching the age of eighteen, and that over eighty percent of abuse cases involve a parent or step-parent. Fifty to eighty percent of all sexual abuse goes unreported. Over ninety percent of abuse is perpetrated by someone the victim knew and trusted.

Secondly; I am legally obliged to report to the authorities any crimes and threats of crime that are revealed here... Did you shoot your father?"

"No."

"Good. Then we can continue. And please... call Tony."

"Yes, of course—right now!"

I have flown to New Zealand to see Hillary, but I cannot visit at short notice—"Against the rules," according to Dr. Moon—but I am permitted to talk with Hillary on the phone.

"You're up with the latest on Carmella?"

"Yes. But what will become of *you* now?" Hillary asks.

"I promised Carmella that I am not filing for divorce," I say. "But why did I dream about losing her this morning?"

"Because you love her?"

"In my dream Carmella visited my room--then excused herself to go to the bathroom. I waited and waited. Suddenly I awoke... and called you."

"I am glad that you called."

"We both have had a lot of bad luck," I say.

"Yes. Both of us."

"But fortunately, Carmella is seeing a counselor, Chris Else."

"A good one. Come over. We'll have an old fashioned meeting."

Hillary selects the pretend Café Alphar as the place for us to meet and make our plans... at the downstairs conference room in the asylum.

Dr. Moon escorts me to Hillary's white room. Hillary's desk is shiny, showing no evidence of her day-to-day responsibilities, or her intense efforts to get Dr. Moon to release her from the asylum... I had not accounted for Dr. Moon lacking an ability to recognize that Hillary is sane. For God's sake! Even I can see the tell-tale signs of sanity when I compare Hillary's room to that of the other inmates: No stacks of soda cans and cigarette boxes like in the other rooms, no childish art, no heavily scored wall diary, and no pin holes on the shiny walls... Just her A6 size leather bound brown diary on the right corner of the desk and a radio mounted on the wall.

The phone rings, but Hillary ignores it. She has the mild mannerisms of swaying forward to smile, and smoothing her eyebrows in reflection. "And where do those ideas come from," she asks me. "They're new to me, but I gather you've been to a Republican convention."

"No," I say.

"Then perhaps you have been to a Narcotics Anonymous meeting?" she asks.

"I have been thinking about that, after seeing this interview by Muleskinner for an AA convention--our lawyer and band leader is now a spiritual giant: *Millions of emotionally healthy people functioning out there will have noticed that many of us have lives which are a dysfunctional collection of compulsions and impulses for instant gratification, for control, for mind-altering chemicals such as alcohol, drugs, tobacco, caffeine, sugar, flour, food, gratuitous sex, and environment-destroying commodities such as oil--to comfort our aching hearts."*

"Yes," Hillary says, "I can appreciate his insight."

"Yes. He's brilliant! Perhaps I can use Simtwo to convince Dr. Moon that you are ready to be released... hopefully before your inauguration date."

## CHAPTER 45: HILLARY February, 2013

Tony recognizes that he has fallen in love. He is in love with the changed, and more attentive, Carmella Meeks. What else could he call it? Not anything as crass as simple happiness, but an aching dependence on another person who compliments his own broad-brush approach to life: With Carmella's attention to the details, and Tony's unbearable awareness of the simultaneous power and transience of now, when his attention deficit interferes with his singular thought pattern.

Love is that singular form of suffering which moves concern from yourself to another, so that you are freed, for a while, from stultifying selfishness and paranoia. More than anything else Tony wishes that he could protect Carmella from the new wave of terrorists who are now flourishing in the hinterland of New Zealand, flouting the law as they abduct pretty young women such as Carmella, abduct them to use as sex slaves. Tony has not heard about these abductions from reliable authorities, such as his hairdresser or his car mechanic. But Tony knows such things intuitively! He has a rare gift of being wherever his imagination takes him. Tony also has a desire to move in with Carmella, containing her fiercely, bringing . . . And simultaneously Tony has a need to lie . . . To lie absolutely still and talk to her in a trusting way that is quite apart from sex. Isn't all that part of love's jumble, so that poise, caution and common sense are upset?

Even though Carmella will not travel to Dunedin for two more days, Tony can surely imagine the smell of the sun block on her skin, and see the winking silver studs in her ears. There is that pale Islamic-crescent-shape of a scar on the underside of her left arm, just like his.

This is how life goes, things held in unique juxtaposition for a moment in time and space... the submarine on the water, and the promise of a home-coming, Tony and Carmella talking, generous intentions and slender gains, then all whirls on again for a different throw.

Carmella is a night person. Tony is a day person. Only moralist convention denies that it's possible to love more than one person at a time, and convention is nothing to Tony now that his life is no longer just a series of fantasies of conquests in unreal places, without TV or newspaper. We are grooming Tony for a huge station in life, so we insist that he not be allowed to be read or view any public media. No! Now his life must be as a beacon, as an epiphany of God's purpose for the great Nation of America, preparing for the final crusade, for the rapture, and for the final judgment... but he can telecommute, from his family ranch in New Zealand, from his new home with Carmella... in the same way that I shall be the President of the USA while living in New Zealand—by telecommuting... A practice which will become mandatory next year. Telecommuting is a new practice where all employees, apart from those performing critical services such as theater nurses and beat policemen--will be compelled to work from home, to eliminate the need for transportation from home to workplace... Telecommuting will be the cornerstone of my new Green Policy to reduce greenhouse emissions.

# CHAPTER 46: PRESIDENT HILLARY CLINTON, February 2013

I am always waiting. It started when I was waiting for the election returns to be finalized last year--but it was certain that I had won... As a write-in candidate. It took a long time for America to get into the trouble it is in now. The problem with all the *work* the government has done to make America better is that it has been done by tackling apparent symptoms and not the real ills--and I have watched it from afar, on the big-screen TV at the Chaytor Ranch in New Zealand.

Last year Tony and Carmella visited Bill and I for the big Election Day, to await the returns. Such a nice couple. And now, so much drama! Psychic vulnerability will be perpetuated for Carmella and Tony unless memories are collectively articulated and shared... they have to talk, acknowledge, apologize, and patiently recreate their lives. Having sex with someone other than our spouse damages our souls and relationships. I've seen couples over the years who thought they would swing a little since, you know, a little affair of the flesh won't hurt anything in the long run. Often it is the beginning of the end of the marriage as the betrayed partner feels devalued, inconsequential, and unprotected. Prayer can be more intimate than sex. A husband and wife that pray together intimately usually get to have a fantastic marriage.

Last month, safely in my white room in Dunedin--while preparing for my inauguration, Tony and I pre-recorded my official acceptance speech. Dr. Moon-- crisp and professional, raises an eyebrow and shakes her head not quite imperceptibly. Delusional people do not understand those signals; the book said so. I have read the book so I know what it is that I do not understand. What I haven't figured out yet is the range of things *they* don't understand: The people who wear the white coats and sit behind the desks in comfortable chairs. I know some of what Dr. Moon doesn't know: Every day Dr. Moon asks what my job is, and I say I am doing public service. She asks if I know what *public* means? She definitely assumes that I am still sick.

I was not pleased about Tony and Carmella pressuring me to go along with their desperate plan for an election campaign. When I questioned the honesty of it Tony scoffed: "When we rise above our illusions, we are no longer *disillusioned*, and we no longer grieve for our past selves."

Tony can be funny some days, I guess. But nobody likes a good laugh more than I do. Except perhaps my husband, Bill. And some of his friends. Oh yes, and that Dubya Bush. Come to think of it, most people like a good laugh more than I do.

Anyway, here is what I am going to do as President. First, since I am not beholden to any special interest group--or to anyone in government, I will take a *no holds barred* approach. I will let Congress know that they are on notice. I will set up a website that anyone in America can go check: It will list what each member of Congress voted on, what *pork* they inserted into bills, what special interest group they received donations from, and who was giving them PAC money.

The media reported, during the 2012 election campaign, that I had been reclusively attending a born-again-Christian retreat--reinventing myself. I have certainly worked my heart out, but now I have to prove my sanity again--to Dr. Moon, before she will release me from her asylum.

I watch it on TV. The High School Band is set-up along the parade route on Inauguration Day, and the Boy Scouts Troop wave up to my window in the White House from a float in the parade... but of course I am not there. The TV footage of my pre-recorded Inauguration interview--that acknowledges the support of my fabulous guru, Dr. Elizabeth Moon, was created by Tony using Simtwo. It definitely had the down home country flavor that originally made Dubya Bush so popular. The showing of my Inauguration Speech on national TV finally persuades Dr. Moon to discharge me from the asylum.

The week following my release Bill and I spend President's Day weekend with Tony and Carmella on the front lawn of the White House. What leaps to the eye are places to pray, play music, and praise the Lord; and all else--rostrums, microphones, flags, journalists who smile then crouch in dark corners to ambush, and the passing of time--is interference from a world that will never be conducive to the divine purpose and allegiance of America: to unite the world under one Christian American government, the government of the write-in underdog, Hillary Rodham Clinton.

This morning I, President Hillary Rodham Clinton, flew with Tony and Carmella into Fort Pierce, Florida for a Democrat fundraising breakfast—my husband is busy at home on a pet project. The Reverend Arthur Blessitt has read about my visit and has paid his $1,000 admission. Hundreds of people are attending the breakfast at a huge private home on the ocean. I speak outside along the waterfront, and am applauded warmly and sincerely after I share my Christian testimony, and my plan to reduce polluting emissions with compulsory telecommuting. There is no way I am going to shake hands with everyone here and leave to catch our plane. The same feisty old preacher, Arthur Blessitt, is waiting near the exit door as Tony, Carmella, and I wade through the huge living room full of people. Arthur later told me that he prayed and figured which door I would come through. Sure enough I came through that door and he is the third person to shake my hand.

"I am Arthur Blessitt, we met at Miami," he says.

I interrupt him. "Yes, you carried the cruciform through the Darien Jungle."

He pulls me to him in a big hug. He tells me briefly that he has carried the cross in every nation and is now going to all the remote island groups. I ask how he is and then he says, "Do you remember when we met and talked about Jesus and we prayed together and you invited Jesus into your life?"

"Oh, yes," I reply. "But not in particular. I invite Jesus further into my life every morning."

Other people are crowding about and can overhear us talking now. He says quietly "I am very proud of you and your testimony for Christ. I would like to have a brief prayer with you again--and your friends."

"Sure, we would like that," I say.

Arthur had typed a prayer the night before, and he prays it aloud now. We follow the words with our finger on the paper he has given us.

*A prayer for Hillary Clinton, and for Tony and Carmella:*

*In the Name of Jesus, I request that God bless you and keep you. May He who formed you in your mother's womb and He who called you and chose you from her womb, protect, bless, lead, prosper and keep your heart pure. May you be a light to many people and show Wisdom and humility, Compassion and justice, Service and sacrifice, both to God and humanity... In the Name of Jesus. May the Lord watch over you in your going out and coming in, now and forever more. May the peace of God fill you even in the face of your adversary. May the fruits of the Spirit: love, joy, peace, longsuffering, gentleness, goodness, faith, meekness and self-control be yours.*

Arthur then says, "How can we keep in touch?"

"I will give you the email address of my assistant," I say.

Arthur tells me that he is thrilled that he has been able to make contact, "It cost me one thousand dollars, but it was worth a million," he says.

Then Arthur whispers a silent prayer, "Oh Jesus put your words in my mouth, and lead our listeners to understand and be saved."

Arthur slowly leans forward, lifts the Bible that is in his hand, and begins to speak.

"What is your relationship with Jesus"? Arthur asks me.

"I'm not sure," I reply.

"Let me ask you this question Hillary. If you died this moment, do you have the absolute and certain assurance you would go to heaven, immediately?"

"No" I say.

"Then let me explain to you how you can have that assurance, and know for sure that you are saved and healed from your shame."

"I'd like that," I say. Arthur is looking at Carmella and holds eye contact until she nods affirmatively.

Arthur then begins to share with the three of us about how to know and follow Jesus:

"All have sinned and come short of the glory of God: Romans 3:23.

This means we all have sinned and fall short of the example of Jesus, of God's Glory. I am a sinner and you are a sinner—and we need healing from guilt. The Bible says, *blessed are the pure in heart for they shall see God.* Matthew 5:8. No one has a pure heart, and here are the consequences of that sin.

*The wages of sin is death but the gift of God is eternal life through Jesus Christ our Lord.* Romans 6:23

Our sin has earned a wage, and that wage is death--or separation from God in Hell. God Has provided a gift of healing (eternal life) and yet to have this new and eternal life we must receive Jesus.

*God commends His love toward us in that while we were yet sinners, Christ died for us.* Romans 5:8

On the cross Jesus paid the price of our sins. He died for us to focus the futility of our guilt. Then Arthur explained that, even in our sins, God loves us:

*For whosoever shall call upon the name of the Lord shall be saved.* Romans 10:13

*Peace I leave with you, my peace I give to you; not as the world gives do I give you. Let not your heart be troubled, neither let it be afraid.* John 14:27.

The call of Jesus is for us to repent and believe!

Jesus changes us from the inside out. The world tries to change us from the outside in. Jesus is not condemning you. He wants to save you, cleanse your heart, and change your desires. He wants to write your name in the Book of Life, and welcome you into His family, now and forever.

Would you rather spend eternity with Jesus, or without Him?"

"With Jesus."

"Madam President, I would like to pray for you and then lead you in a prayer of commitment and salvation. You can all become followers of Jesus now."

I have listened the entire time and ask some questions and Arthur gives further explanations. Arthur leans forward and reaches out his hand as he says, "Hillary, Carmella, and Tony, I want to pray with you now."

"We'd like that," I say.

Arthur has a strong handshake but a tender grip. Arthur prays for us, that we might know and become a true follower of Jesus from this day forth. Then Arthur asks us to pray with him, to read the following prayer with all our hearts, and consider each word to make it our own.

Arthur's grip tightens and we pray, one phrase at a time, a prayer similar to this:

"Dear God, I believe in you and need you in my life. Have mercy on me a guilty sinner, in the Name of Jesus…. I want to become more and more like him. In the Name of Jesus, cleanse me from my shameful guilt and come into my life as Jesus is my Savior and Lord. I believe Jesus lived without sin, died on the cross for my sins, arose again on the third day, and is now ascended unto the Father. I love you Lord, take control of my life. I know you hear my prayers in the Name of Jesus. I welcome the Holy Spirit to lead me in Your way. I forgive everyone—even those who have violated me wickedly, and ask You to fill me with Your Holy Spirit and give me love for all people, including my violators. Lead me to care for the needs of others. Make my home in Heaven and write my name in Your book in Heaven. I accept the Lord Jesus Christ as my Savior, and desire to be a true believer in, and follower of, Jesus. Thank you God for hearing my prayer. In Jesus' Name I pray."

It is an awesome and glorious moment! "We are just three brothers rejoicing in Christ," I say.

"Having repented of your sins and asked Jesus Christ into your heart as Savior and Lord it is important now to consider what has taken place: Jesus has come to live within your hearts.

"Behold, I stand at the door and knock. If anyone hears My voice and opens the door, I will come in to him and dine with him, and he with Me." Revelation 3:20.

"When you open the door (your will) Jesus comes into your heart to stay. This is a personal relationship with God. You can come to Him with every need and receive certain victory. The One who has made us now comes to live within us."

"But if we walk in the light as He is in the light, we have fellowship with one another, and the blood of Jesus Christ, His Son, cleanses us from all sin. If we say that we have no sin, we deceive ourselves, and the truth is not in us. If we confess our sins, He is faithful and just to forgive us our sins and to cleanse us from all unrighteousness." 1 John 1:7-9.""

We are smiling and Arthur is rejoicing! It is a glorious and happy time.

"Before you receive Christ, the Bible declares you to be spiritually dead, but now in Christ you are spiritually alive. Not a temporary life in Jesus, but an eternal relationship with Him. He will be with you every moment from now on. He has promised never to leave or forsake us.

You are now the Children of God.

Your relationships with other people have changed.

We forgive others as we expect God to forgive us. Walk in a forgiving relationship to others.

Forgiveness is a mark of a true follower of Jesus.

"And forgive us our sins, as we forgive those who sin against us." Matthew 6:12.

"And whenever you pray, if you have anything against anyone, forgive him, that your Father in heaven may also forgive you your trespasses. But if you do not forgive, neither will your Father in heaven forgive your trespasses." Matthew 11:25-26.

Arthur, Carmella, Tony, and I, talk for a while more about following Jesus. Arthur encourages us to tell our friends about what has happened *in our hearts*. We tell him we will. Arthur teaches us a *mission statement:* "I need now to grow in the Lord and study the Word of God and be open in my testimony."

Arthur confirms to me that he will *not* get up and announce in the next meeting about me, the President being saved: "You give your own testimony of what Jesus has done and continues to do in your life."

The four of us talk some more then, we have a brief prayer before Arthur and we leave on our separate ways. Carmella is smiling through tears… knowing she has the gift of forgiveness and a fresh start. I tremble at the glorious work of the Holy Spirit. I prayed to receive Jesus Christ in 1966, and have gone on to become the President of the United States of America. What is next?

This evening my husband is noncommittal about my new style of Presidency. But he does get enthusiastic about joining a small group of visitors to the White House, to help prepare my formal State of the Union speech. We rehearse in the movie theatre—they previously used this White House movie theatre to rehearse the former President Bill Clinton's State of the Union addresses. But it is me, the real Hillary--not Bill, or Simtwo--up front of the movie theatre this time. Bill sits with the other two visitors, offering pointers and word changes, but has a hard time staying seated. He leaps up excitedly, advising, "You need to say why you're accepting the job of President here and now."

"Because I'm a crazy and delusional," I say. They all burst out laughing.

Bill begins rearranging the sequence at the end of the speech. "Hillary will accept. They'll cheer and dance around. That's fine. Why not rake in some dough? Why ask to be trashed right now? What I wish you could do, Hillary, is a sentence here: *The overwhelming reason is that I want to devote my life to public service.* That was, after all, your motive for becoming President."

An urgent Tony Chaytor dressed in a yellow sports coat interrupts me: "Our great nation last month made a complete profit of one dollar."

"Only one dollar, Tony?"

"Roughly yes, madam President."

"Tony darling, I'm the President of a multi-trillion dollar economy and you are a very new Treasury Secretary; isn't it possible there may have been some mistake?"

"That's very kind of you Madam President, but I don't think I'm ready to be President. Not yet."

# EPILOGUE:

Carmella has become fully aware of the issues in her life, and has found through Christ, the humility that has led her to a victorious relationship with the Holy Spirit.

We would like to pray for you and then lead you in a prayer of commitment and salvation. You too can become a follower of Jesus now.

You have read this book, and hopefully have some questions, so now here are further explanations: Dear child of God, please lean forward and reach out your hand. I want to pray with you now.

Repeat the following prayer with all your heart and consider each word to make it our own.

"Dear God I believe in you and I need you in my life. Have mercy on me a sinner, in the Name of Jesus, who I want to follow you, cleanse me from my sins and come into my life as my Savior and Lord. I believe Jesus lived without sin, died on the cross for my sins, arose again on the third day, and is ascended unto the Father. I love you Lord, take control of my life. I know you hear all my prayers that are in the Name of Jesus. I welcome the Holy Spirit of God to lead me in Your way. I forgive everyone and ask You to fill me with Your Holy Spirit and give me love for all people. Lead me to care for the needs of others. Make my home in Heaven and write my name in Your book in Heaven. I accept the Lord Jesus Christ as my Savior and desire to be a true believer in--and follower of Jesus. Thank you God for hearing my prayer. In Jesus' Name I pray."

"There is rejoicing in Heaven now! You are saved!" Let me read you some scriptures:"

"There is joy in the presence of the angels of God over one sinner who repents" Luke 15:10

"I now want to share with you what Jesus has done in your and my life. Having repented of your sins, and asked Jesus Christ into your heart as Savior and Lord, it is important to now consider what has taken place:

Jesus has come to live within your heart.

"Behold, I stand at the door and knock. If anyone hears My voice and opens the door, I will come in to him and dine with him, and he with Me." Revelation 3:20.

When you open the door (your will) Jesus comes into your heart to stay. This is a personal relationship with God. You can come to Him with every need and receive certain victory. The One who has made us now comes to live within us.

Your sins are forgiven.

"But if we walk in the light as He is in the light, we have fellowship with one another, and the blood of Jesus Christ His Son cleanses us from all sin. If we say that we have no sin, we deceive ourselves, and the truth is not in us. If we confess our sins, He is faithful and just to forgive us our sins and to cleanse us from all unrighteousness." 1 John 1:7-9.

The Lord is not slack concerning His promise, as some count slackness, but is longsuffering toward us, "not willing that any should perish but that all should come to repentance." 2 Peter 3:9

The Bible teaches when we repent of our sins the blood of Jesus Christ, His Son, cleanses us from all sin. To repent means that we turn our backs upon the old way, to put our trust in Jesus and desire to live for Him from now on. When we repent and ask forgiveness our sins are gone. God forgives us – this is good news. Other people may remember but God erases your past.

You are saved.

That if you confess with your mouth the Lord Jesus and believe in your heart that God has raised Him from the dead, you will be saved. For with the heart one believes in righteousness, and with the mouth confession is made to salvation. For the Scripture says, "Whoever believes on Him will not be put to shame." For there is no distinction between Jew and Greek, for the same Lord over all is available to all who call upon Him. "For whoever calls upon the name of the Lord shall be saved." Romans 10:9- 13

To be saved means that we have been delivered from spiritual death through faith in Jesus Christ. Sin separates us from God, but Jesus bore our sins on the cross and paid the eternal penalty for our sins. When we receive Jesus we are saved from the penalty of sin, which is eternal separation from God. We are being saved daily from the power of Satan, and one day in heaven we will be completely saved from the presence of Satan and sin.

You have received eternal life.

"For God so loved the world that He gave His only begotten Son, that whoever believes in Him should not perish but have everlasting life." John 3:16

Before you receive Christ the Bible declares you to be spiritually dead, but now in Christ you are spiritually alive. Not a temporary life in Jesus, but an eternal relationship with Him. He will be with you every moment from now on. He has promised never to leave or forsake us.

You are now the Child of God.

"But as many as received Him, to them he gave the right to become children of God, even to those who believe in His name." John 1:12

Through faith in Jesus Christ you are now in the family of God, you are the object of God's love and can be sure that your relationship with Him is close, personal and intimate. As a father would love his children and care for them so even God our Father now loves and cares for us.

The Holy Spirit abides within you.

"Or do you not know that your body is the temple of the Holy spirit who is in you, who you have from God, and you are not your own? For you were bought at a price; therefore glorify God in your body and in your spirit, which are God's." 1 Corinthians 6:19-20

God has revealed Himself to us as God the Father, God the Son and God the Holy Spirit. He comes to live within us at the moment of conversion, and makes our body His dwelling place. "Through the Holy Spirit the fruits of the Spirit-filled life: love, joy, peace, longsuffering, kindness, goodness, faithfulness, gentleness, and self-control, can become a living reality. Against such there is no law." Galatians 5:22-23

You have become new people.

"Therefore, if anyone is in Christ, he is a new creation, old things have passed away; behold, all things have become new." 2 Corinthians 5:17

Jesus answered and said to him, "Most assuredly, I say to you, unless one is born again, he cannot see the kingdom of God." John 3:3

Many times people call their new birth in Jesus their 'new birthday'. Inwardly we have become a new person. Things are changed. Jesus Christ changes the heart. The outward actions of our life then become different. God's Spirit lives and abides within us.

Your relationships with other people have changed.

We forgive others as we expect God to forgive us. Walk in a forgiving relationship to others.

Forgiveness is a mark of a true follower of Jesus.

"And forgive us our debts, as we forgive our debtors." Matthew 6:12

"And whenever you stand praying, if you have anything against anyone, forgive him, that your Father in heaven may also forgive you your trespasses. But if you do not forgive, neither will your Father in heaven forgive your trespasses." Matthew 11:25- 26

We now love other people, as we know God loves us. We should be willing to share the material things that God has blessed us with. We should be concerned about the whole of a person, mind and soul--and should seek in every way to meet the needs of others.

"And do not be drunk with wine, in which is excess; but be filled with the Spirit." Ephesians 5:18

When we are saved the Holy Spirit comes to live within us, yet often we are not fully in the control of God's Spirit. To be filled with the Holy Spirit is a moment-by-moment walk. When you realize that any attitude or action is not of God then, at that moment, repent, ask God's cleansing, and have Him refill you with the fullness of His Spirit. We are filled with His Spirit when we repent of all sin, yield our life to His control, and by faith ask to be filled with His Spirit. It is vital for your life to be filled moment by moment with His Spirit. You, as a new person in Jesus Christ, have begun life's greatest adventure.

What to do now!

Pray Daily.

"Pray without ceasing." 1 Thessalonians 5:17 "He spoke a parable to them that we always ought to pray and not lose heart." Luke 18:1

Prayer is a moment-by-moment relationship with God. You can pray at any time, at any place. As we share every need of our life with God in prayer we can know that He hears us. Prayer is also being open for God to speak to our life. It is in this most personal way through prayer that we grow spiritually day-by-day.

Read the Bible Daily.

Jesus said, "Man cannot live by bread alone but by every word that proceeds out of the mouth of God." We need to eat the spiritual food of God's word daily, to study His word, and be obedient to His commandments.

Witness for Christ Daily.

"But you shall receive power when the Holy Spirit has come upon you; and you shall be witnesses to Me in Samaria, and to the end of the earth." Acts 1:8

"And daily in the temple, and in every house, they did not cease teaching and preaching Jesus as the Christ." Acts 5:42

Prayer and reading our Bible daily is to strengthen us and help enable us to bear witness of Jesus to others. We should seek to witness for Jesus to every person we meet wherever we are. We should not be fearful or timid, but we should be loving and open as we tell others of Jesus. We are saved to share our faith, not simply to wait until Jesus comes to receive us. Our commission is to go into the entire world and preach the gospel to every person.

Confess Christ Openly and Be Baptized.

"Therefore whoever confesses Me before me, him I will also confess before My Father who is in heaven." Matthew 10:32

"Go therefore and make disciples of all the nations, baptizing them in the name of the Father and of the Son and of the Holy Spirit, teaching them to observe all things that I have commanded you; and lo, I am with you always, even to the end of the age. Amen." Matthew 28: 19-20.

Jesus always calls His disciples openly to follow Him. We are not to be secret disciples but open witnesses. Therefore Jesus has asked us to confess Him openly, and follow Him in baptism after we have put our faith in Him as Savior. Jesus was baptized in water. He commands us to be baptized, and early followers followed His commandment. Baptism does not wash away our sin, but it is an open testimony that we have died to one way of life--to live a new life with Jesus.

Every follower should be in fellowship with other believers: praying, singing, worshipping, studying the Bible, following Christ's commandments, and seeking to preach the gospel of salvation to other people--and minister to all the needs of our fellow man. It is vital that we assemble ourselves together with others to grow spiritually and help others. This fellowship can be found in many Churches, and also often in small Bible Study and Prayer Groups--perhaps in a Christian friend's home.

Keep Christ's Commandments.

"If you love Me, keep My commandments." John 14:15

Jesus said if we love Him we will keep his commandments. We obey the commandments of the Bible because we want to. A person that loves Jesus desires to be obedient to His will and accepts that the way the Bible has asked us to live is right and proper for us. Therefore we seek daily to walk as He has asked us to walk."

Carmella prays daily, as follows—and I recommend that we all do the same:

**For Protection**

Father, I thank You that You have a hedge of protection around about my life.

I plead the Blood of Jesus over myself; spirit, soul and body.

I declare that I am covered by the Power of the Holy Spirit and the Blood of the Lamb.

I thank you Father that Your angels go before, above, below, behind and totally surrounding me. I thank you that you guard and keep and protect me.

Right now I take authority over every demonic assignment against my life and I break the power of any arrow the enemy would send against me; spirit, soul and body.

I bind every spirit of accident or injury that would try to come against me today and I declare that I am kept safe by YOUR Mighty Hand.

I thank You that angels line the perimeter of this property and protect me spirit, soul and body and also all of my responsibilities.

In Jesus' Name.

### For Character

Father, I thank You that You are interested in everything about me. That You know and desire what is best for me. I thank You that I have a meek and pliable spirit.

I thank You that Your Spirit dwells in me, to lead and guide me into Your Character.

I declare that I am a child that walks in love, joy, peace, patience, gentleness, kindness, faithfulness, tolerance, forgiveness, discipline, self-control, (... anything that you perceive that you might be lacking in, or need)

I bind rejection and I declare acceptance over myself.

I declare I am loved ... that I am free and not bound in any way

In Jesus' Name.

### For Success

Father, I thank You that You cause me to excel in every area of my life ... spiritually, mentally, physically, relationally, and my work environment.

I thank You that Your desire for me is to succeed.

I declare that I will succeed in every thing that I put my hand to in life.

I declare that I will not be held back in or by anything.

I declare that I am the head and not the tail.

I thank You that You have made me to be an over-comer and that greater is He that is in me, than he that is in the world.

In Jesus' Name.

### For Healing

I declare, in Jesus' Name:

"By His stripes, I am healed" Isiah 53 v 5 and 1 Peter 2 v 24

I declare that healing belongs to me, and that Your will is that I walk in divine health. Healing is Your will for me.

However ... I must now build healing in the spirit realm, before I get sick again!

I shall declare healing daily, while well, and if sickness comes, there will be a deposit in your spirit that won't actually allow it in.

It takes time and diligence to establish the Word, for anything, and only in Your spirit.

Faith comes by hearing, and hearing by the Word.

Anything that's written in His Word belongs to me and becomes mine as I declare it out of my mouth ... I shall seek daily to find scripture that is relevant to my needs.

And, His Word is His will. If I know His Word, then I will know His will and He will then reveal His specific will and direction for my life.

You say that Your Word is life and health to my very bones and I believe it!

I thank You Father, that I am healed.

In Jesus' Name.

# BIBLIOGRAPHY:

Contributions to this novel by the following authors are acknowledged:

Philip Roth, Toni Morrison, Michael Riddell, Ben Olson, Philip Temple, Brian Caldwell, Chuck Polahniuk, Drew Stepek, Nick Hornby, Chris Else, Owen Marshall, Chris Abani, Elizabeth Moon, Lloyd Jones, Vanessa de Oliveira, Arthur Blessitt, Curtis Sittenfeld, Janna Levin, Ezeibieli Kingsley Chidi, Robert Byrne, Peter Hoeg, Hillary Smith, Nick Cave, Pankaj Kurulkar and Anne Desclos.

This bibliography contains title details, in chronological order of appearance, of the paragraphs and exerts of sampled literature from outstanding authors displayed in this novel:

Elizabeth Moon: "The Speed of Dark," Ballantine, 2002. See Chapter One.

Janna Levin: "A Madman Dreams of Turing Machines," Random House, 2007. See Chapters Two and Fifteen.

Chris Else: "On River Road," Random House (NZ), 2004. See Chapters Three, Thirteen, Thirty six.

Brian Caldwell: "We All Fall Down," Alphar Publishing, 2006. See Chapter Three, Thirty nine.

Ezeibieli Kingsley Chidi: "Limbus Infantum," Unpublished screenplay, 2007. See Chapter Three.

Peter Hoeg: "Miss Smilla'sFeeling for Snow," Harvill Press, 1996. See Chapter Four.

Toni Morrison: "Beloved," Vintage at Random House, 1979. See Chapters Five, Six.

Hillary Clinton: "Living History." See Chapters Seven, Eight, Twent two, twenty three.

Gail Sheehy: "Hillary's Choice," Random House, 1999. See Chapters Seven, Eight, Fifteen, Twenty two, Twenty three.

Robert Byrne: "Skyscraper," Robert Hale Ltd., 1984. See Chapters Nine, Fifteen.

Vanessa de Oliveira: "The Diary of Marise," Matrix Editora, Brazil, 2001. See Chapter Eleven, Twelve.

Curtis Sittenfeld: "The Man of my Dreams," Random House, 2007. Chapter Fourteen.

Michael Riddell: "Masks and Shadows," Flamingo (NZ), 2000. See Chapter Sixteen.

Nick Hornby: "How to be Good," Penguin Group, 2002. See Chapter Thirty.

Anne Desclos/Pauline Reage: "The Story of O" Jean-Jacques Pauvert (Paris), 1954. See Chapter Thirty five.

Chuck Polahniuk: "Fight Club," Henry Holt (NY), 1997. See Chapter Thirty seven and forty one.

Philip Roth: "The Professor of Desire," Vintage, 1977. See Chapter Forty.

Philip Temple: "Stations," Collins (NZ), 1979. See Chapter Forty two.

Arthur Blessitt: "Praying with George W, Bush," www.blessitt.com, 1984. See chapter Forty six.

Owen Marshall: "Harlequin Rex," Random House (NZ), 1998.